Quintin Jardine was born once up̶ rather than America, but still he gre̶ ̶.̶.̶.̶ ̶S̶e̶r̶g̶i̶o̶ Leone fan. On the way there he was educated, against his will, in Glasgow, where he ditched a token attempt to study law for more interesting careers in journalism, government propaganda and political spin-doctoring. After a close call with the Brighton Bomb in 1984, he moved into the even riskier world of media relations consultancy, before realising that all along he had been training to become a crime writer. Now, more than forty novels later, he never looks back.

Along the way he has created/acquired an extended family in Scotland and Spain. Everything he does is for them. He can be tracked down through his website: www.quintinjardine.com.

Praise for Quintin Jardine:

'Well constructed, fast-paced, Jardine's narrative has many an ingenious twist and turn' *Observer*

'A masterclass in how murder-mysteries ought to be written' *Scots Magazine*

'Deplorably readable' *Guardian*

'Very engaging as well as ingenious, and the unravelling of the mystery is excellently done' Allan Massie, *Scotsman*

'The perfect mix for a highly charged, fast-moving crime thriller' *Herald*

'Remarkably assured, raw-boned, a *tour de force*' *New York Times*

'A triumph. I am first in the queue for the next one' *Scotland on Sunday*

'"Revenge is a dish best eaten cold," as the old proverb goes. Jardine's dish is chilled to perfection with just the right touch of bitterness' *Globe and Mail*

'[Quintin Jardine] sells more crime fiction in Scotland than John Grisham and people queue around the block to buy his latest book' *Australian*

Quintin
Jardine
STATE SECRETS

HEADLINE

First published in Great Britain in 2017 by
HEADLINE PUBLISHING GROUP

First published in paperback in 2018 by
HEADLINE PUBLISHING GROUP

1

Cataloguing in Publication Data is available from the British Library

ISBN 978 1 4722 0576 6

Typeset in Electra by Avon DataSet Ltd, Bidford-on-Avon, Warwickshire

Printed and bound in Great Britain by CPI Group (UK) Ltd, Croydon CR0 4YY

HEADLINE PUBLISHING GROUP
An Hachette UK Company
Carmelite House
50 Victoria Embankment
London EC4Y 0DZ

www.headline.co.uk
www.hachette.co.uk

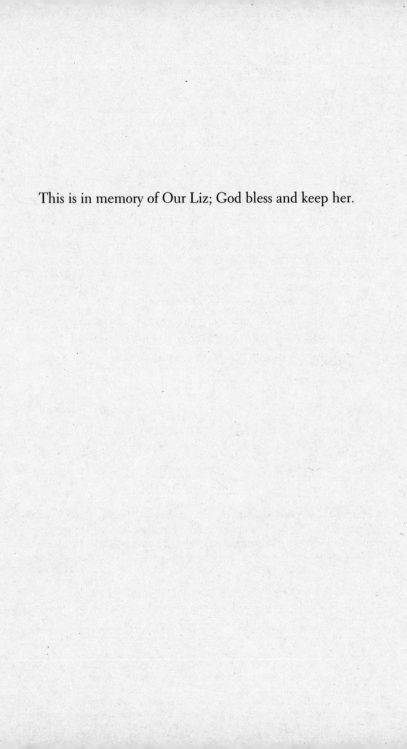

This is in memory of Our Liz; God bless and keep her.

Acknowledgements

My thanks to Baron Foulkes of Cumnock for taking me back to where much of this book is set, to the great Ian Rankin for reminding me of the existence of Soor Plooms, sugar free, at exactly the right moment, and to Kirsti for providing me with the means and the inspiration.

One

Did I really want to be ennobled? Did I see myself as Baron Skinner of Gullane?

No I didn't, when the question had been put. Being Chief Constable Skinner gave me a higher profile than I liked, and I've been happy to be shot of that title. However, I'd been invited to discuss the possibility, in good faith as far as I knew, so it would have been churlish of me to reject it out of hand . . . even though the invitation had come to me via my ex-wife.

And also, as I said to Sarah, the potential Lady Skinner, while I had been a visitor to the Westminster village several times in the later years of my police career, I had never been in their lordships' House; the chance to cross that off my bucket list was too good to pass up.

Not so long ago, I wouldn't have had time to fit it in, not when I was a serving officer, head of Scotland's largest force before it was replaced by one even larger, the controversial and almost universally unloved Scottish Police Service.

My critics, and there were plenty of them, rounded on me when I decided not to pursue my application for the position of chief constable, but it isn't a decision I've ever regretted. The truth of the matter was, I was well past my 'best before' date as a cop when I quit; most of my close colleagues knew that, but none of them ever told me. I like to believe they were too loyal, rather than too fearful, to suggest it.

Any post-career visions or fears I might have entertained of becoming a house parent and scratch golfer were soon blown away, by a couple of private commissions from friends and acquaintances with problems that needed sorting, and another from my older daughter Alex, who is beginning to make a name for herself as a criminal defence lawyer.

They helped me keep my hand in, so to speak, and led me into a couple of situations that got my investigative juices flowing again. One day, chewing the fat with some pals in the golf club, I said I might set up a website and call it 'Skinner Solutions'; they knew I was joking, but a journalist in the bar overheard me and took me seriously. He ran the story; I might have had the devil's own job knocking it down, had I not been well placed to do so.

As a bonus, the first of my private investigations led to me being appointed a part-time executive director of an international media group called, appropriately if unimaginatively, InterMedia. That gives me an office in central Edinburgh, and pays me an almost embarrassing salary, for a theoretical one day's work per week, although in practice I enjoy it so much that I give it much more than that.

Most days you'll find me there, on the executive floor of the building that houses the *Saltire*, the group's Scottish flagship, the only title in the land that maintains its circulation in print form in the face of an all-out assault by digital media.

Not that morning, though, not that fateful morning, as I passed patiently through the detailed but very necessary security process that protects the centre of the British state from the mad, the bad, the fools and the fanatics. It isn't perfect, though; no system ever will be. For example, it didn't find the blue plastic Victorinox SwissCard that I had forgotten was tucked away in a pocket of my Filofax.

There isn't much to it, only a rectangle not much bigger than a credit card, but there are a couple of things in it that should not have evaded the check. I only remembered about it as I was walking into the Central Lobby, but since I had no intention of killing anyone, it didn't matter.

Being Monday, the parliamentary gathering place was less busy than it had been on my previous visits, for security meetings or, once, to appear before a powerless but self-important select committee of grandstanding backbench MPs. There was still some action, though. It was autumn, the party conference season was over, parliament was back from its extended holidays, and political warfare had been resumed.

A Scots voice floated through the rest and caught my ear. I turned towards it, thinking for a moment that it was my one-woman welcoming committee, but saw instead the BBC's political editor recording a piece to camera for the midday news.

In the event, Aileen de Marco was late, ten minutes late. I didn't mind, for I spent the time chatting with a couple of the new breed of Scottish members who recognised me and intro-duced themselves. Both of them knew all about me, or thought they did. One was my constituency MP, a sharp guy; the other was blunt, and just plain curious. It took him only a couple of minutes to ask me flat out what I was doing there, since I wasn't a cop any longer.

I told him I was down on a lobbying mission. It wasn't a lie; I didn't say who was being lobbied, that's all.

He was trying to frame a supplementary question when

3

Aileen arrived, calling out her apologies for the delay. 'Sorry, Bob, I was collared by the Chief Whip.'

She was the Opposition as far as my new acquaintances were concerned, more so than the sitting government. The nosy guy turned on his heel and walked away. His companion was rather more polite. 'Ms de Marco,' he murmured, raising an eyebrow.

She smiled at him; there was no malice in it, only amusement. 'It's okay, George,' she said. 'My former husband and I do still speak on occasion.' Then she frowned, switching to business mode. 'How does your leader intend to react to the defence statement this afternoon?' she asked.

'He hasn't told me. It'll depend on what's in it, I suppose. Have you been briefed?'

'No.' Her frown deepened. 'That's becoming typical of the ruling cabal. They see us as severely wounded and hope to finish us off next time around, so the old courtesies are in abeyance. Have you been given any clue?'

'No, but we wouldn't be,' my constituency member replied. 'We're still the hooligans in the eyes of the PM and her hatchet man, the Home Secretary. They think we'd leak it if we were briefed in advance.' He winked. 'We bloody would too.'

'Nobody's being briefed on this one,' Aileen complained, 'not even the political editors. I'm not sure what that means. I called Mickey Satchell . . . the Prime Minister's pumped-up, self-important little PPS,' she added, for my benefit, I assumed, 'and not even she knows . . . or so she assured me.'

'I tried her too,' her colleague said. 'Same result. Yes,' he chuckled, 'Mickey is up herself, isn't she. Boots on the ground in the Middle East was the speculation I heard on Radio Four this morning.'

Aileen shook her head. 'No. I have a friend on the Army General Staff. They'd know if that was happening and they don't.'

'In that case we'll have killed another terrorist with a drone missile. That's my best guess.' He glanced up at me. 'What do you think, Bob?'

'More likely they've killed civilians by mistake,' I suggested, 'but that would probably have been leaked by the victim's side by now. Seems to me it's either something very big or something very small. If you like, I could call the *Saltire* news desk and find out what they're speculating . . . if anything.'

My new friend pointed across the Central Lobby. 'I'll save you a phone call,' he said. 'I'll just walk across and ask its political editor; whatever their reply is, it'd be coming from him.'

'Collared by the Chief Whip, eh?' I murmured as he left us. 'Parliamentary language never ceases to amuse me.'

'You could be a whip yourself if you come on board in the other place,' she countered.

'If,' I repeated. 'I still don't get this, Aileen; this invitation out of the blue. You know I didn't vote for your lot, don't you?'

'I've always assumed you didn't,' she admitted. 'But you fell out with the SNP as well over the national police force. So I figured that you were at best neutral.'

'And at worst, Tory?' I countered, smiling.

'I never thought that for a second. Have that lot offered you a peerage?' she asked.

'I was offered a knighthood,' I replied, 'which I turned down, twice; a peerage, no.'

'The K is routine for your police rank, regardless of politics, and you know it. If you were a Tory you'd have been offered a seat in the Lords by now.'

I had to challenge her assumption, right or wrong. 'Hold on

a minute; you know very well that through all my police career I was politically neutral. A senior cop has to be.'

'Of course I know that, but we were married, Bob. We got drunk together and you let your real self out, more than once.' She tapped her chest. 'In there you're left of centre. Not very far left, I'll admit, but it's there.'

'Privately, yes,' I conceded, 'but I always steered clear of public politics . . .' I stopped myself, just in time, from adding, '. . . until I married you.' That would have taken the encounter in a direction that I wanted to avoid.

Aileen sensed it and nodded. 'But you voted. You said more than once that it's your duty as a citizen.'

'Yes I voted,' I agreed, 'until last time, the last Scottish parliament elections. Then, I gave myself a day off, because none of the parties were saying anything that I wanted to hear.'

'But you're prepared to hear what we've got to say to you today?'

'Out of politeness, yes, and a bit of curiosity too. Who am I meeting? You and who else?'

'Not me,' she said, quickly. 'Not for the business discussion. I'm just the honey trap they used to get you down here. You'll be met in the other place by Baroness Mercer, our leader in the Lords, and by Lord Pilmar, the senior Scottish peer. Do you know either of them?'

'I've heard of her, but that's all. Paddy Pilmar I know quite well from his days as an MP in Edinburgh. What's the lady like?'

'Academic,' Aileen replied, 'with a journalistic background. She was economics editor on one of the broadsheets . . . I can never remember which . . . then had a chair at a red-brick university in the north-west. Intellectually she's top drawer; she's capable on her feet in the chamber, but she's remote from her troops. Her main job is to keep the party on message in the Lords and to keep Merlin's feet on the ground in the shadow Cabinet.'

'That'll be a task,' I observed. Merlin Brady, the leader of the Labour Party, known inevitably as The Magician by the media, had emerged from the drama that had followed his predecessor's incapacitation by a malignant stomach tumour, having been persuaded to stand as a compromise candidate, acceptable to both warring wings of his party. He had been regarded until then as a career back-bench loyalist devoid of personal ambition, but he was rumoured to be settling into the job.

'Whose idea was it to approach me?' I asked her, bluntly.

'It was a joint suggestion really,' Aileen admitted. 'There was a sense coming out of the Lords that we're not being forceful enough. The government pretty much ignore us. Lord Pilmar and I were tasked by Merlin's office with finding a strong man to go in there and exercise a bit of discipline, without undermining Georgia Mercer.

'We kicked some names around, but couldn't find anyone who suited the job description. Paddy suggested Sir Andrew Martin, now that he's no longer head of the Scottish Police Service, but with his tongue in his cheek. We laughed at that, then went quiet, both of us thinking the same thought, until he spoke it.

'I said you'd never do it, but Paddy was fired up by the idea. He persuaded me that there would be no harm in asking, so we took your name back to the leader's office.

'Merlin didn't know anything about you, but when I told him you'd had a big fallout with Clive Graham, that made him sit up. Anyone who's an enemy of the Scottish First Minister is a friend of his.'

'Clive and I aren't enemies,' I protested. 'I like the man, on a personal level. He's okay as a politician too, but when it came to putting pennies before public protection, there we went our separate ways.'

She smiled. Aileen has a very attractive smile when she isn't thinking about running whatever country she happens to be in at the time. Unfortunately, that doesn't happen very often. 'I know that,' she chuckled, 'but I wasn't going to tell Merlin.'

'Do I get to meet him?'

'Depends on how you get on next door,' she replied, then glanced at her wrist. I noticed that her watch was one I'd given her as an anniversary present . . . not that we had many of those. I wondered if she wore it often or had dug it out for the occasion. 'Speaking of which, it's time you were getting along there.'

I stared at her. 'Aren't you coming?'

She shook her head. 'We MPs aren't welcome next door,' she chuckled. 'I'll take you along to meet Lord Pilmar at the Peers' Entrance, then you're on your own.'

We walked out of the great building, past security and past Westminster Hall. I paused and looked at the impressive space, trying to put myself in the midst of the great events that have happened there, and the history that was made, over the centuries. I'm not a romantic by nature, but that place does get to me.

Aileen knows me well enough to understand that; she was smiling as we moved out into the street and turned left, heading for the House of Lords.

'How's Sarah?' she asked, out of the blue . . . or maybe it was the red, given her politics. I searched for anything in her tone beyond a sincere enquiry, but couldn't detect it.

'She's fine, thanks. She's started her maternity leave. How's Joey?'

It was her turn to throw me a sideways look. Joey Morocco is the Scottish film actor with whom Aileen had a relationship before and during our marriage. It became all too public when a paparazzo took a very revealing photograph of her in his house and sold it to the tabloids.

'Joey's fine,' she said, cautiously, 'as far as I know. He and I were never going to be a permanent thing. Why do you ask? Is he still on your hit list?'

I laughed at her question. 'He never was, not really; you can tell him that if you want. If I'd encountered him when it happened, and nobody had been around, I might have clipped him round the ear, but that would have been hypocritical. Joey, you, me: we've all taken a pretty relaxed view of the sanctity of marriage in our time.'

'So why did you and Sarah remarry, after saying you weren't going to?'

'It was the right thing to do for the baby's sake. We're both old fashioned that way. Also, I've changed. I've had a second chance and I'm not going to blow that.' I glanced at her, raising an eyebrow. 'How about you? If not Joey, who? Your friend on the Army General Staff?'

She grinned. 'That would be a she, and I haven't switched sides yet. I'm unattached and not looking around either. I'm number two in the shadow defence team and I hope to be number one after Merlin's next reshuffle. I can't afford any casual relationships.' Then she smiled again, the Aileen smile that I like. 'Besides,' she added, 'Joey passes through London every so often.'

She walked me up to a police box that was guarding an enclosed forecourt; it was manned by two officers, older cops, the kind whose service had earned them what was probably a nice easy station, most of the time. She spoke to them, quietly, then turned back to me.

'I've told them you're meeting Lord Pilmar,' she said. 'That's the Peers' Entrance over there.' She pointed at a small arched doorway on the other side of the courtyard.

'Not very grand, is it?' I observed.

'We don't have signs over the door in this place. Good luck. I hope it goes well. Please, Bob, give it some serious thought. We're not joking about this.'

'I'll listen,' I promised. I gave her a quick peck on the cheek, then headed for the House of Lords.

Baron Pilmar of Powderhall was indeed waiting for me; he didn't look noble at all, just a cheery wee man with a ruddy complexion. I knew that he was seventy-three years old because I'd done a refresher check on him in preparation for the meeting, but he didn't look it.

'Bob,' he exclaimed, as I came through the double doors, 'good to see you. Come on in and let these lads fit you up with a badge.'

He led me to two more security guards; they were in uniform, but civilians rather than police. There was a security gateway but I couldn't pass through because of my cardiac pacemaker. Instead they gave me a wave down with a hand-held detector, and took my briefcase to put it through an X-ray machine. I told them about the Victorinox card, but they weren't bothered about it.

Once I was official and wearing my badge, Paddy Pilmar returned to take me into his charge. 'Good journey?' he asked, as I hung my overcoat on a vacant peg on one of the racks that filled most of the area. *Search all these for illegal substances,* I thought, *and what would you find?*

10

'Fine,' I assured him. Rather than risk delay and to avoid the remarkable crowds that can gather in Edinburgh airport departures for early morning flights, I had taken the train down the day before and had booked myself into a hotel. With time on my hands after breakfast I had put yet another tick on my rapidly shrinking bucket list by visiting the Cabinet War Rooms, and making a mental note to take my boys there, on a long-promised visit to London.

'Let's go for a coffee,' my custodian said. 'Georgia's in a committee, but she'll join us as soon as she can get out.'

He led me out of the entrance area and up a wide stone staircase. Halfway up, he paused and pointed at a series of coats of arms that decorated the walls. 'Chiefs of the Defence Staff,' he informed me. 'They all wind up here after they retire and lately they've let them put their heraldic crests on this stair.' He frowned. 'I'm no' really sure why.'

I knew Lord Pilmar pretty well; he had always struck me as one of nature's doubters rather than the full-blooded cynic that a thirty-year police career had made me. He had taken an unusual route to the top. He had been a clerk on the old Edinburgh Corporation, before any of the reforms of local government that led to Scotland's present system, but had switched from servant to master by being elected as councillor for a ward in Leith, combining his public duties with a job as a trade union official, created, I assumed, to give him a salary.

Paddy had made his mark on the council, becoming a committee chairman in his twenties, and was earmarked as a future Labour group leader and political head of the Corporation . . . the Lord Provost having the title and the chain of office, but not the power . . . but he had walked away from that in the mid-seventies to contest and win a Westminster seat.

A popular and active MP, he had spent most of his parlia-mentary career on the Opposition benches. The highlight had been a brief stint as shadow Secretary of State for Scotland, but when his party's outlook and tone had changed with the creation of New Labour, he had been moved aside and eventually out, with a peerage as a reward.

Our paths had crossed a few times, occasionally at formal social events, the kind where police and politicians had to be seen, but more often professionally, when my work took me into his constituency. We had been useful to each other over the years. I won't say that he was an informant, but he was as firmly on the side of law and order as was I, and there were occasions when he had access to information that my officers and I did not. In other words, people trusted him to keep their names out of it, when they did not trust us.

While he had helped us, he had also been a thorn in my side. If he ever felt that one of his people had been given an unde-servedly hard time by the police, I was his 'go to' man when it came to sorting it out. It had led to a couple of confrontations, but mostly I had found it as useful as he had. Paddy had marked my card about quite a few officers who were disasters waiting to happen, letting me correct their attitude or when necessary take them out of the picture altogether, by transfer or, in extreme cases, dismissal.

I hadn't seen him for a couple of years when we met that Monday morning. He hadn't aged at all; if anything he looked younger and his bright little eyes had an added twinkle.

At the top of the stairs we turned into a long corridor. It was busy, but Paddy nodded to everybody we passed and stopped to talk to a couple of them, introducing me as 'a visitor from Scotland'. One had been a member of the 'Gang of Four' back in the eighties; meeting him threw me for a couple of seconds as I had genuinely believed him to be dead.

The little baron must have sensed and understood my confusion. 'I know,' he chuckled quietly. 'This place is like an animated Madame Tussaud's, isn't it?'

Our destination was a large room, a bar, but only coffee and tea were being consumed at that time of day. I hadn't gone there to people-watch, but I recognised several of the faces: a former justice secretary in a rejected government, an ennobled television personality, and a female Conservative Cabinet minister from the nineties. Lord Pilmar greeted each of them with a smile, a word or a nod.

The room in which we sat was opulent. Looking at the wallpaper I remembered the scandal when a lord chancellor was pilloried for the cost of refurbishing his accommodation, and found myself sympathising with him. Opulence was the standard set when the palace was built; faking it with a cheap copy would have been wrong.

'What's your thinking, Bob?' Paddy said, bluntly, after our coffee had been served by a breezy lady who reminded me very much of the queen of the senior officers' dining room in the old Edinburgh police headquarters.

'It starts with a question,' I replied. 'Why me? Have I ever given you any hint that I'm of your political persuasion?'

He shot me a sly grin. 'Apart from setting up house wi' our leader in Scotland, you mean?'

'An alliance which was dissolved,' I countered. 'Come on, answer me.'

'No,' he admitted, 'you haven't. But there have been a few folk joined our party, and others, on the same day they were appointed to this place. We've never discussed politics, you and I, but I know what you are: you're apolitical.'

His forehead twitched, into a small frown. 'You're like me,' he continued. 'First and foremost, we're public servants; my branch of the service called for party membership for me to make progress. As an MP I worked on a short-term contract that was renewed at the pleasure of my masters; they were the party, and ultimately the electors. Your warrant card was your entry to the public service; your progress depended on the quality of the service you gave. Latterly you worked on a fixed-term contract too, that was renewable at the pleasure of your masters, the Police Authority. We're the same animal, you and me.'

'The policeman and politician argument?' I suggested. 'The notion that the two words mean exactly the same thing? Often cited, but not actually true; they have different roots.'

'Never mind that; it's no' what I meant. You're a man who gets things done, and you're a leader; folk like you are needed in this place.'

'Nice of you to say so, Paddy,' I conceded, 'but there must be lots of people like me who are actually members of the Labour Party!'

'Bob, don't be self-deprecating; Christ, there's a big word for a boy from Powderhall . . . by the way, I added that to hint that I actually know what "self-deprecating" means. There are not lots of people like you, period. As for being a Labour Party member, that counts for fuck all now.'

Realising that he might have been overheard, he leaned closer to me. 'I'm going to assume,' he continued, 'that to prepare for this meeting you've read our last manifesto.'

I nodded.

'How much of it do you agree with?'

'Quite a lot, but I could say the same about all the manifestos.

14

But I also read Merlin Brady's policy statement when he ran for leader, and I disagree with practically every line of that.'

'Eighty per cent of the parliamentary party have issues with him one way or another,' a female voice interjected, 'which is why it won't become official policy.'

I wasn't facing the door, and so I hadn't seen Baroness Mercer arrive. I looked up at her intervention, then I stood. If anything she was even shorter than her colleague, but her perfectly cut, wiry, iron-grey hair gave her an added presence. Paddy did the introductions, and we shook hands.

'We're the Opposition party,' she continued, once we were seated, 'and we're having our backsides kicked in the Commons on a daily basis. This is the place, the Lords, in which we can make a difference and do most to keep a reckless government in check. The problem is, Mr Skinner, as Ms de Marco and Lord Pilmar may have explained, we need to be better organised, and to be honest, better led.'

Self-deprecation seemed to be the order of the day. 'That's a hell of a thing for a leader to say, Lady Mercer,' I remarked.

'Maybe, but it's the truth. My title is Leader of Her Majesty's Loyal Opposition in the House of Lords, but I was given the job because there was nobody else here that Merlin felt he could trust. My predecessor supported his principal rival for the party leadership, and declined to continue in the post. For some reason he turned to me, possibly because he realised that I am emotionally detached from politics. So are you, from what I've been told.'

I smiled. 'Who told you that?' I asked.

'Your former wife.'

I think my smile widened. 'Did she say that I have an instinctive distrust of politicians that borders on outright dislike?'

'That's not quite how she put it. But she did say that anyone who had you on their side didn't need anyone else.'

'That's a laugh,' I retorted. 'I was on hers, but she did.'

Baroness Mercer seemed to recoil from my bluntness. *Bad start there, Bob*, I thought.

But Lord Pilmar laughed. 'You touched a nerve there, Georgia,' he said.

She recovered her poise. 'She's still a strong supporter of yours, nonetheless. She was forceful in recommending you to me as a person with the qualities we need.'

'Then spell it out for me,' I challenged. 'What are those qualities?'

'We need a fixer, Mr Skinner, a person with authority in any situation, a person who cannot be ignored at any time, someone with command experience.'

'You want me to be a policeman again?'

'When necessary, but the role we have in mind is more motivator than enforcer. We're out of power, Mr Skinner, and our party in the Commons is, to be frank, a shambles. Government is walking all over us, the Scottish Nationalists are showing us up on a weekly basis. But this is a different chamber; here we can be effective.

'It's our job to contain where we can the excesses of government and to moderate legislative proposals for which the majority of electors certainly did not vote. We have a chance of doing that, for the Conservative troops in the Lords are far less malleable than those in the Commons, without the pressure of re-election or even deselection, should they step too far out of line.

'We think that someone like you, operating quietly in the background, could affect the thinking of their wobblier members.'

I was sceptical about that. 'Look, I don't know too much

about your procedures down here, but I do know what whips are. If I was spreading sedition on the Tory side of the House, theirs would catch on in very short order, surely, and put me on some sort of a blacklist.'

'Aye,' Paddy Pilmar murmured, 'but only if you actually took the Labour whip.'

I frowned. 'Explain, Noble Lord,' I commanded.

'You wouldn't necessarily be taking our whip,' he replied.

'I wouldn't?' I exclaimed. 'Then what the . . .'

'If you're reluctant to do that, there is another way.'

'Do you know what cross-benchers are?' Baroness Mercer interrupted.

'Sure,' I said, 'they're neutrals. Members of the House of Lords but with no political allegiance. Much the same as independent members of the House of Commons, or any politically elected chamber.'

'Do you know how they are appointed?'

'Frankly, no,' I admitted.

'They're recommended by the House of Lords Appointments Commission. It has seven members; four are non-political, and one each from the three main parties.'

'That includes the Liberal Democrats, for the moment,' Paddy Pilmar chipped in, drawing a glance of rebuke from his leader.

'It has come to our attention,' she went on, 'that you are being considered by the commission as a potential "people's peer", as cross-benchers are sometimes known. We're wondering whether, if you were nominated and accepted, you would be sympathetic to our cause.'

'If I said that I wouldn't . . . ?'

'Would we prevent your appointment? I don't know that we

could, but we might well oppose it. If we did, it would come down to a simple vote, and I have no idea how that would go.'

'How much of this does Aileen know?'

'Of the cross-bencher thing?' Lord Pilmar said. 'Nothing. Merlin's office asked her to join Georgia and me in looking for effective new peers. We put your name in the frame straightaway. We were sceptical about whether you'd accept, then we heard about the commission looking at you and we thought there might be mileage in it for us if you came in that way.'

I stared at him, then at Lady Mercer. 'Let me be clear about this,' I murmured, slowly. 'You two are saying that if I agree to play on your team, behind the scenes, you'll clear the way for my appointment as a cross-bencher. You're asking me to accept an independent peerage under false pretences.'

'There would be no obligation, Bob,' Paddy insisted. 'We're just sounding you out here. It needn't be full time. You could keep your job with the newspaper group. That's only a day a week, isn't it? And very lucrative, from what I hear.'

He had done his homework. 'You're sounding me out, but what you're saying . . .' I gasped. 'Man, even if I was so inclined, I couldn't agree to that without taking advice from a constitutional lawyer. I'd need to be sure of the legality of the proposition. Christ, is this conversation even legal?'

'Of course it is,' the baroness snapped. 'If you felt unable to accept our proposing you, we're asking whether in certain circumstances as a cross-bench peer you would be amenable to supporting our positions and advocating them.'

'And the bit about putting the fear of God in your troops . . . for no mistake that's what you were saying?'

'That would only apply if you chose to accept the Labour Party's nomination and take our whip.'

'I see.' I paused for a second. 'Who put me forward to the Appointments Commission?' I asked when I was ready.

'I believe it was Lord Archerfield,' Lady Mercer replied. 'He's one of the non-political four.'

He was Ronnie Archerfield, to me; a member of my golf club and also of the Burgess in Edinburgh, and of the New Club, to which I had also belonged until I let it lapse. He was a banker in the days when those people were viewed with respect, one of the last Governors of the Bank of Scotland before it lost its independence. He had to be well over seventy; I had no idea that he was still an active peer, or that he held a place on the commission.

Lord Archerfield barely knew me or anything about me, for our paths crossed only rarely in the club, but I knew one thing about him. He was the father-in-law of Clive Graham, First Minister of Scotland and leader of the Scottish National Party.

As part of its pursuit of Scottish independence, Clive's outfit had always declined to nominate members of the House of Lords, even when its representation in the Commons justified it. I got it in an instant; Clive believed that if I was close to anyone politically, it was to him. For sure, he had persuaded his unimpeachable father-in-law to put my name forward with a view to making me his eyes and ears in the place.

I looked at Baroness Georgia Mercer and realised how politically naive she really was. But Lord Paddy Pilmar was a different animal; he must have made the connection. I knew for sure that the Labour approach had been his idea more than Aileen's, an attempt to head Clive off at the pass.

'You're a clever little bugger, Paddy,' I murmured.

He smiled and made an open-handed, 'Who? Me?' gesture.

'All the same,' I continued, 'you should have told Lady Mercer.'

'Told me what?' she asked.

'The nature of the game, to stop you putting your foot in it. You're not a politician, my lady. I've spent decades around these guys, so I know not to take anything they do or say at face value. I'm worried now that I've started to think like one.'

'I don't understand you.'

'Paddy will explain,' I said.

'Yes, I will.' He looked up at me. 'You might be right about my motives, but you're wrong about something else. You've always been a politician; or thought like one, same difference. You and I used to play each other like fiddles when I was an MP, exchanging information, but always when it suited us, always on our own terms. You'll be great in this place, all the more so if you've got no sworn allegiances. Truth be told, I'd rather have you as a cross-bencher than as a Labour peer. You might do us more good that way.'

'What makes you think I'd want to do you good?' I countered. 'Yes, I read your manifesto, and yes, I liked a lot of what was in it, but if I did what you want, what cause would I be advancing now? You said yourself, you don't have any positive policies.'

'We've got one objective, that's all: to frustrate the Tories. No, two; the other one's to beat them at the next election.'

I nodded. 'Obviously. So let me sum up where we're at here; you want me, as a cross-bench member of this chamber, to do what's best for you, rather than for the government or the SNP, rather than what's best for the people, much of the time.'

'Definitely not the SNP!' Lady Mercer exclaimed. 'Those people are hooligans. They're dangerous, they're destructive and what they know about economics you could write on the back of that visitor pass you're wearing around your neck.'

My Scots hackles rose. 'With respect, madam,' I protested,

'that sounds more than a wee bit xenophobic. The Finance Secretary's a graduate of my university, first class honours in economics.'

'She's talking about the crowd in the Commons,' Paddy said, hastily. 'You're maybe being a wee bit harsh, Georgia,' he told her, trying to repair the damage. 'There are some good people in there.'

'And most of them were elected in preference to your candidates,' I added.

'We know that,' he conceded. 'Bob, you're here, talking to us, and I hope listening to us. I don't expect you to give us an answer now, but will you take time to consider what we're saying?'

'Of course I will,' I retorted. 'I've got a lot to consider. Not least whether to square up old Ronnie Archerfield next time I see him in the golf clubhouse. Neither he nor his son-in-law bothered to ask me whether I wanted to be put up for a peerage.'

'Aye, but now you have been . . .' Paddy's eyes twinkled. Yes, the little bugger could read me.

Since I left the police service I have been able to step back and look at myself, to consider what I was and what I am. There is one thing I have to admit. I have always enjoyed having power: not power over individuals, I don't mean that, rather the power to influence events and to affect their conclusion. The higher I rose in the police, the more power I had, until I reached chief constable rank and found that it was diluted by the need to delegate field control to my deputies and assistants. In the work I've done since I left, those private investigative commissions for friends and for my daughter Alex in her legal practice, and in my role as a director of InterMedia, I have exercised power.

Before I left for London, I had told Sarah that no way was I

21

actually interested in becoming a baron, but with that life behind me, it was inevitable that once I got there and had a sense of what the place was about . . . not only the Lords, but the seat of government . . . that my juices would start to flow.

Yes, I was attracted by the idea . . . and flattered, let me not deny that. Whatever Clive Graham's motive had been in having his father-in-law put my name forward, whatever wee Lord Paddy Machiavelli and his lady companion . . . who was not going to last long as leader of her group, that was for sure, for she was a few feet out of her depth . . . suddenly the prospect of being a player in that place, to my great surprise, appealed to me.

I had to think very carefully about my reply to Lord Pilmar, but eventually I was ready.

'Yes, I will think about what you've said. I will think about the whole situation that's been outlined this morning, but bearing in mind what you've said about the policies I might or might not promote, there's one group of people whose interests come first, and that's my family. If Sarah approves, if my daughter approves, and if my sons approve . . . all of them, mind . . . then I will consider it.'

That's what I would have told him, there and then, if the breezy lady who served the coffee hadn't intervened to tell me that there was a phone call for me.

I would have told her to take a message, and pressed on, if she hadn't added, 'The caller says her name's Amanda.'

Two

Nobody should have been able to reach me in the middle of that meeting. My mobile was switched off and all my secretary in Edinburgh knew . . . I shared her with the editor of the *Saltire* . . . was that I would be away for a few days and contactable only by email.

Nobody would have been able, if I hadn't had a dinner date for that evening. Even then I wouldn't have been contactable if it had been with anyone other than my friend Amanda . . . okay, if Sarah had gone into labour, she and Alex had details of my movements, but otherwise I was completely off the radar.

I've known Amanda Dennis since she was a mid-ranking officer in the Security Service, which anyone who watches modern TV drama knows as MI5. Through those years I watched her rise inexorably to the top, forcing her way past barriers of sexism and racism. She wasn't the first woman to become director general, but she was the first black woman.

When it became known that I was leaving the police force, the first job offer that came my way was from her. She wanted to beef up the service in Scotland, and she asked me if I would head it. I wasn't ready for such a role, not on a permanent basis, and so I declined, but told her that any time she really needed

23

my help on one-off situations, she knew where to find me.

A little while later I had a similar offer from the First Minister of Scotland to do a similar job for him, off the books. I turned that down too, not because I have no interest in the security of what I regard as my nation, but because I'd have been working behind Amanda's back and potentially in opposition to her, if Westminster and Holyrood ever had a conflict of interest in a security matter.

She and I have been in some testing situations together; once I was called in to investigate a security breach within MI5. We worked closely on it and I was in on its conclusion, a memory that will live with me for the rest of my days.

More recently, I worked on another case that led me right inside Thames House and into a confrontation with a man the old boy network had appointed director general over Amanda's head, when she'd been acting DG. That one ended in a knock-out loss for the fool, his removal, and her long-overdue installation in the top job.

Every time I visit London, I meet up with Amanda, occasionally in her office, but usually over dinner. Likewise, when she's in Scotland we see each other. She's been to my home, and met my family, but I've never been to hers. There was a Mr Dennis, but he left the scene years ago. These days she lives alone, and very, very privately, as she must. Bitter experience has taught me that a camera can do more damage than a gun; bullets miss more often than not, but any idiot with a mobile phone and an eye for the main chance can do in your reputation if he catches you in an unguarded moment.

There has never been anything between the two of us beyond friendship, but we enjoy each other's company; we were due to meet that evening, in a restaurant of her choice. As I went to take the call, my assumption was that one of her daily crises was forcing her to cancel.

'Hey,' I said as I picked up the phone, standing at the bar, 'no worries if you can't make it; I'll find a show to fill in the time. My mate's wife's in a West End play just now.'

'Dinner may well be off, Bob,' she retorted, 'but I need to see you before then. Extricate yourself from your meeting as quickly and as gracefully as you can, and meet me. Please. I can't say any more.'

There was a tension in her voice that I'd never heard before. I felt it seize me. I tried to keep it from showing on my face, but instinctively I knew that somewhere close by there was a very large fan, and it had just been hit by a serious quantity of ordure.

'Sure,' I murmured. 'It was heading towards natural break time anyway, so that won't be a problem. Where?' I asked. 'Your place?'

'No,' Amanda said, 'closer. Go back to the Peers' Entrance, and I'll meet you there. But contrive somehow to come alone, I don't want anyone from where you are to see us together.'

'What about the security guys there?'

'They don't see anything; that goes with the job.'

'Okay. Give me ten minutes, to let me manage the graceful part.'

'Okay, but no more.'

As I hung up I realised that she must be very close by. Even the DG goes through palace security and that takes time; she had to be in the building already.

'Sorry about that,' I murmured as I rejoined the two peers of the realm. 'My secretary panicked. I have a board meeting in Spain next week, and someone sent the papers to me without having them translated.' That wasn't a lie, not exactly; it had happened the previous Friday.

'Do you fly over for it?' Paddy Pilmar asked, buying the yarn.
'Of course.'

He grinned. 'Executive jet?'

I scowled. 'Six-thirty flight from Edinburgh Airport; I'm met by a driver, but that's as far as the executive privileges go.'

I looked across at Lady Mercer. 'I think we're done here, don't you? I will think very carefully about the whole situation before making any decision.'

'How long will you need?' she asked.

'End of the week?'

She nodded. 'That will be fine. Please communicate through Lord Pilmar.'

I almost ventured, 'Since we speak the same language?' but thought better of it. The baroness gave the impression of a woman whose sense-of-humour filter had a very fine mesh.

'One thing, Bob,' Paddy added. 'You won't really say anything to Ronnie Archerfield, will you?'

'Not a word,' I responded, sincerely. 'It's down to him to speak to me.' I rose to my feet. 'I'll see myself out,' I said.

Lord Pilmar made to follow, but slowly. 'I'll come with you,' he volunteered.

'Don't be daft,' I replied. 'I'm sure you two have to complete my interview scorecard so you can report back. Then you'll have divisions to divide, marching through corridors, parliamentary stuff like that. Thank you for your offer of consideration. Whether I accept or not, and I'm open minded at this stage, I do appreciate being asked.'

Without giving them an opportunity to counter, I stepped quickly to the door and out into the corridor.

Bit of a bugger really, I thought. I'd been looking forward to a more extensive tour of the building and maybe even to testing out one of the dining rooms of which I'd read so much. *Of course*, I reminded myself, *as a member I'll be able to do that at my leisure*.

It had taken me no more than five minutes to withdraw from my meeting, but when I reached the Peers' Entrance Amanda was there, waiting for me. That was the moment when I knew for certain that whatever had prompted her to call me was very serious, maybe with another very thrown in.

The Director General of MI5 was there, in person, waiting for me, a retired cop from Scotland. She could have sent a flunkey to collect me, she could have sent anyone she damn well chose, but she hadn't. She'd come herself. Friends though we were, in all the times that we'd met professionally, that was most unusual.

I saw the tension in her eyes as I approached her; she threw me a very brief smile. Was it one of relief? I asked myself, returning it with an involuntary frown. I sniffed, theatrically.

'What?' she exclaimed, puzzled.

'I thought I'd smell smoke, but I can't. Where's the fire?'

'You'll see,' she replied. 'Come on, this way.'

'Hold on,' I protested. 'I need to get my coat.'

'Never mind your coat; I'll send someone to fetch it. Besides, we're not going outside.'

'Amanda, where the hell are we going? What is this?'

'You'll find out, soon enough.'

She marched off at a rate of knots, and I followed, obediently; I had no choice. She led me past the security men, who looked as puzzled as I was, but said and did nothing, then through a doorway that led into yet another corridor. I was getting the hang of the geography of the place by that time and realised that we were heading back towards the Commons, with the Lords chamber somewhere above us and on our right. We continued, until we reached a stairway; we ascended it, passed through a doorway, took a right turn and emerged into the Central Lobby, where I had met Aileen.

'Gimme a clue,' I said, as we kept on walking, but she didn't. We were heading straight for the Commons chamber; I could actually see Mr Speaker, in his chair. Remarkably our eyes met; maybe I imagined it, but he looked as puzzled as I felt.

For a moment I thought we were going to walk right up to him, but Amanda veered off left, then right, into another corridor that ran alongside the chamber, under the public gallery, by my reckoning. It was busy but nobody seemed to be in a hurry, and nobody took much notice of us. We made another right turn, then a left, then climbed another flight of stairs, at the top of which we faced a closed door, at which a dark-suited man stood guard. He had a small gold badge in his lapel. In my world and in that of my escort, that was a signal that he was armed.

'Ma'am,' he murmured, nodded, then opened the door for us.

Still silent, Amanda led me through, into yet another of the corridors of which the Palace of Westminster seemed to have been constructed.

Finally, she stopped, at a heavy oak door that was guarded by another dark suit, another gold lapel badge.

'Bob,' she murmured, not out of breath in the slightest despite the pace of our trek, 'what you're going to see, you may never be able to talk about. It can't go into the memoirs that you will inevitably write one day when you're too old to keep piling up material. I've brought you this far, but I can't take you any further other than on that understanding.'

I should have been apprehensive. I might even have been

trembling with excitement. But I wasn't; I was curious, that's all, and I'd have promised her anything to find out what was on the other side of that door.

'There's lots can't go in my memoirs, Amanda,' I replied. 'We both know that. But before we go any further, tell me one thing. On what basis am I going in there?'

She smiled, for the first time since we had met at the Peers' Entrance. 'I thought you'd ask me that.'

She reached into the pocket of her grey jacket and showed me a piece of white plastic, like the Lords pass that I still carried, only laminated.

I looked at it, saw my image, and beside it my name, my full name, Robert Morgan Skinner, QPM. Below that, but above the Security Service crest, was a title, 'Consultant Director'. I whistled. 'Indeed?' I murmured. 'Funny that I can't remember ever attending an interview.'

She ignored the comment. 'As of now,' she said, 'you are an acting member of Her Majesty's Security Service. You told me that if I ever needed you, I'd know where you were. I do, I did, and I've found you.' She handed me the badge of temporary office. 'This has been ready and waiting for you for a while.'

I nodded. 'If that's how it has to be, okay; but I warn you, as soon as this, this . . . thing is over, you'll be getting it back.'

'Whatever you want.' She nodded to the suit, who opened the door and stood aside to let us pass, without, I noticed, glancing inside himself.

I followed Amanda into the room; it was a spacious office furnished traditionally, with pieces that might have been almost as old as the building itself. There was a low central table with a heavy pedestal base, with four worn leather seats set around it. I noted a four-drawer filing cabinet against one wall, and a side table on the one opposite, laden with an array of drinks: sherry, cognac, malt whisky. The only modern items in the room other than a television and a computer were a small fridge that sat beside the filing cabinet, with an electric kettle on top. There was a door beside the filing cabinet. It was ajar, open far enough to let me see a basin and a shower curtain. There was a square window, with heavy green drapes, undrawn, but it was shaded with a white blast curtain that made the room completely private, allowing no prying eyes or lenses. The low winter sun cast astragal shadows upon it.

I took in all that before turning my eyes and my attention to the desk. Delaying the moment? Maybe, I can't say for sure.

In common with the rest of the furniture, it was antique. It had known many famous users, and a couple better described as notorious. That's how I might have classed the current occupant of its big brown chair, but it's possible that I was biased, because there was history between Emily Repton and me.

Whatever that might have been, it was irrelevant. It was clear that the Prime Minister and First Lord of the Treasury had emptied her last Red Box. A slim steel blade with a round wooden handle had been driven deep into her brain and she looked quite, quite dead.

'Fucking hell!' I whispered, forgetting for the moment that there was another lady present and that she was alive.

'Exactly what I said,' Amanda murmured, letting me off the hook.

'Who found her?'

'Her PPS . . . Parliamentary Private Secretary,' she added, although I understood the acronym. 'Michaela Satchell's her name; Member of Parliament for the South Downs.'

'Big woman, is she?'

'No, she's petite actually. Small, young and pretty. Why do you ask?'

'I'm wondering whether she has the strength to ram a knife that deep into someone's head.'

'I would say not,' she ventured. 'But it isn't a knife; it's Emily's letter-opener. Sheffield steel, a gift from a constituent, she told me. I asked about it when I saw it on her desk, when she was Home Secretary, and I was acting DG, before Hubert Lowery was appointed . . .'

'Because he'd been to Eton with her predecessor's uncle,' I grunted, cutting her off. Lowery was a nasty, unscrupulous piece of work, and rather dim witted with it, which made him even more dangerous, in a perverse way. I like to think that I played a part in his downfall.

'Something like that,' she conceded. 'The letter-opener,' she continued. 'The blade's about six inches long.'

I leaned across the desk and peered at it. 'And at least four of those inches are buried in her brain. Was it pointed, can you recall?'

'Not sharply, no. And the blade could open a letter but not cut anything more solid than butter.'

'Then we probably can discount Ms Satchell, although I'll reserve judgement on that until I've seen her. Where is she now?'

'She's with the Home Secretary in his office, just along the corridor, with a guard on the door. By the way, it's Dr Satchell: medical.'

I straightened up and looked at her. 'Why am I here, Amanda?' I asked. 'And when are the police coming? This should be a job for the Met, for the Parliamentary and Diplomatic Protection crew, that used to be SO17. They're responsible for parliamentary policing, as I understand it.'

'On a day-to-day basis, yes, but they do it under contract, through a service agreement with the House authorities. The assassination of a prime minister is a national security matter, and as such my service can pull rank on them. There are special issues here, Bob. Our first priority must be to determine whether any of those have been a factor in Repton's murder.'

'And my role?'

'We want you to conduct an investigation; a quick, short-term investigation, not only to identify the assassin, but to determine, if possible, who sent him.'

I raised an eyebrow. 'That's twice you've used that term; by accepted definition, as you know, an assassin is someone who murders an important person for political or religious reasons. So who's your prime suspect? ISIS? Al Qaeda? . . . Merlin Brady?'

'The list could be longer than that. We're going to be briefed by the Cabinet Secretary; he'll explain. While we're waiting for him . . .' She looked at me, earnestly, her tension showing in the lines around her brown eyes. 'I want to keep the PM's death a secret for forty-eight hours, Bob. I think I can; Emily was in West Africa recently at an African Union summit. I'm going to release a fable that she contracted a virus there and that she's in quarantine at an unknown location. That should hold for a couple of days, and that will be your window.'

That's not a window, I thought. *That's a mineshaft.*

'Amanda,' I said, 'that isn't legal.'

'It isn't necessarily illegal,' she countered. 'Frankly, I don't care. In these circumstances I'll worry about all that after the event. Whatever happens, the buck will stop with me; as my subordinate within the service you'll be absolved from any responsibility.'

'That "only obeying orders" argument didn't hold up at Nuremberg,' I pointed out, but her expression was set firm and I didn't protest further.

'I'm going to need a second person,' I told her, 'someone I know and trust. How about Clyde Houseman, your man in Glasgow?'

'He's on an op at the moment,' she replied. 'Plus, Clyde isn't an investigator.'

'Then I want Neil McIlhenney. He's a close friend of mine, he worked under me in Edinburgh and now he's a commander in the Metropolitan Police, running undercover officers.'

'I know who he is,' she said, 'but I'm not keen to involve the police at any level, not yet.'

'In that case, I need you,' I told her, 'and you're otherwise engaged. There's nobody else. I will not work on the basis you've outlined with someone I don't know.'

She capitulated, with a smile of resignation. 'Okay, you can have McIlhenney, if that's possible. I'll speak to the Met Commissioner, Sir Feargal Aherne, and tell him you're looking into an internal situation I have and need top-level non-service back-up.'

'Good,' I said. 'I know Feargal from when he was in Northern Ireland. Tell him I need Neil here inside an hour; there's no time to watch the grass grow. Make your call, and chase up the Cabinet Secretary too, if you need to.'

She did, moving to the far corner of the room and leaving me with the body of the woman who had taken tea with the monarch on a weekly basis since her appointment a few months before.

Three

I never expected to make commander rank.

For the first ten years of my police service, becoming Detective Inspector Neil McIlhenney was the height of my ambition. I was a conscientious cop, a touch old school, to be honest, when it came to sorting out the occasional troublemaker who didn't take the uniform seriously enough. I had a kindred spirit there, in the solid shape of my great mate, from childhood to this day, Mario McGuire.

He was known as the 'posh kid' among our schoolmates. His Irish dad was a successful building contractor and his Scottish-Italian mum was a member of the Viareggio family, who were among the best-known merchants in the city. The boy Mario could have gone in either direction, career-wise, but he didn't; instead he joined me in applying for the police force. We were in the same graduation class from the Tulliallan training college, and were paired up on the beat in our first posting.

Being big lads, they sent us to a part of the city where our size was more of an asset than our diplomatic skills. It didn't take us long to forge a reputation. We didn't win the respect of the local youth; we put the fear of God in them, and in their dads too, when we had to.

We were pretty much inseparable, on and off duty; we enjoyed our work and we enjoyed our play, although my social life changed on the night in a disco when I met Olive Smith, looked into her eyes and was hooked. Less than a year later we were married, and Lauren was on the way. I'm a bit vague about which happened first.

Mario stayed free and single, although he did come to spend more time at our house and less in the pub. He had a woman problem, of a sort; his feisty cousin, Paula Viareggio, was in love with him, and made no secret of it. Both sides of their family were small c conservative, and might not have approved of such a relationship, but that didn't matter to Paula. Mario? He was in denial, simple as that, or maybe it just didn't dawn on him. It took years and his short-lived marriage to another detective, Maggie Rose, before finally it did, and the inevitable happened.

By the time they settled down, Olive was dead, killed by her smoking habit, but I won't dwell on that.

My friend was the first to catch the eye of Bob Skinner. He happened to be in the right place at the right time, and was pulled in to help the Serious Crimes squad sort out a potential gang war. I came into the gaffer's circle not long after that, and my life began to change.

Even with my family responsibilities, my hopes for myself had been limited. I hadn't even taken the sergeant's exams when I entered the big man's orbit, and I had let myself go a bit physically. That couldn't last: it wasn't allowed to. The ACC, as he was then, didn't preach, or hector, or bully anyone. I don't know if it was deliberate, something he worked on, because even now I've never thought to ask him, but he made you want to do better for him. Once you had, he made you want to do better still.

With that constant self-improvement came rewards, interesting career developments . . . the stint I did in Special Branch prepared me for the job I do now in the Met . . . and regular promotions.

McGuire was always a step ahead of me in that score. I've always thought he was a shade brighter than me, although he's always insisted it's the other way around. Whatever, he took each step up the ladder before I did, until he got very close to the top.

That doesn't mean that when I chose to move to London I did it to get out of his shadow. No, I did it because I'd promised Louise, the second Mrs McIlhenney, that I'd do everything I could to help her go back to the career she'd put on hold to marry me and have our child. She's an actress, a decorated one . . . we have a few garish gongs on our mantelpiece . . . and I was as keen as the rest of her fan base to see her return to work.

The job with the Metropolitan Police Service, heading a unit of deep-cover officers without going into the field myself, could have been created with me in mind. It carried chief superintendent rank, and with Bob Skinner as one of my referees, I passed the interview.

I'm still surprised by how much I like London, and the pleasure I get from seeing Lou on stage can only add to that.

Last year I made commander. (I don't know whether that's me caught up with Mario at last, for rank equivalents have become muddled by the creation of the national Scottish service, from which I'm profoundly happy to have escaped. He's the deputy chief up there now, with Maggie, his ex-wife, as chief constable.) My section gets results, and I get regular pats on the back from my boss, Assistant Commissioner Dina Winterton.

What I do not get, as a matter of routine, is a 'drop everything' summons to the Commissioner's office, but that's what happened *that Monday, out of the blue. It was the first time I had been to the inner sanctum of our new headquarters building; I confess I only found it after a couple of wrong turns.*

When I got there, I was ushered straight into Sir Feargal Aherne's presence. I had met him only twice since his appointment; like everyone else, I'd done my best not to tower over him. If Bob Skinner is the 'Big Man', as he always has been to most of us, then Sir Feargal's the 'Wee Man', for sure. There was a time when he'd have failed the height requirement by several inches.

Behind his vast oak desk he looked even smaller. Maybe he sensed it, for he stood as I entered and moved round to greet me, hand outstretched; a good sign, I reckoned, for a handshake is never a precursor to a bollocking.

'Commander,' he said, 'thank you for coming up on such short notice.'

'You're the boss,' I replied. I was aware of a tension about him, an air of uncertainty. It transmitted itself to me. Had something unspeakable happened to one of my field officers? I haven't lost one yet, but it's a daily risk for most of them. 'Where's the fire?' I asked, as lightly as I could.

A corner of his mouth flickered, in what might have been a tiny smile. 'In the House of Commons, it seems,' he murmured. 'I've just had a call from a former colleague, Mrs Dennis, the DG of the Security Service.'

That was something of a revelation; there were rumours in the senior ranks that the biography released at the time of Sir Feargal's appointment might have been incomplete, and his casual admission confirmed it. I knew that Amanda Dennis was a career MI5 operative, and so he must have served there at some point.

He turned and took a couple of steps to a window, looking out

*at the dull grey Thames, beyond the Victoria Embankment. I
followed.*

*'She told me that she has a situation. That's all she said, and
I didn't press her for more. It's under immediate and very discreet
investigation. I don't know what it is. Mrs Dennis didn't volunteer
and I didn't ask, but it must either be very delicate or very serious,
most probably both, for Parliamentary and Diplomatic Protection
are not involved.'*

*'They're not?' My eyebrows rose, and I felt a surprising flicker
of outrage at PaPD, part of the Met, my force, being sidelined by
MI5 on its own turf.*

*'For the moment, no. The person in charge is a secondee,
someone she's drafted in because of his special experience.'*

I almost laughed, but I cut it off short. 'Bob Skinner,' I said.

*The Commissioner turned and stared up at me. 'Was that a
guess?'*

*'Not really. I know he's in town, and I know why. I'm due to
have breakfast with him tomorrow, although we haven't agreed a
venue yet. I think he's expecting me to invite him in here.'*

*'Then please do so. I haven't seen Mr Skinner in quite some
time. But you may not have time for breakfast. He has asked for
your assistance in his investigation. Are you able to take that on
board?'*

*I thought about it. I had a guy in place in a very sensitive
investigation, more sophisticated than most. He was due to make
contact with his handler on the following morning, and I needed
to be contactable if a policy decision had to be made. But hell, I
could take my phone, and I wasn't going to be far away if I had to
drop out and meet them.*

*'I can do it,' I declared. 'I'll tell Gilly Beevor . . .' Detective
Superintendent Gillian Beevor is my deputy in the unit '. . . that*

the nanny's sick and Lou has a matinee performance. I can be with them in ten minutes, fifteen tops. Where do I find him?'

'*In the Prime Minister's room in the House of Commons.'*

I had to laugh at that; there was no suppressing it. 'Pure bloody Skinner,' I said. 'He never does anything low-key.'

Four

Emily Repton and I had met once, when I was acting chief constable of the old Strathclyde Police Service in Scotland and she was Home Secretary. It wasn't exactly amicable. Each of us had something on the other, and each of us had been prepared to use it.

My weakness was a series of compromising photographs of Aileen, to whom I was then legally still married, taken at a party when she'd been filled up with drink by a couple of female spooks and persuaded to inhale something she shouldn't have.

Hers was another reel of images, featuring her husband, the then Justice Secretary, Lord Forgrave, having congress with a lady who had set up a hidden camera to record the encounter, in considerable detail.

In the event, neither of us had won, nor had either of us lost. I'd laid hands on the originals of the Aileen pictures, by a means I need not disclose, and she had neutralised my threat to her by the simplest means. She'd divorced her husband, and engineered his sacking from government. To top it off she'd been reshuffled into the Department of Work and Pensions, from which position of safety she had watched the former Prime

Minister, the Right Honourable George Locheil MP, tear himself to pieces during the shambolic EU referendum.

When he fell she had been the Conservative Party's choice as the new tenant of 10 Downing Street, the second woman to hold the office. She had moved in without invoking the principles and examples of any saints, probably because she didn't know any.

I had loathed the damned woman at our only meeting, and for a while after that, but watching her subsequent career moves I had come to admire her just a little. I was pretty sure she would have made a very good prime minister, and so I found myself with mixed feelings as I observed the crumpled little figure lying across the desk, stripped of all glamour and dignity by the four inches of stainless Sheffield steel that had been slammed into her head.

Assassination? I thought. I've seen the aftermath of a couple of those and in neither case had the murder weapon been improvised. Nor had the assassin been able to get inside what had to be the most secure part of one of the most secure buildings in the world.

There may have been political motives, there could conceivably have been religious motives . . . although I wouldn't have bet a penny on that, not even at the most ridiculous odds . . . but I was certain of one thing from the very start.

Statistics vary according to circumstances and location, but overall, more than fifty per cent of murder victims are acquainted with their killers. Emily Repton was not among the minority; nobody she didn't know or who hadn't been vouched for was getting into that room.

As I walked around the room, my investigator's instinct kicked in, and I realised that I was breaking one of the basic

41

commandments of modern policing: *Thou shalt not fuck up the crime scene forensically.*

'We need to get out of here,' I told Amanda as she pocketed her phone and moved back towards me. 'And you need to call in a CSI team; I assume you have those at your disposal.'

'Yes,' she conceded, 'but not all with the security clearance required for this. You're going to have to do without scientific back-up. Mickey Satchell's a doctor; she will certify death for the record, but that's the only formality we can have here.'

'Jeez,' I whistled, 'thanks very much. You've got me investigating with one hand in my pocket. We? Us? Am I getting Neil McIlhenney?'

'Yes. He's on his way. So is Norman Hamblin, the Cabinet Secretary; but not here. He wants us to meet him in Downing Street, you, me and Roland Kramer, the Home Secretary . . . who's also the Deputy PM,' she added, but I'd known that.

'Fuck that,' I declared, instinctively. 'I'm not leaving this building. I've just had a meeting with the leader of the Labour group in the Lords and one of her senior colleagues. It was private in theory but plenty of people knew about it, on the Opposition side of the house. I know enough about this place to be aware that word always got around here at Twitter speed, even before the blogosphere was invented.

'You might be the chief spook, Amanda, but these days everybody knows who that is and what she looks like. People know I'm here. If we're seen together anywhere, other than having dinner in Shepherd's, word will get out and questions will be asked. So please get back on to Mr Hamblin and tell him he's coming here. Now, who normally has access to this corridor? How easy is it to get in here?'

'Too easy, obviously,' she replied. 'Honest answer, I don't

know. The woman you should ask is the Serjeant-at-Arms. She's the chief constable of this place.'

'Does she know about this?'

'Not the whole story, no.'

'Then who does?' I asked, sharply. 'Apart from the Satchell person.'

'When she found the body, she went running into Roland Kramer's office. As Home Secretary, he's my immediate boss, and he called me; he has a direct line to me. I advised Xanthe Bird, the Serjeant-at-Arms, that we had a red security issue and that I was taking control of the premises. She probably thinks it's an exercise. We have contingency plans for all sorts of situations; every so often we try them out, but we play it for real. I told her I was sealing off the ministerial corridor until further notice. She accepted it as routine, and she'll have advised her staff.'

'They think there's a security drill under way?'

'Yes.'

'How long do these normally last?'

'Until I say they're over; there is no norm. Let me call Hamblin again,' she said, reaching for her mobile.

Locked in a room with a dead prime minister, I was still trying to get my head round the situation, to think of all the questions that needed to be asked, and to put together a plan of action. Was I up to this task? I don't remember ever coming close to panic before, but I was then.

I closed my eyes and pictured things as they should have been, not as they were, with someone having been able to walk into Emily Repton's Commons office, drive her letter-opener through her skull then walk out again.

'CCTV?' I asked, hopefully.

'Not in this corridor,' Amanda replied. 'There used to be, but a previous prime minister had it removed. It was never reinstated.'

No easy fix, then.

'Protection officers,' I said. 'The PM's close protection team. Where the hell were they?'

I've known a few of those people over the years. They were all calm, unflappable, very well trained, and fiercely loyal to the leader they served.

'They were in Downing Street,' she said, 'and they still are. Emily didn't like them being here. She said this place is a fortress, so they'd only be getting in the way. They would ride with her in the car that brought her here, then go away, and come back to collect her when she was ready.'

'They can stay where they are for now, but I'll need to speak to them, at some point.' I paused. 'There's something I think you should do,' I added, 'if you haven't already. Extend your so-called security drill by instructing the protection officers for the other Cabinet members to stick to their charges like ticks to a dog. We can't assume that this was a one-off. In fact we have to assume the opposite, that this is an attack on the state and there may be other targets.'

'Really?' she exclaimed. 'One loose word and we could start a panic, Bob.'

'Who's going to panic over an exercise?' I countered. 'Is Hamblin on his way?'

'Yes, under protest. He says do nothing till he gets here.'

My moments of self-doubt were over and things were beginning to slip into place.

'I wasn't planning to.' I checked my watch; it was approaching midday. 'We have one immediate problem,' I told her. 'The big story of the day was supposed to be the Prime Minister's mystery statement on defence. Nobody knows what she's going to announce. Well, she's going to say nothing now.'

'What do we do?'

'Put your plan into action: take that knife out of her head and get the body out of here in a stretcher. Put her in an ambulance and take her to a tropical diseases hospital, the same one they treat the Ebola patients in. Is it possible to do that without her being seen?'

'Not without clearing the whole place.'

'Could we stage a fire alarm?'

'That's possible, but even then the ambulance will be visible from Parliament Square.'

'Okay, we wrap her up and put an oxygen mask on her. If someone does snatch a photograph it'll fit with the cover story.' My mind was working at full speed, as I visualised Repton's extraction from the building.

'What about the paramedics?' I asked. 'We can't risk a leak via one of them talking to his mates in the pub tonight.'

'We'll use my people,' she replied quickly. 'She's bloody dead,' she added. 'They only have to look like an ambulance crew.'

'The protection officers,' I said. 'If they always collect her, they'll have to be there, and wearing biohazard suits. They'll still be recognisable, and they should be, they're part of the story.'

'You mean the legend,' she chuckled, grimly. 'Spook-speak,' she added. 'Should they be told that she's dead?'

'Let them see for themselves in the ambulance; not before then. You need to have someone senior from your service in there, in control of the situation. These guys are trained to react in a certain way. We don't want them shooting your fake paramedics.'

She grimaced. 'That would be unfortunate, I agree.'

A solution presented itself. 'No, not someone from MI5,' I said. 'Mr Hamblin can go in the ambulance. The protection people know him; he can explain as soon as the doors close.'

'If he agrees,' Amanda warned. 'Norman Hamblin is not a man who takes orders.'

'He will from me,' I growled, 'after I've told him he's a fucking suspect.'

'The Cabinet Secretary?' she gasped. 'Are you crazy?'

'How many people have open access to the Prime Minister in her private House of Commons office?' I retorted. 'Every one of them is a suspect until I decide otherwise.' I winked at her. 'As for me being crazy, I like to think I'm a way short of that. However, my friend, you have just handed the bull the keys to the china shop. Don't be surprised if some valuable crockery gets smashed along the way.

'Go on,' I insisted, 'get your plan under way. While you're doing that,' I added, taking out my phone and selecting its camera, 'I'll do the best I can to create a full photographic record of the scene.'

Five

I was stepping out of the late Prime Minister's bathroom, phone in hand, a couple of dozen images shot, when the office door opened. I glanced across the office, expecting to see Amanda return with the Cabinet Secretary, a man I'd recognise only because his image had accompanied a *Saltire* story a few weeks before. Instead it was Commander Neil McIlhenney, God bless him, who stepped into the room.

He didn't look at me, not immediately; his gaze was drawn to the desk and what was sprawled across it. I heard his gasp, and I saw an expression flash on to his face, one that I'd never seen on my friend and former subordinate, an instant mix of shock, panic and terror.

It didn't surprise me, for I knew that I must have looked much the same less than an hour before.

'For fuck's sake, Bob,' he gasped, as he became aware of my presence, and as he recovered the composure that was one of his trademarks. 'Do we know who did this?'

I liked his use of the personal plural. He would have been sent to the scene by the Commissioner, his big boss, without explanation. Possibly he hadn't even been told that I was there.

But in an instant he understood that an old team had been re-formed and was back in action.

His second question confirmed it.

'Is McGuire coming too?'

Deputy Chief Constable Mario McGuire, second in command of the Scottish Police Service, was Neil's closest friend. They had been kids together, then plods, kindred spirits whose love of life, as much as their love of the job, had earned them a nickname that had been recognised all across Edinburgh, and feared in some parts: the Glimmer Twins.

They had been, in their youth, the most formidable pairing ever sent out on the streets of Edinburgh in coppers' uniforms. As their reputation grew, trouble faded away on the merest whisper of their approach. I don't care what anyone says, every city needs police officers who will put fear and trepidation into its hooligan element.

They were massive, each of them, hard as nails, but their personalities, while different . . . McGuire the extrovert single lad, McIlhenney the quiet family man . . . were complementary. Mario always had Neil's back, and Neil always had a hand on Mario's shoulder, lest he become over-enthusiastic. I've influenced the careers of many young cops. Most have pleased me, a few have disappointed me, but I'm more proud of McGuire and McIlhenney than of all the rest put together.

'I wish,' I replied, in answer to his second question. 'As for who did it,' I continued, 'that's what we're here to find out. We have forty-eight hours, tops. I hope the situation can be contained, but it can't be for longer than that.'

'Who's doing the containing?' he asked.

'We are,' I told him, showing him my Security Service credentials. 'You're seconded to work with me until we've identified the perpetrator, or until we run out of time.'

He smiled, grimly, as he studied my badge. 'So she's finally got you. Mrs Dennis. She's finally drawn you into the Dark Side.'

'Only for this situation. That card is temporary; she gets it back on Wednesday at the latest.'

He glanced at the ID again, then handed it back. 'Bob, it doesn't matter where the damned card is. Your name's on it, your image and no doubt the same biometric detail that's on your passport. The signature at the bottom reads "A. Dennis". What I don't see is an expiry date. As soon as you put that in your pocket you were in.'

He had a point. 'Hell of a place, Westminster,' I growled. 'I've been here for one morning, and I've had two job offers already.'

'Let's concentrate on this one. You said this situation can be contained. Tell me how.'

I explained the plan for removing the corpse of Emily Repton from the palace, and keeping the truth under wraps. When I was done, he nodded. 'I see how it'll work, but is it legal? Last time I looked, failure to report a crime wasn't against the law, but there's still malfeasance in public office.'

'You're here; in effect the crime has been reported to the police.'

'Concealing a death?'

'It hasn't been concealed from you. Concealing it from the general public isn't a crime. We're not going to take advice from the Attorney General here, Neil. I'm comfortable that we're both legally in the clear and even if some obscure law says we're not, we're acting in the national interest.'

'Are we?'

'Amanda Dennis says we are, and the Cabinet Secretary's on his way here to tell us why. That's all I can tell you.'

'Where is Mrs Dennis?' he asked.

'She's making arrangements for the removal of the body.'

Neil sighed. 'In that case, the very least I'm going to do as a conscientious detective is bag the murder weapon. That's if I can get it out,' he added. 'It looks like the sword in the bloody stone.' He moved behind the desk.

'Wait a minute,' I called out before he could begin. 'I'd better video the removal process. This is history, mate.'

'Make sure it is video,' he exclaimed, 'and not a still. I don't want anything that could be interpreted as me putting it in there.'

He stepped up to Repton's chair, putting on a pair of disposable gloves that he took from his pocket. Raising her lolling head and holding it still with his left hand, he drew the blade slowly and steadily from her skull. It came out easily, the embedded section caked with blood and brain tissue.

'Sssssss.'

'What the . . .' We exclaimed, in unison. We stood, staring at each other, listening; the sound was not repeated, but we were both sure that we had heard it and that it had come from Emily Repton.

'Air escaping?' McIlhenney suggested, nervously. His left arm was still cradling the Prime Minister's head.

'Hardly,' I murmured.

He laid the weapon on the desk, peeled off his right glove with his teeth, and pressed two fingers to her neck feeling for a pulse. 'Nothing,' he whispered.

'Keep holding her like that,' I ordered, as an idea came to me, and I reached for the briefcase that I had laid on the coffee table. I snapped it open and grabbed my Filofax, then slid my Victorinox SwissCard from its pocket. I carried it because James Andrew, my youngest son, had given it to me for my last birthday. I knew the thing would come in handy one day.

Among its many gadgets is a torch. It's tiny, but close up it's quite effective. I switched it on and held it no more than an inch from Repton's right eye, focusing its beam directly on the pupil, looking for any reaction to the light.

There was none. I transferred it to the left eye, holding it even closer, almost touching. I was about to put it away, when I saw the slightest movement in the right eye, the slightest widening of the black centre of the eyeball, then a contraction as I moved the silver shaft of light away. I repeated the process, and saw the same reaction, then did it a third time, for confirmation.

'Hold her, Neil,' I said, 'gently. 'I'll be back.'

I headed for the door, stepping out into the corridor. 'Where's Mrs Dennis?' I asked its Security Service guardian. He glowered up at me, unsmiling, uncooperative.

I took my new symbol of authority from my pocket and held it in his eyeline. 'This is who I am,' I snapped. 'Now answer my question.'

'Sorry, sir,' he said, attitude adjusted. 'The Director is in the Home Secretary's office, with him and Dr Satchell.' He nodded across the passage. I didn't have to ask which door he meant. Another dark-suited man with a gold badge and a bulge in his jacket told me.

This one had a goatee beard and a reddish, receding, V-shaped hairline. I showed the badge again as I moved towards him; he nodded, rapped on the door, then opened it.

I felt the tension grab at my stomach as I stepped inside. The layout was similar to the office I'd just left, a little smaller, that's all. Amanda was seated at a coffee table with two other people, a man and a woman, as the door guard had said. He was very familiar to me from hundreds of TV bulletins and media stories: the Right Honourable Roland Kramer, MP, Home Secretary and Deputy Prime Minister.

He had been Chancellor of the Exchequer in the administration of Emily Repton's predecessor, Locheil, and her only serious rival for the top job, with each of them having the added benefit of not being an old Etonian. She had held him off in the final ballot thanks to her greater support among the membership at large; and then she had neutralised him, by moving him out of the Treasury and into the Home Office, the post that she knew from her own experience to be the most difficult in government.

Kramer was a social animal, no stranger to the celebrity magazines, and he had a reputation as something of a dandy. He lived up to it that morning, in a dark blue three-piece suit that might have graced the frame of a Premier League footballer turned TV pundit, with a gold watch chain hanging across the waistcoat.

Yes, I knew him well enough by sight, but Michaela Satchell rang no bells at all. She was a plain little person. She didn't seem petite, as Amanda had described her, just very small in her big chair. She was still in shock, but so was I, and I wasn't about to go easy on her. As the three of them looked around at my entrance, I glared at her.

'What sort of a bloody doctor are you?' I barked, then switched my gaze to Amanda.

'Director,' I continued . . . I don't know why I addressed her formally, I never had before; I suppose I may have wanted to preserve her authority in the eyes of her boss, 'you'll need some real paramedics in that ambulance. You'll also need a neuro-surgeon wherever it is you're taking her. The Prime Minister is still alive. Only just; there's no detectable pulse, but one of her pupils is reactive to light when it's shone into the other eye. It's weird, but there's definitely neural activity.'

'And what sort of a bloody doctor are you . . . whoever you are?' the wounded Mickey Satchell shouted.

'I'm not,' I replied, calming myself, 'but my wife's a professor of forensic pathology, and I know she wouldn't be opening up the Prime Minister just yet.'

'Home Secretary,' Amanda said, quietly, looking at Kramer to maintain a degree of order.

He stood, extending a slim hand. 'You're Mr Skinner, the fortuitous police officer.'

'No longer a police officer,' I replied as we shook. 'Now I'm just fortuitous.'

'Nevertheless, I'm grateful to you for being here and agreeing to help . . . as it seems you've done already, very significantly.' He glanced at Amanda. 'DG, you'd better act on Mr Skinner's findings, and get those people in place. You and I, Mr Skinner,' he continued, turning back to me, 'we have a briefing by the Cabinet Secretary, whose feathers you have ruffled well and truly.' He winked. 'Don't worry, I've smoothed them . . . although I don't suppose you're the worrying type.'

'What about me?' Satchell asked, as Amanda left the room.

'You go away,' Kramer replied curtly, 'with your lips buttoned tighter than they've ever been, difficult as that may be for you.'

A couple of minutes before I'd been barking at the woman, but the Home Secretary's coldness had won her some of my sympathy.

'Go to her, then go in the ambulance,' I suggested. 'She's

catatonic at the moment and clearly she has massive brain damage, but on the slim chance that she might say something coherent and relevant, we need someone to hear it.'

'You're suggesting that Emily's a witness to her own murder?' Kramer exclaimed; his sceptical grin shocked me.

'All murder victims are, Home Secretary,' I reminded him. 'I've even known one or two who were able to give evidence.'

'Written in their own blood?' His smile widened. I couldn't decide whether the man was as callous as any I'd ever met or whether under the urbanity he was just plain terrified. Then I took a closer look and realised that Roland Kramer hadn't clambered up the greasy pole of politics by being afraid of anything.

I frowned at him. 'Or in other media,' I replied, coldly. 'Death isn't always instantaneous.'

Sensing my hostility, he changed his manner, to match mine. 'I take your point. Let's see how it pans out in this case, but from what I've been told, if Emily does survive by some miracle, she won't be the woman we know.'

He reached into his waistcoat with his left hand, took out a gold full hunter pocket watch, flipped open the case and peered at it impatiently. 'Come on, Hamblin,' he muttered. 'We need you here, now.'

I nodded. 'Yes, we do,' I agreed. 'As yet I haven't seen any reason for keeping PaDP out of this, or anything to justify the massive deception that we're engaged in. Amanda talked about national security, but government's continuous. As deputy, you must surely be the acting Prime Minister as of now. She talked about special issues, but I haven't seen any, just a woman with a blade rammed into her head and left for dead.'

'Nonetheless,' Kramer replied, 'there are, as you will discover.'

'When I do, I want my colleague in here.'

'Absolutely not!' the Home Secretary exclaimed, switching back into aggressive mode in an instant. 'This has to be on a need-to-know basis.'

'And Commander McIlhenney needs to know; he's been seconded to work with me on this investigation. I can't have knowledge that I'm unable to share with him. You must understand that.'

'I do, but he's Metropolitan Police, and when this is over he'll go back there, free to tell his colleagues anything he chooses. Work your way round any difficulty. I'm sorry, but that's the way it has to be.'

'Then I'm sorry too, but I'm leaving.' I started for the door.

'You can't,' Kramer called out. 'I can't allow that.'

I stopped in mid-stride, turning to stare at him. 'Would you be threatening me, by any chance?' I looked him up and down. 'Because I don't think you're up to stopping me.'

'The man on the door is. He's Security Service but he's mine, and he does what I tell him. So is the one on the PM's door.'

'You'll need more than him,' I warned.

His thin lips formed a thin, smug smile. 'Really? Are you armed?'

'I will be by the time the second of those men comes for me.'

'Then we'd better avoid that possibility. Richard!' he shouted. In less than two seconds, half the time it would have taken me to reach it, the door opened and its keeper stepped into the room, pistol in hand, aimed at me.

'His name is actually Daffyd,' Kramer said mildly, pleased with his show of power. 'Richard is a code word that means weapon drawn.'

I ignored him and looked at the minder, unblinking eye to unblinking eye. *Yes, he would*, I decided.

I nodded in the general direction of his boss. 'Okay,' I murmured, 'I'll stay. But I am telling you now, Daffyd, that I am no threat to the Home Secretary, and I seriously do not like people pointing guns at me. You've done your job, now lower it, or you'll have made it personal. In that case you'll have to live with the possibility that one day, maybe even tomorrow, I'll have the power to send you to the Security Service version of Siberia, in which event you can pack your thermals.'

Kramer may have nodded to him; I couldn't tell because my back was to him. Whether he did or not, Daffyd reholstered his pistol.

'That'll be enough for now,' the Home Secretary declared. 'You can resume your station.'

'That goes for you too, by the way,' I advised him as the door closed. 'I never forget a threat.'

'You imagine you'd ever be able to harm me?' he chuckled.

'I have no idea,' I conceded, 'but you can't say for certain that I won't, so bear it in mind.'

In the silence that developed I began to think of what I might achieve as a cross-bencher in the Lords, or even as a Labour peer. In that moment the idea was attractive; then Sarah seemed to whisper in my ear, '*Best thing you can do, Bob, is make sure our kids don't grow up like him*,' and I knew she was right.

I kept looking at him, though, until he grew fidgety and turned away, to peer through the blast curtains that shrouded his window.

'We've got off on the wrong foot,' he exclaimed, changing his tone once more. 'We've got to work together on this. Agreed?'

'Agreed,' I replied, 'but only for as long as it takes.'

He turned back to face me. 'If you do succeed, Mr Skinner, if you do find Emily's attacker and keep the genie in the box, what's your price?'

'What makes you think I have one?'

'Everybody does.'

'Scottish independence,' I ventured, half-seriously.

He laughed. 'Not something I can grant, I'm afraid, much as I'd like to. How about a peerage? Join our team in the Lords. I'd make you security minister.'

I laughed in return, but he had no idea why; offers from both sides, and the one in the middle. 'Not my style,' I retorted.

'Then how about Mrs Dennis's job? Your record speaks for itself; yes, I do know all about you. Emily told me that you and she had, sorry, have, history. Amanda is very good, but I am not quite convinced that she's completely on message.'

'Amanda's better than that,' I countered quietly. 'She's the best person in the land to be holding her job. She's also a very close friend, and if you think I'd ever agree to supplant her, then you certainly do not know all about me. In fact you know fuck all about me. In the last five minutes you've offered me threats, then flattery, and now inducements. You should have had Neil McIlhenney in here; he'd have stopped you after the first of those.'

Kramer shook his head. 'Sorry,' he said, 'I can't help misjudging situations this morning. Not that I care too much,' he added, casually.

'Then let me mark your card about another one. It isn't Amanda's role to be "on message", not yours or anyone else's. She has to be independent of people like you and she has to work with a free hand. If I was in her chair, I'd be your worst fucking nightmare based on what I've learned about you since I walked in here. So would she be if I told her everything that's happened.'

I let that sink in, then continued. 'I will work with you on this, Kramer, because I know Emily Repton, and though I didn't like her when we met, I like what's happened to her even less. But once it's done, whatever the outcome, you'll be my next project. If there's a way to stop you succeeding her . . . yes, she's probably going to die, maybe before the ambulance reaches hospital . . . then I'll find . . .'

I broke off, as the door opened again, and an angry man flowed into the room. That's the best way I can describe it; he had a liquid way of moving that made me think of mercury. Angry? That's how he seemed from the glare in his brown eyes and the way that his sandy hair bristled, as though he'd just been on the end of a low-voltage shock.

'Mr Hamblin,' Kramer exclaimed, his expression telling me that he was grateful for the intervention. 'You made it, finally. I'm sorry we couldn't answer your summons to the Cabinet Office, but Mr Skinner here was quite right in his insistence that this secret should be contained within this building, for now.'

He nodded in my direction. 'You don't know Mr Skinner, do you? A chief constable in recess, was how Mrs Dennis described him to me, the man best suited to investigating the attack on the Prime Minister with the discretion that the situation demands. Mr Skinner, this is Mr Norman Hamblin, the Cabinet Secretary.'

The angry eyes blazed at me briefly, then switched back to Kramer. 'Home Secretary,' he murmured in a soft voice that was at odds with his fierce appearance. 'Surely the situation changes with the Prime Minister's death. The decision that was taken: with her gone, should it not be reviewed, and at the very least endorsed by her successor? This afternoon's statement . . .'

'. . . must be postponed,' Kramer concluded for him. 'Yes, that's obvious. That will be announced as soon as the Prime Minister has left the building. She's not dead, by the way. Mickey Satchell's clinical skills seem to have been eroded by three years in the House. Damn near it, though. Still, she's alive and that means she's still PM. Even if she wasn't, why should the decision be reviewed?'

'The dynamic changes, even with her incapacity, Home Secretary,' Hamblin said. 'The core group . . .'

'That will not be changed in any meaningful way.' Kramer raised an eyebrow. 'Are you suggesting that if there's a new leadership election I might not win it?'

'We can't assume that you will, Home . . .'

'For Christ's sake stop being so bloody formal, Norman,' he exclaimed. 'We're three men in a room. Best case for the PM is that she survives, but I've seen her, Mr Skinner here has seen her, and neither of us would count on that. Whether she stays in limbo, or whether she dies, I'm acting PM. If there has to be a contest to choose a new leader, I know how the numbers stack up, I know who'll oppose me and I know he hasn't a chance. So, Norman, if you're trying to reverse a decision to which I know you are personally opposed, forget it. Now please, put an end to Mr Skinner's ignorance of what the fuck we are talking about! Brief him. Come on, let's all sit.'

The Cabinet Secretary was shaking with indignation; Mr Angry had become Mr Furious. I've known a few top-level civil servants in Scotland; all of them were used to being obeyed without question and none of them was pleasant if they were crossed. He glared at me as we sat; his eyebrows were a continuous russet line.

'Have you signed the Official Secrets Act?' he demanded. Next to me, Kramer sighed.

I made myself smile at him. 'Several times more than was necessary,' I replied, 'for once is enough. But I'm happy to sign it again,' I added, then grinned, 'in your blood if you like.'

His lip curled at my humour; I wondered if he was having trouble suppressing a snarl, or if there was a human being imprisoned in there.

'Then be warned,' he murmured, 'it has never meant as much as it does now.'

I nodded, and as I did so, my phone vibrated in my pocket. I took it out, to turn it off. 'Sorry,' I said as I looked at the screen, which displayed a text from Sarah, just two words, 'My Lord?'

I smiled and was about to silence it, when a very large potential problem hit me. 'Bloody hell!' I whispered. 'Mr Kramer, I need to use your computer, now. I need to access my iCloud account.'

'Why?' he asked, curious rather than impatient.

I held up my iPhone. 'In the absence of a forensic team, I took photographs of the scene in the PM's office, and some video as well. They'll have uploaded automatically to the Cloud. In theory all user accounts are secure, but we both know that's only true up to a point. I have to delete them, pronto.'

'Yes, you have,' he agreed. He rose and led me to his desk. 'Hold on a second, and I'll log you in.'

When I opened the account, sure enough, all the stills and video I had shot were there, if not for all the world to see, then certainly those at GCHQ, Langley and anyone else with the technology and skills to hack in there. I deleted each image individually; it took me several minutes and all the time I was hoping that no damage had been done.

When I was finished, I cleared the history on the computer, and rejoined the other two at the table. Hamblin looked at me with evident smugness, and the closest to a smile I'd seen him display.

'That hasn't filled me with confidence in your ability to guard the information that I'm about to give you,' he said.

I felt my hackles move into lift-off position.

'Just get on with it, man,' I sighed, 'or give me a Snickers; I turn into a right diva when I'm hungry, and it's closing on my lunchtime.'

Hamblin's lip curled again; he made a sound like a hissing snake, then began.

'Last week,' he said, 'a decision was taken. The Prime Minister was going to announce it in the House this afternoon. The statement prompted much speculation when it appeared on the Commons business, because nothing had been trailed and no one had been briefed, contrary to what has become standard practice in this place.'

'I know,' I told him. 'My ex-wife was completely in the dark when I saw her earlier, and she's on the shadow defence team.'

Hamblin recoiled, with a shuddering gasp. 'Home Secretary,' he exclaimed, looking wide eyed at Kramer. 'In all conscience, do you really think . . .'

'Yes I do,' Roland Kramer snapped. 'We knew about that relationship. And if you knew as much as you should about the key people on the Opposition benches, it wouldn't have come as a surprise to you either. Now please, Norman, carry on.'

I was struck by the open hostility between two of the most

powerful people in the country, but I kept silent, waiting for the civil servant to regain his composure.

'At three thirty this afternoon,' he continued, when he was ready, 'the Prime Minister was scheduled to make an announcement that will have the most profound effect on this nation. She was intending to announce the cancellation of the renewal of the Trident missile system.' He paused, looking at me. 'You know what Trident is, I take it.'

Those sensitive hackles of mine couldn't have risen any higher. 'The Faslane base lay within my operating territory as Chief Constable of Strathclyde,' I growled at him. 'My force had contingency plans for every sort of disaster, including the disappearance of the city of Glasgow. So yes, I rather do know what it is. Are you telling me that the government is cancelling the upgrade of the system? If so, what's the point of keeping it? It'll soon be obsolete, if it isn't already.'

'We're not keeping it,' Hamblin replied.

That did surprise me.

'We're abandoning the deterrent? You'll make the people of Scotland very happy.' I glanced at Kramer. 'What happened? Was the independence referendum result too close for your liking?'

'We're not abandoning the deterrent either,' the Cabinet Secretary said. 'It will be maintained, but the "continuous at sea" principle will be superseded by a new delivery system, one which will be much more effective and also much cheaper. Instead of large solid-fuelled rockets launched from nuclear submarines on continuous patrols, it will be based on a projectile with a laser propulsion system. These will carry miniaturised warheads to multiple targets. The package will be much lighter, and will be capable of launch from aircraft, vessels, and from the ground in tactical situations. Once the payload has been delivered, the projectile will return to base, or proceed to any designated point. And,' he added, 'it will be unique to the United Kingdom. The system will be called Spitfire, in tribute to a familiar British icon.'

'That sounds like nothing else on earth,' I observed.

'You are absolutely right,' Hamblin declared, with a sudden burst of enthusiasm. 'It will transform our global position. From being at best the third-ranking member of the nuclear club, we will be out there on our own in terms of strike power and effectiveness. Because it isn't a ballistic missile, the rocket-based defence systems that the Americans have developed will be useless against Spitfire . . . not that it would ever be directed at them, of course. Its range will be unlimited, Mr Skinner.'

'That's not to say the missile submarine fleet will be redundant,' the Home Secretary added. 'As the Cabinet Secretary said, Spitfire can be launched at sea and so the Trident boats will be adapted to carry them instead of rockets. The only difference will be that they'll have to surface, although the Aldermaston people are working on a version that can be launched from a submerged vessel.'

'How the hell have we managed to keep the development of such a system secret?' I asked.

'By keeping the circle of knowledge as small as possible,' Hamblin replied, 'and also by keeping it compartmentalised. Those working on the project only knew their own part; the totality is known to very few people, even within the core group . . .'

I held up a hand. 'Stop; what's this core group?'

'The core Cabinet,' Kramer volunteered. 'The Prime

Minister, me, the Chancellor, Defence Secretary and Foreign Secretary, plus the Cabinet Secretary. We took the decision to commit to Spitfire. What Mr Hamblin was about to say was that even within the core group, there is restricted knowledge. The whole package only exists in Mr Hamblin's safe keeping in the Cabinet Office, and not on paper either. Treasury has the financial models and Defence has the operational models; Foreign Office is briefed on international fall-out . . . unfortunate term but you know what I mean.'

'I do,' I said, 'and I guess that will be considerable.'

'Absolutely,' the Home Secretary agreed. 'All sorts of people will be very pissed off with us. The Americans will be very piqued at having lost effective control of the British deterrent as the providers of Trident, and at no longer being the nuclear superpower; our NATO allies will take some talking round, and as for our relations with the EU, they'll go from worse to worst. As for the other side, our trading relationships with China will be vulnerable, and as for the man in the Kremlin, I can see the veins on his neck standing out already . . . especially when his generals realise the benefit of Spitfire that we'll keep out of the announcement.'

He frowned, paused, reflecting; then he made a decision and continued.

'As far as hostiles are concerned, wherever they are, we will have virtually undetectable first-strike capability. The system can literally fly under the radar, faster than you can imagine.'

'So a nuclear war could be over before the losers even knew it had begun?'

'Precisely; their command centres would be destroyed before they had a chance to retaliate. That's how fast the projectiles travel.'

64

'That is fucking scary,' I conceded. 'Morally scary too,' I suggested.

'Yes, but so what? If the North Koreans had this technology, would their signature on a treaty make you sleep easier at night?'

'Not a lot,' I admitted. 'How did we develop this thing anyway?' I asked. 'What defence establishments do we have that are capable of that?'

'We didn't develop it,' Kramer replied. 'We bought it.'

I stared at him. 'Amazon has gone that far?'

'Very funny, but your humour is actually pretty close to the mark. The Spitfire projectile and its propulsion system was developed by a private individual, an American citizen named John Balliol, a billionaire who describes himself as a high-tech entrepreneur.'

'Balliol?' I repeated, as the name jumped up and bit me. I knew it well, for it had figured a couple of times in my past.

'Any relation to a man named Everard Balliol, a crazy American who owned a large chunk of the Scottish Highlands?'

Kramer nodded. 'His son. Everard Balliol died five years ago when one of his household, a Korean bodyguard, robbed and killed him. John inherited; he'd been playing around with private projects for years with the limited cash that his father let him have, but once he inherited he committed to his dreams. One of them was laser propulsion. There's nothing new about the concept, it's been explored for years as a way forward in powering spacecraft.'

'As in ion rockets?'

'Yes, but they only work in space; laser propulsion, or some forms of it, have capability within the atmosphere. That's what Balliol's team focused on, in a secret establishment in Brazil . . . hence the Amazon link. They succeeded, not in producing an engine that would take us from Miami to Mars, as he had imagined, but in miniaturising the system. When he saw what he had, he brought it to us.'

I asked the obvious. 'Why us? Balliol's American.'

'Yes,' Hamblin said, forcing his way back into the discussion, 'but he is an Anglophile, as was his father, with a dislike of his own nation that borders on hatred. I don't know why, but it's not relevant.'

More of a Scotophile, I thought as I recalled crazy old Everard, but I let it pass.

'Balliol didn't realise his system's full potential,' the Cabinet Secretary continued, 'but he knew enough to believe that it should not be given to a nation with the potential to elect a war-mongering demagogue as its commander-in-chief, so he brought it to us. His price was one billion sterling, and his team's participation in future development, that to be funded by the British government.

'Oh yes,' Hamblin murmured, 'and one other thing; a British passport. John Balliol is now a citizen of the United Kingdom.'

'When did this happen?' I asked.

'Two years ago; during the Locheil administration. That's when the agreement with Balliol was struck. Since then his development team has been working at Aldermaston, the Atomic Weapons Establishment, which was rebranded at the beginning of the century as AWE, in a burst of "Cool Britannia" enthusiasm.

'Its staff have been working on warhead miniaturisation for years; when the Balliol people came on board, it was just a natural fit. And yet,' he added, 'none of the research staff know the totality of the project, only Balliol himself.'

'Outside the core group you spoke of, who else knows about this?'

'Mrs Dennis, the Chief of the Defence Staff, and the heads of the three services, Army, Navy and RAF. They know the outline, but not the detail. Also the head of MI6, the Secret Intelligence Service; his department has an operational brief to look for any sign of development of a similar system in other parts of the world.'

I frowned. 'Might that be because you don't trust Balliol not to have sold the technology to a second buyer?'

'It might,' the Home Secretary conceded with a faint smile. 'There is no sign of it, I must say. It looks as if the man is on the level, but it's a sensible precaution to have taken.'

I nodded. 'How advanced are we? How close to deployment?'

'We have battlefield systems available now,' Hamblin replied, 'and the manufacture of longer-range projectiles is under way; we have a viable prototype already. Within two years, continuous-at-sea deterrence will be no more, in its current form.'

'How have you been able to achieve this without it being detected? The missile tests must have left some sort of a trail, surely.'

'Or again, these aren't missiles as such, Mr Skinner. We refer to them as projectiles, but they are remotely pilotable aircraft. Any nation, hostile or otherwise, that's had us under surveillance will have assumed that we were testing drones. Effectively that's what they are.

'Flying bombs, with a delivery speed at least five times that of the fastest conventional aircraft, global range and a propulsion system without a heat signature. The fact is, we could launch one from Aldermaston now, and obliterate Pyongyang by teatime.'

I whistled. 'From what you're telling me, I reckon there should be an international treaty to ban these things.'

'You may be right,' Kramer acknowledged, 'but the genie's left the bottle and the cork's been lost. Be grateful that we have the system and our enemies don't.'

'We have the system,' I countered, 'but do we have to deploy it?'

'That's the decision that the core group took.'

'The core group,' I repeated. 'Not the Cabinet, not parliament.'

'Sometimes leaders have to lead.'

'And now one's had a blade stuck in her head.'

'Precisely, and you can see what Mrs Dennis and I are wondering. Has there been a security leak? Is there a connection between the attack on Emily and the announcement? Is this an attempt to sabotage Spitfire? That's why you're here, Mr Skinner, you and Commander McIlhenney. We are hoping that you can find out. What will you need?'

My head was swimming through the flood of information that had been dumped on me. 'I don't know yet,' I replied, 'but a full forensic examination of the crime scene would have been a good place to start.'

'Noted,' the Home Secretary said, testily, 'but in its absence?'

'We need a plan of this building showing all means of access to this corridor. We need to have access to CCTV as close as it gets to here, even if the scene itself isn't covered. We need to interview every person with knowledge of the announcement, and of Spitfire,' I looked at him then at Hamblin, 'including you two.'

'Us? We've just told you all we know,' Kramer exclaimed.

'No, sir, you've told me all you think you know. We will require to interview you both again, individually, and we'll need to interview the other three members of the core group.'

'As suspects?' Hamblin snapped. 'Surely, Mr Skinner . . .'

'As witnesses,' I countered, as patiently as I could.

'Okay,' his political master said. 'You will have all the cooperation you ask for. You can interview all of us, with the exception of the military, at this stage at least. If it becomes necessary, we'll see. Where do you want to base yourself? Thames House?'

I was on the point of agreeing with him; the Security Service headquarters building is a stone's throw from the Palace of Westminster and its security was guaranteed. But a potential problem stopped me short. All the people I had named were high profile; they rarely travelled alone and wherever they went they tended to draw attention.

'No,' I replied. 'It'll be more discreet if we're somewhere that the people we're interviewing would normally go.'

Kramer nodded. 'Yes, that makes sense. If the Chancellor was seen walking into the MI5 building, God knows what sort of rumours would start. Mr Hamblin, please arrange for Mr Skinner and Commander McIlhenney to be accommodated within the Cabinet Office. That's adjacent to Downing Street. Will that be okay?'

'Yes, that'll do,' I told him. 'Now, in addition to the core group, there are others we'll need to interview. We'll begin with Dr Satchell, and then we'll want to speak to Ms Repton's protection officers. As soon as they've delivered her to hospital, have them all come to see us.'

'Mickey I can understand, but why do you need the protection people?' he challenged. 'They weren't here when Emily was attacked.'

'Maybe not, but I think you'll find they want to help trace her attacker. I know, I know, you've given us a specific remit, to seek out any link between the attack and the Spitfire announcement, but I don't propose to stick to it. We will find out who did this thing, whatever the motive. I need to talk to these two officers to determine whether anything has happened recently that might give us a line of inquiry.

'One other thing,' I added. 'It is not possible for Neil McIlhenney to operate alongside me without knowing at least some of the story. You will leave me to include him as far as I need to, and that will be at my discretion. I'm talking here about a man whose job is to run deep-cover police officers infiltrating organised crime. For you or anyone else to suggest that he can't be trusted with information, well, frankly, that offends me.'

'Have it your way,' Kramer sighed, with a shrug. 'What about Balliol?' he asked, suddenly. 'Do you want to see him?'

'He's here?'

'No, but I can bring him up from Aldermaston at a couple of hours' notice.'

'Then I may need to interview him also. I'll tell you if I do.'

As I spoke I heard movement in the corridor outside. 'Now,' I said, brimming over with pleasure at the experience of laying down the law to the two guys who, on that day, in that place, were running the country, 'I need to get to work, so that means I need to get back to Mrs Dennis. Mr Hamblin, the plan was that you go with the PM to hospital, but as this is now a genuine emergency admission you'd probably just be in the way, so you'd be better employed back at the Cabinet Office arranging our accommodation and arranging for the people we need to interview to come to see us, pronto.'

He stared at me with something that I couldn't define; it

could have been fascination or it could have been hatred; either way I wasn't bothered, not at that time.

'You, Home Secretary,' I continued, 'have an announcement to make about the Prime Minister's sudden indisposition, and you've had a stroke of luck. The fact that she's unexpectedly still alive . . . if she still is . . . means that if your press office people are any good, they'll be able to draft something for you that doesn't require you to tell a flat-out lie.' I winked at him, with the memory of his stunt with his bodyguard fresh in my mind. 'That'll probably be a new experience for you.'

Six

I went back to the Prime Minister's office, with a brief nod to Daffyd as I passed him, to find Neil and Amanda waiting there, but nobody else.

'She's gone?' I asked, as I eased myself into a chair beside them.

'Yes,' he said, 'two minutes ago.'

'They couldn't wait for Hamblin,' she added.

'There was no need anyway,' I said. 'He has other things to do than wringing his hands by the bedside. From the haste, I take it the Prime Minister is still alive.'

Amanda nodded. 'Yes. They're not sure of her level of awareness, for she's unable to move, and completely unresponsive. The paramedics were not hopeful, to say the least.'

'The real ones or yours?'

She returned my smile. 'Mine were stood down, given the change in circumstances. She's been taken to the high-level isolation unit in the Royal Free Hospital, in line with the original cover story that we agreed when we thought she was dead.'

'Which makes me ask . . .' I said, 'how's Dr Satchell? I think I owe her an apology. I went a wee bit over the top at her along in Kramer's office. None of the three of us had any doubt that

Ms Repton was dead when we saw her lying there, and we've seen a fair few who were. Even the sound she made could have been a reflex, gases escaping from somewhere, and the reaction of her pupil was minimal.'

'Don't waste your sympathy on the woman Satchell,' Amanda snorted. 'She's an unctuous little twat, without a friend in the House of Commons. I don't know why Emily Repton ever chose her as her aide.'

'What do you know about the Prime Minister?' I asked her.

'In what respect?' she countered, cautiously.

'In every respect. Don't tell me you don't have a file on her.'

'We did, as we do on most leading politicians, but when she was Home Secretary she had Hubert Lowery, my predecessor, destroy it. When I took over I'd have rebuilt it, but by that time she'd moved to the DWP and the Civil Service there built a wall around her.'

'And since then?'

She shook her head. 'No, she's PM now. That makes a difference.'

'Do you have a file on Roland Kramer?' Neil asked. 'Or has he had his destroyed?'

'We do,' she admitted, 'and the Prime Minister was fully aware of its contents. He was over-stretched financially five years ago, but his wife is a hedge fund manager, and one of her bonuses took care of all of that. There are a couple of bones in his closet maybe but nowhere near a full skeleton. He was a little fast and loose with his parliamentary expenses before the great scandal, but who wasn't? His family are respectable . . . his father paid all his taxes; he was a solicitor, like yours, Bob . . . his mother was chair of Ladies Circle, and his sister is married to a bishop. Roland had a promising career at the Bar, before being elected. He was Solicitor General at the start of the last administration, then Minister of State in Defence; his first Cabinet post was Welsh Secretary, then made a big jump to the Treasury, as Chief Secretary at first, then Chancellor. He was there when he contested the Conservative leadership election. He was never expected to win, but he emerged as the recognised number two, which Emily made official.'

'Private life?'

She smiled at my question. 'It's very difficult for politicians to have one these days. *Private Eye* was bad enough for them but these bloggers we have now, Jesus!'

'That wasn't an answer, Amanda,' I pointed out, quietly. 'I know he's your boss, but . . .'

'He's a straight arrow,' she replied, firmly. 'He has a few female friends from his university days that he still sees, but never one on one with any of them, only at gatherings. He's a faithful husband, no question, and devoted to his two sons, Billy, who's twelve, and Jay, who's ten.'

'But . . . ?' I said, for I sensed one.

'But.' She paused. 'We think that Siuriña, his wife, might play away games. We don't keep her under twenty-four-hour observation, but given her own political position, there is some oversight, for her sake. There's been a pattern of unexplained absences that have raised the question, but I've never let anyone try to confirm it.'

'What is her political positon?' Neil asked.

'She's the chair of the Conservative Party.'

'How long might this thing of hers have been going on?'

'At least three years. George Locheil appointed her as party chair a year before the last election. If our suspicions are correct, and she does have a bit on the side, she's been able to sustain it because she has a professional life that allows her to explain periods away from home.'

'Is she still involved with her hedge fund?'

'No, that had to end when Roland went to the Treasury.'

'Why haven't you tried to verify this possible fling?' I wondered.

'Because she's the bloody Home Secretary's wife,' she laughed, 'and he's my boss. How would you handle it if you were in my shoes?' she challenged.

'If I was in your shoes I'd be struggling to keep my balance,' I retorted. 'But yes, I get that,' I carried on. 'That's Kramer's back story; now, fill us in on the other members of the core group, for we're going to be interviewing them all.'

'You are?'

'Of course,' I said. 'The brief that Kramer has given me is to establish whether there's a link between the attack on the Prime Minister and the announcement she was due to make this afternoon, whether it might have been a desperate attempt to scupper the Spitfire project.'

'The what?' Neil exclaimed.

I realised that I'd just broken Kramer's injunction, but I wasn't too concerned. 'Tell you later,' I said, then continued.

'If there is, it would indicate that the thing has leaked beyond the need to know group. And if that's happened, who has advance knowledge of what we're up to? The Americans? The Russians? The French? ISIS? From what I've been told, if this system was deployed in Syria it could end that conflict in a couple of days, even if only conventional weapons were used. It's fucking Star Wars, Amanda. So, too damn right I'm going to interview anyone I need to.'

'Fair enough, but remember you're doing this as a member

of my service, so don't start any fires that I'm going to have trouble putting out once you've gone. Christ,' she chuckled, 'listen to me! I might as well look out my extinguisher now.

'Okay, let's see,' she continued. 'Where to begin? Start with Leslie Ellis, Chancellor of the Exchequer. He's one of the old brigade, age fifty-eight and a member of parliament since nineteen ninety-two.

'He was Emily Repton's political mentor; he took her under his wing when she was elected in two thousand and one. Fifteen years on, he ran her leadership campaign and was rewarded with the Treasury, after a career of mostly low-level Cabinet and shadow Cabinet posts, until he became Defence Secretary in the previous administration.

'He's a sound pair of hands, been a good Chancellor so far, and they say that he has absolutely no ambition to be Prime Minister. His family business background was metal bending in the Midlands, producing wire components for various industries, but he sold his interest when he was elected to parliament. He was married for twenty-eight years but was widowed five years ago. He has one son, James, age thirty, who's a PR consultant, for want of a better term.'

'And on the debit side?'

'Apart from a penchant for dressing in ladies' underwear, which he was silly enough to buy on Amazon, under an assumed name but using his London address? Well, for ten years he was an active shareholder in a company that owned and managed rental property in Leicester, which adjoins his constituency. In fact, those properties were virtual slums, poorly managed and maintained, with inflated rents. There was a fatal fire in one of them; an Asian family, parents and three kids, all died. Scandal followed and Les Ellis sold his shareholding. It was held through a company, but it's traceable, and it might still crush him if it became known. To put an extra spin on it, he was shadow Housing Minister at the time.'

'What about the son?' McIlhenney asked. There was something in his tone that made me curious.

'James is clean as a whistle,' she replied. 'Educated at Winchester and Cambridge; openly gay, in a permanent relationship and due to be married next spring.'

'And his partner?'

'London born, Pakistani origins, a currency trader; Shafat Iqbal by name. They met at Cambridge and have been together ever since; that's according to Les, not my people. Shafat's family are Muslim, but he's an outcast because of his sexuality and the fact that he hasn't been to a mosque since he was fifteen.'

'How close,' I chipped in, 'are father and son, Les and James? Would he have access to the Chancellor's papers?'

'In theory, he would if his father allowed it. To answer your first question, the two are very close. Les owns a house in leafy Wimbledon which he shares with James and Shafat, and no, he doesn't claim it as a second home on expenses.'

'What do we know about Shafat?' I asked her.

'No more than I've just told you.'

'Then find out the rest.' The expression that crossed Amanda's face, however briefly, pulled me up short. I smiled inwardly, but kept it from showing.

Skinner, I scolded myself, *you're not a chief constable any longer. You're a seconded member of maybe the most powerful organisation in the country and this lady is your boss. For once in your life, show respect.*

'I'm sorry, Director,' I said, contritely. 'I need to get over myself and stop issuing orders. We have to assume that the

Ellis/Iqbal household is as relaxed and imperfect as anyone else's. So Shafat Iqbal, who's about to be the Chancellor's son-in-law, might see anything that was left lying around, if only for a second or two, and would be part of any casual conversation across the dinner table. And who doesn't talk business occasionally?'

'Granted,' she acknowledged. Then she smiled. 'Apology accepted also, but it wasn't necessary. When I brought you in on this I knew how it would be. In fact, it was one of the reasons I did. I know that you're no respecter of office, and that you won't let anyone or anything get in your way. So just carry on and if you see a red rag, charge at it.'

I remembered an exchange less than an hour before. 'I'm not that reckless,' I countered, 'but I do break a lot of china.'

'I'll sweep it up. Okay, I will put people on Shafat.'

McIlhenney coughed. I know that cough, so it got my attention. I frowned at him. 'What?'

Seven

T alk about being dropped in it. I watched Bob and the head of the Security Service butt heads, I listened to their exchange and all the while I was hoping that she would win. Of course I should have known better.

When he came out on top, I knew I couldn't sit silent any longer, as a crazy Keystone Cops situation was about to develop.

'Don't,' I said, quietly. 'He's one of mine.'

They stared at me. 'Yours?' Mrs Dennis gasped; yes, that's what it was, a gasp of incredulity. 'SCD10?' My, she was on the ball; very few people remember the designation of my section.

'Yes.'

'Then his cover's bloody good.'

'It is, ma'am,' I agreed, with due deference; I've always been more respectful of rank than Bob Skinner has. 'Most of it's true, as well. He and James Ellis did meet at Cambridge, and he was indeed a currency trader, until he was twenty-three. Then he quit and became a cop. He was noticed early, because he's bright and, I suspect, because he's Asian, and he was posted to my team. It all happened before I arrived there.'

'Go on,' Bob urged. I could tell that they were both intrigued *by my revelation. Me? I was quietly chuffed that I knew something MI5 didn't.*

'He did a couple of operations,' I continued, 'long term, deep cover, with a new identity. The first was abortive when the target was murdered in a dispute with a rival. In the second he infiltrated a crew who were importing fake electrical goods from Bulgaria, and flogging them at street markets all around the country. That might not sound too glamorous, when compared with narcotics and the like, but there was a level of violence involved that peaked when they killed a security guard in a lorry park. Shafat got a result there, twenty convictions with total jail time of over two hundred years, and he earned himself a promotion to DS. That's what he is now.'

'So why do we think he's still a currency trader?' Mrs Dennis asked, pointedly.

That was when it got tricky. I almost said, 'For your ears only,' but I remembered who and what she was.

'Because he is,' I said, 'as far as the world's concerned. I have an operation in place in the City that's been going on for a couple of years; I won't go into detail because it isn't relevant, but there's an organised, multi-multi-million pound scam going on in the money market, and we are in there, through Shafat. When I was tasked with getting into it and breaking it up, he was the obvious guy to infiltrate it; I didn't have to change his name or much of his background. All I needed to do was invent a reason for a seven-year absence from the trading floor and give him a new address. Ostensibly, he's living in a flat across the river that's worth a couple of mil and was confiscated from a Russian gangster, and his CV has been doctored so that it includes a spell working in Singapore.'

'How exposed is he?' Bob asked.

'Very; we're talking very serious money and there are dangerous people at the top of the chain, Indians, not your usual east European hoodlums, but just as vicious. He's due to report to his handler tomorrow morning. He's very close to success, but this job is as risky as any other, so please,' I looked at the chief spook, 'Mrs Dennis, do not do anything that might put him in danger.'

'Of course not,' she replied, then glanced at Bob. 'I'm glad you brought him in,' she added.

Eight

I could tell that, inwardly, Amanda was boiling mad that her people had been taken for a ride by Neil's cover yarn for Shafat Iqbal, complete with fake CV. I didn't envy the operatives involved in what would be coming their way when she found time to deal with them.

At the same time, I was pleased with the way that my mate had handled a delicate situation. She recognised it too, as she made clear when Neil had finished. Then she set it aside.

'In any event,' she continued, 'going back to the Chancellor, leaving out Commander McIlhenney's operative, and a potential security leak through James Ellis, no, I can't rule it out, Bob, but remember that Spitfire is so secret that there is minimal reference to it on paper and even then it's coded. James could look at it and probably not have a clue what it was.'

I nodded. 'Point taken, who's next?'

'The Right Honourable Montgomery Radley, MP,' she replied, 'age sixty-two, Her Majesty's Principal Secretary of State for Foreign Affairs. I give him his full title because he's so far up himself it wouldn't seem right just to call him Monty. When the inevitable next leadership contest happens, if anyone runs against Roland Kramer it'll be him . . . if he can find enough backers to get on the ballot paper.'

'Will he?'

'Probably, because he does have a degree of support in the traditional wing of the party, and among the Commons dinosaurs who went with Emily because they don't like Kramer. He won't get anywhere near winning, though; if I thought he had a chance, I might have to do something about it.'

'Why?' I asked, puzzled.

'Because he drinks too much and he beats his wife. Oh yes, and because he's a rapist.'

Both Neil and I stiffened in our seats. 'Alleged, or for sure?' I asked.

'Alleged, but I believe it. It happened in the year of his election to the Commons, nineteen eighty-seven. He strolled into his safe seat in Hampshire, and as the victory party was drawing to a close decided that he fancied his female agent's fifteen-year-old daughter, who'd had a couple of glasses of champagne and was passed out in a spare room. The mother caught him in the act. The kid was moaning and she'd been sick; she didn't know what was going on, and to this day I don't think she knows for sure that it happened.'

'The mother hushed it up?' Neil exclaimed.

'Completely. I'd like to think it was for the daughter's sake, but I'm not so sure; political professionals are often real zealots. She carried on as Radley's agent for another eight years, until she died of spinal cancer. When she was terminal, she told her husband about the incident. He went ballistic, as one would at such a story, but he knew that if he went to the police, it could ruin his daughter's life. However, he was a Grade Six in the Home Office and he knew enough to come to me. I went to see his wife myself. She told me the tale, and I believed her. Then she died.'

'I see,' I murmured. 'Didn't the husband want to tackle him, even privately?'

'The husband wanted to horsewhip him on College Green, but I talked him down. We had a crime whose victim had no knowledge of it, and the only witness was dead.'

'Dying declaration?' Neil suggested.

'To me? Forget it. To the husband? Try that on the Crown Prosecution Service, Commander. No chance. Even if the victim's memory of the rape could be stimulated, there would never be an absolute guarantee of conviction. No, guys, it stays with me; but if there was ever a chance of Radley moving into Number Ten . . . that would be my secret weapon.'

'What about the domestic abuse you mentioned?' I asked.

'That comes from his protection officers. They've had to intervene on a couple of occasions when he's given Valerie, Mrs Radley, a slap. And once when she had some of her own back. It's a volatile household. She's a formidable lady. She's his second wife; they married eight years ago. She was his researcher, and eased the first Mrs Radley out of the picture. Not an uncommon occurrence in this place,' she added, although I knew that well enough.

'She runs a charity now,' Amanda added. 'It's pretty high profile; it advertises on Sky TV. It raises money to fight eye disease among African children, and she has no qualms about using her position as wife of the Foreign Secretary to win special treatment.'

'Does that give her contacts . . .' I began.

'In some pretty unstable countries,' Amanda finished. 'Yes it does.'

'Children?'

'Two daughters, Faith and Chloe, from the first marriage. They're very much on their mother's side and don't see much of him. In fact Faith sees nothing at all; Chloe's married to a racehorse trainer and their paths may cross when the Right Honourable Montgomery and Valerie show themselves off at Royal Ascot.' She peered at me, as if she was wearing spectacles and looking over the top. 'Are you sure you want to meet this man, Bob?'

'I don't want to, Amanda,' I replied, 'but I have to. He's a wife-beater with a deep dark secret who's managed somehow to elevate himself to one of the high offices of state. If that doesn't make him worthy of attention nothing will.

'Who's next?' I continued. 'Apart from Ellis, is there anyone running the country who isn't a shit?'

'Yes,' she laughed. 'There's the Defence Secretary, Nicholas Wheeler MP, age thirty-four, and the youngest member of the Cabinet by quite a margin. You'll have read all about him, I'm sure. The chattering classes call him the acceptable face of the Tory Party, and that's what he is; good-looking boy, an ad-man's dream. He's Emily Repton's protégé as she was Les's. He's also the second cousin of her former husband, Murdoch Lawton QC, Baron Lawton of Forgrave, but that's by the by.

'Nick Wheeler is the archetypal modern professional politician. His father, Cotton Wheeler QC, was in the same chambers as his cousin Lawton, and young Nick could have gone there too, to a long and comfortable career as a barrister, but he chose not to. Instead he took his firsts in international law and economics into the Conservative Research Department. He did a few years there, became a department head, and then was appointed special adviser to the shadow Foreign Secretary.

He came into parliament in twenty ten, and was appointed straightaway as PPS to his cousin, Lord Forgrave, the new Justice Secretary. At the first reshuffle he became a junior minister in the same department, and two years later went to Defence as Minister of State for the Armed Forces.'

McIlhenney held up a hand. 'Isn't that an odd career path, given that he has such a strong background in law?'

'International law,' Amanda pointed out. 'Given the ructions over the Iraq war and the fifteen-year debate over its legality, the last prime minister decided that there was a need for exactly that expertise within Defence at ministerial level. His successor agreed. When everybody thought that his connection to the adulterous Lord Forgrave might get him the sack, Emily confounded them by promoting him into the big chair in Defence.'

'How does a thirty-four year old manage the Defence Staff?' I asked.

'Very well, apparently. Unlike too many of his predecessors he lets them do their job, he fights their corner in Cabinet when cuts are being decided, and when an operation requires a legal decision, he makes it on the spot, without passing the buck to the Attorney General.'

'How do he and Roland Kramer get on?'

'They're good, from what I hear. Nobody can dislike Nick Wheeler, and Kramer has no need to fear him, any more than Emily had. He won't run for leader, not yet, and he wouldn't have even if the Repton administration had run its natural course. He knows that government is cyclical, that the electorate wants change after two or three terms, and that the next leader might well be on a loser. He wants to be prime minister, yes, but he's able to take the long view, because he has time on his side.'

'How do you know all this?' Neil put my thoughts into words. 'Are you watching him that closely?'

'We don't have to. That analysis comes from him, from newspaper articles he's written, from things he's said on TV programmes like *Question Time* and from a speech he made a couple of years ago in an Oxford Union debate on proportional representation. He spoke against the motion, arguing that the present system guarantees a continual refreshing of government and that PR would bring stagnation. His side won hands down.' She grinned. 'His *Private Eye* nickname is Galahad,' she added.

'Mmm,' I grunted. 'He didn't last too long, as I recall. And Emily Repton found her Holy Grail but look what it got her. So he's the golden boy of politics,' I said, 'but what about his personal life?'

'Heterosexual, unmarried, and determined not to acquire a wife simply because it's expected of him. He has relationships, and he's discreet, so rumours swirl around him, inevitably.

'Wheeler is very careful whom he gets into bed with, literally; we've never had to worry about any of his flings.' She paused for a second; when she continued I detected a slight change in her tone. 'Although there is a friendship developing that we're keeping an eye on, even though it is outside our remit, there being no security issues attached.'

'Another politician?' I murmured.

'Public figure.'

'Two sword lengths apart?'

'As in the distance between the two sides in the Commons?' she laughed. 'Ah, are you thinking it might be your ex-wife?'

'That had crossed my mind,' I admitted. 'She was a wee bit mysterious this morning.'

'Then cross it off. No, it's not an MP. It's a member of the royal family, albeit a junior one; she's also a constituent. The palace gets very nervous about any political relationships, and we're just a little nervous too, because this individual has a couple of media contacts.'

'Can we interview her?'

'Not unless Wheeler tells you something that means you have to. I doubt that he will, though. It hasn't got as far as pillow talk yet.'

'Okay, but we might ask him about her,' I warned.

'As discreetly as you can, if you have to,' she warned. 'These guys all know we monitor them, but they don't like to be reminded of it.'

'Guys,' McIlhenney repeated. 'I thought the number of women in government was on the rise, but I don't see too many female faces in the current Cabinet, and none at all in this core group we're talking about.'

'There's a woman at the head of the House,' Amanda reminded him, 'and that has a lot to do with it. Emily Repton isn't our first woman prime minister, remember.'

'Who could forget?'

She smiled at his muttering. 'If you look at the record of the other one,' she continued, 'you'll find that she didn't share the ladies' room at Cabinet level with anyone. It was part of her make-up, and many commentators remarked upon it at the time. Why didn't she promote more women? In fact, there were actually fewer of them around in those days; the talent pool was smaller. But there may have been more to it than that. She intimidated most of her male colleagues; the handbaggings at Chequers are still talked about by the survivors with nervous awe. But could she have done that to another woman and got away with it? I doubt it.'

'I see what you're getting at,' I conceded, 'but Emily Repton's hardly . . .'

'Your knowledge of her is limited,' she pointed out, cutting me off. 'You met her once in special circumstances . . .' she winked at me, '. . . plus you're a bloody old misogynist.'

I opened my mouth to protest the allegation, but she laughed, waving me to silence.

'Just kidding; you wouldn't be my friend if you were. There's a lot more to La Repton than you saw at your only meeting. She's cut from the same cloth as the last one, and her instincts are the same. There's something Shakespearean about them.'

'Mmm,' I murmured. 'I'm trying to remember which of Shakespeare's women survived.'

'None of them did too well, but think of King Lear and his daughters and you'd be getting close.'

'Which one would Emily resemble?'

'Her admirers would say Cordelia; her enemies would say Regan or Goneril.'

'They'd all be right given what's happened to her,' I said. 'Whatever, that's the core Cabinet,' I went on. 'What about their Secretary?'

Amanda grinned. 'Norman Hamblin has been described as a dinosaur more times than I've had a gin and tonic before dinner, but he isn't; dinosaurs became extinct because they lacked the ability to adapt to survive a crisis. Hamblin's still here because he's done exactly that all through his career. They say that the Civil Service is managed independently of government, but it's not exactly true, not at the top level. At the top level it's very difficult to be a servant of two masters. The Cabinet Secretary is right at the top of the tree. In theory he isn't the head of the Civil Service, but in practice nobody will ever countermand him. He oversees the ministerial behaviour code and also my service and MI6, through the National Security Adviser. That makes him the top dog, whatever the organisation chart says.

'As you can imagine,' she went on, 'the holder of the post works so closely with the Prime Minister of the day that it becomes very difficult for him to maintain the political neutrality required of the civil servant. When there's a change of government, then generally there will be a change of Cabinet Secretary, not immediately but not far into the new administration.

'But it doesn't happen with Norman Hamblin. He's a peppery son of a bitch, he's a bully with his staff, with junior ministers and even with some of the lower ranks in the Cabinet, but he gets away with it because he's so damn good at the job. The man has now served four prime ministers, and that hasn't happened for over fifty years. Nobody likes him, but so what? Roland Kramer actively hates him.'

'So I noticed,' I remarked.

'He doesn't bother trying to hide it any more. But still the man goes on.'

'Why?' Neil asked. 'What makes him fireproof?'

'He's my Civil Service boss,' she answered. 'That gives him a head start over the rest.'

'Does he have access to the information you hold?'

'If I encounter a situation that threatens national security I'm required to report it to him and the Prime Minister.'

'What about Hamblin himself? He's bound to have been vetted at some point in his career.'

'More than once. Yes,' she admitted, 'we keep a discreet eye on him also. Apart from being a cold, emotionless little sod, he has no issues.'

'Personal life?'

'He barely has one. He lives with his sister, Constance Hamblin; she was an assistant secretary in the Foreign Office until she retired ten years ago. They've both devoted their lives to the state. I know that sounds corny, but it's true.'

'Come on, Amanda,' I insisted. 'Nobody is that self-contained. I've just met the man. He's petty, arrogant . . .'

I held up a hand as my phone vibrated in my pocket. I'd meant to switch it off but had been distracted by my rush to clear the crime scene photos from the Cloud. 'Sorry,' I murmured. 'Let me take this; it might be Sarah and . . .'

She nodded. 'Yes, I know; given her condition. Go on, take it.'

I took it out and peered at the screen; yes, it was her, but as my thumb moved to take the call, the icon vanished and the trembling stopped. I shrugged, and was about to put it back in my pocket, but Amanda told me to call her back. 'You won't be focused until you do,' she said.

I pressed recall; she picked up in an instant.

'Bad time?' she asked. 'I'm sorry, lover; you know my patience threshold.'

'Only slightly above mine,' I admitted.

'Is it done? Did they win you over?'

'Yes, and not yet. I'm tempted but there are a few things to consider. I'll probably stay down here for an extra night or two to sort it out.'

'Do they measure you for a coronet?' she laughed.

'No, I think you buy them off the shelf.'

I waited for her comeback, but she fell silent. 'Hey,' she exclaimed, after a few seconds. 'What's this about the Prime Minister? I've just had a flash on my tablet from Sky News about her being hospitalised with a suspected tropical disease. Have you heard about it?'

'What are they saying?' I retorted, avoiding a direct lie.

'Just that. She's been taken to an isolation unit. They're linking it to a trip she made to Africa. If so, she's been pretty unlucky; I'd have thought that national leaders would have been kept well away from any dangerous sources. Seems not. I'm reading the story now; they're being very guarded about her condition, not saying how serious it is. They're not even identifying the virus. It won't be Ebola, not where she was. Did you know about this? Have you heard about it where you are?'

'I knew something was up,' I replied, trying not to sound evasive.

'Where are you anyway? Still in the House of Lords?'

'I'm in the palace, yes. Never mind me. How are you? Are you taking it easy like you're supposed to?'

'I'm fine,' she drawled. 'I'm bored out of my skull, if you want the truth. I wish I'd come with you; I could have, since you went by train.'

'You'd have been too long on your feet. Anything else on Sky?'

'No, that's it; another bulletin at eight they're saying. And some defence statement's been cancelled, apparently. The reporter's curious about that. She's asking why that needed to happen, why the Defence Secretary couldn't make it.'

'Has anyone given her an answer?'

'Not so as you'd notice,' she admitted, 'but she's speculating that the Prime Minister's condition might be more serious than they're letting on. If you hear anything, let me know.'

'Will do,' I promised insincerely. 'I have to go now. Take care. Love you.'

As I pocketed the phone I saw that Neil was smiling. 'That was good to hear,' he said. 'You're at your best when you're with Sarah.'

'Let's see if we're both still at our best when we're up at three in the morning with a new baby,' I chuckled, then turned back to Amanda.

'The story's out and accepted,' I told her, 'although the media are wondering why Wheeler isn't making the defence statement.'

She shrugged. 'Let them. The situation is contained, for now.'

'You're happy that the hospital is leak proof?'

'As happy as I can be. Very few people will have access to her. We can live with all the speculation there's bound to be about the nature of the disease.'

'Won't the press want to know who's treating her?' Neil asked.

'We won't tell them.'

'There can't be that many people in the field.'

'Enough,' Amada retorted. Neither of us was sure whether that was a comment or an impatient warning.

I took it as both. 'Back to Hamblin,' I said. 'You say he's a man with no issues, but how long have you known him?'

'For the eight years I've been at deputy or director level. He's a team-spirited little man, he has a mind like a mainframe and if you cut him open you'd find "Loyalty" running through him like "Blackpool" in a stick of rock.'

'What about his sister? What did she do in the Foreign Office?'

'Commonwealth relations, latterly. She's a dry old stick, Bob.'

'Was she a dry young stick? She made it to assistant secretary; that suggests a university education.'

'She and Norman both went to Christ's, twelve years apart. She got a two one, he pulled a first, then came top in the Civil Service examinations.'

'So she'd be there early to mid-sixties,' I suggested. 'A volatile time; students were just as political then as now and CND was very active. Did she have any affiliations?'

'We don't know,' she admitted, 'but we've never had any reason to ask. I'll see what we can find out now.' She rose to her feet. 'What do you need?' she asked.

'A working base; Hamblin's getting us a room in the Cabinet Office, and lining up the people we need to interview. I've asked for CCTV footage as well if it exists.'

'It does; I've requisitioned it already from the Serjeant-at-Arms. When I have it I'll send it on to you. If we can, we'll look at it together. Shall we go?'

I shook my head. 'You should go, but Neil and I need to stay here for a while. Before we do anything else we need to start behaving like detectives and take a proper look at the crime scene . . . or what's left of it.'

She headed for the door, until I called out to stop her. 'One thing, Amanda,' I said. 'Neil, you have the weapon.' McIlhenney nodded, then retrieved the bagged letter-opener from his case. 'Have the forensic lab go to work on that, please. Fingerprints, blood spatters, anything else they find. Got another bag, chum?'

He nodded and produced one. Carefully, I picked up a mobile phone that lay on the desk, encasing it in the see-through plastic. 'This was hers, I'm guessing,' I murmured. 'I'd like to know who she called in the period leading up to the attack, on this and on the landline.'

'I'll get people on it right away. There's a secure Home Office lab that can look at the knife; my people will handle the phone issues.' She took both items from me and left.

Nine

When Mrs Dennis left us, and it was just Bob and me, reality kicked in for a moment.

'I'm still bloody nervous about this, man,' I confessed as the door closed behind her. 'This should be a police matter; it's not for spooks.'

'I'm not arguing with you,' he admitted, 'but in practice, it's what Roland Kramer says it is. He's the Home Secretary, which would give him all the authority he needs, and on top of that he's acting Prime Minister.'

'And if he misuses that authority?' I countered. 'We're expected to go along with it, are we?'

'In the circumstances, yes,' he said, but with less conviction than usual.

'But what are the circumstances?' I protested. 'All I've seen is a woman with a blade buried in her head. At any other time, in any other place, the full resources of the police would be thrown into finding out who put it there. What makes this different?'

'The context.' He paused, as if he was considering his next words very carefully, until he nodded, as if he had made a decision. 'Fuck it,' he muttered.

He took my breath away then, by launching into a staggering

tale about a top-secret defence project called Spitfire, the name he'd dropped earlier, which was going to revolutionise global nuclear policy and put Britain in a position of unprecedented power. Emily Repton had been due to announce it in parliament that afternoon, but the attack on her had put paid to that. Were the two related? Yes, I got that.

When he was finished he gazed at me as if he expected me to react, with either awe or outrage, but I didn't. I was still taking it in.

Bob never was the most patient of men. 'So you see . . .' he continued, but I cut him off.

'To be honest,' I confessed, 'I see a crime scene, that's all; one that's being wilfully concealed. Okay, there are national security issues, but what if this crime has eff all to do with national security? And another thing. Was Repton the only target? We don't know that for sure. What if she wasn't? What if other senior politicians are at risk?'

'No we don't know that,' he agreed, 'but I think you'll find that all the protection officers are on increased alert. Kramer gave me a demonstration earlier on.'

'Bugger Kramer,' I exclaimed. 'What if I took my phone out right now,' I challenged him, 'and reported this to PaDP. What do you think would happen?'

He looked at me, seriously, and replied, quietly, 'I think your career would be over before you hung up.'

He hadn't needed to tell me that. I knew he was right, but nonetheless I grinned. 'You'd have to shoot me, would you?'

He laughed, in turn, shaped an imaginary pistol with his right hand and pointed it at me. 'That's all that I have to do it with,' he chuckled. 'Amanda's only given me a warrant card so far.'

He sighed, his humour evaporating. 'Come on,' he said. 'It's a weird situation, I know, but don't tell me you aren't just a wee bit excited. And you are fireproof; don't worry about that.'

I shrugged. 'Aye, fine. All my training and all my procedural nous has just gone out the window, but what the hell. Let's do what we can. Which,' I pointed out, 'in the context of a crime scene investigation, will not be very much.'

'I agree,' he conceded, 'but let's do what we always do and try to imagine the crime.'

He took out his phone and showed me some of the photos that he had been taking when I arrived; they had been saved in a folder named 'Emily'. He scrolled straight to one that showed the Prime Minister lying face down on her desk, with her right cheek on its surface, and the blade in situ in her skull, in line with the top of her left ear, a couple of inches in front. The handle was touching a notepad, which was stained with a small amount of blood that had leaked from the wound. Her left hand was beside it, palm down, fingers curled.

He swiped the screen to enlarge the central area of the image. As I studied the detail, I noticed that she wore a large diamond cluster on her third finger but no wedding band. At first glance I had thought that the central stone was a ruby, but on closer inspection I realised that a spot of blood had settled on it.

He pointed to it. 'We'd better add Lord Forgrave to our interview list,' he murmured.

'Who's he?' I asked. The name was familiar, but I couldn't pin it down.

'Her former husband, and former Justice Secretary.'

I felt my eyes widen as I recognised the name and title. 'Ah yes,' I said. 'The guy who was caught shagging . . .' I let it fade away.

I only knew whom he'd been caught shagging because Bob

had told me. The relationship had surfaced during an investigation in which we had both been involved. There was photographic evidence, he had said, but I hadn't seen it. Even so, when Forgrave and Repton had split, it was clear to me that the full story had been kept well away from the tabloids, or they'd have had a field day.

'You don't think this could be a domestic, do you?' I ventured.

'Most murders and attempted murders are,' Bob pointed out, 'but in this case Forgrave will only go to the top of our list if he shows up on the CCTV footage. We should talk to him, possibly. Emily binned him because he was a liability politically; for all we know they may have stayed close. That does look like her engagement ring she's wearing.'

'Given the timescale, we're going to have to talk to a lot of people very quickly,' I observed.

'Agreed, so let's finish up here and get ourselves over to the Cabinet Office.' He seemed to allow himself a brief moment to gather his thoughts, before he voiced them.

'It could be that the Prime Minister will recover consciousness,' he said, 'and that she'll be able to tell us who attacked her, but if not, you're right; we have to move fast. So,' he asked, 'what do you see here? Where was the attacker positioned when he stabbed her?'

'It's a long reach across the desk,' I suggested, 'probably too long.' I took another look at the photograph, enlarging as much as I could. 'Also, there's no sign of any defensive reaction that I can see, no wounds that suggest she might have tried to grab the blade, or to ward it off with her hand or arm.'

'No, there aren't,' he agreed, 'which suggests to me that the blow was struck from her left . . . but if it was, it would still have been within her line of vision, and we should have been able to see

some sign of a reaction . . . or from behind, taking her completely by surprise.'

'In that case,' I ventured, 'the assailant is left handed, almost certainly.'

'Assailant? Get you with the English police-speak,' he mocked. 'But you are on the button with that supposition. We're looking for a left-handed man; that's a start.'

'Man?' I repeated, questioning that assumption like the good sidekick I was.

'Okay, that's a supposition too,' he admitted, 'but . . .' He found another image on his phone and showed it to me. It was one that he'd taken of the Prime Minister's bathroom. 'What do you see there?' I asked.

I peered at it, looking for some tiny detail, then smiled as I saw what he'd meant me to see. 'You foxy sod,' I murmured. 'The toilet seat's up.' I got the message. 'We need to get Amanda's Home Office forensic specialist in here,' I said, 'to print that door, toilet handle, taps, every-bloody-thing, and they need to do it before anyone else comes in here and contaminates the scene even further.'

Ten

When Neil and I had finished our study of the crime scene and the images that I'd taken, we agreed that a specialist examination was essential.

I called Amanda at once; she was back in Thames House by then, having travelled even that short distance by car. I gave her an update, and asked her to send the Home Office team to the PM's office to do what was needed.

'They don't need to know what has happened there,' I pointed out. 'You could tell them there's been a robbery; that would do.'

Asking wasn't something I'd done for a while; in the final years of my police career I had given instructions, interspersed with the odd suggestion. While it was happening, I'd never thought of myself as an autocrat, but looking back, I realised that I had been.

As we left, I showed my brand-new badge to the Security Service operative on door watch who had replaced the guy there earlier. The man had never seen me before that morning, but the fancy title got his attention. I gave him strict instructions that nobody, repeat nobody, was to enter that room until the CSI arrived, then we headed out of the Palace of Westminster, and along Whitehall, towards the Cabinet Office.

I wasn't sure where the entrance was, but Neil knew; just past Downing Street, he said. Like most British people, and quite a few foreigners, I was familiar with the names of these places from news programming, but not so clear about their locations. One of the surprising things about the seat of our government is how compact it is. The great departments of state are crammed close together with only the Home Office being any distance from the rest.

We stepped into the foyer, to find that we were expected. A uniformed escort met us, led us to a lift, and accompanied us all the way to the Cabinet Secretary's eyrie on the top floor. There was a small staff in an outer office, presided over by a woman with heavy eyebrows and an even heavier build. Her hair was in a bun and she had a large bulldog-like jaw. She only had one head, but even so, she was 'Cerberus' to me from that moment on.

She eyed us up and down as our escort departed, then pointed over her shoulder at a door behind her desk and announced, 'You may enter.'

Norman Hamblin was waiting for us inside; I could tell at first glance that his humour had not improved. He frowned at me, ignoring Neil altogether. 'Mr Skinner,' he snapped, looking down his nose as if I'd come to clear a blocked toilet. Metaphorically I had, but everyone deserves to be treated with respect, even those who do the smelliest jobs.

I met his glare with one of my own. 'Cabinet Secretary,' I growled. 'What's the word from the hospital?' I asked; I wasn't in a mood to be deferential and my tone let him know that.

He winced, slightly; my question had reminded him that at

the heart of the crisis, a woman, someone he knew and served, had been grievously injured.

'The Prime Minister is still alive,' he replied, 'but only just. I've just spoken to Sir Sajid Chaudhry, the consultant neuro-surgeon who's looking after her. They've given her a brain scan. As you would expect, that shows there to have been considerable bleeding. It seems to have stopped but a clot remains. Sir Sajid says that it would be too hazardous to attempt to remove it and that in any event there would be no point. The damage has already been done. If she survives, which he thought to be on balance unlikely, she will be severely impaired, physically and possibly intellectually.'

'And no longer capable of exercising her office,' I said.

'Exactly,' he sighed. For the first time his eyes showed me something other than hostility. 'Mr Skinner, the Home Secretary does not seem to have taken the time to consider that this is a massive constitutional issue.

'The Prime Minister exercises executive power on behalf of the monarch. If she is temporarily incapacitated then her deputy, in this case Kramer, may fill the gap. But if her disability is permanent, the Queen should be advised.

'Normally, the handover process is quite clear; where a prime minister falls, be it after a general election defeat or for other reasons, established practice is for him or her to go to the palace and tender their resignation in person. At that time he or she would advise Her Majesty to summon their elected successor and invite him or her to form a government.'

'But Emily Repton can't do that,' I observed.

'Nor may she ever, or so I am advised by the consultant. And the fact is that our constitution, such as it is, does not provide specifically for such a situation. The office of deputy prime minister is not recognised in British law, the perception being that if it was, there would be a presumption of succession, which would limit the prerogative of the monarch to appoint her head of government.'

'Kramer knows this, presumably?'

'Yes, and I have just restated it to him; forcefully, I might add. His reaction was that the present national security situation justifies his course of action. He went on to forbid me from discussing it with anyone else . . . a prohibition which I now realise I have broken by speaking to you. I told him that I was of a mind to consult the Attorney General; he replied that if anyone does that it will be him.'

'And you accept that?'

'I have to,' Hamblin replied, quietly. 'I am a civil servant and he is my political master. I am still of a mind to consult the Attorney General but only in respect of my own position in law. If the Prime Minister dies, the situation will be unequivocal, and the constitution must be defended. As it is, we are at an unprecedented moment, but I am concerned that what Kramer is doing is borderline illegal. Of course,' he added, 'that might also mean that what you are doing falls into the same category.'

'Except,' I countered, 'I have a badge that says I'm an official of the Security Service, and that makes Kramer my boss, just as much as he is yours.'

'You could always resign.'

'So could you, but you're not going to, are you?' The Cabinet Secretary lowered his eyes and shook his head. 'As it happens,' I continued, 'I tried that; it resulted in a confrontation with a man called Daffyd.'

'Kramer threatened you?' Hamblin's frown deepened. 'He's that serious?'

'Seems to be; I can't say how serious he is without calling his bluff, but his attitude is that I have no way out. Besides, Amanda Dennis is my friend and my loyalty is to her. She's brought me in to do a job, and I have to see it through for her sake. So, please, can we get on with it?'

'I suppose so,' he conceded. 'I have procured an office for you on this floor. You'll find all the equipment you need in there. Let me show you where it is.'

He led us back through his outer office, where his staff carried on working, oblivious to the drama that was unfolding, and along a high-ceilinged corridor to an unnumbered door. He threw it open; there were four desks crammed into the modest space, each with a terminal and two phones.

'The Cobra staff use this, when there's an emergency situation . . . an acknowledged emergency that is,' he added. 'I suppose it's appropriate. I'll leave you to begin. If you need me, you know where I am.'

'We need you now, Mr Hamblin,' I told him. 'You're on our interview list, remember.'

'Is that really necessary?' he sighed.

'Yes, it is. Come on, let's get it over with. There's something else you can help us with as well, when the CCTV footage we've asked for is available to us. We're not going to know many of the people we might see on there. You can help us identify them.'

I led the way into our temporary base, with a reluctant Hamblin following. 'Take a seat,' I told him, as I chose a desk that faced the door. Neil grabbed the one on my right, leaving the Cabinet Secretary facing me.

'This is an informal situation,' I began, 'within the context of a discretionary investigation, but for all that we will proceed formally. This interview will be recorded, as best we can, using a phone if we have to.'

'We don't,' McIlhenney said. He opened his briefcase and took out a dictation device. 'I didn't know what I was walking into when the Commissioner ordered me here, but I brought the basics.' He inspected the palm-sized recorder, checked the battery status, switched it on, and placed it on the desk.

'In that case, let's get under way. I am Robert Skinner, currently seconded to the Security Service, accompanied by Commander Neil McIlhenney, of the Met.'

Our interviewee leaned forward. 'I am Norman Hamblin, CB, Cabinet Secretary,' he announced, in a loud clear voice, 'and I would like to put on the record my discontent at these proceedings.'

'Noted,' I said. 'However, we are here to investigate an attack this morning on the Prime Minister which has left her severely injured. Mr Hamblin, how did you come to hear of the incident?'

'I was called, on my direct telephone line, by Ms Repton's parliamentary private secretary, Dr Michaela Satchell.'

McIlhenney intervened. 'You were in this building at the time?'

'Obviously,' Hamblin sighed, with a show of forced patience. 'It was a landline.'

'Did you make a note of the time?'

'No, but when I took the call, I was looking at my computer screen. I had barely put the instrument to my ear when the clock in the corner moved from ten fifty-nine to eleven.'

'What did Dr Satchell say?' I asked.

'She was in a rather agitated state. She called me by my forename, not something she would do normally. She said, and

I remember quite clearly, "She's dead, Norman, Emily's dead." Naturally, I was stunned. It took me a second or two to absorb what she had said. When I had, I asked her to control herself, and to repeat what she had just said. She did. I asked her where she was, and she told me she was in the Prime Minister's House of Commons office. She said that the Prime Minister was at her desk and that there was a blade embedded in her head.'

He paused and I stepped in. 'What was your immediate reaction?'

'Disbelief,' he retorted. 'Dr Satchell has a history of prescription drug abuse. There was a psychotic incident when she was a junior doctor in a hospital in Berkshire. She was treated in the Priory clinic in Roehampton, and it was discreetly excised from her records by a sympathetic hospital administrator, who happened to be a friend of her father. There has been no sign of a recurrence, but what she described to me was so bizarre, that was what I feared.'

'What did you do?'

'I instructed her to stay where she was, to lock the door and to admit nobody until I got there.'

'Did she comply?'

Hamblin's eyes flashed fury. 'No she did not!' he hissed. 'When I arrived, five minutes later, the Home Secretary was already in the room, and had assumed command. I asked Dr Satchell whether there was any part of nobody that she did not understand, but Mr Kramer intervened to say that she had quite correctly summoned him.

'At that point we believed, on Dr Satchell's say-so, that the Prime Minister was dead. I told Mr Kramer that I would call Her Majesty's Private Secretary at once, but he forbade me from so doing. He said that the Spitfire announcement offered a potential motive for what we then believed to be a murder, and that the situation should be contained to allow immediate and thorough investigation. At that point Mrs Dennis arrived, and was given the instruction by Mr Kramer that has led to your involvement, gentlemen.

'I returned to the Cabinet Office at that point, since I felt that my position had been usurped.'

'You went off in a huff?' I ventured.

His eyes widened. I expected him to be outraged by my temerity. Then he confounded me by laughing quietly and nodding. 'On reflection, Mr Skinner, that is exactly what I did.'

'Who would have been in the Prime Minister's Commons office as a matter of routine?' Neil asked him. 'She must have a considerable Civil Service staff. Were none of them there?'

'No,' Hamblin replied. 'Mostly they work in Downing Street. The principal private secretary and his senior assistants would have been there had it been a Wednesday, to help her prepare for Prime Minister's Questions in the House, but there was no reason for them to be present at that time, on a Monday morning.'

'How accessible was she? Could any MP have knocked on her door?'

'Any MP, no. Backbenchers and lower echelon ministers would have to arrange to see her through Dr Satchell. Her most senior colleagues, yes.'

I intervened again. 'Particularly those within the Spitfire circle of knowledge?'

'They were all required to be on hand today, to help her prepare the announcement.'

'Are you saying it wasn't finished?'

'No; sorry, yes, that's exactly what I'm saying. She was still working on it over the weekend. For reasons you will understand, having been briefed by Mr Kramer, the draft could not be entrusted to her private office for preparation. None of her immediate staff, not even the principal private secretary, knows about Spitfire.'

'How does she work?' I asked. 'Did she do everything on screen?'

'No, she was a scribbler. She would possibly have typed up the final version, but the drafts would usually have been hand written.'

'But there was nothing there,' I exclaimed, 'no notepad, no paper at all.' I stared at him. 'Think back, please,' I said. 'When you walked into that office and saw the scene for the first time, was the desk clear, as it was when I arrived?'

'It was as you saw it.'

'Is it possible that if she was interrupted by someone, she put anything she was working on in the Red Box, the secure case in which ministers' papers are kept, that was on the desk?'

'It's possible but if she put it in there, it wasn't secure. I'm sure there was a key in the lock.'

'Hold on,' I said. I reached for my phone, called up the photos that I'd taken, and found one that showed the desk from the correct angle. I swiped to enlarge it, then nodded. 'For the tape,' I continued, 'a photographic record of the scene confirms that there is a key in the lock of the Prime Minister's Red Box. Mr Hamblin, I would like that box to be retrieved and brought here, but . . .' I remembered my instruction to the MI5 man on the door.

I paused the recorder and called Amanda Dennis on her secure mobile. I explained what needed to be done and she took it on board. 'It'll be with Mr Hamblin in ten minutes,' she promised. 'I can't take a Red Box into my custody, but I can ask for it to be sent to the Cabinet Office.

'While I have you on the line,' she added, 'I can tell you that the CCTV footage is available. I'll text you a link that will take you into it on the server where it's stored. Don't wait for me, look at it.

'I've found out from the protection officers that they dropped the PM off at the Commons an hour and a quarter before Mickey Satchell found her, at a quarter to ten. You'll have to wait to interview them, I'm afraid. They refused to leave their charge as long as she's breathing and I can't argue with that. They're hurting and they're angry, as I'm sure you can understand.'

'Of course,' I agreed.

'I did ask them if anything had happened recently that had given them cause for concern. They both said, "No, absolutely not." Emily Repton is still in her honeymoon period as PM. Most places she goes, the reaction is positive.'

'Okay. That saves some time. How about the phones and the letter-opener?'

'Still working on all that, top priority. I'll get back to you as soon as I have reports.'

I cut the call and looked across at Hamblin. 'The box is on its way,' I told him, 'and so is the CCTV footage.' As I spoke, my phone played the tone that told me a text had arrived. 'How do I get into this computer?' I asked, pointing to the screen on my borrowed desk.

'Switch it on,' the Cabinet Secretary replied, 'and it will ask you for a user access code. There is a default, though.' He began to recite it, then stopped as he remembered that he was being recorded, scribbled it on a notepad and passed it to me.

I followed his instructions; my monitor went live instantly. I passed the code to Neil so that he could do the same, then copied Amanda's link into the address bar, digit by digit. I did the same for the others, arranging things so that we were all looking at the same frozen frame, from a camera looking along a corridor that I recognised as one I'd walked along myself. Neil and I had been there only for an hour or so, but it seemed like an eternity.

'Press the "Play" arrow on my word, please,' I began, 'and pause on my command as each person comes into view. Okay, now.'

I clicked on the white triangle, watched, and waited, but for only a couple of seconds. The recording appeared to be motion-activated; the first figure to appear was walking away from the camera, but I recognised her back view. 'Dr Satchell,' I said, for Neil's benefit. The time was shown in the top right corner of the image: one minute past ten.

Playback was at double speed and so her movements were jerky, like an old silent movie, but shot in full colour. She passed out of view in a few seconds; the screen froze once more, but briefly until another figure appeared, a grey-haired man I didn't know.

'Pause,' I called out, stilling his movement.

'That's Mr Dunlop,' Hamblin announced. 'Graham Dunlop, the deputy Serjeant-at-Arms. Quite normal for him to be there. Remember, not everyone you see will have been going into the PM's office corridor.'

I took his word for it and we moved on. At ten sixteen another male figure appeared. I thought I recognised him but I paused for confirmation.

'That is Mr Radley,' he said, 'the Foreign Secretary. The only reason he would have to be there would be if he was going to see the PM.'

'Thank you,' I acknowledged. 'We need to ask him why. He goes to the top of our interview list.'

'You may need to make an appointment,' Hamblin warned me, 'to suit his convenience. As you may well have heard, Monty Radley sees himself as a very important man.'

'I don't have time to pander to anyone's bloody ego,' I retorted. 'Either he sees me without delay or I'll have him brought to me.' I thought I detected a flicker of a smile on the Cabinet Secretary's face, as he considered the prospect of the Right Honourable Mr Radley having his collar felt by the Security Service, but I didn't dwell on it, carrying on instead with the review of the recording.

Faces popped up, individually and in groups of two or three, mostly heading towards the corridor, or the area behind the Speaker's chair, only a few walking in the other direction. Hamblin recognised them all, and was able to discount the possibility of any of them dropping in on the Prime Minister. In the main they were Commons officials, or backbenchers whose presence there was unexceptional.

'Members like to keep their faces in front of the Speaker,' he explained. 'If there is a question on a list with a direct bearing on their constituency, they make sure he knows about it, and that they're called when it comes up.'

The timing of each sighting was shown on screen; as we watched, the clock advanced towards ten fifty-nine, the hour at which Mickey Satchell had found the stricken Repton. It showed ten twenty-six when Radley came back into vision, heading in the direction from which he had come. He was striding briskly, almost aggressively, so much so that he might have collided with the person who came into our view just as he disappeared from it, had she not stepped out of his way.

The newcomer was a woman; she wore a dark suit that even I could see was expensive, with silver high-heeled shoes that reminded me of a Jimmy Choo pair that Sarah wears on special occasions. Her hair was auburn with what I'm told are called autumn streaks, although she looked very much in the summer of her years, around the forty mark. No question, she was dressed to make an impression, and she was heading somewhere in a hurry.

We froze our three screens on my word. 'Who is she?' I asked.

'Who is she indeed?' Hamblin murmured, suddenly looking more animated than I had seen him since our first meeting. 'That is Mrs Siuriña Kramer, the wife of the Home Secretary, and chair of the Conservative Party, and she very definitely does not have business with the Speaker's clerks.'

'So what was she . . .' I pondered. 'Let's move on.'

We did, staring at the empty screen until the clock changed and action resumed. The clock changed to ten fifty-three, and the back view of Siuriña Kramer came into shot. The playback speed made it appear that she was moving as fast as her medium-high heels would carry her. 'Pause,' I called to my companions.

'What the hell?' McIlhenney murmured.

'My thoughts almost exactly,' I said. 'Does she have the right to move freely in the House of Commons?' I asked Hamblin.

'Within limits, yes,' he replied.

'And that corridor, does it fit within those limits?'

'Not really, no. She has her official position within the Conservative Party, and because of that she has a pass that gives her access to the public areas of the building without having to queue, but the precincts of the chamber itself should be off limits to her.' He paused. 'But she's the wife of the Home Secretary, and she's well known about the place, so who's going to stop her? As for her presence at that time, I can only imagine that she was visiting her husband.'

'He wasn't there,' I pointed out. 'We know that Kramer arrived at his office just as Satchell was finding the Prime Minister. Let's finish this,' I said, 'then think about it.' We restarted the recording but there was very little more to see, the clock showing ten fifty-six as one of the people we had seen and discounted earlier moved in and out of shot, then ten fifty-eight as Mickey Satchell reappeared, on her way to find her stricken boss.

The recording ran on until four minutes past eleven, when a Speaker's clerk made another appearance, and then the screen went dead as it ended.

'Hold on a minute,' Neil exclaimed. 'If the Home Secretary didn't arrive until the very moment that the PPS found the victim, why isn't he on the tape?'

'He will have used the other entrance,' Hamblin replied.

'Excuse me,' I said, heavily. 'I thought the senior ministers' offices could only be accessed from the corridor we've just been watching. I didn't see any other way when I was there.'

'Ah, but there is one. There is a doorway just past the Chancellor's office. It opens on to a stairway that goes down one level to another door, beyond which you're outside the building on a vehicular throughway; usually the Prime Minister will be dropped off there by her official car, also the Home Secretary and the Chancellor.

'Earlier this morning Mr Kramer had a public engagement; he addressed the Prison Governors' Association in the Central Hall conference centre. The speech was timed for ten, it will have lasted for around forty minutes, and given the proximity of the venue he would have returned to the Commons at the time stated.'

'Travelling by car?' McIlhenney asked. 'Central Hall's on the other side of Parliament Square.'

'To be honest, I am not certain,' the Cabinet Secretary admitted. 'But even if his protection officers were happy with him walking, he could still have been back within that timescale, and he would still have used that entrance as it's the closest.

'There is a permanent police presence there, always experienced officers. They don't log people in and out of the entrance, but there are no more than a dozen people who are entitled to use it, so they will know who passed through it this morning and will be able to confirm Mr Kramer's arrival.'

'Then it needs to be checked,' I decreed. 'Not just him but everyone who used it this morning, in and out.' I glanced at McIlhenney; he had read my mind, and was halfway out of his chair.

'Siuriña Kramer,' I said to Hamblin as the door closed behind my friend. 'Where do I find her?'

'You could begin with Conservative Party Office in Matthew Parker Street.'

'Where's that?'

'Behind and alongside the Central Hall.'

'Where her husband was speaking?' I murmured. 'There's no way she wouldn't have known that.'

'What does that signify?'

'I don't know,' I admitted. 'Possibly nothing at all, but it does beg a couple of questions. Why would she visit her husband's office at a time when she knew he wouldn't be there? Alternatively, did she go to his office or to one of the others? I know that the Chancellor's room was locked when I arrived, but do you know if he was there at any time this morning?'

'I know that he wasn't. He chaired a Cabinet subcommittee meeting in this building from nine forty-five until shortly after eleven.'

'Therefore there was only one person in that corridor when Mrs Kramer got there: the Prime Minister. She couldn't have been going to see anyone else. Would she have known that? Would she have known that the Chancellor wouldn't be there?'

Hamblin raised his eyebrows. 'I can't say for certain, but the Cabinet sub is a regular weekly event. The Chancellor's special adviser is always there. She is on the party payroll, not the Civil Service; as its chairperson, those people are under Mrs Kramer's overall supervision. Yes, it's probable she would know, or could have found out.'

'Then she's at the very top of my list.'

I reached out and restarted the recording device. 'Finally, Mr Hamblin,' I continued, 'I'd like to ask you about the last time you saw the Prime Minister. You've told me already that you were here in the Cabinet Office when you were made aware of the attack. Were you in the House of Commons at all today before being called there by Dr Satchell?'

'No, I was not. I did meet with Ms Repton at eight forty this morning, but it was in Downing Street.'

'Why?'

He glared at me; his initial prickliness was back. 'We discussed matters of state, Mr Skinner. That is all I am prepared to say.'

'How did she seem?'

'I would say that she was her usual self.'

'What does that mean?'

'Serious, thoughtful, calm and in control; that's the Emily Repton I knew.'

'Knew?' I repeated.

He nodded, tight lipped. 'You've heard the prognosis, Mr

Skinner. Even if the hospital manages to save her life, it will be a different woman who emerges.'

'Do you like her?'

He blinked, surprised by the bluntness of my question. 'Like her? That's immaterial: she's the Prime Minister. It's not for me to have a personal view of any minister. My position gives me oversight of the ministerial code of conduct, so personal feelings would be inappropriate.'

I nodded. 'Then let me rephrase that. What does your sister think of her?'

Hamblin stared at me; and then he surprised me again by laughing. 'You are well briefed, sir, are you not?' He pointed to the recording device. I read his signal and switched it off.

'My sister Constance,' he said, 'has no constraints. She has met Ms Repton on two social occasions, once when she was Secretary for Work and Pensions and once since she has been in Downing Street. She couldn't stand her. "Cold, calculating and opportunistic"; those were the words she used to describe her.'

'But in the classic mould, you couldn't possibly comment?'

'Exactly, Mr Skinner, exactly. But why do you ask about my feelings?'

'I'm trying to get a sense of how all of her colleagues see her, that's all.'

'I don't regard myself as a colleague. There is a clear distinction between ministers and their servants . . . as there is between the public and the police, if I may say so, although I don't know too many police officers who really see themselves as public servants.'

'Me neither,' I confessed.

'As an observer,' he continued, 'I see no great fondness for Ms

Repton among most of her senior colleagues, although I do see great respect in most of them. They all have their cliques, you know, all PMs; kitchen Cabinets, they are often called, and as each administration goes on, they tend to gather more and more influence, until all of the key decisions are taken within that tight little circle. The present incumbent is still relatively new in office, so hers hasn't developed fully; now it never will, it seems. If it had, I suspect that it would have been very small, perhaps only three or four people.'

'Who will they be?'

'I would imagine they would have been the Chancellor, then Grover Bryant, her official spokesman, and the Defence Secretary.' He paused. 'Yes, definitely the Defence Secretary. Of all of her colleagues, Nicholas Wheeler is closest to her.'

'So even now, you see a core group having developed within the core group, do you,' I said, 'with the Home Secretary and Foreign Secretary on the outside?'

'Not completely on the outside, perhaps; you can't freeze those two individuals out altogether. But in terms of influencing the PM's thinking, the three I've mentioned have the greatest influence. You asked me how Ms Repton's colleagues feel about her: I'd say that Kramer actively dislikes her, and that Radley dislikes everyone. Leslie Ellis, on the other hand, appears to like everyone.'

'Appears?'

'Yes. I find him inscrutable. He is unfailingly courteous, and endlessly patient. None of my colleagues in Treasury have a bad word to say about him.'

I made eye contact. 'But you think he's too good to be true?' I asked.

'I suspect that he might be. I have held my position for a long time now. I have, as they say, seen them come and seen them go. All of them, the good, the bad, the excellent and the barely competent have one thing in common, their sheer driving ambition. But the Chancellor is an exception; he doesn't appear to have any.

'I have observed his rise to that office and I have to say that it was like watching someone being washed in on the tide. I believe that the Prime Minister, and also the Home Secretary, I have to say, are, were, comfortable with him because they don't see him as a threat.'

'Likely it doesn't matter to her now, but is Kramer wrong about that? From what he said to me, he doesn't think he has any threats, other than one that I took to be Radley and he's not worried about him.'

'Nor should he be,' Hamblin said, 'but possibly he isn't as popular within the parliamentary party as he thinks he is, and those are the people who decide on two candidates for a leadership election among the general membership. Radley has a minority support that will not grow but will stay loyal. But if Leslie Ellis was persuaded to run, and those with doubts about Kramer swung behind him, the Home Secretary might not get on to the final ballot paper that goes to the membership at large.'

I wasn't aware that I was smiling, but I must have been for he said, 'That prospect would please you, I see.'

'Could I give a toss?' I retorted, but he was right. I had met the stricken Emily Repton when she had held Kramer's office, spent the same amount of time with each of them; I found myself wondering which I'd disliked more and decided it was a draw.

'What about the man Bryant?' I asked. 'His name hasn't been mentioned until now.'

118

'That was remiss of both Mr Kramer and Mrs Dennis,' Hamblin remarked.

'Is he within the circle of knowledge on Spitfire?'

'In theory no, but I can't be certain of that. In fact my suspicion is that the Prime Minister will have shared at least some of the secret with him. I worry, Mr Skinner, about him being kept out of the loop on what's happened to her. He came to see me, just before you arrived, wondering what the hell was up, to use his words. I could tell that he was sceptical about the tropical disease story.'

'What's his role, other than official spokesman?' I asked.

'He doesn't have one; he isn't part of the communications department, but he is the de facto information minister. Ms Repton brought him into the Home Office, took him to the DWP, and brought him here. His background was broadcasting, as an independent documentary maker, before he went into public relations, where he founded a successful consultancy. He's more of a political animal than most of the Cabinet.' He paused, bringing his hands together in a steepling gesture. 'He's also Emily's half-brother.'

'Bloody hell!' I exclaimed. 'He's family? And we're feeding him the cover story about his sister having fucking swamp fever? What will he do when he finds out the truth?'

'He will either accept Kramer's national interest view, or he will blow the lid off everything. You see? That's why I worry.'

Eleven

In the time I'd spent in London, I had never been in the Houses of Parliament before that morning. My daughter Lauren had; she'd lobbied our MP as part of a youth group pushing for the vote for sixteen year olds. My son Spencer had, with a group from his school. My wife Louise had, years before, giving evidence to a select committee investigating tax breaks for the film industry. But not me; I work less than a mile from the place, and I've walked past it nearly every working day since I moved to the Met, exiting Westminster Underground station. On just about every one of those days I've glanced across at the place and said to myself, 'I must go in there.'

I'd probably still be saying it if I hadn't had that summons from Bob Skinner, via my big boss, and been dispatched on the instant to the scene of the biggest drama I have ever encountered in my twenty-odd-year police career.

When I pitched up there I had no idea what I was walking into, but it was made very clear to me very quickly that if I wasn't in over my head, I was certainly up to my neck.

A world-shaking announcement about a new delivery system for the nuclear deterrent, put on hold by what appeared to be the murder of the Prime Minister . . . only for it to turn into an attempted murder, to everyone's surprise.

A home secretary who had taken command and overridden normal police procedures, not to mention the law, by throwing a cloak over the truth and placing the initial investigation in the hands of the Security Service.

Add to that the coincidental presence of my old Edinburgh mentor, who was obviously loving every bloody minute of it, and no, Commander McIlhenney, it was not your average day at the office.

That's what I was thinking as I retraced my steps from the Cabinet Office, back to the House. I wasn't entirely certain where I was going, but a helpful PC, one of a pair of armed officers manning the gateway closest to Big Ben, pointed me in the right direction, past the entrance to Westminster Hall and on a few yards, to a spot where a taxi was disgorging passengers.

The drop-off point was manned by two more uniforms, guys significantly older than the twenty-something on the gate: a dark-skinned constable, and a pasty-faced sergeant who clearly hadn't run anywhere in a couple of years. He was chatting to the taxi driver, laughing at something he had said, unaware of a woman who had exited from a cab behind and who would have walked straight into the building had his colleague not stepped in to check her credentials.

As I moved towards him, he glanced at me and called out, 'With you in a second, mate.' He handed the driver what appeared to be a twenty-pound note.

I shook my head and replied, 'With me now, Sergeant,' with an edge to my voice that isn't normally there.

He frowned. 'Have a little patience, mate,' he barked, irritably. 'I'm busy here.'

My warrant card hangs on a lanyard inside my jacket. I produced it, held it up and beckoned him to me. 'That would be Commander, mate,' I said.

He gulped visibly, muttered, 'See you, Art,' to the driver, and came towards me.

'Commander McIlhenney, to be accurate,' I told him, 'Sergeant . . . ?'

'Fowler, sir. Sorry, didn't realise. It won't 'appen again.'

'I know, so let's not dwell on it. Except . . . what was the twenty quid about?'

'He's putting a bet on for me. Three twenty at Ludlow, a sure thing.'

'Who told you that?'

'He did.'

I suppressed a smile. 'Good luck with that, then. Have you and Constable . . .' I looked at his colleague.

'James Rasani-Hastings, Commander,' he obliged. 'Jimmy, usually.' The PC's uniform was noticeably neater than that of his colleague, and his equipment belt was strapped tightly in place, unlike the sergeant's, which sagged on the slope of his belly. I glanced down; his heavy shoes were cleaner too.

'Thanks. Have you been on duty here all morning?'

Both uniforms nodded. 'Since nine, sir,' Fowler volunteered.

I half turned and nodded towards a large brown painted door. 'Does that lead up to the PM's office?' I asked.

'Yes, sir,' Rasani-Hastings replied.

'Terrible what's 'appened, sir,' Fowler sighed. 'We was here when they took her away in the ambulance. All wrapped up she was; white as a sheet from what I could see of her. How's she doing? I asked Rob and Barry, her protection officers, but they were saying nuffin'. Have you heard, sir?'

'No, I haven't. There'll be a hospital bulletin this evening, I understand.'

'It must have come over her quickly,' Constable Jimmy observed.

'She was fine when she arrived this morning.' There was a look in his eye that made me think he was a man not given to taking too much at face value, unlike his colleague.

The promotion system isn't infallible in any police service, and the Met is so big that it gets it wrong more often than anywhere else. Looking at the pair I suspected they were two examples of its failure.

'She used this entrance when she arrived?' I asked.

'Yes, sir,' Jimmy confirmed. 'The car dropped her off at nine forty-five.'

'Alone?'

'No, Mr Bryant was with her.'

Not a name that I'd heard. 'Who's he?'

'Grover Bryant, sir. He's the PMOS: the Prime Minister's official spokesman,' the constable replied. He smiled. 'We're big on acronyms here.'

'When did he leave?'

'He didn't, not through this doorway anyway. But that doesn't mean he's still in there. He could have gone out through St Stephen's Entrance, or through the gate that leads into the tube station.'

'That's right,' Sergeant Fowler confirmed. 'This door here's used more often as an entrance than a way out.'

'Who've gone through it today?' I asked him.

'Only those as is allowed. The PM and Mr Bryant, like we said. The Chancellor was in early, before we arrived, 'cos he left at ten past nine. Mr Kramer came in just as he was leaving, then he went off in 'is car, just as the PM and Mr Bryant arrived.'

'He came back in again, of course,' Rasani-Hastings reminded him.

'Can you recall the exact time?'

'Ten fifty-nine, sir, exactly. I checked my watch and entered it in my notebook. He was gone for an hour and a quarter, give or take a minute.'

'Is there any other log of the use of the entrance?'

'No, just my book.'

'Is that a standing instruction?'

Constable Jimmy smiled at me. 'No, sir, it's a standing precaution.'

'In case someone like me comes along asking questions?'

'Spot on, Commander,' Fowler declared 'Our inspector's a fu . . .' He stopped in mid-imprecation, realising that anything he said could be noted down and used against him.

'Sir,' Rasani-Hastings ventured, 'can I ask? Where do you fit in? Are you PaDP? We're a uniformed body, I've never heard of us having a plainclothes commander on the strength. And if you're not, can you tell us what's going on, and what are the questions about?'

I looked him dead in the eye. 'Do you like it here?' I asked him, directly.

His gaze dropped. He shifted his weight from one foot to another. 'Sorry, sir. Not my place; I get it.'

'No,' I said, 'I've got no problem with your curiosity. That was a straight question. You don't need to answer it in front of your sergeant,' I took a card from a pocket and tucked it into his equipment belt, 'but if you ever fancy being something other than a glorified doorman, get in touch with me and we'll bring you in for assessment. No promises, though.'

He took the card and peered at it, eyes widening.

'Okay,' I said briskly, looking at Fowler, 'that's the lot, is it? Nobody else has used this entrance this morning, coming or going?'

He didn't reply, but I sensed a reaction from the constable. I frowned at the sergeant. 'What?' I snapped.

'Well, sir,' he murmured, 'there was one other. It was a bit unusual like and Jimmy here, give him his due, was a bit reluctant, since he ain't on the list, but he said he had an appointment with the Prime Minister, and well, sir, I wasn't about to tell him he couldn't get in, him being who he is, so I let him in. Then we let him out again, about twenty-five minutes later. Struck me 'e was in a bit of a state when 'e left.'

I held out a hand. 'Notebook, Jimmy.'

He handed it over, open at the last page used. I looked at the final entry, which recorded the departure of the Prime Minister in her ambulance, then scrolled up, past the note of Kramer's return. 'MB: exit ten fifty-two,' the entry before it read.

I had to flip the page to see the one before it. 'MB: entry ten twenty-eight.'

I looked at Rasani-Hastings. 'MB? Please tell me it isn't the MB I'm thinking of.'

He looked me in the eye. I had a strange feeling that each of us was trying to read the other's mind.

'No, you'll have got it right, Commander. You're not going to tell me he's one of your people, are you?'

Twelve

I had hoped to keep clear of Grover Bryant for as long as I could, but that wasn't to be.

The Cabinet Secretary and I finished his recorded interview, and parted company on decent terms, a big improvement on our first encounter. He returned to his own office, leaving me to prepare a list of priorities.

Based on what I had learned, and subject to any feedback from Neil following his visit to the House of Commons, I installed Siuriña Kramer as my top target. I had just noted the name of Montgomery Radley as number two, when my phone's embarrassing ringtone, 'Margaritaville', sounded.

Making my twentieth mental note to change it for something more dignified, I took the call. The number was withheld, but I guessed the caller correctly.

'Bob, it's Amanda. I have information for you on the Prime Minister's telephone activity this morning. There is nothing on her landline, either in her Commons office or in Downing Street, that strikes me as suspicious, although three of them do stand out. At eleven last night, six o'clock Washington time, she called the President of the United States on her secure line. It wasn't recorded, but my assumption would be that she briefed her on the Spitfire announcement. They were on the line for thirty-two minutes. Next she spent fifteen minutes speaking to the President of Russia and after that a further twenty in conversation with the President of China.'

'So add three more to the circle of knowledge,' I said. 'I don't imagine that any of them was too pleased. Has there been increased chatter through their three embassies this morning?'

'Bob,' she chuckled, 'we don't spy on other nations' embassies.'

'Not bloody much we don't!'

'Well, maybe on certain issues and at certain times we keep an eye on them. The answer is no, there hasn't. The Americans will want us to share the technology with them, of course.'

'Will we?'

'That would cause great difficulties with the Russians,' she said.

'Those would be the same Russians that claim to be developing a space plane that will be capable of doing much the same as Spitfire?'

'Yes. It will be bad enough that we have the capability before them, that's assuming their version ever works, which I doubt, but if we gave it to the Americans . . .'

'Yes,' I agreed. 'Their reaction would be unpredictable.'

'Exactly.'

'So,' I continued. 'We think she told the three presidents. Anyone else?'

'Not that her phone record shows, landline or mobile. However, the latter does reveal something of interest. Very few of the calls recorded are incoming, for an obvious reason: very few people have the number. But she did have one, at nine fifty-four this morning. Thing is, we can't trace the caller. It came from a one-off, over-the-counter SIM card. It took my people five minutes to trace it, but all they learned is that it was bought for cash from a shop in Clapham and only ever used once, for that call.'

'Can you trace the source?' I asked. 'Do you know where the mystery caller was when he phoned her?'

'GCHQ can't even trace the SIM. They tried to ping it, but got no response. It'll have been destroyed: use it then lose it, standard practice.'

'Standard practice among the sort of people that you and I have spent our careers chasing,' I pointed out, 'but not among the people who should have the Prime Minister's mobile number. Nine fifty-four, you said?'

'Yes.'

'Did she make any calls on her mobile?'

'Three. She rang Nick Wheeler at sixteen minutes past ten; no reply. She tried him again ten minutes later, and once more at nine minutes to eleven, but she didn't get through.'

'That's important,' I exclaimed. 'Hamblin says Satchell called him at one minute to eleven. She must have been attacked within that eight-minute window.'

'Yes,' Amanda agreed, 'that's progress.'

'Do you know where Wheeler was at the time?'

'No,' she said, 'but it's not really important.'

'Maybe not, but if she left a voicemail,' I pointed out, 'it might be useful to know what it said.'

'She couldn't have. She wasn't on the line for long enough on any of the attempts. What's your thinking?'

'I don't have any, Amanda,' I confessed. 'I know, you're wondering whether the mystery caller led her to phone Wheeler, but that's far from being an automatic assumption. Let's go back to that SIM card. If you've identified the shop where it was sold, I'm assuming that your people have spoken to the staff. Did they get any sort of a description of the buyer?'

'No such luck. It was one of ten cards sold in a batch, four months ago. The assistant who served the customer no longer works there. The manager remembers the transaction, because he was asked if it was okay, but he was in his office at the time and didn't see the buyer.'

'As we say in Scotland . . . bugger!'

'And here. Another piece of bad news. You won't be getting that Red Box. The Prime Minister's Civil Service private secretary won't release it without her authority. Nobody can overrule that; not even Kramer. It may be academic, though: I was assured there was nothing in it but correspondence, official and personal.'

'Okay, annoying but not vital,' I agreed. 'Anything else?'

'Apart from the phone records,' she continued, 'the lab has reported back on the letter-opener. There's a section of a palm print on it, and several partial fingerprints. They're clear and we assume they're Emily Repton's but we can't check.'

'If she comes round, it may not be necessary,' I pointed out. 'If she doesn't . . .'

I was in mid-sentence when the door of my temporary office was opened, wide, and a man strode into the room; a very large man, six feet four perhaps, and heavily built, but most of it fat, from the size of his jowls. He was jacketless; the sleeves of his white shirt were too long, but were restrained by bands, the kind that my father used to wear, but I never have. His blue tie was twisted and his dark hair was tousled, as if he had run his fingers through it.

He glared at me, then shouted, 'Who the hell are you?'

'I have to go,' I told Amanda quietly, pocketing my phone as I stood.

'Who's asking?' I retorted. 'The office manager?'

'Don't get clever with me, chum,' he barked, advancing on me, chin jutting out. I gave a moment's thought to hanging one on it, but contented myself with putting a hand on his chest, then slowly pushing him back on his heels.

'Take a seat,' I ordered him, 'and quieten down. My name's Bob Skinner and in this room, I ask the questions today. The first one being . . . who the hell are you?'

He peered at me. 'So you're the famous Skinner,' he exclaimed. 'Emily told me about you, and the trouble she had with you when she was Home Seccy.'

'Sit down,' I repeated.

'If you insist.' He planted his bulk on the chair that Hamblin had vacated. 'She told me you're a rough sod.'

'I wouldn't quite put it that way,' I said. 'I'm a perfectly affable guy, with people that I like. Now,' I added, although by that time I had guessed the answer, 'level the playing field. You are?'

'Grover Bryant, PMOS. If you weren't a hick from up north, you'd have known that.'

I stared at him, poker faced. 'Are you telling me that the Prime Minister trusts you to take her message to the media?' I exclaimed. 'That makes me worry about her judgement, on the basis of what you've shown me so far. Now, tell me, with no further bluster, how you came to burst in here. How did you know that anyone was in this room?'

'Sources.'

'Who?'

'Can't say,' he murmured.

'Won't say,' I countered. 'If I could be bothered, I could find out in a couple of minutes, just by calling Norman Hamblin. Obviously he wasn't your informant or you wouldn't have had to ask who I was, but only his office staff know I'm here. Ergo . . .'

I smiled. 'But as I say, I can't be arsed, for now. Maybe I should, though. If I was in Hamblin's chair, I'd want to know I could trust everyone around me.' I nodded. 'Yes, at some point, I will deal with it. I'm temporarily an MI5 officer, so I suppose I have to. You have a very small window to have your friend transferred out of here, if you can.'

'That's noted,' Bryant snapped, 'but please, Mr Skinner, don't try to blow smoke up my arse. I want to know what's going on. My . . . informant told me that Hamblin was summoned to Emily's office in the Commons, not by her, but by Kramer. Not long afterwards we had this cock and fucking bull story about Emily being hit by a tropical disease, and then Hamblin arrived back here and instructed that this room be prepared for you and a colleague.

'I'm not an idiot, man. I was on that African trip; everywhere we went was completely fucking sanitised, so no way did she contract Ebola, or schistosomiasis or dengue fever or anything else. Nor was she displaying symptoms of anything the last time I saw her, which was little more than three hours ago. So what the hell has happened?'

'How much do you know about the business of the day?' I asked him.

His eyes narrowed. 'What business?'

'The defence statement this afternoon. The one that's been cancelled because of the Prime Minister's absence.'

'I know nothing about it. I asked her but she said she wasn't ready to tell me.'

'Why do I have trouble believing that?'

'I don't give two fucks whether you believe it or not. What is wrong with her?' A look of pain came into his eyes. 'Mr Skinner, she's my half-sister; we came out of the same womb. I'm her closest living relative after her father. I have a right to know.'

Fat, bombastic arsehole or not, he had a point.

'You said you saw her this morning,' I continued, quietly. 'When?'

'I took a ride in her car across to the Commons. We went in through the side entrance and up to her office. I carried the Red Box; heavier than they look, those things. I dropped her off there then went up to the tea room. I'd arranged to meet a couple of the tamer lobby correspondents, to mark their cards about some of this week's government business.'

'How long did you spend in her office?'

'A couple of minutes, no more. I made her a coffee, but didn't have one myself.'

'Why did she go there, at that time of day? Is that normal?'

'There is no normal with Em,' he chuckled. 'If she wants to get away from Downing Street, sometimes she'll go over there just to hide out. This morning she said she wanted to prepare herself in private for the defence statement.'

'But she didn't tell you what was in it?'

'No, she didn't. Obviously I asked her, but she told me that it would be better for both of us if I didn't know. Whatever it is, it's strictly embargoed. By not telling me she was removing the possibility that I might let something slip. I confess I have made a couple of errors of judgement in briefing people I thought I could trust.'

I nodded; I'd spent only two minutes with the bloke, but that was enough for me to understand her caution.

'Do you know if she was expecting visitors over there?'

Bryant frowned. 'No. The opposite, in fact; she went over there early so she could be alone. Mickey Satchell has access to her when she's there, and Kramer too, I suppose, and I know she invites the Chancellor in for a coffee sometimes, because he's one of her sounding boards . . .'

'One of?' I queried. 'Who are the others?'

He stared at me. 'There's me, for a start; even more so since she got rid of Murdoch, that pillock of a husband of hers. When she wants a woman's perspective, she might talk to Valerie Radley, the Foreign Secretary's wife. Not that they're friends as such; oh no, Ems doesn't have friends who are remotely political.' He paused, and smiled. 'Apart from young Nick of course, Nicholas Wheeler, the Defence Secretary. He has very blue eyes where she's concerned.'

'What about Siuriña Kramer? Would she talk to her?'

'Whoa,' he boomed, in a great exhalation. 'Not a chance of that happening, not even if they were the last two people on earth. They can't stand each other.'

'Hold on, doesn't the leader, the Prime Minister, appoint the party chair?'

'Yes, she does, but Siuriña was put there by the last regime, by George Locheil. Emily would have fired her when she took over, but I persuaded her that doing so would have made things tricky with her husband, and that she should be seen to be magnanimous. So she's still there, although Emily did revoke her automatic access to Cabinet meetings. Get it?'

'Got it.'

'Right. The thing is, Siuriña's power crazy. She believes that Roland should be PM, not Emily. During the leadership campaign she did a lot of whispering, about her and about

Murdoch, suggesting that she used MI5 while she was Home Secretary to catch him playing away games, so she could get him out of the way while covering up her own marital misdemeanours.' Bryant wrinkled his nose. 'Maybe she did. I wouldn't put it past her.'

'She didn't,' I said, firmly, for I know who did fix Lord Forgrave. 'Were there any?' I asked. 'Marital misdemeanours?'

'Not that I know of,' he replied immediately. 'Emily is a very smart woman; she knows that sleaze will finish you in politics, faster than a speeding bullet, and sleaze involves one or both of two things, basically: sex and money. Also, she did love the idiot, in her way. I think she only got rid of him because he'd become a liability.'

'Are they still in touch?'

'Occasionally. Their paths cross in parliament, for he's still a Tory peer. He hopes she'll bring him back into government. She won't, but if he goes back to the Bar and keeps his nose clean, he might well wind up on the Supreme Court bench one day.'

He glowered at me again. 'Now,' he rumbled, 'if you have no more questions, will you answer mine. What's wrong with my sister?'

'I do have one more question, although it will seem very odd. When you were in the Prime Minister's office this morning, did you use the lavatory?'

'Odd?' he exclaimed. 'It's almost bloody offensive. No, I did not.'

'You certain?'

'Absolutely. I went into her bathroom for water to fill her coffee machine, but that's all.'

'Was the seat up or down?'

He stared at me as if I was crazy. I couldn't blame him; it was an odd question in any circumstances.

But he replied. 'Down, definitely. I know this because I had the coffee capsules in one hand and the jug in the other. I put the capsules down on the lid to turn on the tap. Does that actually help you in some way?'

I nodded. 'It does. Now, to your question. I'm going to answer it, but the truth stays between us. That is not a request, it's an order, and you can take it as coming from the acting Prime Minister himself.'

He leaned forward in his chair. 'Acting PM? Who do you mean?'

'Kramer.'

'Does that mean . . .' His eyes had a glazed dazed look.

I held up a hand. 'The Cabinet Secretary was called across to the Commons because your sister was found by her PPS, slumped across her desk. It was apparent that she had been attacked. Initially, Dr Satchell believed that she was dead. Without waiting for Hamblin to arrive, she went to the Home Secretary, who had just returned from an engagement.'

Colour was draining from Bryant's florid face. 'Kramer took command,' I continued, quickly, before he could recover himself and intervene, 'and called in Amanda Dennis, the head of the Security Service. Without going into detail about the content of the defence announcement, their concern was that it might have a connection with the attack. Kramer's view was that it was a national security matter. Therefore, even when the PM was believed to be dead, he decided to conceal the fact, to allow an immediate and urgent investigation.'

'Hence the tropical disease story?'

'That's right.'

'And that's where you come in?'

'Yes. I was around, Mrs Dennis knew it and seconded me; in fact she pretty much conscripted me.'

He leaned closer. 'But Ems isn't dead?' he whispered.

'No, she isn't. But don't get your hopes up,' I warned. 'She has a severe brain injury, and her surgeon isn't able to give a positive prognosis.'

The big fellow leaned back, his shirt sticking to folds of belly. 'Do you have any idea,' he murmured, 'what the media would do with this story?'

'I'm a director of a newspaper group, Mr Bryant,' I replied. 'I know exactly what they'd do with it.'

'Do you know what the Opposition would do with it?'

'Probably twice as much as the media would.'

'Exactly. Merlin Brady would call this a coup d'état, and he wouldn't be too far off the mark either. How long have you got for your investigation?'

'Forty-eight hours, Kramer said.'

'Can you catch the attacker in that time?'

'If I can't catch him in twenty-four hours,' I confessed, 'I'm probably not going to catch him. On the other hand, if I can rule out any connection with the defence announcement, I'll expect Kramer to call in the police at that point.'

'Do you have a suspect?'

I frowned. 'To be honest, you're as close to a suspect as I have.'

'Me!' he spluttered. 'You can't be serious.'

'I don't do flippant,' I retorted: 'You're the only person I know to have been in there this morning, until Satchell found her.'

'The journos I met in the tea room. They'll vouch for me.'

'I'm sure they will,' I agreed, 'but that wouldn't eliminate you. The only person who could do that is lying unconscious in the Royal Free Hospital.'

'You can't . . .' he repeated.

'I can, but . . . until I can figure out a way for you to have covered yourself by making three calls from her mobile between a quarter past ten and ten to eleven, then getting it back into her office without being seen on the CCTV, I'm not going to take you too seriously as a would-be killer.' I picked up a plastic ballpoint pen from my temporary desk and tossed it to him. Automatically, he caught it, with his right hand.

'That too,' I said.

'Eh?' he squeaked, puzzled.

'Never mind. So, Mr Bryant,' I continued. 'What's it going to be? Are you going to let me get on with the job of finding your sister's attacker, or are you going to get in the way?'

'Put that way, what choice do I have?'

'You can do whatever you like,' I assured him. 'I'm not going to try to detain you, or coerce you. I'm following Kramer's brief at the moment. I don't have any option, because he was clever enough to tell me exactly what your sister was due to announce this afternoon, thereby wrapping me up tight in the Official Secrets Act, which I am duty bound to respect. But I haven't told you about it, have I? All you know is the truth about what happened to your sister, and that is not a state secret as such, but an unreported crime.'

'If I go public, will it harm Emily?'

'No, but it will destabilise the government you serve, through her. What would she want you to do?'

He nodded. 'She'd tell me to go back out of that door and pretend I'd never met you. And that's what I'm going to do, Mr

Skinner, for those twenty-four hours you mentioned. After that, we'll see.'

He heaved himself out of the chair. 'Can I visit her?' he asked.

'Of course. In fact you should; it would look bloody odd if you didn't, would it not? But just one thing,' I added. 'Her protection officers are there just now, standing guard over an unconscious woman like a couple of Greyfriars Bobbys. If they found out what really happened to her, the outcome would be unpredictable, and nobody needs that complication, least of all your sister.'

'Okay,' he said. 'I'll say quiet.' He paused in the doorway. 'This defence announcement: was it the cause of what's happened to her?'

'I fucking hope not,' I growled, 'otherwise I'm going to have to add the people in the White House and the Kremlin to the suspect list.'

Thirteen

As soon as Bryant had gone, I walked along to Hamblin's room and told him about his visit.

'Will he behave himself?' the Cabinet Secretary asked, gazing up at me anxiously from behind his desk.

'I hope so,' I replied. 'I think so. We had a difficult beginning, but by the end we'd reached a meeting of minds.' I frowned. 'Tell me something,' I said. 'Why is it that everyone here is so bloody rude? You, Kramer, the man Bryant; I'd barely been introduced to the three of you before we were locking horns.'

'Physician,' he murmured.

'Excuse me?'

He smiled. 'Physician heal thyself. If I may say so, you also have an abrasive side, Mr Skinner.'

'I'd prefer to say that I don't take shit from anyone, regardless of rank or status.'

'Same thing,' he countered. 'But I respect it. I admit that I also recognise your description of us. In this world, we live inside a glass bubble, visible to those outside but for most of the time untouchable by them. The three of us you have encountered so far are all, make no mistake, very important people in the great scheme of things, and we are treated as such. The entire Civil

Service defers to me, and I defer to Roland Kramer. But at the same time they do not, and I do not. Forelocks are not touched to us as individuals, but to the offices at we hold.

'As for Bryant, most people find him a distasteful man, as clearly you did, but he attracts cautious deference too, not necessarily because of his place in our world, but because he is closer to the Prime Minister than any of us, she being the bestower of rank and privilege.

'Living as we do, and treated as we are, it is all too easy for us to become self-important. Inevitably, most of us do, and frankly, it is good for us to be challenged. It happens to me every day.'

I felt my eyebrows rise. 'In here?'

'God no,' he laughed. 'At home, by my sister, every evening after dinner. She throws me an apron, and a look that says "the dishes won't wash themselves". Every time I suggest that we buy a dishwasher, she says, "Why? I already have one." Often I have barely hung up my coat before she hands me a list of tasks, about the house or in the garden. She insists that having grime under my nails will make me a better person.'

'Does it?'

'No. I'm still the same autocratic shit that I've always been. I don't simply respect the great offices of my political bosses, I respect my own.' He sighed. 'All very different from your world, I imagine.'

'I don't know what my world is any more,' I confessed. 'I've drawn a line under one career but I'm not sure yet what my next one will be.'

'If Mrs Dennis has her way you've already begun it.'

'I wasn't asked,' I told him, 'and I didn't volunteer. In fact I tried to walk away, but Kramer told me that I didn't have that option. He even gave me a demonstration of power, through one of his attack dogs, the man Daffyd I told you about earlier. That's something he and I are going to discuss when this investigation is over.'

'Indeed?' Hamblin murmured. 'Be careful of that man Daffyd. He failed SAS training because of excessive zeal. That was one of the things that commended him to our Mr Kramer.'

'I've met bigger zealots than him,' I retorted. 'The last one was a Russian; he'd have had Daffyd running for cover. But speaking of Kramer,' I continued, 'I need to see his wife. How do I do that?'

'Get yourself along to Conservative Party headquarters. She's pretty much full time as chair. Would you like me to arrange a meeting through her office?'

'Thank you, no,' I said. 'I'd rather it was a cold call; I don't want to give her any preparation time.' I waved the card that was my badge of rank. 'I imagine this will get me through the door.'

'I imagine it will. Will you advise the Home Secretary?'

'No way.'

'He will not be pleased,' Hamblin warned, 'when he finds out that you've interviewed his wife without his approval.'

'Good.'

'Were you always insubordinate, Mr Skinner?'

'I've never had to be. My senior officers, when I had any, always knew that I was right.'

'Mmmm.' The Cabinet Secretary frowned. 'In the unlikely event that Mrs Kramer confesses to the attack on the Prime Minister, what will you do?'

I hadn't thought about that, but I didn't really have to. 'I'll call in Neil McIlhenney and let him take it from there.'

He shuddered.

'By the way,' I said, 'one more thing before I head for the

Tory HQ. You've got a leak in your office; someone's feeding information to Grover Bryant.'

'I know,' he replied, 'but I choose to leave her in place. Some of the information she passes on isn't factually correct. In any event,' he added, 'Mr Bryant may not be around here for much longer, unless the Prime Minister makes a miraculous recovery.'

I left him nurturing that thought and headed for the exit. As I walked I consulted an app on my phone; it showed me exactly where the Conservative Central Office was located, a ten-minute walk away.

I had just turned into Parliament Square when Jimmy Buffett sang his song in my pocket. As I took it out, I found myself hoping it would be Sarah, offering me a reminder of what sanity and stability were like in the midst of the madness, but it wasn't. It was Neil.

'Bob,' he exclaimed, 'daft as this sounds I can actually see you.'

'Where are you?' I asked, stopping in my tracks.

'Look across the square to the gate into the Commons.'

I did, and saw him standing beside one of the armed officers on guard duty. 'Gotcha. Come across and join me.'

'Fine,' he said, 'as long as we're going for a sandwich or something similar. I never told you, but I was diagnosed with mild type two diabetes a few months ago, and I need to refuel.'

I glanced around, looking for a Greggs sign, even a Starbucks, but seeing none. 'Where can we do that around here?'

'No worries. I'll show you. Stay where you are.'

I ended the call and watched him as he made his way across the junction, waiting twice for the signs to turn green. As he approached I studied him, looking for any signs of physical change. He might have been a little less chunky than before, but he looked none the worse for that.

'Are you on insulin?' I asked, as soon as he reached me. 'Do you need to go somewhere to inject?'

'Hell no,' he laughed. 'I told you, Bob, it's mild. My last medical showed raised sugar levels, and diabetes turned out to be the cause. I control it by diet, for now, and hopefully that will always be enough, but I can't take liberties. Come on.'

I fell into step beside him as we headed for the north side of Parliament Square, then past the Supreme Court and the Queen Elizabeth Conference Centre, towards a massive stone building. High above the entrance the words 'Methodist Central Hall' were displayed in gold lettering; I realised that was where the Home Secretary had addressed his prison governors that morning, and said so.

'Yes,' my friend agreed, 'but there are public facilities too.'

He led the way into a spacious entrance area. 'There must be more Methodists than I realised,' I murmured as I looked around.

We turned off to the right, then down a flight of stairs into a big, well-illuminated, self-service cafeteria. It was busy, but there were plenty of available tables. We loaded a tray with sandwiches, wraps and sparkling water, then commandeered one of them.

'This is good,' I said. 'I never knew it existed.'

'Neither do most of the tourists,' Neil observed, 'which is a blessing. When I was in the old Met building just round the corner, I came here quite often. Even now we've moved, I still do. I meet my undercover people here if they develop a pressing need to report in.'

'Here, rather than in New Scotland Yard?'

'Yes, and you know why.'

I did indeed. The officers who were reporting to him were in so deep that even in a city as populous as London, they could not risk being spotted walking into the Met HQ, or any other police building. He might even have been implying that they would not have been safe inside. Corruption exists, and the larger the force, the likelier it is to go undetected.

'So,' I said, after a mouthful of tuna mayonnaise sandwich, 'did you get anything useful over there?'

'I hope not,' he replied. 'I've got the Chancellor leaving at ten past nine, the PM logged in at nine forty-five, with the official spokesman, a guy named Bryant . . . who will need to be interviewed . . . and Kramer leaving as they arrived, then coming back at exactly ten fifty-nine.'

'Don't worry about Bryant,' I told him. 'He came looking for us; he's under control for now, although he could still become a problem. Ten fifty-nine, you say Kramer got back. How sure are you of that time?'

'Pretty sure. It was recorded by a PC who seemed to understand that record-keeping has to be accurate if it's to be any good.'

'If his watch squares with the timer on the CCTV footage it puts Kramer outside the building when Repton was attacked.' I frowned. 'I suppose I'm happy about that,' I grumbled.

Neil laughed. 'Were you hoping it was him?'

'It would have been good for my memoirs.'

'Hold on. The next one could be even better.'

'You mean there was somebody else? There are only three offices in that corridor and only three people who can access them through that gate: you've just placed them all within the timeframe of the attack.'

'Maybe so, but there was one other person admitted. The sergeant in charge got a bit shifty about it, but he realised he had no choice but to cough up. The person he identified was admitted at ten twenty-eight according to the PC's log and was in there for approximately twenty-three minutes before he left by the same doorway. They let him in because he said he had a meeting with the Prime Minister, and because the sergeant didn't have the bottle to make him go the proper way.'

'So who was he, your mystery man?'

'Merlin Brady.'

The remainder of the tuna mayonnaise stopped halfway on its journey to my mouth. Filling leaked out as my fingers tightened on it.

'Merlin fucking Brady?' I gasped. 'The leader of the fucking Opposition? You're telling me that he blagged his way into Repton's office corridor, then left again, appearing agitated, a few minutes before Mickey Satchell found her on her desk with a blade sticking out of her scone?'

'That's what happened,' McIlhenney confirmed. 'Sergeant Fowler, on his own, might have got the timing wrong but not PC Rasani-Hastings. I'm in no doubt.'

'What time exactly was he logged out?' I asked.

'Ten fifty-two.'

I did some sums in my head. Based on the times of the phone calls that Emily had made to Wheeler, Brady had left within the timeframe for the attack.

'Then I think we should search the cellars as well,' I declared. 'It's coming up on November the Fifth and you never know, we might find one of Guy Fawkes's descendants hiding in there with a few barrels of gunpowder.'

'What are we going to do? Do we need to go to Kramer with this?'

'Let me think about that,' I said. 'I was heading somewhere when you called, and I still need to go there. First things first. Let's tackle Mrs Kramer in her lair.'

Fourteen

*I*n all the time I worked for Bob Skinner in Edinburgh, I never aspired to match him, not in any way. None of us did, not me, not Mario, not Maggie Rose, not Brian Mackie, not the late, lamented Stevie Steele, not Sammy Pye, and not even young Sauce Haddock . . . although one day he might. The Big Man was our leader, and the thing that drove us all was a desire to live up to his expectations of us.

We didn't always succeed; when we failed, as sometimes we did, he never held it against any of us, but took the blame upon himself, as a failure in his guidance. Looking back, I can see that his gift was his ability to spot people whose talent was not tainted by personal ambition, then to nurture it. And as it's turned out, all of us, even me who never dreamed of it, attained senior ranks.

But hold on, I'm wrong; there was one who was always striving to catch up with Bob; but the fact that I forgot to include him in that list of his protégés says it all.

Andy Martin was the first of us to be taken under his wing, and for a while he was the closest to him. Later he was even closer to Alex, Bob's daughter. That relationship drove a wedge between them for a while, but eventually the big man accepted it.

Andy rose fast, but he was never content with anything; there was a cold, cruel streak in him and an excess of self-esteem that Bob never saw. Andy had his eye on the prize from the beginning, and I'm sure that he only ever saw the boss as a stepping stone. He proved it, in fact, when he leapt into the vacuum created by Bob's refusal to countenance applying for the chief's job in the national police force, the creation of which he had failed to prevent.

Sir Andrew accepted the knighthood that his mentor had declined, but that was all he had to take with him when he proved to be an absolute disaster as a leader. I was gone by that time, but I was a witness from four hundred miles away as he alienated all of the people on whose shoulders he had climbed, and came close to inflicting terminal damage on the fledgling service before he was quietly eased out of the door.

Bob was a witness too, but he stayed silent; he would have helped Andy, I'm sure, but he was never asked to do so. In fact he was kept at a distance. Most foolish of all, Alex was alienated too, and that probably sealed his fate. I don't imagine that Bob engineered the newspaper stories that triggered his fall, but I do believe that if he'd intervened and backed him publicly he might have saved him.

All that was running through my mind as I concentrated on finishing my carefully selected chicken salad wrap in the Central Hall cafeteria, on the most bizarre day I could recall from a police career that has never been what anyone would call normal. I looked at my old boss as I held my water bottle to my lips, feeling a mix of pleasure and pride to be working for him again.

I say 'for' rather than 'with', because that's how it's always been, and because I recognised that I was only there beside him because he'd had the power to insist upon it.

'So, gaffer,' I said, 'do we just walk in there cold, and demand to see the chairlady?'

'Less of the "gaffer", Commander,' he grunted, wiping his lips with a paper napkin. 'Pretty much so, yes.'

He produced a laminated card from an inside pocket of his jacket and handed it to me. It was smaller than a police warrant card, but it bore the crest of the Security Service, a crown over a circle of stars and portcullises surrounding a heraldic lion, his name and the title 'Consultant Director'. It bore his photograph also, and a gold chip that I guessed had biometric information that would match his passport. Amanda Dennis hadn't knocked that up at a moment's notice. I knew she had tried to recruit him; she must have been waiting for the day.

'That ought to get some attention,' I agreed.

'She'll see us, I'm sure,' he said. 'When we get in there I'm going to try to assess whether she was expecting us.'

'Do you think Kramer will have told her what's happened?'

'That's the question, isn't it? I don't know. This isn't a normal couple we're dealing with. She's the chair of the governing party and at the moment he's its acting leader. How much does he tell her? Hamblin says she doesn't attend Cabinet any longer, so does he keep the secret stuff away from the dinner table or does he share it?'

'When Louise is in rehearsal she'll share her script with me,' I volunteered. 'We run through them at home.'

He grinned. 'Reading the lines in Macbeth hardly equates with discussing the nuclear deterrent.'

'The Scottish play,' I corrected him. 'You never call it by its name . . .'

'I know, but only in a theatre.'

'This building is a theatre of sorts. There are performances in here from time to time. Trust me, it's a serious thespian superstition.'

148

'If that's so, since I have said "Macbeth", what do I have to do to placate the evil spirits?' he asked.

'Turn around three times and spit over your left shoulder, I believe. That usually cuts it, Lou says.'

He stood. 'In that case they can bring it on; I can be a fucking evil spirit myself. Come on,' he said, 'screw your courage to the sticking place. From what we saw in that TV footage we may be paying a call on Lady Macbeth herself.'

I stayed where I was, for something was troubling me. 'Hold on a minute,' I said.

'Problem? Do you need to eat more?' he added, a little anxiously.

You have to be diabetic to understand it properly. Mild cases can be managed quite simply, and so far I've been able to do that, more or less. 'No, I'm fine,' I assured him. 'It's got nothing to do with that. I'm wondering whether we should go in there without letting Kramer know first. Didn't you say he told you to keep him informed every step of the way?'

'He did indeed,' Bob laughed, 'and that's an instruction I intend to ignore. Siuriña Kramer showed up where she shouldn't have been, and I'm going to treat her like any other suspect. If the Home Secretary has a problem with that once he finds out, he can bloody well fire me . . . and I don't think he's going to do that.'

'He might fire me,' I countered.

'Not a prayer. He doesn't have that level of control over the Met, not any longer. And if he tried,' he added, 'I think he'd have to fire that wee Commissioner of yours as well.'

He was in such high humour, as we left the building, it was clear that he was enjoying being back in the saddle. He seemed to know where he was going, for he led the way down Tothill Street then turned into Matthew Parker Street, where the Tory lair is situated. (*Like the majority of Scots, I've never voted for them; I don't know for sure but I doubt that Bob has either.*)

The reception area had a guardian, a man in a black suit that might have been a uniform of sorts, but he didn't have any obvious deterrent value. I was surprised by the lack of obvious security, until I realised that the mirror behind him was probably more than that, and that we were being observed by more than the TV camera set in the ceiling.

'Yes, gentlemen,' he said, rising, and walking round to greet us. His lapel badge bore the name Gwynn Edwards. 'How can I assist you?'

Bob produced his credentials. 'I realise this is a little unorthodox,' he replied, quietly, 'but we need to see Mrs Kramer. It's a matter of some urgency.'

'I'm not sure she's in the building, sir,' Mr Edwards murmured, with a soft Welsh lilt. 'Let me find out.'

'If she isn't, then please tell me where she is. This isn't going to wait.'

The man moved back to his desk, picked up the phone that sat there and punched in four digits. He kept his back to us, but my hearing is sharp enough for me to pick up the odd word: 'Shirley', 'Five', 'rid of', the last with a question in the tone. I thought I saw a small shrug as he replaced it in its cradle.

He turned back to us. 'In fact the chairman is in, gentlemen, and she does have a minute or two free. Her office is on the first floor. I'll buzz you through, then just take the stairs. You'll be met by her secretary.' He pointed to a double door behind him, to his right, then stretched an arm across and under his desk. He must have pressed a button, for we heard a loud, continuous buzz. We followed his instructions; there was a loud click as the door closed behind us.

The dark-haired, middle-aged woman who greeted us at the top of the stairs wore no badge on her white blouse, but she identified herself as soon as we had reached her level.

'Shirley Oxford,' she said, hand outstretched towards Bob. We were side by side, she didn't know either of us, and neither of us was displaying ID but she locked straight on to him. 'I'm Mrs Kramer's chef d'equipe.'

The big man beamed. 'Indeed?' he exclaimed. 'I thought we were leaving Europe. Sorry,' he added quickly. 'I shouldn't be flippant. I'm Bob Skinner and this is Neil McIlhenney.'

Shirley didn't appear to be riled by his wisecrack. She smiled. 'You may have a point about the title,' she murmured. 'It may be passé.' I liked her counter. 'Siuriña introduced it when she became chairman,' she explained. 'She said she wanted the office to have a cosmopolitan feel, combined with greater authority. Before that I was the chairman's secretary, plain and simple. To be honest, I still am to most people in here. Now,' she continued, 'do you really have to see her? She does delegate to me quite extensively.'

'I'm sure she does,' Bob conceded, 'but this time she can't. It's a security matter and we have to discuss it with her, in person.'

'I see, but I'm puzzled,' she confessed. 'Security matters rarely land on the chairman's desk. In fact, I can't remember anything like this ever happening, and I've been in this post for eight years.'

He grinned, amiably. 'First time for everything.'

'Indeed.' She asked the question I'd been expecting, and fearing. 'Does the Home Secretary know you're here?'

'I don't report to the Home Secretary,' Bob replied. 'My boss is Mrs Dennis, the Director General; call her if you need confirmation of my authority. Besides,' he added, 'the Home Secretary has suddenly become an even busier man, with the indisposition of the

Prime Minister. He's running the whole damn country. I'm sorry, but I have to insist; we need to see Mrs Kramer.'

She hesitated. For a moment I thought she was going to call his bluff, and phone Amanda Dennis, but finally she nodded, discounting that last option, and said, 'In that case, you must; we're not here to obstruct MI5 in any way. Follow me, please, gentlemen.'

Our discussion had taken place on a carpeted L-shaped landing, and had been interrupted only by the sound of an elevator heading to and from the upper floors. There were only three doors; none bore a name or a number, but the 'chef d'equipe' turned and led us to and through the one immediately behind her. We found ourselves in a large anteroom, with three desks; a man and a woman, neither of them any older than mid-twenties, were busy at two of them.

Another door led out of the anteroom; Shirley ushered us through it, without introduction, then withdrew, closing it behind her.

The first of two things that struck me about Siuriña Kramer was her height. She was standing when we entered the inner sanctum of the Conservative HQ; she seemed taller than she had appeared in the jerky CCTV footage, at least five nine by my estimate. Then I realised that the only perspective available on the screen had been her near-collision with Montgomery Radley, the Foreign Secretary. He was pointed out to me at one of Louise's premieres and I'd observed that he was something of a skyscraper.

The second thing was that she was an extremely attractive woman. I'd seen her on television news reports a couple of times and once on Question Time, where she'd more than held her own against a predominantly left-wing panel, and a studio audience that seemed to have been seeded with hostiles, but not even a large curved OLED screen had captured the deep blue of her eyes, or the height of her cheekbones, or the sheen of her hair. I'd like to have added, 'or the warmth of her smile', but the look she gave us was on the chilly side of cool.

She faced us along rather than across a polished mahogany conference table. It was drawn up against her desk, with five chairs on either side and another at the end, facing her own. She said not a word, simply standing her ground as if she was trying to stare us . . . or freeze us . . . out.

If it was a contest she won it. 'Thank you for receiving us, Mrs Kramer,' Bob said, more formally than I'd ever heard him.

'I haven't, not yet,' she responded. 'You're presumptuous and I'm still deciding. Show me your credentials, please. And by the way, in this building people usually address me as "Chairman".'

'They would be the faithful, I imagine,' he replied. 'Don't mistake me for one of those.'

He took out his MI5 ID and slid it along the table. I followed suit with my warrant card, but walked along and handed it to her.

She thanked me and frowned at Bob as she picked up his card. 'Consultant Director,' she read. 'How long have you been with the Security Service, Mr Skinner? My husband has never mentioned you.'

'As of this morning, as it happens,' he told her. 'Unless you and he had lunch together, he hasn't had an opportunity to mention me.'

'No, we didn't. I haven't seen him since breakfast.' She pushed the ID back towards him and looked at mine. 'Commander McIlhenney, Metropolitan Police Service. What are you doing shadowing MI5?'

'I'm on secondment,' I volunteered, and left it at that.

'Very well,' she said, her decision made as she returned my

card. 'I'll give you ten minutes; you must appreciate that the Prime Minister's sudden illness has put this place on high alert. So, what do you have to tell me?'

'Nothing,' Bob replied. 'We've come here to question you.'

The blue eyes grew even more chilly. 'Question me?' she exclaimed. 'Why on earth should you want to question me? Did I jump a red light taking my daughter to school? Two Scotsmen,' she laughed harshly. 'Are you the heavy squad?'

'We are, as a matter of fact,' he said, and there was something in the quietness of his tone that made a flicker of apprehension show in her eyes. 'I have to tell you, Mrs Kramer, that so far I dislike you as much as I dislike your husband, and that saddens me.'

Uninvited he took the seat at the table nearest to hers; I chose the third of the five, to give me a clear view of her. 'Sit, please,' he murmured.

She complied; her face looked a little flushed.

'How does Emily Repton feel about you?' he asked.

'How would I know that?' she retorted.

I saw his grin reflected in the window opposite. 'Somehow I'm pretty sure you would. She has no reason to like you, has she? You did your very best to shaft her during the last leadership election.'

'I supported my husband's candidacy,' she insisted. 'Nothing wrong with that.'

'There is when you put the word out that she misused her powers as Home Secretary, and hint that it wasn't only Lord Forgrave who was playing away games.'

That was news to me, but I could see that it had stung Siuriña Kramer.

'Those were stories that she spread around herself; then she accused me of doing it, to discredit Roland,' she protested.

I had to jump in on that one, if only to remind Bob that I was still there. 'Chairman, are you trying to say that she accused herself of adultery to make you look bad?' I asked.

Bob nodded to emphasise my question; also, he got the message, pulling his chair back and changing its angle, so that I could eyeball her directly.

'That's right,' he said. 'Come on, nothing's going to leave this room, so let's be honest about it. You call it briefing down here, isn't that right? You were briefing against her and she found out.'

'She reappointed me as Chairman of the Party,' she countered.

'Because she wanted to keep your husband onside and on the Front Bench,' he shot back, 'but she kicked you out of the Cabinet, did she not? Let's just accept it as fact, shall we? You and Emily Repton are the best of enemies.'

'Very well,' she snapped. 'Let's accept it. I can't stand the woman and she can't stand me. She's a manipulator and she's an upstart; Roland should be in Downing Street, not her.'

'You really believe that, don't you?' Bob murmured.

'Of course I do.'

'If she doesn't recover from this mysterious tropical disease, chances are he will be. Will that make you happy?'

'Ecstatic. I admit it quite freely.'

Bob slapped the table with his right palm. 'Excellent,' he exclaimed. 'I like it when people are honest with me. So tell me,' he said, 'given your antipathy to Ms Repton, why were you seen hurrying towards her office corridor this morning?'

She stared at him, then at me, then back at him, for several seconds. 'Why do I have the feeling,' she mused aloud, 'that in other circumstances this is where I would insist on having a lawyer present?'

'We're not there yet,' I said, 'unless you're about to admit to a *criminal act.' I paused, as the policeman in me took over. 'Maybe I should caution you formally, just in case.'*

'There's no need for that,' she replied, then she looked back at Bob. 'Who told you that? The Right Honourable Montgomery, I imagine.'

'No, he didn't,' he told her. 'We haven't had time to speak to him yet. I'm surprised you noticed his presence; you seemed to rush past him without a word.'

'I never speak to that man, unless it can't be avoided. He's a loathsome creature.'

'What? The nation's representative in the wide world?'

'The best thing about Monty Radley being Foreign Secretary is that it involves him being out of the country for long spells.'

'Why don't you like him?'

'He doesn't have a likeable bone in his body. He's a bully, he drinks too much, and he alienates practically everyone who comes into contact with him. And he's a lech, a great lumbering lecher. Ashley, the first Mrs Radley, was a very happy lady when he left her for Valerie. She only stayed for the girls' sake; not that she was doing them any favours.'

'If he's that much of a swine, how did he rise so high?' I asked.

'He appeals to a certain type of Tory, within the parliamentary party and among the more right-wing membership. And he's rich, of course.'

'And all that compensates for him being a boozer and a bully?'

She frowned at me. 'Nothing compensates for him slapping Valerie around.'

'You're saying he's violent towards women?' Bob murmured.

'There have been stories,' she replied, 'but I'm saying no more about it, or him.'

'I agree,' he said. 'Let's concentrate on you, Mrs Kramer. You

were in the PM's Commons corridor this morning. Did you go into her office?'

'No, I did not. Why do you ask?'

'Hasn't your husband told you?'

'I've told you, I haven't spoken to Roland since he left home this morning. What might he have told me, suppose I had?'

'Let's just say that her indisposition is still a bit of a mystery. We've been asked to find out all we can about its onset so we're speaking to anyone who might have seen her around the time it happened.'

'I thought she has a tropical disease: that's what the news bulletins are reporting, according to my press office people.'

'Yes, but if we can find out how she reacted when it struck, or how she behaved just before it, that might help the medical team.'

'In which case I can't help you, I'm afraid.'

'You heard nothing? No sound from her office?'

'Nothing at all.'

'You saw nobody else in the corridor, heard nobody?'

'I might have seen the Chancellor.'

Bob smiled. 'That's a yes or no, surely; you did or you didn't.'

'Well no, I didn't,' she acknowledged, 'but I thought I heard sounds coming from his office.'

'I see,' he murmured. 'If I might ask, Mrs Kramer, if you didn't go to the Prime Minister's room, you didn't go into the Chancellor's office, and your husband was out at the time, why exactly did you go there?'

'I'm not sure that's any of your business,' she said, archly.

'Neither am I,' he conceded, 'but I won't know for sure until you tell me.'

She sighed. 'Very well, if it'll get you out of here. I was looking for something in Roland's room.'

'You have a key to his Commons office?'

'Yes, I do.'

'What was it? What were you looking for?'

She shrugged, impatiently. 'Just something I needed, that's all.'

'Something you needed?' Bob repeated. 'It must have been urgent if you couldn't wait another few minutes for him to be clear of his engagement in Central Hall. Come to think of it, wouldn't it have been quicker for you to have nipped round to Central Hall and collared him there, asked him for whatever it was, or if it did turn out that it was in his office, have his driver drop it off here, when he got back? Wouldn't it have been easier to do that?'

'With hindsight, yes,' she agreed, 'but I didn't.'

'Or was it something else,' he suggested, 'something you wanted to see that Mr Kramer hadn't shared with you?' She would have replied but he held up a hand to stop her. 'How much do you know,' he asked, 'about the content of the defence statement that Ms Repton was due to make this afternoon?'

'Nothing!' she snapped, vehemently. 'I asked my husband but he wouldn't tell me.'

'I'll bet that annoyed you: you being Chairman of the Party and him telling you that something is above your pay grade. Yes, I'll bet it did.'

She said nothing but her cheeks were flushed.

'So here's what I'm seeing,' he continued. 'The whole Westminster world wants to know what's in it. They expect you to know, but you don't because Roland's kept you out of what they're calling "the circle of knowledge". You're embarrassed; you're furious, but you can't admit it; so at a time when you know he'll be out you go round to the Commons, you go into his office, and you go through his desk, through his papers. But you don't find a *damn thing, because there is nothing to find, because the project is so damn secret that there is hardly anything about it on paper.' He smiled again. 'That's what I'm seeing, Mrs Kramer. Am I right?'*

The lustre of her veneer dulled; her control dissolved. 'Okay,' she shouted. 'Okay, have it your way; that's what happened. Now get the hell out of my office.' She stood, drawing herself to her full height.

We did too, withdrawing as gracefully as we could. 'I hope you find what you're looking for about Emily's illness,' she called after us; her accent had slipped, a hint of Brummie had appeared. 'And I hope it does her no good at all. In fact, I hope she fucking dies!'

Fifteen

'What the hell was all that about?' Neil exploded as we emerged from the Conservative Party HQ, after a lively meeting with its lady chairman.

'Cage-rattling, that was all,' I told him. 'I didn't take to the woman and I wanted to make her as uncomfortable as I could.'

'You went beyond uncomfortable,' he said glumly. 'You lit a fire under her, and I can see my pension going up in its smoke. She's going to give her old man, the Home bloody Secretary no less, chapter and verse and he is going to come after us with everything he's got.'

'I'll deal with it if he does,' I promised him, as we walked out of Matthew Parker Street, and back into Tothill Street. 'But it's not going to happen, because she won't say a word to him. She was ferreting around in his office when she knew he was out; I'll bet you she's more worried at the moment about us telling him than you are about her shopping us.'

'You sure?' he asked, doubtfully.

'Stone cold certain.'

'How did you work it out, that she went there to find out about Spitfire?'

'I didn't; I flew a kite, that was all.'

160

'It caught a nice air current then.'

'Don't be so sure. I'm not convinced. The only thing I know for certain was that she wanted us out of there, as fast as she could. If I'd said she was looking for last Saturday's Lotto ticket she'd probably have admitted to that as well.'

'You don't believe her?'

'Not a word of it. Not even her claim that Roland wouldn't tell her about Spitfire. She was too quick with her denial, too insistent; I suspect he did tell her, maybe not the whole story but some of it.'

'Do you believe she didn't go into the Prime Minister's room?'

'Why should she?' I countered. 'She hates her. She didn't stab her, that's for sure. "I hope she fucking dies!" isn't something I've heard too many murder suspects say. No, Neil, she was up to something, but I'm not going to get drawn into pursuing it. We have other priorities.'

'Yes,' he said. 'Merlin Brady for a start.'

I nodded. 'Merlin, yes, but not for a start. We have to interview Radley before anyone else.'

'Where?'

'Hopefully in the Cabinet Office. Hamblin hoped that he'd be able to persuade him to meet us there. If not, we'll have to go to the Foreign Office.'

'And if he won't agree to see us at all?' Neil asked.

'He doesn't have that option. This is an investigation into an attempted murder. Unorthodox maybe, but that's what it is. We have a man with a history of violence against women being seen approaching and then leaving the area of the crime scene. The timing of those phone calls to Wheeler may suggest he didn't do it, but one way or another, I'm talking to him.'

We walked in silence for a while, until, as we approached Whitehall, I spotted a coffee sign that I hadn't noticed before, in a small cloistered shopping area. We crossed the street and picked up two lattes to go, in polystyrene beakers. We had just emerged when my phone sounded. Awkwardly, I retrieved it, and took the call, when I saw that it was from Amanda.

'Any progress?' she asked, briskly. 'I've just had the Home Secretary asking me for an update.'

'And that's all?' I chuckled. 'We've just interviewed his wife; let's just say she terminated the meeting abruptly.'

'God, Bob! He didn't say anything about that.'

'That's not a surprise. I may not be finished with her,' I said. 'Our focus at the moment is on the Foreign Secretary, but there's one other person of interest.'

'Who's that? There was nobody else on the video who attracted my attention.'

'I didn't say he was. You do know there's another entrance, don't you?'

'Yes, but it's manned and used only by the three occupants of those offices. Are you trying to tell me that the Chancellor was there too? Or the Defence Secretary?'

'Neither. I'll deal with it. I'll need to be cute to set up a meeting, but I know how I'm going to do it. What's the news from the Royal Free Hospital?'

'O'er the wire the electric message came,' she chimed. 'She is no better, she is much the same.'

'What?'

'Lines by Alfred Austin, Poet Laureate,' she explained, 'on the illness of Edward the Seventh. It was my attempt at black humour. I'm sorry, my friend, it's been a trying day so far.'

'Learn something new every day, Amanda,' I said, with

a smile. 'That's my motto, so thanks for that piece of trivia. I need to go now, though; I may have a Foreign Secretary to arrest.'

I ended the call before she could come back on that, and crossed Whitehall to catch up with Neil as he headed slowly towards the Cabinet Office. When we reached our temporary base, there was an envelope with my name on it on the desk I'd been using. I opened it and saw a handwritten note, that read, 'MR will visit you: 4 p.m.'

I checked my watch and saw that it was just short of three thirty, the time at which Emily Repton should have been on her feet in the Commons, telling the world about Spitfire. That had been aborted, but the good news was that it allowed me to make a phone call before Radley arrived, and still have time to prepare for his grilling.

If the announcement had taken place, Aileen would have been on the front bench as a member of the Opposition defence team, and the House would have been packed, but with its cancellation it would simply be business as usual, and only those MPs with a constituency or personal interest in the day's subject would be in the chamber.

Hoping that she would not be one of them, I phoned her. When she answered, her voice told me that she was smiling.

'Have you chosen your title yet?' she teased. 'Paddy Pilmar called me to say that all in all he thought that it had gone well. He said he could see that you were feeling the buzz about the place. He was disappointed you didn't stay for lunch though. Georgia Mercer was very impressed, he reckoned, even if she didn't let you see it, and he was hoping she could get to know you a bit better.'

'Did you know about the cross-bencher idea?' I asked.

163

'What cross-bencher idea? No, I don't know what you're talking about.'

'Paddy's got wind that my name's been put forward for consideration as a people's peer. He suspects that Clive Graham's behind it as a way round his party's policy of not nominating people for the Lords. He and Lady Mercer were trying to recruit me as a sympathiser before Clive could, to destabilise wobbly Tories or some such nonsense.'

'Are you serious?' she exclaimed.

'That's what the man said.'

'Not with my blessing, he didn't. We were tasked by the leader's office to recruit a Scottish Labour peer, to do the job that Paddy's too nice a bloke to do himself.'

'Thanks for that one,' I chuckled.

'You know what I mean. Someone less malleable than him.'

'Yes, I get it, but Paddy reckoned that I could operate more effectively on your lot's behalf from the cross benches.'

'If that's so, he didn't discuss it with me, or with the leader, I can promise you that. Merlin would never go for that; it's improper and it's impractical.'

'Paddy has a different agenda from you; he's looking for a spy rather than an enforcer.'

'Then he should have come clean to me about it,' she said. 'Now I'm embarrassed.'

I laughed. 'That's a fucking first, Aileen.'

'Don't start,' she warned, but once again I could hear a smile in her voice. 'I mean I don't want you thinking that I lured you down here on a false prospectus.'

'My dear, you never lured me anywhere I didn't want to go, including into your bed.'

Aileen and I might have ended our marriage in acrimony,

but things weren't bad from the outset. Her opponents, in the media and in the political morass, have accused her, sometimes openly, of coming between Sarah and me, and wrecking our first marriage. That's not true; Sarah and I made a first-class job of that by ourselves, without any outside assistance. Aileen didn't make a pitch for me, nor I for her; it happened spontaneously, as these things do.

It combusted spontaneously too, after a fairly short period, burning out on the twin rocks of her political ambition and my obduracy. Now I can see that we didn't spend enough time getting to know each other, other than biblically. We started as new friends, we parted as enemies, and now I would say we're friends again, old friends this time.

I never ever think of Aileen, ever, when I'm close with Sarah, but I'll admit very privately that when Aileen and I were a couple it didn't always work that way.

'I'm serious,' she said. 'Georgia Mercer came back to me too, after your meeting. She said one word, "Go". That's as close to enthusiasm as she can get. A Labour peerage will be yours if you want it, and on your terms, if they're reasonable.'

And that was where I got cute.

'At the moment,' I told her, 'I am thinking "No thank you". But, before I reach a final decision, I would like to meet with your leader.' There wasn't a word of a lie there, so why did I feel guilty?

'With Merlin?' she said. 'Of course. I'll speak to his office and get back to you.'

'Could it be today?'

'I'll try. It should be okay, although I can't promise. Things are a wee bit chaotic with the Emily Repton situation. Have you heard about that? "A sudden illness that they suspect is related to her African trip last week." That's what they're saying. Whatever, it blew that defence statement we spoke about clear out of the water, leading to even more speculation about what was in it. And on top of that, it leaves Roland bloody Kramer running the country.'

'You don't like Kramer?' I asked, casually.

'Not a lot, but I don't like many people on the Tory front bench; not even Repton, although she's supposed to be a role model for women in politics.'

'What about Kramer's wife? The Tory Party Chairman.'

'The less said about her the better,' she replied, abruptly. 'Nick Wheeler, I like him; I've faced him at Commons questions a few times, when my boss has been away. He's polite, calm, funny, and there's nobody else in the government with the command of his brief that he possesses.'

'You sound as if you fancy him,' I suggested.

'A little young for me, perhaps, and besides, they say his interest lies elsewhere; minor royalty, no less.'

'Where did you hear that?'

'Normally I'd protect my sources,' Aileen said, 'but in this case I don't like the creep, so I'm happy to grass on him. Grover Bryant, Emily's mouthpiece half-brother.'

'He's that discreet, is he?'

'I know,' she agreed, 'it might seem odd that he should be whispering to me, of all people. But Grover's not very subtle, and his half-sister is still watching her back. Wheeler would be very much a threat to her if he chose to be; if he did, close personal ties to the palace might not work in his favour. So I read it as a mild form of counter-briefing.'

'That's a Westminster buzzword, isn't it?'

'Too right. Fucking spin doctors,' she growled. 'If I'm ever

166

prime minister I'll ban them from the precincts of the House.'

'Would you ban Tories too?'

'If I could. Maybe not all: Nick can stay, and Les Ellis, the Chancellor. Emily Repton too because she's a woman, but grudgingly in her case. The rest? The Kramers, they'd be proscribed. And as for that man Radley . . .'

'The Foreign Secretary?' I said, gauchely.

'That's the one.'

'What have you got against him?'

'Other than him being a Tory? The man's self-importance knows no bounds, he's a boozer, he's a borderline fascist, a thinly disguised racist, and he has the bizarre notion that he's attractive to women. Do you know, he actually tried to hit on me in the Strangers' Bar one night.'

'Some women might be impressed by the Foreign Secretary making a pass.'

'Not this one. Ugh! He really was persistent, Bob; I was glad the place was busy, or . . .' She stopped in mid-sentence. 'Enough; just thinking about him makes my blood boil, and my flesh creep.'

'Both at once?'

'Indeed. Away from the spotlight, he's that sort of creature. Please, let's end this discussion so that I can fix your meeting with Merlin. Where are you? Are you close by?'

'Yes, I'm not far off; seeing the sights, you know.'

'Then enjoy them. I'll be in touch.'

I pocketed my phone and turned to Neil. I guessed he'd been trying his hardest not to listen. 'I could get to see Merlin this evening,' I told him. 'I may have to do that one on my own,' I warned.

'Understood,' he replied. I realised that he'd heard enough of my side of the conversation to know who was arranging it. 'Let's concentrate on Montgomery Radley first, though.'

'Yes,' I murmured. *Yes*, I thought, *let's*.

The man himself arrived a few minutes later, at four o'clock on the dot, shown in by one of Norman Hamblin's staff. He looked even more florid in the flesh than he had on TV. Thick veins stood out on his nose and on his cheeks. His shiny hair was slicked back, and he sported sideburns. He was dressed like a barrister, black jacket and pinstripe trousers.

'Skinner?' he barked.

'That's me,' I replied, rising to greet him. As we had realised when we met Mrs Kramer, he was tall, on a par with Grover Bryant, but not carrying quite so much bulk.

He pointed at Neil, who was still seated. 'Who's this?'

'Commander McIlhenney, Metropolitan Police Service,' I told him.

'Met?' Radley exclaimed. 'Hamblin told me you were a Security Service gumshoe.'

'That's true, but Mr McIlhenney's sitting in on this one, at my request.'

'And what is it, exactly, this inquiry?' he asked, as he took the chair that Bryant had occupied earlier.

'It has to do with the Prime Minister's indisposition,' I replied. I chose my words carefully; I couldn't be certain that Kramer hadn't let him in on the truth, or Mickey Satchell for that matter.

'Indeed? Damn strange that. Thought they knew what it was.'

'They're treating her now, but they don't know anything about the onset of the problem. It would be helpful in reaching a resolution if they did.'

Montgomery Radley gave me a long look, down his nose; I

didn't care for it. 'And they've brought someone from MI5 in to find out?' He gave a short spluttering laugh. 'My people on the other side of the river will have their noses well out of joint about that.'

'I don't see why, Foreign Secretary,' I countered. 'MI6 has different expertise, and a different remit.'

'So what's your remit, and why do you want to talk to me?'

'I want to know why you went to the Prime Minister's office this morning.'

'What the fuck's that got to do with you?' he snapped.

'Humour me,' I said. 'Answer the question.'

'How do you know I did?'

'CCTV footage rather suggests it. Why did you go there?'

'She asked me to.'

'How?'

'Phone.'

'There's no record of that call,' I told him.

'Not if you're looking at today's log. She rang me last night, from Downing Street, asked me to meet her in the Commons at ten fifteen.'

'How did she seem to you when you saw her?'

'Right as rain, same old Emily. She didn't show any signs of jungle fever, if that's what you mean.'

'More or less. And when you left?'

'Just the same. Why? Do you think I attacked her?' he laughed.

I looked him dead in the eye, without a flicker of a smile 'Did you?' I asked.

'Did I . . .' he spluttered, then turned to Neil. 'Has your guv'nor had a liquid lunch?'

'Sparkling water, sir,' McIlhenney replied.

'Then he can't fucking handle it.'

'You can assure us,' I continued, 'that you had no disagreement with the Prime Minister when you saw her, yes?'

'Absolutely.' He frowned. 'Look, this is going beyond jungle fever and the like. What's up?'

I busked it. 'The consultants believe that there may have been a trigger to Ms Repton's condition. We're exploring all possibilities.'

'They can forget that one. Emily and I had a perfectly amicable meeting.'

'What did you discuss?'

He shook his head. 'Again, Skinner, you're going too far.'

'Why are you being reticent?' I asked him.

'Because we were talking state secrets, man!' he shouted.

'Don't raise your voice to me, Mr Radley,' I replied, quietly. 'Did you discuss the Spitfire project?'

He stared at me. 'How the hell do you know about that?'

I took out my credentials and displayed them. 'That's how I know. The Home Secretary and the Director General trust me with the knowledge, so take me seriously and stop yanking my chain. What did you and Ms Repton discuss?'

He took a deep breath. 'She instructed me to have our ambassadors in France, Germany, Spain, Italy and Israel, and the High Commissioners in India, Pakistan, Australia, New Zealand and Canada, on standby at the time of the defence statement, ready to brief heads of government in each country. She told me that I would be provided with the briefing material at the time of the statement.'

'That was all?'

'That was all. Now, what the hell does that have to do with her illness?'

'Nothing at all. Did you use the lavatory while you were there?'

'Did I what?' he gasped. 'That's preposterous, man.'

'Why, do you have a problem in that department?'

'Now look here, Skinner . . . No, I did not. Satisfied? You'd better be, for I am out of here. And by the way, my next conversation will be with Roland Kramer, advising him of everything that's been said in here this afternoon. He's lost his fucking mind, entrusting a maverick like you with the business of the nation.'

I stood, nodding. 'You may well have a point there, Mr Radley,' I agreed. 'Yes, you tell him everything. And you can report this promise to him as well. If I ever hear another whisper of you sexually harassing my former wife, I will jump on the first available transport, wherever I am, whatever I'm doing, and knock the living shit out of you. I know all about you and I'm watching you. Thank you for your cooperation.'

Sixteen

*B*ig Bob has never been a respecter of persons, political persons least of all, but the way he signed off our interview with Her Britannic Majesty's Secretary of State, as our passports describe the Foreign Secretary, was disrespectful even by his standards.

As his warning sank in, I studied Radley's face; I'll swear that it turned purple, and that his eyes seemed to pop forward in their sockets. I'd never met the man before, having seen him only the once from a distance at Lou's premiere, but I knew from his reaction that nobody had ever spoken to him in that manner, not his housemaster at Eton or whatever public school he attended, not his commanding officer in his service in the Guards, not even his Opposition shadow across the floor of the House of Commons.

For a few seconds I held my breath; Radley seemed to be still drawing his in, ready to explode in outrage when his lungs wouldn't hold any more. He didn't know my old boss, and I wondered if he would misread the signs. If he did, I thought, I might be needed.

There are a couple of simple truths about Bob Skinner. When he shouts at someone . . . not that it happens very often . . . it's okay; it doesn't mean he's angry, it's just his way of telling people they could do better.

It's when he doesn't shout that you have to watch it. When he's confronted and it's serious, his reaction is quiet, and something that I can only describe as danger emanates from him. When that happens, push him any further and it can be messy.

I'll never know whether Monty Radley realised that he was over his head or whether he was simply a coward at heart. Whichever, all he did was utter a sound that sounded remarkably like 'Bah!' and stalk out of the room.

'That went well,' I murmured.

Bob looked at me, still stone faced. Then it cracked, and the tension gave way to laughter.

'What a bag of wind and piss!' I exclaimed, as we both dropped back into our seats.

Bob nodded. 'The face of Britain abroad,' he chuckled.

'The last part,' I said, 'warning him off, did he really . . .'

'Yes, he did. Aileen told me, just before he arrived. He has a bad reputation with the ladies, very bad. I'm not having that, any more than you would have if he'd come on to Lou at that event he attended.'

Nothing like that has ever happened to us, but he had a point. If it did, I might well revert to my days as a young plod and discourage the perpetrator.

'What did you think of his account of the meeting?' I asked.

He shrugged. 'Much as I'd like to be able to prove that he and Repton had an argument that ended with him lashing out at her, I don't believe for a second that he did, even without the subsequent phone calls to exonerate him. In fact, I pretty much know he didn't.'

'How? Why?'

He glanced across at me. 'You and I, two experienced CID officers, agree that she must have been stabbed from behind by a left-handed man, yes?'

'Yes. I'm convinced of that.'

'Radley's right handed.'

'How can you be so sure?' I asked. 'He didn't do anything while he was here to demonstrate that.'

'He did,' Bob replied. 'He opened the door: when he stormed out of here, he opened the door with his right hand. Look at the side it's hung on; it favours a left-handed person, but Radley reached cross and opened it with his right. Then there was his jacket. There was a pen in his breast pocket. A southpaw wouldn't do that.' He picked up a plastic pen from the desk with his own left hand and demonstrated the action. 'You see how awkward that is?'

He had a point. 'Yes,' I conceded. 'That's true. It doesn't mean he's in the clear, we're not infallible, and there could be an explanation for the phone calls that we haven't thought of, but it makes him less likely.'

He nodded, then smiled. 'However,' he said, heavily, 'I have met one man today who is left handed.'

I frowned, trying to recall details of everyone we had encountered. 'Who?' I asked, once I'd admitted failure.

'Roland Kramer. I noticed that when I was with him.'

'But he can't be a suspect,' I pointed out, 'since we know he wasn't here at the time of the attack.'

'I know.' He grinned, again. 'Bloody annoying, isn't it?'

'Where does it leave us?' I asked.

Bob shrugged. 'Dunno about you, but it leaves me puzzled. Siuriña Kramer can't be ruled out yet, but without scientific evidence that puts her in the room, we have nothing to counter her denial.'

'Not unless she likes the feel of porcelain on her bum when she pees,' I suggested, 'and forgot to lower the seat. Can you get an arse print, I wonder? I must ask a CSI next time I see one.'

174

'Lord save us,' he muttered. 'You can take the boy out of Edinburgh, but you can never take Edinburgh out of the boy. That doesn't hold water though,' he added. 'She's a woman; she'd never leave a toilet seat up, regardless.'

'Touché. So?'

'So,' he repeated, 'that leaves us with . . .' He broke off as his phone sounded. He retrieved it and peered at the screen, then produced a pair of reading glasses and put them on. 'Text,' he mumbled, then beamed.

'As I was saying,' he continued, 'it leaves us with the surprising late entrant, Merlin Brady. That was a message from Aileen; she's fixed it for me to see him at six o'clock, across the road.' He glanced at me, apologetically. 'As I said, just me on that one, I'm afraid, chum.'

Missing an interview with the leader of the Opposition, in which he would be quizzed as a suspected assassin? No, that didn't bother me at all.

Seventeen

I've never been a believer in the maxim that power corrupts, but I was prepared to make an exception for Montgomery Radley. I'd met some highly placed people that day, and had taken an instant dislike to at least three of them, but the Foreign Secretary stood out. *If his power ever becomes absolute*, I thought, *God help the nation*.

I would have loved to have been able to prove that he was Repton's attacker, but I knew that he wasn't. I wasn't entirely convinced by his account of their meeting . . . she could have given him those instructions in an email, without summoning him to her presence . . . but he didn't fit the physical profile upon which Neil and I were agreed.

For a while our room felt as if it had been polluted by his presence, but a text from Aileen blew away those bad odours.

'Merlin can see you at 6,' it read. 'Meet me Central Lobby 5:55, I'll take U to his office. Want me to sit in?'

I messaged her back: 'Tks, but no tks. 1 on 1 is better.' I hoped that she didn't feel slighted or, worse, that she didn't insist on being there, but an immediate reply put my mind at rest. 'For the best. Both of us working on U, U'd have no chance.'

I thought about the rest of my day. I couldn't guess where my impending encounter with Merlin Brady would take me, but once it was over I'd be at a dead end for the day. I planned that Neil and I should interview Mickey Satchell, and speak to the PM's protection officers, even if that meant going to the hospital, but both could wait until the next morning.

I needed some thinking time, and my friend needed to get home to his wife and kids. And then, of course, there was my dinner date.

I called Amanda. 'Are we still on for tonight?' I asked her.

'I'll be free if you are,' she replied. 'Shepherd's at seven thirty as arranged?'

'Fine by me,' I said, 'but isn't it a little . . . public? A place where people go to be seen?'

'Hell no! You're thinking of the Groucho Club. Shepherd's is discreet enough.'

'Will you book?'

'I have done already.'

'What are we doing here, Bob?' Neil said, as I hung up, pulling my attention back to the present.

'I've been asking myself the same question,' I admitted. 'So far the only thing I know for certain is that I'm thirsty. Fancy a pint?'

'No, but I'll have a diet something. Let's go.'

Norman Hamblin was busy, so I left a message with Cerberus that we were through for the day, but would require the room again next morning, then left the building in search of the nearest pub.

We didn't have to go far: the Red Lion was just across the street, an old-fashioned place that's survived the era of knee-jerk modernisation, and still offers good ale in unpretentious surroundings. It was ten minutes short of five when we went in;

the early evening rush of civil servants hadn't begun. Neil asked for a bottle of sparkling water and coffee, an odd combination; I chose a pint of Chiswick bitter, and was pleased to see that it didn't have too many bubbles in it.

There were a couple of unoccupied tables; my friend pointed a questioning finger towards one of them.

'Nah,' I said. 'Let's drink standing up. I haven't done that in God knows how long.'

'Not even on Friday nights in Gullane?'

'Even there I have a bar stool.'

The Chiswick was well kept, with a nice hoppy tang that we don't find in many Scottish beers. 'Good?' Neil asked as I put my glass back on the bar.

'Yeah,' I murmured. 'Washes away the bad taste of Montgomery fucking Radley.'

'You really didn't take to him, did you?' he laughed.

'Like something I've scraped off my shoe.'

'And yet he's the Foreign Secretary.'

'So fucking what? He'll be gone in a couple of years, maybe sooner if Emily doesn't make it and the Tories choose a new leader. You, on the other hand, are a commander in the Met and you haven't finished climbing the ladder yet. He's transitory, you're not.'

'What if they choose him?' McIlhenney countered. 'Their electoral system is famously unpredictable.'

'They won't. He'll be stopped.'

He frowned. 'By whom? Who could do that?'

'Me, if I had to,' I replied. 'I don't mean that I'd waylay him at midnight and chuck him in the Thames. No, I have strong media contacts; I could give the *Saltire* a story that would take him out.'

'Spook stuff? MI5?'

I nodded.

'But he didn't attack Emily Repton?'

'No, but there is something about the situation, about the timeframe, that doesn't knit together. Maybe I'll know more after I've had half an hour with Brady.'

Neil smiled as he sipped his coffee. 'Does he think you're going in there to discuss the peerage offer?'

'Yes. I may have to do some apologising to Aileen afterwards. That'll be no new experience; I've done it often enough.'

He shot me a quizzical look. 'You are going to turn it down, yes?'

'Without a moment's hesitation,' I replied, with more assuredness than I felt.

'Why?' he challenged me. 'Man, you would be great for the House of Lords, no kidding. I see them on BBC Parliament occasionally, sprawled across those red leather benches, most of them looking no more than half awake. I'll swear I heard someone snore once. They need people like you, to breathe some life into the place.'

'I'm not in the CPR business, pal. Look,' I exclaimed, 'the only way I would consider it would be if I was middle aged, free and single, but I'm not. I have a wife I love, three children of school age, soon to be joined by another, an adult daughter who is starting out on a career change and grateful for my help whenever she needs it, which is often, and a grown-up son I never knew about until last year who gets out of fucking jail next month! I can't put all of them to one side to join an archaic institution four hundred miles away from my home base.'

'Have you told Aileen that?'

'Of course. The first time she raised the subject I laid it on

179

the line. She asked me if I'd do them the courtesy of listening to their pitch, and I agreed. I'm here out of curiosity, Neil, nothing more. If the Scottish parliament was bicameral with a second chamber in Edinburgh, I might be interested in that, but it isn't and it won't be, unless we do achieve separation from England.'

He frowned. I could see that he was mulling over something. 'She must know you well enough,' he said, when he was ready, 'to realise that you'd never change your mind, suppose they offered you a bloody dukedom, so why did she persist?'

'I do not have the faintest Scooby-do about that,' I admitted, 'but you are right. That's a question I'll ask her.'

I drained my glass, and checked my watch. 'I'd better amble across there,' I said. 'Even with my nice new credentials I have to go through security. Give my love to Lou and the kids. I'll see you in the Cabinet Office tomorrow . . . that's unless Merlin admits to attacking Repton,' I laughed, 'and I need to call you in to make an arrest.'

'If you don't see him as a suspect, then . . .'

'He told your two cops on the door that he had a meeting with the Prime Minister, yes?' He nodded. 'That being so, my assumption is that she had decided to brief him about Spitfire in advance of the announcement, as a courtesy. I expect him to confirm that.'

Neil wasn't convinced. 'She would do that, knowing Merlin Brady's known ambivalence towards the nuclear deterrent? Could she trust him not to spill it to the first lobby correspondent he could find?'

'I'll know in about half an hour,' I said. 'See you tomorrow.'

Eighteen

The queue at security was much smaller than it had been in the morning. As a result I was ten minutes early for my appointment with Aileen, but she was five minutes early herself; the receptionist was about to call her when she appeared from the Commons Corridor.

There were only two other people in the Central Lobby, deep in conversation. I recognised one from telly as a failed contender in the last Labour leadership election, but her name hadn't stuck with me.

'I wonder what they're plotting,' Aileen whispered, as she waved to them, with a comradely smile.

'Dinner?' I suggested. 'Why should they be hatching a plot?'

'In my party most people are involved in the hatching of plots. Stability went out the window about ten years ago. Mind you,' she added, 'after today's sensation, the Tories will be at it too.'

'Have you heard any more about the Prime Minister's condition?' I asked, innocently.

'Nothing beyond what's in the public domain. Grover Bryant's gone to the hospital and none of the Downing Street communications department will offer anything without his say-so, on or off the record. The whisper is she's going to die.'

'And if she does?'

'People are watching Roland Kramer already. He's holed up in the Home Office; been there all afternoon. His lovely wife,' she added, acidly, 'is in Castle Blueskull, the Tory HQ, and I'll bet she's melting the phone lines. If Emily does snuff it, the Kramers will want a coronation. They won't want to risk a ballot of the membership even if it is against Radley. My spies tell me he was summoned to see Norman Hamblin, the Cabinet Secretary, this afternoon. That's unusual, but they don't know what it signifies.'

'Would they be the only candidates?'

'That's the consensus view among the lobby journalists, but I'd keep an eye on the Chancellor. He's a Repton loyalist and if he thought that Radley had the remotest chance, he might step up to the plate himself.'

'Fascinating,' I said. 'I've chosen a good day to come down. I didn't expect all this excitement.'

'It's not every day the Prime Minister drops in her tracks . . . hours before a major announcement.'

'Has anyone found out what that was going to be about?' I asked casually. 'Are you any closer to knowing than you were this morning?'

She pursed her lips. 'I think,' she murmured, leaning closer to me, 'that she was going to announce the cancellation of the Trident renewal.'

'Is that a guess?'

'Sort of. I asked my friend on the General Staff if that was it, and got blanked. A very firm no comment.'

'Some people simply don't like to admit that they're out of the loop,' I pointed out. I was pretty sure that was true of Aileen's friend. I wished I could tell her, but my hands were tied securely by that damn Official Secrets Act, and the pieces of paper that had my signature on it.

'That's true,' she conceded, 'but that's as close as I can get to answering your question.'

'Your leader will be chuffed if you're right.' I paused. 'Sorry, correct; I know you can't use the word "right" where Merlin Brady's concerned.'

'Don't take the piss,' she chuckled. 'Come on, we need to be on time.'

'Aileen,' I ventured as I fell into step beside her. 'Why are you doing this? Tempting as the offer of a seat in that place might be, you must have known from the start that it was long odds against me accepting. I'm flattered, but I don't get it. You're not trying to destabilise Sarah and me, are you?'

She glanced up at me as we walked out of the lobby. 'I'm not that much of a bitch, Bob,' she replied. 'I'm very happy for you and Sarah; there are no hard feelings at all. You and I were only compatible in one way; when we weren't horizontal we had completely different agendas. Truth is, I approached you and put your name forward because I believe that you are exactly the man for the job we need doing. Truth is, I knew you'd be very hard to convince, probably impossible.'

She stopped at the top of a flight of stairs. 'I went ahead regardless for a selfish reason. I wanted you to see me down here, to see the life I'm living now, and to show you that I'm happy with it.'

'I get that,' I said as we descended the short staircase. 'I can see you're enjoying it, but enjoyment and happiness don't overlap completely. I don't think you'll be completely happy until you get to where you want to be.'

'Oh yes?' she probed. 'And where do you think that is?'

'I know where it is. You want to go all the way. You want to be prime minister.'

'We all want to be prime minister,' she laughed, 'but most of us are realists who know our level. Mine is front bench, shadow Cabinet.'

'Which you will achieve fairly soon, I'd say. I've seen your present boss in action, what's-his-name, Len McSkimming, the shadow Defence Secretary. He's a tube; you'll see him off.'

'He's a tube with the backing of the unions,' Aileen countered. 'Merlin has to have him in his team.'

'But not there, and not for long; he'll move him to Transport, or Industry, where his union connections will do him more good.'

She glanced at me, smiling. 'You have been paying attention in class, Skinner.'

'I had a good teacher, de Marco. Being married to you taught me a lot; it made me look beyond my own areas of interest. It didn't make me like politicians any better, but it helped me to understand them. There are two basic motivations in those who stand for elected office: some are in it because they want to make people's lives better, some are in it for themselves, for power and influence.'

'In which group do you see me?'

'You're in both. You're a fully committed socialist, but you've got the brains to understand that you can't improve the lot of the average family unless you have the power to do it. And you will not be happy, truly happy, until you've had a crack at it, in the top job.'

'Will I get there though, Bob?' she countered, not trying any longer to deny my assertions. 'I've got baggage; my fling with Joey Morocco, that paparazzo shot in the tabloids.'

I grinned. 'That's not baggage, love. Half the women in the country want to fuck Joey . . . the other half probably have. You'll get there if you're patient and choose your moment.'

'My moment may never come,' she said.

'It will. I'll have a better idea of how soon when I've spent some time with your leader.'

'It is a formality, this meeting, isn't it, a courtesy? You're not going to accept, are you?'

'No. You're right, it's a courtesy. Plus, I'm insatiably curious; I want to see if there's anything about Brady that I've missed.'

'Between you and me,' she murmured as we arrived at his office, 'I've been looking for that since he was elected leader. He's a charming, gauche, lonely man, but I've yet to find a scrap of charisma.'

She rapped on the door. A cry of 'Enter' came from within.

'Merlin,' Aileen said as we stepped inside, 'may I introduce Mr Bob Skinner.'

I stepped forward and shook hands with the leader of the Labour Party, the man whose election had taken most of the country by surprise, but not those with a finger on the pulse of Westminster.

Merlin Brady had been a peripheral figure in the previous Labour administration and had held only minor office in his party's last government before being returned to the back benches in Opposition.

After the decimation of the previous general election, there had been no stomach within the parliamentary party for a leadership battle, but the power brokers in the trade union movement, which had quietly rebuilt its influence after a quarter century in the background, had insisted on it. After a split between the two leading contenders had weakened them both, Brady had stepped forward, or rather had been pushed, as a unity candidate, and had won the nationwide ballot by a wide margin.

Most of those who voted for him had known little or nothing about him, but the contest had been decided by the two biggest trade unions, who had given him their backing and urged their members to support him. When he took office, and came into the spotlight for the first time in a twenty-year career, the nation had seen a quiet, diffident, gentle guy from Manchester, whose main strength seemed to be that anyone who was rude to him would be seen as school bully, and so nobody ever was.

He had been presented as a throwback to the left-wing, anti-nuclear firebrands of the past, an inspirational leader who would shake up his party and make it electable again. It had taken six weeks at most, and a bland speech to the Labour conference, for it to become apparent that he was nothing of the sort.

He was left of centre, and no fan of the deterrent, but that was as far as he resembled the picture his backers had painted. His polite, non-abusive style at Prime Minister's Questions in the Commons had allowed Emily Repton to brush him aside on a weekly basis. His shadow Cabinet was drawn entirely from his own left-wing; to my eyes, most of them mediocrities. Behind them, in the second tier, Aileen was one of a dozen ambitious and more talented people. She was the best of them, though, and as she left me alone with Brady, I was still unconvinced by her explanation of why she had put me in there.

She might have been less keen if she had known my real agenda.

'Mr Skinner,' he began once she had left us on our own, 'good of you to come down. Please, take a seat.'

He directed me towards one of two chairs on the visitor side of his desk. His office was much smaller than Repton's but it was much tidier. His papers were arranged in neat piles, each with a pen beside it; the newspapers on his coffee table sat one on top of the other, neatly placed so that each one's masthead showed . . . I was surprised to see a copy of the *Saltire* displayed beneath the *Guardian*.

The man himself was as impeccable as his surroundings. I knew that Brady had been a single man for many years and I'd been expecting him to look the part. He didn't. There wasn't a hair or a speck of dust on his jacket, and his red tie was absolutely centred. His salt and pepper hair was perfectly parted and there was no suggestion of stubble on his chin. I was showing the wear of a busy day, and felt scruffy opposite him.

'So,' he said with a diffident smile, 'have we won you over? Ms de Marco said from the outset that it would be tough, but that if we could persuade you to join us you would transform our performance in the Lords. How did you feel your meeting with Lady Mercer went?'

I bounced his question back at him. 'How did she feel? I've no doubt she'll have reported back by now.'

'She has,' he acknowledged. 'She said that she wasn't sure what you'd decide; she thought that if anything you might be more amenable to a cross-bencher situation.'

'She got that wrong,' I replied. 'That would be disingenuous at best, dishonest at worst. If I went in there, my colours would be nailed to the mast. Also I have to say that the concept of me winning over wobbly Tories doesn't appeal. I don't do gentle persuasion. It isn't in my skill set.'

'If you did join us,' he continued, 'what would you want? If I offered you the chance to write your own ticket, what would you ask for?'

As I had never considered seriously accepting the Lords

proposition, that was a question that I hadn't put to myself, but I knew the answer. 'I'd want to be your leader in the Lords, because you don't have one at the moment. Gloria Mercer is a Premier League economist, I'm sure, but she couldn't lead a Girl Guide troop. I'd probably want to be shadow Home Secretary as well, because the guy you have there, Mark Malone, is the son of a man who was jailed for violence on the Orgreave picket line during the miners' strike, and he's never forgiven the police for it.'

Brady's grey eyes widened. 'Are you sure about that?' he asked, softly. 'It's news to me.'

'I'm sure all right. Malone was a Labour MP in Midlothian when I was deputy chief in Edinburgh, before he went south; Special Branch had a file on him and I've seen it. His father's name was Alfredson. Malone started using his mother's name when he went to university.'

He scratched his chin. 'That could be a problem.'

'No, Mr Brady, it is a problem, if your party wants to have any sort of a relationship with the police in England and Wales. Have you read any of the man's speeches? Did you see his *Guardian* article, where he accused the police in a couple of cities of institutional fascism?'

'I was told that his special adviser wrote that piece, and that somehow it slipped through the screening process.' He sighed. 'What would you do about the situation, if you were in my shoes?' he asked.

'That would depend on him,' I replied. 'I'd confront him with the truth about his background, and suggest that he adjusts his attitude, sharpish. If he agreed, I'd wait till the next reshuffle to move him. If he didn't, I'd leak the story to the tabloid of my choice, probably the *Sun*. I'd give it a day then accept his resignation with profound regret. Then I'd replace him with a proper politician who's a match for Roland Kramer, or whoever succeeds him, if he succeeds Repton.'

He smiled, thinly. 'Can you help me with that choice too?'

'What do you think? You have a woman in your team whose political CV includes a spell as First Minister of Scotland and you don't have her in the shadow Cabinet? You're off your fucking head, man.'

The smile became a soft chuckle. 'You don't pull your punches, Mr Skinner, do you?'

'No,' I agreed, 'and that's why I'd be a terrible appointee to the Lords or any other political job. It's one reason why I'm probably going to decline your offer, the other being that I'm not sure I want to see your party in government in its present form.'

As soon as the words were put there I wished I'd bitten my tongue, hard. I hadn't got to my main reason for the meeting, and I'd gone and given him a chance to terminate it.

But he didn't. Instead he continued to smile, his eyes seemed to shine, and I realised how decent a man he was.

'It's nice to meet an honest man who speaks his mind,' he said. 'You wouldn't last a week in this place. You'd be ostracised, because everyone would be afraid of you.'

Suddenly, to my surprise, I felt an awkwardness that I realised was shame.

'In the spirit of honesty,' I continued, 'there's something I have to tell you.'

'Would it have something to do with Emily Repton?' he asked, quietly.

Wow! I thought. *Have I underestimated this man!*

I nodded. 'My presence here today attracted attention,' I told him. 'I have a longstanding friendship with Amanda Dennis, the Director General of the Security Service, and our paths have crossed professionally too. There are aspects of the Prime Minister's indisposition,' I continued, thinking, for a change, about every word I was saying, 'that have caused concern. Its onset was sudden and needs to be explained. I've been asked by the Home Secretary and by Mrs Dennis to find out what happened, if I can.'

'Is Emily dead?' he asked, bluntly.

'No.'

'You mean not yet?'

'None of us are dead yet, but I'll concede she's closer than most.'

'Have you seen her?'

'Yes. Now my job is to find out who else did, around the time that she was overcome.'

Merlin Brady frowned. 'Oh dear,' he murmured. 'She doesn't have a disease, does she?'

'No.' I'd shared the truth with Grover Bryant, because I knew he'd protect his sister. I took an even bigger leap of faith with Brady, because I felt I could trust the man. 'Between the two of us, she was attacked in her office and left for dead.'

'Thank you,' he murmured. 'I know what you just did, and I'll respect it. Today of all days,' he added.

'Meaning?'

'The day of the mysterious defence statement that she was due to make this afternoon, the one that's defied the norm in this place, in that it hasn't been leaked and spun in advance. Is it your thinking that the attack is related to that announcement?'

'I'm not ready to commit myself, not yet. Do you know what she was going to say, Mr Brady?'

'No, I don't. I had hoped for advance notice of the content, but it didn't happen.'

'Did you ask her this morning and did she refuse to tell you? And now I'm going to go all the way: did you lash out at her in frustration?'

The gentle grey eyes settled on my cold blue ones. 'Do you see me doing that?' He smiled. 'Even if I had the opportunity. It would be the crime of the century.'

'No I don't,' I replied, 'but I have to ask. I know that you were admitted to the vicinity of her office by the cops on the door, after you told them you had an appointment with the Prime Minister.'

'Yes, that's true,' he agreed, with a nod, 'but that meeting never took place. I didn't see Emily.'

'Why not? There's no indication that she left her office at any time. And you were there for well over twenty minutes. So?'

Then I thought about that timeframe, and about what I'd seen on the CCTV footage; a cartoon light bulb clicked on above my head.

'No,' Brady said. 'I didn't see her. Mr Skinner, can I be as frank with you as you were with me?'

'If you feel you can't,' I advised him, 'it's best that you say nothing and I leave now.'

'If I am, can I rely on your discretion? That's what I'm asking.'

'If what you tell me relates in any way to the attack on Ms Repton, no you can't. Otherwise, of course.'

'I'll take that chance,' he decided. 'I misled those policemen. I did have a meeting but it wasn't with her. Mr Skinner, for the last three years, I've been in a relationship with a lady, a married woman. When it began, I was a background figure in the Labour Party with no prospect of advancement, and no such ambition either. If we'd been outed then it would have been damaging to her marriage, but no more than that. If it came out now, when I am where I am, it would blow the roof off, off everything.'

Someone turned up the dimmer switch on that light bulb.

'Siuriña Kramer,' I exclaimed. 'You're having an affair with Siuriña Kramer.'

'How did you know?' he asked.

'She's on CCTV, heading for the office corridor. I interviewed her earlier and she told me that was where she was going, to look for something in her husband's office. She was there for around the same length of time as you. Look,' I said, 'maybe you shouldn't tell me any more. I have to report to Kramer, and I have to assume he has access to the same footage I've seen.'

Another light clicked on. 'You knew what I'm doing before I came in here, didn't you?' I asked.

He gave me the briefest of nods. 'Siuriña called me after you saw her, as soon as you'd left. She was afraid you were on to us. When Aileen asked me to meet you, I thought I might find out.'

'What the hell? Your meeting this morning, what was that about? Please don't tell me you fancied giving her one across Roland's desk. I don't like the guy, but that would be rubbing his nose in it.'

'No, no,' he retorted, dismissively. 'We have a little more style than that.'

'Has it ever occurred to you,' I ventured, cautiously, 'that she might be using you?'

'Has it occurred to you,' he countered, 'that I might be using her? The truth is that we're using each other to an extent, and we know it. Siuriña is driven by her ambition for her husband. I'm driven by my ambition to unseat the Tories. She doesn't believe that I can ever do that; she sees me as no more of a political threat to her than I was when the affair, as you called it, began. However, she does see me as useful, if she can help me undermine Emily Repton. I see her as useful for the same reason.'

'Do you actually care for each other or is your thing pure bloody politics?'

'Oh we do; we care very much. Siuriña is a kind, compassionate woman confined by circumstances in a loveless marriage. If Roland wasn't what he is, I believe she'd leave him for me.'

I pitied him for his naive, misplaced confidence; the woman I'd encountered that afternoon hadn't given me a glimpse of the one he was describing.

'Where do you meet?' I asked him. 'Other than in the Home Secretary's Commons office,' I added.

'Is it relevant to your investigation?'

'No, I'm just curious,' I admitted. 'Given that each of you is a public figure, how have you kept it secret for so long? When Aileen and I got together the whole bloody world knew in a week.'

He smiled, turning slightly in his chair. 'We met at an event in the Tate Modern, the opening of an exhibition by a Welsh artist. Siuriña didn't have a Conservative Party role then, and I was a junior shadow minister on Overseas Development . . . my predecessor thought that by tucking me away out of sight he'd keep me silent on the many issues where we disagreed.

'I hadn't a clue who she was, but she recognised me as we were mingling. We struck up a conversation and . . . it's been going on ever since. It started innocently enough, with a few dinner dates, and it evolved from there.

'Where do we meet, you asked? I have a small flat in Putney. Siuriña came there for the first couple of years, and no one was any the wiser. However, since I've been leader and she's been party chair, well, as I'm sure you'll appreciate, it's been much more difficult. This morning was the first time we've been alone together in six weeks. The last time, I was driving to my constituency in Manchester, and she was driving to see her mother in Chester.'

'How do you communicate?'

'We have second phones. Everyone does in our world.' He paused and looked at me. 'I don't know why I'm telling you all this,' he murmured.

'Because you need to tell someone,' I suggested. 'The bigger the secret, the more stress it generates. I've uncovered it, and now you're spilling your guts as if I was your parish priest. Trust me, it's something I've seen often in my career. Also, you have a naive belief that I'm not going to share it with another living soul.'

'Is that misplaced?' he asked, but with no sign of anxiety.

'No, it isn't. I don't condone what you and Siuriña are doing, but my disapproval comes from the guilt of having been in a couple of furtive relationships myself.' I took out my MI5 badge and displayed it. 'As long as you don't threaten national security, it's none of my business. I don't see that you are, as long as you can explain to me the purpose of your meeting this morning. That does seem reckless, and for the purpose of my investigation I do need an answer.'

Brady nodded. 'It won't sound very honourable, I'm afraid,' he said. 'I asked Siuriña if she could find out the content of the defence statement.'

'So you could leak it and sabotage Repton's big moment?'

'Definitely not; that would have triggered a major inquiry. It would have compromised Siuriña. No, I'd have used it to prepare

my reaction in the chamber once she had made the announcement. She told me it was very tightly guarded and that she
couldn't hope for a sight of it until today. Her plan was to copy
what she could and pass it to me. Meeting in Roland's Commons
office was her idea; she said it was the only place where we could
guarantee privacy.'

'You told me earlier that you didn't know what was in the
statement,' I pointed out.

'I don't. When I arrived, she was furious. She said that Roland
had refused point-blank to discuss it with her. They had a massive
argument, but he wouldn't budge. He claimed that Repton had
ordered absolute secrecy, and that by staying silent he was
actually protecting her.' Brady smiled again. 'He didn't know
how true that was.'

'I take it she wasn't best pleased with the Prime Minister.'

'That would be putting it mildly. She spent most of the time
we were together railing against her. "Paranoid" and "megalo-
maniac" were probably the gentlest words she used. Others, I
will not repeat. She accused her of distrusting everyone around
her; if so,' he chuckled, 'that was wise on Emily's part. I wonder
what went wrong.'

I didn't return his smile. 'What you're telling me is that
Siuriña was sounding off about the Prime Minister less that
twenty minutes before she was found unconscious in her room.
Which of you left first?'

'I did,' Brady replied.

'Nobody saw you?'

'No, but there was one close call as I left. I opened the door
slightly to check that the corridor was empty. It wasn't, there was
someone standing there, a woman. I stayed where I was.'

'Did you recognise her?'

'No. I only had a back view, a fleeting one at that, for I closed the door very quickly. I waited for a minute, then took another look out; the coast was clear.'

'That would be around ten to eleven?'

'Yes, that would be right.'

'Then you left? Before Siuriña?'

'Yes, that's correct.'

'So you left her alone in the Prime Minister's corridor, still bubbling with anger against her, with nobody else there and only a door between them. Any wonder I'm asking myself again, did she step through it?'

'She didn't, Mr Skinner, I can assure you of that. As I reached the door at the top of the stairs I turned and looked back. I think I was intending to blow her a kiss, or something equally silly, but she had her back to me and was striding away. I watched her walk past Emily's door, out of the corridor, and out of sight.'

'She could have returned, once you were safely on your way.'

'If she had done,' the leader of the Opposition countered, 'she'd have been caught on camera, wouldn't she?'

'A fair point,' I agreed.

He frowned. 'Mr Skinner, you are going to keep this to yourself, aren't you? I'm not afraid for myself, but for Siuriña's sake. Roland is a cold, ruthless man. He'd take it out on her if he ever found out.'

I returned his gaze. 'I'll make you this promise,' I replied. 'I'll report only what's necessary, and nothing at all to Kramer. I'll speak to Amanda Dennis and nobody else, but I'll only tell her what I have to.'

I paused, looking at him more closely. 'Why is it, Mr Brady, that I'm thinking you might not be all that bothered if scandal erupted and you had to step down?'

'Because I wouldn't,' he replied. 'In all walks of life people are prisoners of circumstance. I never wanted to lead my party, but I was persuaded. I will do the job to the best of my ability, and hound the Tories out of office if I can, but inwardly, Mr Skinner,' he tapped his chest, 'I still feel a bit like a fish on a bicycle.'

Nineteen

'You are telling me that the leader of the Labour Party is sleeping with the Tory Party Chairman?' Amanda Dennis exclaimed.

'Yes,' I said, 'but only because you need to know in the context of this investigation. It doesn't go any further or appear on any file. Agreed?'

'Agreed,' she sighed.

'Are you telling me you didn't know?' I asked.

She held my gaze for a few seconds, then smiled ruefully. 'No,' she admitted. 'I knew. I was hoping you wouldn't find out, that's all. There are some things I don't share with anyone.'

'Least of all the Home Secretary, in this case.'

'Least of all him.'

'When did you find out about the liaison?' I asked.

'Shortly after I became Director General,' she replied. 'The service had paid no attention to Merlin Brady until he suddenly popped up as a serious leadership contender. When he did, while the campaign was in process, I ordered a security check on him. Very early on my people reported back to me that a lady had spent a night at his flat when Kramer was away at an EU summit in Prague.

'They didn't know who she was but they had photos. I

198

recognised her straightaway; I told them to keep him under surveillance throughout the leadership campaign. They met on another two occasions during that period. When he was elected leader I ended the operation.'

'Do you still have the evidence?'

'Yes, but it's in my safe.'

I looked at her over my wine glass. 'For use in what circumstances?'

'None that I can imagine,' she replied, 'but you don't flush gold dust down the crapper.'

I leaned back and looked around the cellar restaurant. We had a corner booth, but the place was only half full, and there was no danger of us being overheard by other diners. There was even less danger of us being overheard by anyone else. It was a popular venue for politicians, and the Security Service had it swept for bugs at least once a week.

We had eaten in relative silence; I had worked off my lunchtime sandwiches long since, and was more than ready for the Caesar salad that I ordered and the lasagne that followed. Any chat was purely personal. Amanda asked me about Sarah, and the soon-to-be-forthcoming baby. She enquired about Alex also. 'I hear from my people in Scotland that she's making progress at the criminal Bar.'

'Some,' I said. 'She had a big case quite recently that would have boosted her reputation, but it never got to trial. The Crown case collapsed before they even served the indictment.'

'And your eldest son? How's he making out?'

'Ignacio's university bound, once he's released on parole. He's going to live with his sister during the week and with us at weekends and vacations. I'm having an apartment built above my garage that will give him some independence.'

'Are you comfortable that he's not going to slip back into bad ways? Won't his mother still have influence over him?'

'Mia's two outstanding characteristics,' I responded, 'are her innate luck and her pragmatism. She should have gone to jail with Ignacio, and for longer, but the Crown couldn't charge her because all the evidence was against the boy and not against her.

'I'm sure that if she could have swapped places with him she would have. If I could have made that happen, it would have. But it wasn't possible; all I could do was use what influence I have to minimise his jail time. She was left out there, with no choice but to get on with her life. She went back to what she does best, radio, and she landed on her feet yet again. She married the owner of the radio station, and many other things besides.'

'Lucky break,' Amanda acknowledged. 'Where does the pragmatism come in?'

'It will stop her from doing anything that would rock the boat. Cameron McCullough, her husband, is not a man to mess with, and he's certainly not someone who will tolerate any indiscretions. Mia has only two options, make him happy, or put cyanide in his porridge.'

She laughed. 'Would you rule out the latter?'

I smiled back. 'Not completely, but that pragmatism will stop her. He's very rich and she's twenty years younger than him. She'll be a dutiful wife and wait him out. Will she influence Ignacio?' I continued. 'Probably, but I'll make sure it's always in his best interests, and so, I think, will Cameron.'

'I'll watch with interest,' she said.

'I'm sure you will, but not too closely, okay? How about you?' I asked, turning the discussion around. 'Are you still with your toy boy?'

'No, I set him free,' she admitted. 'Nothing to do with the age difference, but when I moved into the top job, he was a luxury I felt I couldn't afford. Now I'm all alone in my little house, looking forward to the day when I can retire to the seaside and write thrillers that everyone will buy because they assume they're based on my career experiences, but are in fact completely fictional.'

She put her cup back in its saucer, signalled our waiter for another coffee with Bailey's liqueur, and leaned forward, forearms on the table. 'And now, Consultant Director . . . I hope you like the title, by the way . . . to business. Do you know who stabbed Emily Repton?'

'No,' I replied, 'but something very surprising has come to light.'

That's when I told her about the astonishing intertwining between Merlin Brady and Siuriña Kramer, and she confirmed my suspicion that she'd known about it.

'The report will stay in my possession,' she continued, 'for as long as I deem it necessary. As soon as I don't I'll burn it; my job is to maintain the security of the nation, not to ruin the lives of decent people.'

'Decent isn't a word I'd apply to Mrs Kramer,' I said.

'No, but he is. Are you saying she might have attacked Repton?'

'Merlin swears she didn't.'

'Do you believe him?'

'Yes, I do. Do I think he might have done it himself after Siuriña had gone? Not for a millisecond. He doesn't have it in him, although the timeframe does fit. He was logged out of the building after Emily made her last phone call. I wish the same was true of Montgomery Radley,' I moaned.

Amanda grinned. 'Ah yes, the Foreign Secretary. I had a visit from him just before five; he actually turned up at Thames House unannounced and unaccompanied, and insisted on seeing me. I'm under orders to withdraw your credentials and fire you, before this day is out. Happily, I don't take orders from Mr Radley. What the hell did you say to him, Bob?'

'I gave him a lecture on the consequences of sexual harassment. Aileen complained to me that he'd been all over her in a Commons bar. I told him that if he did it again I'd punch his ticket. What was his version?'

'That you were an offensive upstart, that you'd been gratuitously rude and that you'd virtually accused him of attacking the Prime Minister.'

'I asked him the question,' I admitted. 'He denied it. Unfortunately, it seems that he didn't. How did you handle him? Am I fired?' I smiled. 'Please tell me I am.'

'No, you're not. In fact, I may promote you. I'd had enough of Mr Radley by then, but when he threatened to set his MI6 people digging into your American connection through Sarah, that was the last straw. I went into my safe and I showed him the transcript of the deathbed statement that Angela Berkeley, his late agent, gave me about the rape of her daughter, and promised him that unless he did what I was about to tell him, a copy would go to the Director of Public Prosecutions.'

'Alleged rape,' I pointed out.

'Spoken like a true copper,' she retorted. 'It doesn't matter whether it's alleged or proven, he bought it. He did try to bluff it for a second or two until I added that Mrs Berkeley's misplaced loyalty to him hadn't prevented her from keeping the girl's pants, cum stains and all.'

'Did she?'

Amanda nodded. 'Oh yes, and there's a DNA match. It's probably inadmissible as evidence because there's no proper chain of custody, but he's too dumb to work that out.'

'What did you tell him?' I asked. 'What was your ultimatum?'

'If . . . when . . . Repton steps down, is declared medically incompetent or just dies, Radley will not contest the leadership. When the next administration is formed, he won't be a part of it. When the next election comes, he won't be a candidate.'

'Nice work,' I said. 'Nevertheless, he didn't attack Emily. Have you made any progress with that incoming mobile call?'

'No, none. Is that the only line of inquiry you have left?'

'Not quite; I'd like to talk to Satchell tomorrow.'

'Why? Will she have anything more to add?'

'I'd like to interview her when she's more in control of herself than she was today. Also I need to apologise to her for going off at her when we found that Ms Repton was still alive.' And I had a third reason to see her again, but I wasn't ready to share that, not even with Amanda.

'As well as her,' I continued, 'I still have to complete the circle of Spitfire knowledge. That means talking to the Chancellor and to Wheeler, when he surfaces. He couldn't be found this afternoon.'

'When will you be ready to report back to Kramer?' Amanda asked.

'Never,' I retorted. 'Kramer's a witness, and I don't report to witnesses. I'll submit my findings to you and you alone, that's if I have any findings.'

'Sorry, Bob,' she said, 'but how is he a witness? He didn't arrive in the building until after she'd been attacked.'

'True, but he was there earlier, and he met her at the side entrance door, as he was leaving and she was arriving. I need to ask him if they spoke and if she said anything that might be relevant.'

'Okay, do that,' she agreed. 'But promise me you won't cross-examine him about his wife's movements.'

I smiled. 'I'll assume you're joking. No way will I drop any hints that might send him after Merlin Brady or, worse, send that guy of his after him.'

'Daffyd Evans? Yes, if Kramer's using him for anything other than personal protection, I should do something about that. He's on my strength, recruited by my predecessor, Hubert Lowery. Hubert used him as his driver. When I took over I decided that I didn't want him in that role, so I attached him to the Home Secretary's protection team. Kramer took a shine to him and now he seems to be leading it.'

'Yeah.' I told her about the stunt he had pulled on me that morning.

Her eyes blazed with anger. 'He did that?' she gasped. 'He drew a weapon on you?'

'Yes, and he seemed to enjoy the experience. What he doesn't realise is that a gun's fucking useless unless you're actually going to shoot somebody. If you're not, it's just something you have in your hands when the other guy's coming at you, and it's absolutely no insurance against a kick in the balls.'

'To hell with it!' she hissed. 'I'm not having one of my people behaving like that, regardless of who gives the orders. I'll pull him off Kramer's team tomorrow.'

I shook my head. 'No,' I said, 'leave him where he is. I don't want to antagonise Kramer; not yet, not until I'm ready.'

She winked at me, unexpectedly. 'Let me know when you are,' she said. 'I'd like to be there.'

Twenty

I *don't always wait up for Louise, but I did that night.*

Being married to an actress . . . woe betide anyone who calls her an actor; she hates that . . . is an odd situation, when she's appearing in a play. With her being on stage in the evening, and me working during the day, we see very little of each other through the week. On the other hand, child care isn't a problem, as one of us is always at home.

It's even less of a problem now that Lauren, my daughter from my first marriage, is old enough to be left in charge of her pre-school half-brother, our Louis. She's a living reminder of her mother, which is good for me and for my son Spencer, although I have to say that both of my kids took to Louise from the moment she walked through the door.

We don't live too far from the West End; she's chauffeured home and is usually back by eleven thirty, but if the audience is generous with the curtain calls, it can stretch out to almost midnight.

The evening of my unexpected reunion with Bob Skinner was one of those, but my head was still full of it when she came in. She was surprised to find me waiting for her, with a half-bottle of Prosecco in an ice bucket.

'Special occasion?' she asked, after she'd kissed me and flopped

into a seat. Her face was absolutely free of make-up; the heavy slap she wears on stage is a necessary part of her trade, but it comes off as soon as she does.

'You might say so,' I said, as I opened the fizz: managing the diabetes means that I drink very little these days, but Lou likes a glass of something to unwind when she gets home. 'You'll never guess who I've been partnering today.'

'You're right,' she agreed, 'so tell me.'

I did, and her eyes widened; I liked the shine that I saw in them. Louise has known Bob Skinner for a hell of a lot longer than I have. They were friends at university in Glasgow, close friends, although it never developed into anything more than that.

One of the ties that bind Bob and me is a shared experience of widowhood. When I lost Olive to the black wraith that hits smokers at random, he was there for me. He took me into his circle of friends, even fixing me up with a regular game of five-a-side football on Thursday evenings.

He fixed me up with Lou as well, although he didn't realise it at the time. She was working in Edinburgh when she came under threat from a stalker. The big man detailed me to look after her, and the rest, as my son Spencer observed, is geography. (Spence has always had trouble with his metaphors.)

'Will he have time to visit?' she asked.

'I don't know about that, he's fully occupied at the moment.'

'What brought him down here? I thought he was keeping himself busy in Scotland with his media work.'

I smiled as I told her he was in town to discuss a possible seat in the House of Lords.

She did too, and then she laughed, out loud. 'The House of Lords isn't ready for Bob Skinner . . . or maybe he's five hundred years too late for it. He'd have been in his element as a Shakespearean kingmaker.'

'Kingbreaker, more like,' I countered. 'The princes in the Tower wouldn't have been a mystery for long if he'd been around; Richard the Third would never have made it as far as Bosworth.'

'Yeah,' she nodded, raising her glass to her lips. 'Bob would have straightened him out.' She looked sideways at me as I settled myself beside her on the couch. 'You said you've been partnering him? How did you fit in time for golf?'

'Not golf; work.'

She frowned, puzzled. 'Run that past me again,' she murmured. 'Bob's retired from the police.'

'But he still has a contact in the Security Service, at the very top. He's been co-opted, drafted in, conscripted . . . any of those apply . . . to investigate a very sensitive situation, and he asked for me to work with him.'

'What did Assistant Commissioner Winterton have to say to that?'

'I imagine she said, "Very good, Sir Feargal," that's assuming she was consulted. The request went right to the top.'

'What the hell is it, this "situation"? Have the crown jewels gone missing?'

'Not quite. It involves government, but that's all I'll say.'

I didn't think she'd settle for that. 'Come on,' she exclaimed, 'you're not going to leave it here.' I could almost hear her mind working; it didn't take her long to make a connection. 'The big news story today is the Prime Minister's illness. Is that what it is? It all sounded very mysterious.'

'It is very mysterious,' I replied. 'That's why we're involved.'

'Have you met anyone famous?'

I smiled. 'Apart from Bob? Well, there's the head of MI5, Mrs

Dennis; a very impressive woman. Mr Hamblin, the Cabinet Secretary; he's so much of a Civil Service mandarin that he almost looks Chinese. Mrs Kramer, the chair of the Conservative Party; a glamorous, ambitious and devious woman. The Right Honourable Montgomery Radley, MP, the Foreign Secretary; he's just a berk.'

'Berk? That's not one of your usual words.'

'I chose it carefully,' I assured her. 'It's Cockney rhyming slang, short for "Berkshire Hunt". I'll let you work out the rest.'

'Easily done,' she said. 'It came off him in waves when we saw him at that reception a while back. How about the Defence Secretary? Nicholas Wheeler? Did you meet him? I did, a few weeks ago; he was in a box at the theatre with his little royal friend and he was invited backstage.'

'How royal?' I asked.

'Cousin several times removed. I don't think it's serious; my impression, and don't ask me why, is that she was camouflage, something to have on his arm, like the Queen's handbag.'

'Gay, probably, but not ready to come out,' I surmised. 'The nation is used to women prime ministers, but I'm not sure it's ready to go a step further. In fact I'm damn sure the Tory Party isn't.'

'He may be, but I doubt it. I like him; he struck me as his own man, not the sort of Tory MP who'll acquire a wife because it's an expected part of the package.'

'I'll form my own view if we meet him. Bob decides who we need to interview, and I don't know what he's got planned for tomorrow.'

She glanced at me. 'Does she really have a tropical disease? I haven't heard a word about any of her staff being quarantined.'

She's a very shrewd woman, is my wife.

Twenty-One

I'd picked my hotel because it was the closest to the Palace of Westminster that I could find. It was above a pub and it wasn't pretentious but it was clean and had everything I needed, namely a comfortable bed and an en suite bathroom.

Amanda and I talked until they were ready to chuck us out of the restaurant. She called a cab, but I decided to walk back, through the maze of streets and squares, with Westminster Abbey as my lighthouse.

The pub was still open when I reached the hotel, but I wasn't tempted; I wanted a clear head for the next day, and also I was tired. I will never admit to feeling my age, but only because I don't know how it's supposed to feel.

My phone had been switched off during dinner; it was only when I put it on the bedside table that I realised I'd forgotten to switch it back on. I decided that it was too late to call Sarah, but I was wrong; she called me.

'Where have you been?' she asked, a little anxiously. 'You've been off air for hours; that's not like you. Did you go to see Lou's play?'

'No, sorry, dinner with Amanda.'

'Is she still trying to lure you into her tangled web?' She chuckled but it was a serious question.

'Not exactly,' I replied.

'So come on,' she exclaimed. 'I've been waiting all day for this. Are you going to make a Lady out of me?'

'Your parents did that, love,' I retorted, then winced. Sarah lost her mother and father tragically; she doesn't talk about them very often.

'No, I don't see that happening,' I added quickly, moving on. 'Paddy Pilmar and Lady Mercer made their pitch, during which I found out that there may be a second offer on the table, courtesy of Clive Graham. I tell you, if Machiavelli was still alive, he'd come a bad runner-up to our First Minister.

'But either way, I don't fancy it. Everything down here is a fucking plot. I've met a lot of people today, and only one of them was open and above board. Because of that, he, poor sod, has no chance. The knives are out for him already, and it's a matter of time before he's gone.'

'Who's that?'

'Merlin Brady.'

'The Labour Party guy? I thought he was a wild-eyed leftie.'

'He's left wing,' I agreed, 'but there's nothing wild about him. He's a nice man, he's honest, and he's open about his beliefs and intentions. In his public life, what you see is what you get. Because of that he has absolutely no chance of ever being prime minister.'

'In his public life,' she repeated. 'What about his private life?'

'Rather more complicated; that's all I'll say.'

'Oh yes?' she challenged. 'How do you know about that? Has your friend Mrs Dennis been telling you stories?'

'No, I did my own digging.'

'Have you dug out anything about the Prime Minister? The bulletin they put out at eight o'clock said nothing, only that they were continuing to treat her, but I can't work out how they're doing that if they don't know what's wrong with her.'

'They do know,' I said. 'It has nothing to do with her trip to Africa; that's a cover story dreamed up by the Home Secretary and Amanda. But don't go spreading that around in the hair-dresser's.'

'As if,' she snorted. 'What is the truth?'

'Rather more complicated. What you asked me earlier, about Amanda recruiting me: she has done, on a one-off basis, and that's what I'm working on. It might mean me having to stay here for another day or two.'

'My God, Bob,' she gasped, 'be careful.'

'I'm not in any danger, I promise you. It's a very discreet and focused investigation and I have help. Neil's on the case at my request . . . but don't go phoning Lou, for he may not have told her.'

'I knew it,' she murmured. 'The way you've been every time I called, your phone being off tonight, I knew there was something. I'm glad you told me, or I'd have worried about it. I shouldn't be, should I? Honestly?'

'Honestly. It's not like that. Now,' I said, 'forget me. How about you? How did your appointment go?'

'Fine,' she answered. 'Too fine in fact; they think they've made a mistake with the due date. They think I have another two weeks to go. If you have to stay there for any more than a couple of days, I may jump on a train and come down. It'll either be that or go back to work. If I hang about the house without you here to distract me, I'll get on Trish's nerves in no time.'

I doubted that. Our children's carer is one of the calmest women I know. 'In that case, take it out on the builders,' I said. 'Keep yourself busy. I'll be back as soon as I can.'

Twenty-Two

The first thing I did when I woke next morning was to take my phone off charge and check the *Saltire* news app. It's constantly updated and I was confident that it would tell me if Emily Repton hadn't made it through the night.

It didn't. Instead it told me that a condition update at six thirty had described her as 'stable but still in a medically induced coma'. The news report added that the cause of her collapse remained to be determined. It quoted her official spokesman, Grover Bryant, as expressing 'cautious optimism' as he left the hospital the night before.

That wasn't how he put it to me when he arrived in my commandeered office at eight twenty-five. 'She's clinging on,' he said, as he took one of the spare seats. We were alone; Neil had called to say that he was stuck in traffic but had reached the Met HQ and would be with me by nine.

'I called them half an hour ago,' he continued. 'I spoke to the neuro consultant. He admitted that he can only guess how it's going to end, but he did say that with every hour that passes her chances improve. He reckons that from having a one per cent chance of survival when he did the head scan, she's now up to about fifteen per cent.' He held up his right hand, fingers crossed.

'I've just been in my office,' he said. 'I spoke to the communications director, Shami Patel. She told me she's been ordered to report to Kramer until further notice. He's in Number Ten now, making his presence felt. I tried to get in to see him but my way was blocked by his Welsh minder. He did send me a message, though. He said that at the moment I have no one to put words in my mouth, so I should keep it firmly shut.' Bryant scowled. 'He'll be relishing this. Bastard!' He peered at me through heavy, hooded eyelids. 'How's your investigation going?' he asked.

'It's going,' I replied. 'That's all I'm prepared to tell you. I haven't exhausted my lines of inquiry. That said, I am no nearer finding the answer than I was yesterday. All I can ask you to do is pretty much the same as Kramer said: stay silent. You might as well get back to the Royal Free.'

'That's where I'm going.' He dug into his trouser pocket and handed me a card. 'Do me a favour,' he said. 'If you do turn something up, give me a call.'

I said that I would, to keep him onside and under control, then watched him as he left.

The coffee that I'd bought on my way into the office was only half consumed, but what was left was stone cold. I binned it and walked along to Norman Hamblin's office. His formidable doorkeeper told me to go straight in.

'Good morning,' he said, with a courteous nod.

I reflected on the warming of our relationship over less than twenty-four hours. At first the Cabinet Secretary had seen me as an intruder into his domain, but that seemed to have changed. I had seen enough during his exchange with the Home Secretary to decide that he wouldn't last long in the event of a Kramer premiership. I reckon that he saw me as an ally; if so he was over-thinking my role. I was there to establish who had knifed Emily Repton, not to interfere with party politics.

Nevertheless, I fed him a prompt. 'I hear Roland's moved into Number Ten,' I said. 'Grover Bryant's been put on notice.'

He nodded. 'And I've been summoned,' he replied. 'He wants to see me at ten thirty, to discuss the rescheduling of yesterday's postponed announcement.'

'Can he do that?'

Hamblin frowned. 'It was actually questionable whether Ms Repton could have done it. By that I mean whether she could have implemented such a far-reaching executive decision that was taken by what I'm sure the media will describe as a cabal within the Cabinet.

'The Opposition will demand a debate, and there will have to be a vote. I'm fairly sure that Mr Kramer knows that: I suspect that he will hold it within a week and that he will rally his own party behind Spitfire and enough of the pro-nuclear Labour people to pass it quite easily.'

'What if Emily recovers?' I asked. 'I know it's long odds against, but what if?'

Hamblin shook his head. 'For as long as the Prime Minister shows the faintest possibility of recovery, she will be kept in a medically induced coma. If she does begin to improve, it will be maintained to help her brain injury repair itself. She isn't going to be conscious in the next two days, or anything like it. While she does hover, Kramer is effectively in charge, with the backing of his senior colleagues.'

'Can Labour challenge that?'

'Not a chance. You're obviously not a student of Westminster, Mr Skinner. I shouldn't say this even to you, but this is the worst Opposition party I've seen since I entered the Civil Service in the early eighties. Mr Brady is completely hopeless; at PMQs he keeps going off on wild goose chases and keeps on being politely squashed by Ms Repton. I don't know who's briefing him, but they should be sacked.'

I had a fair idea who was briefing him, but I wasn't about to share that with my new friend, not yet and probably not ever.

'On the matter at hand,' he continued, 'what have you discovered in the last twenty or so hours?'

'I know who didn't stab the Prime Minister,' I told him ruefully. 'I still need to speak to the Chancellor and the Defence Secretary, but I don't expect too much from either of them.'

Hamblin glanced at his watch. 'The Chancellor has a very full diary,' he said, 'but I've squeezed you in there. He'll see you and Commander McIlhenney at nine fifteen, but not here, in the Treasury. As for the Defence Secretary, I'll get back to you on that when I've spoken to him, and that will be when they can find him.'

Neil had arrived when I went back into our office. 'Enjoy your dinner?' he asked.

I nodded. 'Of course. It's always good to catch up with old friends.' I knew he was fishing, so I took the bait. 'No, she wasn't able to tell me anything that helps our investigation and no, I didn't agree to any connection with MI5 beyond the next day or so. Don't get too comfortable in that chair,' I added. 'We have to find the way into the Treasury building and I have a feeling that won't be easy.'

I wasn't wrong there. I chose the wrong entrance to the vast edifice, and had to be redirected by the security staff. By the time we found the Chancellor's inner sanctum and talked our way in there, it was nine fifteen on the dot.

Leslie Ellis greeted us at the doorway of his office. 'Gentlemen, come in,' he said. 'I've always wanted to see what MI5 operatives actually look like. Pretty large, it seems.'

The Chancellor of the Exchequer is one of the most powerful finance ministers on the planet, and I'd been expecting a personality to match. The incumbent was a plump little man, no more than five feet eight inches in height, bald, save for a semi-circlet of white hair around the back of his dome-like head. He ushered us into his room with a diffident smile.

'Seat yourselves, please.' He pointed at a group of three chairs, round a table on which a coffee pot and three mugs stood, on a silver tray. 'The least I could do,' he said as he poured. 'It would have been much easier for me to find you, as Norman Hamblin suggested, but I do have a permanently tight schedule; also, to be honest, once I'm in here I tend to take root.' He handed Neil a mug, then filled one for me. 'I'll leave you to add milk and sugar. Now, who is who?' he asked, as I added a little milk.

'My name is Bob Skinner,' I replied, 'formerly a chief constable in Scotland, and my colleague is Commander Neil McIlhenney from the Metropolitan Police. My commission with the Security Service is short term, for as long as this investigation lasts.'

'That's a task I don't envy you.' The smile was replaced by a look of concern. 'All I can tell you is that it wasn't me,' he added.

'Who did what?' I murmured, as I sipped my coffee. It was, I realised immediately, a hell of a lot better than the takeaway variety that I'd binned earlier.

'Who stabbed Emily in the head with her letter-opener.' He smiled once more as Neil and I exchanged glances. 'My colleague, the Home Secretary, favoured me with the truth. I understand the reasoning behind the subterfuge that's going on and I agree with it, so worry not, Mr Skinner; I have a couple of secrets of my own, so this one is safe with me.' He paused. 'How long can it stay safe? That's the question.'

'Not for much longer,' I replied. 'Possibly for as long as Grover Bryant can live with being kicked out of his sister's office by Kramer. He promised me twenty-four hours, but they'll be up soon.'

Ellis nodded. 'Compassion was never Roland's strong suit. You're right, he should be treating Grover gently, and not simply for political reasons.' He laid down his mug and peered at us. 'What would you like to ask me, gentlemen?'

'When was the last time you saw Ms Repton?' Neil ventured.

'The night before last. I looked in to see her just before I left. I should explain,' he said, 'that I don't actually live in Number Eleven Downing Street. The accommodation is there when I need it, but most of the time I live in my own house in south London, with my son and his partner. Male partner,' he added, 'but I suspect you know that.'

I nodded. 'Yes but it's irrelevant. How did the Prime Minister seem?'

'Excited,' he replied, immediately. 'She was working on the statement that she was to deliver in the House yesterday, and she was looking forward to it.'

'Spitfire?'

'Yes.' He looked surprised. 'You know about it?'

'We do,' I said. 'The Home Secretary felt I should know all the background; I felt we both should. It's going to cause a major sensation when eventually it does become public knowledge.'

The Chancellor's grin returned. 'I understand now why Roland described you as a man of independent mind.'

'Were those his exact words?'

'Well, no,' he admitted. 'Awkward and Scottish were two of them; I needn't trouble you with the other.'

'I've heard that before,' I laughed. 'To me that's a compliment, not an insult, especially, with all due respect, when it comes from a politician. I did a class in constitutional law at university; because of that, as a point of principle I've never taken an order from one of your crew in my life . . . apart from when I was married to one, and even then it never went further than "Clear the table", or "Pour me a glass of Chablis". My ex-wife is a socialist,' I added, 'but she has expensive tastes.'

'I've made similar observations myself, around this place,' Ellis confessed. 'Most commonly in the House of Commons restaurant, where the Côtes de Nuits Village outsells the house Merlot by quite a margin among the members of the Opposition benches . . . even under the new regime.'

Neil must have felt we were getting too chummy, for he cut in. 'When you saw the Prime Minister, Chancellor, did she say anything to you that was out of the ordinary? Anything that might make you think in hindsight that she felt threatened?'

'No, Commander,' he replied, firmly. 'Emily is a very confident woman. She never feels threatened; she never has done, not even at the height of the leadership election when things were fraught, to say the least, between her and the Kramers. And she was right; she won a clear majority in the ballot of the membership, in spite of all the whispering and the briefing against her.'

'Is it all forgotten now?' I asked.

The little man pursed his lips. 'What do you think?' he murmured. 'If someone suggested, quite improperly and without a shred of proof, that you as a chief police officer used your access to sensitive files on individuals to brief against their interests and in your own, would you forget it?'

McIlhenney laughed. 'Chancellor,' he exclaimed, 'if that happened, that man there would carry a grudge to the other person's grave.'

'Exactly, Commander; and believe me, Emily has an equally good memory, and an appetite for retribution.'

'Could she have been planning to move against them?' I asked.

'She is,' Ellis retorted, 'but in her own time. This parliament has another three years to run, and three years is a hell of a long time for anyone to survive as Home Secretary without dropping the ball, particularly if he's also saddled with the title of Deputy Prime Minister. All she has to do is wait, and a year or so down the line she'll have an excuse to demote him.'

'If she recovers,' I pointed out.

He winced. 'True. If she recovers. Let us pray she does.' He paused for a second or two, then said, 'I'm guessing that you saw her, Mr Skinner. What's your view?'

I had to think about that one. 'When we went in there,' I answered, when I had done so, 'into her room, we were told that she was dead. You're looking at two guys who have seen more murder scenes than either of us cares to remember. And neither of us doubted that she was, until a very small reaction showed otherwise. That's all I can tell you, factually. Beyond that the only view I'll put on the record is that if she does come back to office, it won't be for a while. During that time the country will need to be governed, and it will be down to you people to . . . how do I put this . . . make arrangements to the satisfaction of the monarch. From what I hear, Mr Kramer has made a start on that already.'

'Yes,' Ellis agreed, 'I hear that also; from the horse's mouth in fact. He called me in to see him this morning and told me he would chair Cabinet in Emily's absence.'

'Did he also tell you that he's planning to reschedule the Spitfire announcement?'

'Yes, he did; I have no problem with that. As for his position, in the unique circumstances in which we find ourselves, that will require at the very least to be endorsed by Cabinet, although I suspect it will take more than that.'

'Why?' Neil asked. 'If he's the Deputy Prime Minister, isn't that automatic?'

'No, Commander, it isn't because he wasn't elected to that position, he was appointed to it by Emily Repton. In her extended absence, it's my view that Cabinet should choose the acting Prime Minister. I may as well tell you that I advised the Cabinet Secretary, just before you arrived, that it should be the first item on the agenda for today's meeting.'

I drained my mug, and reached for a refill. 'Will it choose Kramer?'

'That will be a close-run thing. Monty Radley will support him, and so will Transport and DEFRA; Justice will be for, and the rest will split evenly.'

'Who will oppose him?'

For the first time, I saw a hint of steel in the little man. 'The person with the best chance of winning the vote.'

'And that will be?'

'One of two people: Nick Wheeler, the Defence Secretary, if he can overcome his reluctance, or me.' He peered at me, his eyes trying to read what was in mine. 'Do you see Roland Kramer as a suspect?' he asked, quietly.

'No,' I replied at once. 'I wouldn't shy away from the

possibility, if it existed, but he didn't have the opportunity. He returned to the palace from Central Hall just as Dr Satchell found Ms Repton . . . the victim, as we'd call her normally.'

'His wife?'

'No.'

The Chancellor looked at Neil. 'You, Commander? Do you have any views or are you sticking to the party line?'

McIlhenney grinned. 'Not at all,' he shot back. 'I'm actually the ranking police officer here. Bob didn't just ask for me because he wanted a mate to back him up, He did it because he knew that whatever the Home Secretary thinks he has the power to do, he can't legally exclude the police from a major criminal investigation.'

The truth is that had never occurred to me, but he piled it on. 'Effectively he was protecting Mr Kramer from himself, because this will come out and people . . . by that I mean the Opposition parties, and the media, when they find out they've been misled . . . will demand to know the whole story, step by step.'

'Put that way,' Ellis said, 'the government should be thanking you both.'

'Noted,' Neil said. 'As for the party line, there isn't one but I agree with Mr Skinner on this. Mr Kramer didn't do it, because he couldn't have. Mr Radley didn't do it because we know Ms Repton was active after he left her room.'

I nodded agreement. 'I don't know if you're fearing some sort of conspiracy here, Chancellor, but I'd have trouble believing there was one, because it wasn't that sort of crime. It was sudden, it was violent, it was committed with the most unusual of weapons: not a knife, a letter-opener. It penetrated the skull by sheer chance; nine times out of ten it would have skidded off, but the angle was exactly right. That doesn't say premeditation to me. It says spur of the moment anger, someone picking up the first thing to hand and lashing out.'

'I see.' He frowned; his forehead wrinkled. 'If it wasn't Monty, and it wasn't Roland, who was in her room and did have the opportunity?'

'That's the bugger of it; we can't find anyone who was. Nor, to be completely frank, despite the obvious ambition and manipulation of the Kramers, can we find any reason for it either. Can I ask you about Spitfire, Chancellor?' I asked, switching tack.

'You can try, but I won't volunteer anything about it.'

'You don't need to. As I said, I know what it is, thanks to Mr Kramer. I know also that it was discussed and agreed in conditions of great secrecy, that only the most senior Cabinet ministers know the totality of it, and that it was to be announced yesterday. Part of our brief is to determine whether knowledge of the project has spread outside that core group. At this moment in time we can find no indication that it has.'

Ellis's eyes narrowed just a little. 'Is this where you ask whether I've been careless and shared the secret with my family? If so, the answer is no. The very limited documentation on the subject has very rarely left this room, let alone this building, and I assure you there has been no discussion round the dinner table with James, my son, or Shafat, his partner.'

'Thanks for that,' I said, 'but it wasn't what I was going to ask. My question is, were you all agreed on the switch from Trident to the new delivery system, or was it a majority decision?'

'We are all completely behind it. The Balliol project, as it was called initially, was begun by the previous Prime Minister, George Locheil, in conditions of absolute secrecy. Within

Cabinet, only three people knew about it: the PM, myself, as the Defence Secretary of the day, and Roland Kramer as Chancellor. Also, Mr Hamblin, the Cabinet Secretary,' he added. 'He knew too.'

'What about the money? Didn't that leave a trail?'

'Smuggled out of the Trident budget; if the thing hadn't worked, it would have been hidden as an overspend. But it did. When Emily moved into Downing Street and formed her administration, Hamblin was able to brief her about the full potential of Spitfire. She imposed the same secrecy level as her predecessor, but brought Monty Radley and Nick Wheeler into the group that would decide what to do with it.'

'Were you agreed from the start?'

'Absolutely. As soon as John Balliol showed us what it could do, we knew we had to adopt it. Look,' he said, 'we know the Russians will make a terrible noise, but that will be all. They know we have no aggressive intentions towards them, although if they rein in their recent truculence that will be nice. The North Koreans, on the other hand, will stay silent, because they will realise . . . at least the saner part of their high command will . . . that it has been adopted with them in mind.'

I nodded agreement. 'Let's go back to the circle of knowledge. You've already added someone to it, the former PM.'

'George Locheil was never briefed on the completion of the project. When that time came, the government was being torn apart by the EU referendum. Norman Hamblin was effectively running the country with the leadership wholly occupied elsewhere. He sensed that the PM would go if the result went badly for him, and decided to sit on it until everything became clear. So no; Locheil knows the theory of the Balliol propulsion system, but only insofar as it was seen as a drone with global range. He doesn't know what it became. Besides, he's gone now, lecturing in the US, last I heard.'

'What about Balliol's team?' McIlhenney asked. 'How many of them are there?'

'There are a dozen working on the laser propulsion side of it, and twice that number on design and construction of the vehicles. They have no interface with the nuclear scientists, the bomb-shrinkers, I call them. The Balliol team all live on the Aldermaston complex and are under constant surveillance by MoD intelligence. Nick Wheeler knows what they had for breakfast. You can't find any leaks, Mr Skinner, because there aren't any.'

He stood. 'Now,' he said, 'I must ask you to excuse me. We have rather an important meeting in less than three hours.'

Twenty-Three

There was something about Dr Michaela Satchell, maybe nothing more than the way her hair was cut, but it reminded me of a young springer spaniel Alex and I encountered on Gullane Bents, on a Friday evening many years ago. She'd lost her owner, or vice versa, and was panicking; then she saw us and latched herself on to us with a mix of hope and gratitude in her eyes. Alex was nine at the time; she wanted to keep her, but I said we couldn't do that.

'We have to do something,' she insisted. She was right; it was autumn and the sun was low on the western horizon. There are foxes in the grassland, looking for rabbits and other small furry things; if we'd left her she'd have been in trouble.

She had slipped her collar, and it was long before dogs were microchipped, so there was only one thing to be done. We took her home, and next morning I put a notice in the post office window. Gullane being the village that it is, she was back with her owner within three hours. As she left, she gave me that same look; if a dog can say 'Thanks', she did.

Mickey Satchell had lost her owner too, and she was panicking. I could see that as she walked through our office door, in answer to Norman Hamblin's politely framed order that she call on us.

'Mr Skinner,' she began.

'Dr Satchell,' I said, cutting across her, 'before we go any further, my apologies for barking at you yesterday.' That springer spaniel was still in my head. 'We were all under pressure yesterday, you most of all.'

'Thank you,' she replied. 'Apology accepted, but it was nothing to what I said to myself later on. Have you seen Emily?' she asked. 'Her doctors wouldn't let me in.'

'What about her protection officers? Couldn't they help?'

She looked across at Neil as he spoke. 'They weren't inclined to,' she said. 'They blame me, sort of. They take the view that when she's in the Commons she's in my care.'

'That's hardly fair,' I observed.

'I agree, but I can understand them feeling that way. I'm supposed to control access to the Prime Minister in parliament. Anyone who wants to see her over there has to come through me. In Downing Street, the Civil Service looks after her; in the Commons and on party business, I do.'

'Anyone?' I repeated. 'Even senior colleagues?'

'Not all,' she admitted. 'The Foreign Secretary, for example, he makes his own rules. The Chancellor and the Home Secretary have offices in the same corridor; they're always calling in on each other. Have you seen Emily?' she asked again.

'No,' I told her. 'We've been fully occupied trying to find out what happened to her. That's why we needed to speak to you again; we need to go over the sequence of events yesterday morning. Before you discovered her, injured and unconscious, when was the last time you saw her?'

'Just before ten. She usually arrives from Downing Street

between quarter to and ten to; I always check in with her to see what she wants and what she needs. When I got there, Grover . . . Grover Bryant; you know who he is?' I nodded. 'He was just leaving. He'd come over with her in the car, made her coffee and got her settled in.'

'How long did you stay with her?' Neil asked.

'No more than five minutes. She was working on a very important statement she was due to deliver in the House yesterday afternoon.'

'That would be the defence announcement that everyone was anticipating?'

Mickey Satchell looked at me, with a look of caution that hadn't been there before. 'Yes,' she murmured.

'Are you aware of its content?'

'No,' she replied. 'I know no more about it than any other backbencher. Emily trusts me, but I'm not party to everything that goes on in Cabinet.'

'Neither's the Cabinet,' I muttered quietly, carrying on before she had time to react. 'Did you have a sense that this announcement was out of the ordinary?'

'Oh yes,' she said. 'It was all kept very close. Most of the stuff that goes to ministers is in green folders; the most sensitive stuff is in red folders. This thing doesn't appear to have a folder at all. If it does, then I certainly haven't seen it, although I have noticed the last few days that Emily's been keeping her Red Boxes locked all the time. Usually, if it's just the two of us in her office, she'll leave them lying open.'

'This might seem like a loaded copper's question, Dr Satchell, but answer it anyway, please. Did you resent the obvious truth that Ms Repton was keeping you completely in the dark?'

She frowned. 'No, of course not; I know my place. My

job's a stepping stone, that's all. Some of my backbench colleagues would kill to be in my . . .' She broke off as she realised that her turn of phrase wasn't the best, in the circumstances. 'That's to say, it's a privilege to be chosen as the PM's parliamentary aide, and it's a marker that you have a frontbench future.'

'Fair enough,' I acknowledged. 'In the last week or so, have you been asked about the content of the announcement?'

'God yes!' she exclaimed. 'Everyone and his uncle's been bending my ear looking for hints. It's actually been a relief not to know what's in it. That means I can't be accused if there is a leak.'

'Can you recall anyone in particular who's asked you about it?'

'It would be quicker to tell you who hasn't. My phone died of exhaustion on Sunday evening: I've had calls from lobby correspondents, defence correspondents, sketch writers, parliamentary colleagues who want to know in case their constituencies are involved, and my opposite numbers on the Labour and SNP benches demanding that their leaders are briefed in advance. Latterly I was reduced to saying, "I am from Barcelona. I know nothing!" in a Spanish accent like the waiter in Fawlty Towers.'

'Was anyone particularly pushy?'

'The Labour woman Aileen de Marco; she was. She refused to believe I had no knowledge of the content. She left me feeling quite inadequate.'

McIlhenney laughed.

'What's the joke?' Satchell asked, crossly.

'I think he's suggesting she had the same effect on me when I was married to her,' I volunteered.

She drew me a long, appraising look. 'I can understand that,' she murmured.

I assumed she was insulting me, but I let it pass. 'Anyone else?'

'Nobody who stands out.'

'Fair enough. So, yesterday morning, you saw Ms Repton around ten, and left her at five past; the next time you saw her was . . . ?'

'When I found her body . . . sorry, what I thought was her body. Honestly, Mr Skinner, I couldn't find a pulse. It can happen, with some kinds of injury, and in comatose patients; the heart rate drops way down. I should have tried for longer, but I didn't, I panicked, and reached the wrong conclusion.'

'Did she have any appointments in that hour? Was anyone booked in to see her?'

'Not that I know of, but that isn't definitive. She could have called someone, anyone, and asked them to drop in. I'm not keen on her doing that, for I like to have a record of all of her meetings to guard against her being misquoted. Usually she filters her callers through me, but not always.'

I nodded; my assistants used to make the same complaint about me, but there were times when I didn't want them to know what I was up to. 'One last question,' I said. 'In the brief period of time that you spent with the Prime Minister yesterday, how did she seem?'

'Tense. Emily is a very calm, controlled person, but yesterday she was on edge. I put it down to this mysterious statement, but maybe it was more than that. I can only guess.'

I smiled. 'I'm sure she'll tell us when she wakes up,' I said, trying to reassure her.

Her eyes dropped for a second, then found mine. The lost

puppy look was back. 'Thanks for the optimism, Mr Skinner, but I'm a doctor. I may have screwed up yesterday, but normally I'm pretty competent. If nobody else has said this to you, I will now: she isn't going to wake up, not any time soon.'

Twenty-Four

'*That's it, isn't it?*' *I said to Bob as the door closed on Dr Michaela Satchell as she left, with our thanks for her cooperation, to contemplate the possibility of being a run-of-the-mill back-bencher once more among all the people she had undoubtedly snubbed during her period of privilege. I'd liked to have been able to offer her more comfort, but I couldn't.*

I thought Bob had been too kind to her; the way I saw it, Satchell, a doctor, had declared someone dead who wasn't. We'd found the pupil of her right eye slightly reactive to light. If she'd done that test, she'd have dialled 999 rather than call Norman Hamblin, and who knows what difference that might have made to an outcome that was highly uncertain, at best.

As a consequence, we, believing her to be dead, had withdrawn the supposed murder weapon from the wound. If she died, had we played a part in killing her?

Perhaps Bob was thinking the same thing, but if he wasn't, I didn't want to plant the seed of guilt in his mind.

'Almost but not quite,' he countered my remark. 'I'd still like to talk to the Defence Secretary, just to complete the set. There's the forensic people too; that toilet seat still bugs me.'

'Me not so much,' I replied. 'I reckon you may be reading too much into that. For all we know, it may have been up for days. Maybe Emily is an atypical woman; not all of them care how the damn lavvy seat's left.'

'Grover Bryant thought it was down,' he argued.

I'd seen Bob before when his stubborn streak set in, but he was my boss then, and it wasn't my place to argue with him. He hates it when all of his lines of inquiry shut down, one by one by one, and he's likely to clutch at the thinnest of straws.

'Maybe he did,' I argued, 'but Grover Bryant's half-sister is clinging on to life by her fingernails. That doesn't make for the most reliable of witnesses. If you put the thought into his head, he might say "yes" because he thinks that's the answer you want. You know this, gaffer; we get it all the time.'

'Granted,' he conceded grudgingly, 'but still . . .'

He went no further because the door opened, and the Cabinet Secretary insinuated himself into the room. I say that because to my eyes he didn't move like other people; he didn't walk, rather he flowed. I'm not saying he was oily but if his middle name had been Olive I wouldn't have been surprised.

'I saw Dr Satchell on her way out,' he said. 'Did she have anything to add to your understanding of yesterday?'

'No,' Bob replied. 'There was something I hoped she could help with, but it seems not. I'll need to go back to Mrs Dennis about that.'

I wondered what he meant, but the time wasn't right to question him about it.

'I've hit a roadblock too,' Hamblin continued. 'I've been trying to arrange a meeting for you with the Defence Secretary, but without success.'

My colleague shrugged his shoulders; I had the sense that

his mind was still in Emily Repton's en suite. 'What's the problem?'
I asked.

'The problem, Commander McIlhenney, is that I can't find
him. His Civil Service staff say he hasn't been in the office this
week, neither yesterday nor today. His parliamentary aide says
that he isn't in the Commons, and likewise hasn't been seen there
since last Friday. His protection officer told me that he and his
colleague were due to collect him from his flat in Smith Square
yesterday lunchtime, but he stood them down. Normally they'd
have been with him round the clock, but he dismissed them some
time on Sunday evening.'

The Cabinet Secretary had regained one hundred per cent of
Bob's attention. 'Are you telling us, Mr Hamblin, that the Defence
Secretary is missing?'

He nodded. 'Yes, effectively I am.'

'What the hell does that mean, I wonder?' Bob grunted.

'Your guess is as good as mine. All I can tell you for certain is
that it doesn't involve his royal friend. I made a discreet inquiry of
Her Majesty's staff, and received a very dusty answer. The young
lady in question is currently skiing in Colorado, with the British
Winter Olympic squad, of which she is a member.'

'He goes off the radar on the day of the Spitfire announcement,'
I exclaimed. 'That suggests to me that he decided to leave
the Prime Minister to take the flak from the Opposition and the
thousands of people whose jobs are dependent on Trident renewal.'

'Yeah,' my friend agreed. 'Me too. And,' he continued, 'it makes
me wonder about the unanimity about Spitfire in the core group
that took the decision.'

'I assure you,' Hamblin told him, 'that it existed. In the final
analysis, there was no dissenting voice. All ministers were in
agreement.'

I raised a hand, to attract his attention. 'This might be naive,' I said, 'but I take it that this new system actually works.'

'Oh yes,' Hamblin replied, with barely a second's delay. 'Balliol's team computer-simulated a pre-emptive attack on Ascension Island, and then, under their control, it was done for real, using a prototype vehicle with a payload matching the weight of several independently targeted miniaturised warheads.'

'Neil's right, though,' Bob muttered. 'Wheeler's chosen an extraordinary time to go walkabout from his duties. What are you going to do about it, Mr Hamblin?' he asked.

'What can I do about it?' he countered. 'I am a servant, that's all. If the man decides to take a couple of days to recharge his batteries I can't order him back to work. Only the Prime Minister can do that.'

'Or her deputy,' I suggested. 'Isn't Mr Kramer concerned?'

'I don't know that he even knows about it. I haven't advised him of the situation.'

'He'll work it out,' Bob said, 'when he sees an empty chair at the Cabinet table in an hour or so.'

'Very true.' He turned towards the door, having been standing since he came into the room. 'And that is something for which I must now prepare.'

He was reaching out for the door handle when it turned, and his hound-like assistant stepped into the room. She didn't look like a woman who exuded happiness at any time, but her expression was doom laden as she handed Hamblin a note, then pivoted on her heel and left.

He read it and his face changed, to match hers. It was noticeably paler as he looked at us. 'Gentlemen, this is a message from the Prime Minister's consultant. Ms Repton went into cardiac arrest half an hour ago, and could not be resuscitated.

This puts everything on hold; I must convey this news at once, and cancel the Cabinet meeting.'

'Sure, you have to tell Kramer,' Bob agreed, 'but won't he want to press on with the meeting, more than ever?'

'He might, but he can't, not in that format. It's not the Home Secretary that I have to advise of the Prime Minister's death, it's Her Majesty's Private Secretary. The Queen didn't invite the Conservative Party to form a government, nor did she appoint its ministers. She invited Emily Repton, and the authority of the Crown was vested in her, and her alone. Constitutionally, that's not something she could delegate, or bequeath.'

He paused, and we could both see that he was trembling with excitement. 'There's no modern precedent for this situation. It's no exaggeration to say that at this moment we don't have a government.'

Twenty-Five

When Hamblin told us that Emily Repton had finally lost her tenuous grip on life, I could see that Neil was rattled, and I thought I could guess the reason. I'd been wondering whether pulling that blade out of her head had done even more damage; if I had, I was pretty sure he had too.

'I would be grateful if you would remain here, gentlemen,' the Cabinet Secretary said. 'I have no idea what will happen in the next hour or so. The one thing I do know is that you are no longer investigating an attack on the Prime Minister but her murder. There can be no more subterfuge. The truth must be told, and as you have played a major role so far, you will need to be available to whomever carries the matter forward.'

'Who's going to do the truth-telling?' I asked him. 'You and I both know that the cover-up was Kramer's idea, but do you see him putting his hand up and admitting it? I'm bloody sure I don't. Watch yourself, Norman, that man will throw you to the wolves.'

'I am quite sure . . . Bob . . . that the Home Secretary will ask me to explain the course of events to the media, and my guess is in line with yours. Somehow he will try to divert blame to the Security Service or to me, or both.' He threw me a shrewd glance.

'That's not going to happen,' I snapped. 'If there's any suggestion of that, I'll sit beside you when you meet the press.'

'That is not going to happen either,' he declared. 'Whatever Mr Kramer may say, it is for the next Prime Minister to explain what happened. If it's him, so be it, but I've been in this post too long to step in front of a bus. If I go under it anyway, I'll make damn sure the world knows who pushed me. Now I must go; I'll advise you as matters evolve.'

He left us and headed off to play his part in an event that was truly historic, way beyond Olympic gold medals and similarly hyperbolic uses of the word by today's media.

My thoughts went back to Neil's unspoken worry. 'Not to be dwelt on,' I said.

'What?'

'Drawing out that letter-opener. If you hadn't pulled it out, it could easily have stayed there until she was on the autopsy table, and maybe . . .' I stopped; no point in expressing the horrible vision I was seeing in my mind, a pathologist making a Y incision to reveal a beating heart.

But as I fell silent, another thought occurred to me, one to be considered at length.

'Okay,' Neil replied, 'but I'm still going to have nightmares about it for a while, that I know.' He paused. 'What do we do now?'

'We do what Hamblin says. We wait here. And while we're doing that . . .' I took out my mobile and called Amanda. 'Have you heard?' I asked her.

'Yes,' she replied. 'Where are you?'

'Cabinet Office.'

'What's happening there?'

'Mr Hamblin's gone off to save the world, we're on standby: for what, I don't know.'

'Are you all right with that?'

I laughed. 'You're twenty-four hours too late to ask me that. I'm beyond the point of walking away. And anyway, I don't want to; my blood's up and I want a kill.'

'Anyone in mind?' she asked.

'The people with most to gain have conspicuously good alibis, apart from one. Do you know where Nicholas Wheeler is?'

'No. Why should I?'

'Because they've lost him. He hasn't been seen for a day and a half.'

'Don't be daft,' she spluttered. 'You can't lose the Defence Secretary.'

'According to Hamblin that's exactly what's happened. He's stood down his protection team and disappeared. He called off his pick-up yesterday morning.'

'What does it mean?'

'It means,' I told her, 'that when Emily Repton was stabbed, Wheeler was unaccounted for.'

'He's a suspect?'

'A person of interest,' I suggested. 'No more than that, for now. You might want to have a word with his Ministry of Defence staff; he may have a private channel to them, but if he has they're keeping it from Hamblin.

'Now,' I continued, 'how about those scientists of yours? Neil says I'm fixating about the Prime Minister's toilet, but have your people come up with anything?'

'Lots,' she replied, 'on the seat, the door handle, taps, every-where you'd expect to find prints, they're there in abundance.

Nearly all identifiable; they've identified hers, Grover Bryant's, the Chancellor, Dr Satchell; they're all pretty smudged up, but there's one clear set on the underside of the seat, on the flushing lever, and on the door handle. Those have not been identified, not yet, but they're still trying.'

'Are Merlin Brady's prints on file?' I asked.

'No. Bob, you're not suggesting . . .'

'No, I'm not, but we know he was in the vicinity at the time, so don't let's rule him out yet.'

'On the other hand,' she murmured, 'he is on a DNA database. We don't talk about it, but we keep samples of prominent people in parliament in case of, em, extreme situations.'

'You mean in case someone blows them to bits and there isn't enough left for conventional identification?'

'That or a plane crash.'

'Yuck.'

'Yeah, I know. I'll ask the scientists to extract DNA from the unidentified print. Anything else you need while we're all stuck here in a governmental vacuum?'

'Just one more thing,' I said. 'That CCTV you sent us. Was it yours?'

'No, we don't do that in Parliament. It came from the Serjeant-at-Arms' office. Why?'

'Just something I want to query about the timeframe.'

'The man you want is Rudy Muttiah,' she volunteered. 'That's if you're still around once the smoke clears and Kramer's officially installed in Number Ten.'

'Don't count your chickens,' I suggested. 'He may have miscalculated.'

'Twenty-four hours in town and you're a pundit?' she chided me.

'Let's wait and see.'

And that's what we did; we waited. Pretty soon we ran out of things to say to each other. Neil passed the time by checking in with his office. His job is extremely sensitive, the kind that requires twenty-four seven availability, and it's full of anxiety, assuming that you care about the people under your command, the men and women you are sending into dangerous, volatile situations. Big McIlhenney might look like a boulder with legs, but he's one of the most caring people, so I knew that his role weighed heavily on him. His HQ was less than a mile from where we were sitting; I suggested that he go back there to see for himself that all was well, but he refused. 'I've started so I'll finish,' he grunted.

I called Alex while we waited; she had a high-profile case on her hands, on top of an ever-growing pile on her in-tray as a criminal defence advocate, as we Scots call our barristers. She had been instructed by one of the co-accused in a case on which we'd both worked very recently, on that occasion for the original accused. The Crown had declined to accept her client as a prosecution witness, leaving her with a defence of impeachment as her only option.

'Any progress?' I asked her.

'There won't be any until we get to trial,' she replied. 'The indictment will be served on Thursday, and a date set. The sooner the better.'

'You do know that your client's as guilty as sin, don't you?'

'The jury decides that, Pops. The Crown is alleging a con-spiracy to murder; they have to prove all of that. The conspiracy part is easy, there was one, but my client will argue that murder was never part of the plan, that the co-accused was alone with the victim at the time of the crime and acted of his own volition and without premeditation in the killing.'

'Good luck with that one, my darling daughter,' I chuckled.

'I won't need it. My defence is logical and the Crown can't prove intent to kill on the part of my client, only intent to abduct . . . and rather carelessly, that won't be in the indictment. I can sniff a result, I'm telling you.'

'Sure,' I said. 'Aileen told me once that in elections, every candidate, no matter how unpopular their party or their cause, or how far they're behind in the polls, has a moment of irrationality when they believe they can win.'

'They have to persuade thousands,' she countered. 'I only have to persuade eight people out of fifteen. Have you seen the witch, by the way?' (Alexis and her one-time stepmother never did hit it off.)

'Yes, I've seen Aileen,' I replied, refusing the bait. 'She's fine; this place is where she's belonged all along.'

'Will you be joining her?' she asked me, bluntly.

'It has its attractions,' I admitted, 'but they aren't overwhelming.'

'There might be a vacancy for a prime minister soon, I hear from the telly. That's about your entry level, Pops.'

'It's arisen already,' I murmured. I hadn't planned to tell her; the words just fell out of my mouth. From the age of around fifteen, my first-born daughter has been my closest confidante. I keep nothing from her, nor she from me, not any more. The only time we've ever fallen out seriously was the one time that she did, when she became involved with Andy Martin, my former friend, who was closer to my age than hers.

I heard a gasp. 'What? She's dead?'

'Yes. It'll be announced soon, I think. There are formalities to be gone through, and maybe stuff after that. This situation hasn't arisen for over two hundred years.'

'Did they identify the illness?'

'You didn't hear what I said; for over two hundred years, not since Spencer Perceval.'

There was a silence, as Alex trawled through her memories of high school history. 'Spencer Perceval: are you saying she was assassinated, like him?'

'That's maybe not the word I'd choose, but effectively, yes.'

'Bloody hell, Pops. How do you know all this?'

'I got bloody roped in, didn't I? Somebody knew I was here, and before I could catch a breath . . .'

'Do you know who did it?'

'No. It's fucking Holmesian,' I murmured. 'Not quite a locked-room mystery, but near as damn it.'

'What happens next?'

'Dunno. I think the Indians gather round the camp fire and have a pow-wow . . . the ruling tribe, that is.'

As I spoke, the door opened, framing Norman Hamblin. He was carrying a tray with a pot of coffee and three mugs. 'Got to go,' I whispered. 'There's a man coming in who might tell me.'

There was an aura around the Cabinet Secretary; at that moment in time he was the most important person in the country and he knew it. He laid the tray on the spare desk as one of his junior assistants closed the door behind him.

'I need this,' he said, as he poured. 'I have just seen *homo politicus*, to coin a phrase, at the apex of his preening cycle. Already I regret not having the event recorded in some way, on video or in an official minute. Now what happened will be coloured for history by the individual recollections of everyone in the room.'

He handed us a mug each, milk added, and sat down.

'So who's in charge?' I asked.

'I am, I suppose. As soon as I left you earlier, I advised Dame Julia Atkinson, Her Majesty's Private Secretary, of the Prime Minister's death.'

Neil raised an eyebrow. 'Not Kramer?'

'No. It wasn't his place to be informed first. I had to tell the Queen and then await her instructions.' He paused, sipped his coffee and then sighed, as the edge was taken off the tension. 'The possibility must have been discussed, for Dame Julia came back to me half an hour sooner than I'd anticipated, fifteen minutes before the scheduled Cabinet meeting.'

'What was the decision?' my friend asked. 'Send for the Deputy Prime Minister?'

'No; as I've explained, that is not an office of state. The view was that as the Conservative Party continues to hold a majority in the House it is for the party as a whole to make a recommendation to Her Majesty. In a normal course of events,' he explained, 'that would be done by the outgoing Prime Minister.'

'Abnormally?' I chipped in.

'That was what I had to determine. I decided to allow the Cabinet to assemble; before it could be brought formally into session, I advised the members of the Prime Minister's death and of the command of the monarch. The Chancellor asked me for guidance, and I told him that it was a matter for the party to determine within its constitution and rules.'

'You passed the buck,' I suggested.

'Not quite. I then went off minute, and said that from what I knew of those rules, if the parliamentary group can agree unanimously on a candidate, that would obviate the need for a ballot of the membership. And I went a little further; I told them that in my view they had around two hours to get that done, so that the new Prime Minister can go to the palace this afternoon.'

He smiled, unashamedly pleased with himself. 'The Chancellor and the Foreign Secretary took that advice. The Home Secretary remained silent. The Defence Secretary,' he added, 'remained absent.

'After very little discussion, it was decided that Cabinet should adjourn and summon the officers of the Nineteen Twenty-Two Committee, the backbenchers' body, to join them. I believe that its chairman is the returning officer in leadership elections.' He drained his mug. 'I have no part in those deliberations, so I withdrew. Before I did, though, I heard the Home Secretary propose that Mrs Kramer be asked to attend also.'

'How did that go down?'

'Very badly with the Foreign Secretary; the Chancellor defused matters by saying that was a decision for the chair of the Twenty-two Committee.' He stood once more. 'We're in limbo, chaps, and so is the nation, although it doesn't know it. I must go back and await developments.'

'What about the announcement of the Prime Minister's death?' Neil asked. 'Has that happened yet?'

'No,' he admitted, 'but it can't be delayed much longer. The hospital is in lockdown, awaiting instructions that nobody is willing to give. The palace wants to make it public, but ministers won't agree on who should do it before a successor is chosen.'

'It seems obvious to me,' I observed. 'It has bugger all to do with ministers. She's dead, out of the picture, as private as any citizen can ever be. It's a family matter, so let big Grover make the announcement.'

Hamblin gave a small nod. 'Yes, I was thinking along those lines too. It's time for an executive decision; I will ask Mr Bryant to make the announcement from the podium in Downing Street, where all the media are gathered. There may be consequences, but frankly I don't care any longer. The venality of some of these people disgusts me. They always opt for expediency rather than what's right.'

He left us closeted once more. I'd have given a couple of wisdom teeth to have been a fly on the wall of the Cabinet Room. If the Chancellor had gone through with his stated intent to challenge Kramer for the leadership, I wondered if he would have the voting strength to carry it off, or indeed the strength of will.

In a face-off between the two of them I wasn't entirely sure that I'd have voted for Ellis as Prime Minister. He'd struck me as a fixer but not necessarily a doer, a wise counsellor, no doubt, but not necessarily a leader. Truth be told, I didn't fancy either of them. Further truth be told, I hadn't met a single person in London that I'd have trusted to run the country, other than Norman Hamblin and, God help me, Aileen.

I was contemplating the lesser of two evils when my phone sounded. I checked the screen and saw that it was June Crampsey. I took her call.

'Bob,' the *Saltire*'s managing editor began breathlessly, 'are you still in Westminster?'

'Right in the middle of it,' I replied.

'Are you getting any sense down there that something momentous is happening? That Emily Repton might have died and they're not telling us?'

'Why should I? What makes you ask that?'

'It's . . . ach . . . I have a correspondent in London, he's damn good and he thinks she is. He's close to the action and he knows just about everyone, including Repton's protection officers. He's just called me to say that he's seen them leaving the Royal Free Hospital, both of them together. He said they wouldn't have done that if they'd had a live body to guard, and he added that from the look on their faces, she's a goner. Can you find anything out from any of the people you're seeing?'

'Lord Pilmar and Lady Mercer wouldn't be among the first to know,' I pointed out.

'Come on, I know you better than that. You've been there for two days. You've seen more than them. I'm asking you, straight out, have you heard anything that would justify me running this story?'

I frowned. Talking to my daughter was one thing, talking to a newspaper editor, even one from my own team, was something else. On the other hand . . .

'If I could see out of the window of the room I'm in now,' I began, 'and into Downing Street, I think I'd see them setting up the podium that they use for special announcements. Would I be expecting Emily to come out and declare a miraculous recovery? No, I would not. Trust your reporter, and trust your instincts. That's all I will say to you.'

She drew a deep breath. 'Cheers, Bob. I'll quote you as a source close to Downing Street.'

'Don't you bloody dare!' I laughed.

'Why are we still here?' McIlhenney exclaimed, suddenly, as June went off to break her story. 'Bob, I've had enough of this; bugger the politicians, bugger the national crisis. I'm a serving police officer, and I know of a murder that's taken place, one that hasn't been reported. Yet here I am, sitting on my hands, doing nothing about it. This is a historic moment, man, truly;

the assassination of a prime minister. It's going to be written about and pored over; when it is, I want to be seen to have done my duty, not to have been part of a cover-up. Don't you?'

His outburst took me by surprise, but I knew that he was right. 'Yes,' I admitted. 'I do.'

'Good. What are we going to do about it?'

'I think we should tell Hamblin that we're going for lunch. On the way there we should call in at your office, go straight to the Commissioner and tell him what's happened. It's his watch; he needs to know.'

'Thank God,' Neil sighed. 'An outbreak of common sense.'

'There's just one more thing,' I added. 'I've gone too far to stop n—'

The phone on my desk rang, halting me in mid-sentence. I picked it up, and heard Norman Hamblin's voice in my ear. 'Mr Skinner, I am calling from the Cabinet Room. I'd be grateful if you and Commander McIlhenney would come here at once. The Prime Minister designate wishes to speak with you before he goes to the palace. You can access Number Ten from the building you are in. The security staff are expecting you.'

'Lunch is on hold,' I said to Neil. 'They've chosen a new leader and we've been summoned to meet him.' He looked doubtful. 'Come on,' I cajoled him, 'we can go straight from there.'

We'd have had no idea how to find our way through the maze of corridors that led to the heart of our government but for Hamblin's assistant, Cerberus. She tried to explain, but gave up and led us there, through security and all the way to the door of the Cabinet Room. The Cabinet Secretary was waiting for us; he didn't look overjoyed.

'The Prime Minister is ready for you,' he said.

'Who?' I asked, although his expression told me the answer.

'Mr Kramer. He and the Chancellor offered themselves as candidates. The chair of the Twenty-Two Committee decided that given the urgency of the situation, the normal rules should be set aside and the matter decided by a secret ballot within the Cabinet. He sought the agreement of the Chairman of the Party, who had been summoned and was present, to this procedure; unsurprisingly, this was forthcoming.'

'In the continued absence of the Defence Secretary?'

'Indeed. However, it was academic; the Chancellor withdrew his candidacy before it went to the vote. He must have worked out that he would lose. With Wheeler being absent he was probably right.'

'What would have happened in the event of a tie?'

'The chair and the two vice-chairs of the Nineteen Twenty-Two Committee would have exercised a casting vote. Two of them have served in Cabinet and from what I know of them, I believe they would have supported Mr Ellis.'

'Lucky old Roland.'

'Be that as it may,' the Cabinet Secretary said, dispassionately, 'he is about to be invited to form the next government. I think it will look very much like the old one, but with his people in Defence, the Foreign Office and the Home Office.'

'How about the Chancellor?' Neil asked.

'He'll stay and will take Mr Kramer's place as Deputy Prime Minister; that has to happen to hold the Cabinet together. Now, come on, he's waiting for you.'

He swept the door open and ushered us into a room that both of us had seen countless times in television, but neither of us had ever contemplated entering.

Roland Kramer was in the big chair, at the middle of the long table, facing the windows. He rose as we stepped past Hamblin. 'Mr Skinner,' he exclaimed, 'thank you for joining me.' He glanced at Neil. 'I'd prefer it if your colleague remained outside.'

I looked him in the eye; there was something new in there, a look of triumph, the gleam of a gold medallist on his lap of honour. What I didn't see, or hear in his tone, was any sign of regret that he had taken a dead woman's chair while it was still metaphorically warm.

'Commander McIlhenney will stay,' I replied. 'He's been a party to this business all the way through, and he's not being excluded now.'

'I said I'd prefer it,' Kramer murmured, glacially. 'Must I make it an order?'

'Don't waste your time, or mine. Get on with it.'

A quick mirthless smile twisted his mouth. 'Bang goes your peerage,' he chuckled.

'I wouldn't accept one, not from you. What do you want?'

'I want you to prepare a detailed report of your investigation, and have it ready for me when I return from the palace. It should not be copied to anyone else, not even to the head of the Security Service, particularly not to Mrs Dennis in fact, as I'm thinking of replacing her.'

'With a white Oxbridge Tory?' I shot back, wiping the smirk from his face. 'Hands off Amanda, no kidding.'

'I'm afraid that you're out of your usual arena, Mr Skinner, and out of your depth.'

'I'm a strong swimmer,' I retorted, 'and I've never minded playing away games.'

'No? I'm afraid this one is over. Once you've completed your report, you can leave your temporary MI5 accreditation with Mr Hamblin. You should be able catch a flight home this evening, I'm sure.'

I took out my laminated card. 'I'll hand this back to Amanda,' I told him, 'to nobody else, and only when she asks for it. You may think you're the centre of your own universe right now, but let me show you the real world. At this moment, until you've been to the palace you don't have any authority. When you do, you will be an unelected prime minister fast-tracked into post by a national emergency, leading a parliamentary party containing a fair number of people who are sceptical about you and, I suspect, quite a few more who hate your guts.'

'I can live with that,' he retorted. 'I can win over my enemies.'

'You mean you think you can bribe them,' I snapped, 'with government jobs and other favours. Maybe you can, but sure as hell you can't afford to make any new ones. Remove Mrs Dennis, and I can tell you, you'll alienate the entire Security Service; given the risks this nation faces, that is not something that you want to be doing. In the process you'd also make an enemy of me. You may see me as a provincial hick, but when I set my mind to breaking someone, they wind up broken.'

'I will consider what you say,' he said, quietly, but I knew he'd do more than that. Kramer was far from stupid.

'No, you will do what I say; you'll leave Amanda in place, for the country's sake. As for me reporting to you, that's not going to happen; I report to her alone, and I will. Before that, though, Commander McIlhenney and I are going straight to New Scotland Yard, to put the investigation of Ms Repton's murder on to a proper footing.'

The Prime Minister-in-waiting frowned, then nodded. 'It doesn't seem that I can stop you,' he sighed. 'You won't mention

Spitfire, though. That has to be kept under wraps for twenty-four hours.'

'If it's relevant, the investigating officers will pursue it,' I replied, 'but we won't draw it to their attention.'

'Very well.' He looked at the Cabinet Secretary. I wondered how long Hamblin would stay in post; a few weeks perhaps but he'd be on Kramer's hit list for sure. 'Show them the side exit, please, and let me know as soon as the car and the security detail are in place.'

He turned his back on us; we were dismissed.

Twenty-Six

The only thing that Bob Skinner has ever seen is the person in front of him. I've never known him to be impressed by anyone's status, nor dismissive of it either. It was obvious to me and to Mr Hamblin that Kramer didn't know how to handle him, so I wasn't surprised when he chose the better part of valour and backed down.

It was wise of him too; we were guardians of a secret that could have unseated him, although he didn't know it at the time . . . or so I assumed. Or did he know about his wife and Merlin Brady? Even now, it's impossible to say for sure.

I did fasten on one thing that Bob said to Kramer: that he would only hand his MI5 authority back to Amanda Dennis . . . and only when she asked for it. To me, that was a significant change in his attitude; I wondered if he'd meant it or if it was simply a bluff.

As we left 10 Downing Street by the tradesman's entrance . . . it's more of a complex than a building . . . I saw that the big armour-plated Jaguar that is the Prime Minister's personal vehicle was waiting. So were the driver, and two men that I knew were the PM's personal protection officers, because of the umpteen times I'd seen them alongside the late Ms Repton on TV. There was a fourth man also; he was vaguely familiar, but I couldn't place him . . . until Bob shot him a sideways look and I remembered that I'd seen him standing outside Kramer's office in the Commons, twenty-four hours earlier.

We moved towards the street then paused. A white podium stood in the middle of the road. A man I definitely didn't recognise stood at it, facing a throng of journalists, cameras and almost unbearably bright lights.

'That's Grover Bryant,' Bob whispered. 'Hold on.'

He was a great, pallid lump of a bloke with wild, greasy dark hair. He was wearing a pale green linen suit; it was crumpled, and hung on him like a sack. The media crew were silent as they gazed at him; they knew that something momentous was about to happen.

He grasped the sides of the lectern and held them tight. 'Ladies and gentlemen,' he began, then his voice faltered. He seemed to brace himself, and started again. 'Ladies and gentlemen, it is with enormous regret that I must inform you that the Right Honourable Emily Repton, MP, the Prime Minister, my sister Emily, died a short while ago in the Royal Free Hospital. The precise cause of her death is as yet unknown, but further information will be shared with you by the appropriate authorities as it becomes available.'

He paused for breath and as he did so the media crew erupted and became a jostling, yelling mob.

Bryant held up a hand to still their questions, waiting until silence was restored. When it was, he continued. 'I am advised that the Right Honourable Roland Kramer, MP, Home Secretary and Deputy Prime Minister, has been called to Buckingham Palace, where he will be invited to form a new government. Thank you and goodbye.'

The babble of shouted entreaties broke out once more, but he ignored them, turned on his heel and walked back into Number Ten.

'Historic' is a word that's overused in the modern world, in my opinion, but at that moment I felt a frisson of excitement; that moment had been historic, in the truest sense of the word, and I'd been there. People who are older than me say they can remember where they were when Kennedy was shot, or when Elvis died; now, I understand.

Bob nudged me, breaking into my thoughts. 'Okay, let's get moving before somebody spots us. It's going to be really crazy here for a while.'

We headed for the gates at the end of the street, where the uniforms on duty let us through.

'How are you doing?' my friend asked. 'Do you need to eat, with your . . . thing?'

'I need to eat because I'm hungry,' I replied, 'but it can wait. What we have to do is more important.'

He agreed, perhaps a little reluctantly, and we began to walk, briskly, towards the latest incarnation of New Scotland Yard, which is very close to the first one. I prefer it; I didn't like the Broadway building. 'How are we going to play this?' I wondered aloud, as we approached the Embankment. 'Technically we should probably be reporting this to Charing Cross Police Station, or to PaDP.'

'You're the cop,' Bob observed. 'It's your decision. But my view is that it's already been reported to you. There's only one other man in the Met who knows that something's up and that's the Commissioner himself. Unless you tell me otherwise, I'm heading to see him.'

'Fair enough,' I agreed. 'He ordered me to the Commons

255

yesterday, personally, so it's logical that I should report back to him, even though he didn't tell me to.'

Bob laughed. 'Possibly because he didn't want to know what was happening. But it's too late for that. He needs to know now, for he's the man who has to determine how we proceed.'

When we reached the HQ building, with its iconic sign relocated, I talked my companion through security and got him a visitor's pass. That done, I took him up to my office, and from there called the Commissioner's executive officer, a chief superintendent named April Colquhoun. I expected a wait when I asked her for an appointment with the boss, but she told me to come straight up. 'He's been expecting you, Commander,' she said. 'I don't know what's up, but it has him on edge.'

'I won't be alone,' I warned her.

'That's all right,' she replied. 'He anticipated that.'

Sir Feargal was standing by the window when April ushered us into his presence. He smiled when he saw Bob. 'How are you, Chief Constable Skinner?' he exclaimed as he stepped towards us, hand outstretched. 'It's been too long.'

'I'm no longer lumbered with that title,' he laughed. 'Good to see you, Feargal. Where was it last time, Northern Ireland?'

'That's right. I thought Belfast was hypertension city, but it has nothing on this job. I imagine you feel happy to be out of the Scottish police service hot seat.'

'I did until yesterday,' he agreed. 'I was down here on a harmless reconnaissance mission, then I was dragooned by Amanda Dennis.'

'There are worse people to be dragooned by. What have you two been up to for the past twenty-four hours?' He looked at me. 'Fill me in, Commander. You can miss out the part about the Prime Minister being dead; I saw the man Bryant's tearful

announcement, but I knew before that, through the protection officers.'

I glanced at Bob. He nodded and I ran through the story, or at least the parts to which I had been a witness. I said nothing about Spitfire; officially I didn't know, and wouldn't have at all but for my friend Bob's disregard for Kramer's orders. I omitted anything about Merlin Brady also; I hadn't been a party to his revelation.

I thought Bob might have volunteered the fact of the relationship between the Labour leader and Kramer's wife, but he didn't, not even when the Commissioner asked him if he had anything to add.

'Nothing that's relevant to the Prime Minister's murder,' he said.

'Why do I suspect that there is something and you're not telling me . . . Consultant Director?' He smiled as he added the temporary title.

My friend shook his head. 'There's nothing that's relevant, Feargal,' he repeated, 'that I promise you. Anything else, you do not want to know.'

The boss laughed. 'Christ, man,' he exclaimed, 'I always thought you were a spook in a police uniform.'

'Rarely in uniform, Commissioner,' he retorted. 'Only on ceremonial occasions.'

'Lucky you. I have to wear mine all the bloody time. The Mayor, whom we must all obey these days, insists that we wear the tunic as the rule rather than the exception . . . apart from Commander McIlhenney's unit, that is. That would be a bit of a giveaway.

'So,' he continued, 'where is your investigation now?'

'At an end,' Bob told him, 'according to the new Prime Minister.'

'Fuck all to do with him,' Sir Feargal muttered, curtly. 'I knew that you and he were a personality clash waiting to happen. I rather hoped that someone else would succeed Emily Repton.'

'It was a close-run thing,' he said. 'It might have come down to one vote in the end, but Ellis backed down. You're right about me and Kramer. He's a dangerous man; arrogant shit. I've served my purpose as far as he's concerned. I've investigated the attack, and I've come up empty handed. That suits his book, and now he wants me out of the way.'

'And have you? Come up empty handed?'

'So far, yes. But I still see lines of inquiry that the new investigating team need to follow up.'

'And who might they be?' the Commissioner asked. 'This new investigating team?'

'How the hell would I know?' Bob exclaimed. 'It's your call. Whoever's in your major crimes unit, I imagine.'

'I don't quite see it like that,' Sir Feargal countered. 'I would prefer it if you two continued. This is beyond a major crime; it's as big as it gets, and until all possibilities are explored and exhausted or until a perpetrator is found, there's no doubt that it impacts on the security of the nation. I've discussed this with Amanda Dennis, and she agrees.'

'You haven't discussed it with me, though,' he complained, 'and neither has she.'

'No, but we both know, and so do you, that you don't want to walk away from this. Carry on, please; call in whatever assistance you need, but finish the job.'

'What about the legality of it?'

'I'll swear you in as a special constable if you like; you can wear two hats.'

'One will be fine, thanks. That's not what I meant. If I was in

258

Scotland, as a police officer I'd be an agent of the Crown and reporting to the procurator fiscal. Don't you have to report to the City of Westminster coroner?'

'In this case,' Sir Feargal replied, 'I choose not to, at this stage. The crime took place within the Palace of Westminster, which makes it a bit of a grey area. Don't worry, you're both at liberty to proceed as you think fit. I've advised the head of the Parliamentary and Diplomatic Protection Unit, the Parliamentary Security Director, the Serjeant-at-Arms, and the Speaker. They're all only too happy to leave it to you . . . not that they have any choice, since it's my call, as you said. The Security Director is not best pleased about having been kept out of the loop, but that's tough; to me it's quite understandable, since the attack on Ms Repton happened on his watch, so to speak.'

'That's good,' my friend and co-investigator said, effectively declaring himself on board. 'There's something I'm not happy about. It may involve me leaning on some people; if I do, I won't want any comeback.'

'You have a free hand, I assure you.'

'We'll need a base; the Cabinet Office won't be open to us from now on.'

'Use Commander McIlhenney's office.' That could be a tight squeeze, I thought, but I said nothing.

I thought we were finished, but Bob wasn't. 'There's just one more thing,' he continued. 'Forensic pathology services in England are under the control of the Home Office pathology unit. In these circumstances I don't like that; I don't want Kramer, or his placeman as the new Home Secretary, to have any access to the autopsy findings.'

'How will you avoid it?' the Commissioner asked, but I knew what was coming.

'I want to bring in my own. My wife holds the chair of Forensic Pathology at Edinburgh University. She's eight months pregnant, and champing at the bit. She's too far gone to fly, but I can get her on a train this afternoon. I want to use her.'

'Then go for it, Bob. Kramer will instruct the Home Office to appoint someone, I'm sure, but I'll countermand it.'

'What if he complains to the Mayor?' I asked.

'That would not pose a problem, Commander,' my boss laughed. 'The Mayor hates Kramer too.'

Twenty-Seven

'Pack a bag with enough for a few days,' I said to Sarah, as Neil wolfed down some sort of Mediterranean wrap in the canteen, 'take a taxi to Waverley Station, get on the four o'clock London train, and I'll meet you at King's Cross. Don't eat on board; we'll go somewhere flash.'

'Too damn right we will,' she replied. 'What's this about, Bob? Are you missing me that much? Hey,' she paused, and I could almost see her eyebrows rise, 'are you bringing me down to check the place out? Have you decided to accept their lordships' offer?'

'I haven't made any irrevocable decision yet,' I insisted; technically that was true. 'I want you with me, that's all; it would help me in my thinking. If you feel fit enough for it . . . if you don't, speak now.'

'I've had two kids already. I know I'm not going to drop for at least three weeks, whatever they say. I'll ask Trish to call the taxi while I pack. Do you want me to stick a couple of shirts and stuff in for you? You must be running short.'

She was right. I'd packed for two nights, maximum. 'Yes, please, that would be good.'

'Okay,' she said, cheerily, 'I'm on my way. It had better be something flash, mind.'

261

It was; I had already checked that there was a room available in the Savoy. As soon as I hung up on Sarah I called back to confirm it, then rang my original hotel to cancel my booking and settle my account by card. I asked them to cram everything in my room into my case, and arranged through Neil for a police car to pick it up and deliver it to New Scotland Yard.

When all that was done, I turned back to the business in hand. 'I need to go back to the Commons,' I told Neil. 'I need to see Brady again. Want to meet him?'

'If it's relevant to the investigation,' he replied, 'why the hell not?'

I sent Aileen a text: *Can you fix it to see Merlin again, ASAP?*

She came back within five minutes: *Chaos here with PM death; MB about to tour TV studios, but has a slot within next half-hour.*

'Come on,' I said, grabbing my Filofax and heading for the door.

I had visions of being delayed by security, but the cops Neil had met the day before had told him of a pass-holders' entrance at basement level, accessible from Westminster tube station. We took a chance and it paid off; we got through with our badges, our rank, and a quick frisk.

I was beginning to have a feel for the building's geography: I found the Central Lobby without difficulty and from there the Labour leader's office was accessed easily. When I knocked, the door was opened by a shovel-faced woman wearing a red suit. 'Don't keep him long,' she warned as she let us in, then left the room, as I introduced Neil to her boss.

'Sadie Finch,' Brady advised us. 'She's the party's head of communications. You can imagine what sort of a day she's having.'

'And you too, I guess,' I added.

'Not really. The TV people expect me to say something appropriate about Emily, and to comment no doubt on the speed with which Kramer has been installed as her successor. There's nothing difficult in that; she was politically ruthless, as most party leaders are, but there was a decent woman beneath it all. As for the rush to replace her, I don't go in for posturing. It was necessary; I hope that Kramer will seek a fresh mandate from the electorate, and I'll say as much. I don't suppose he will, though, any more than Emily did when her predecessor fell on his sword in mid-term.'

He smiled. 'However, it does give me a chance for a small reshuffle, to adjust to his altered front bench, and to fix some other things. You made a good point yesterday about your ex-wife's special experience.'

'Don't raise her up too high,' I chuckled. 'She's after your job.'

'I know she is. More than half of my shadow Cabinet are after my job. Two or three of them are even capable of doing it. What about you?' he exclaimed. 'Yesterday you said you'd want to be leader in the Lords if you joined us. I think that's an excellent idea; it would put some excitement into the place.'

'You're joking,' I said, glancing to my left, 'or you're flattering me. Either way, you're making Commander McIlhenney feel awkward. We didn't come here to talk politics. There's something I want to ask. Yesterday you told me that you saw a woman in the corridor, as you were trying to leave, with her back to you. I want you to think about that. What was she doing? I mean was she standing still, or was she moving?'

Brady scratched his chin. 'I saw her so briefly, that to be honest I couldn't say.'

'Can you describe her?'

'Medium,' he replied. 'That's the only word that comes to mind, medium height, medium build, medium-length hair.'

'Hair colour?'

'That didn't register.'

'Clothing?'

'Nothing red, but that's all I can tell you. I really had the briefest glimpse.'

'Where was she in relation to the Prime Minister's office door?'

'She was beside it.'

'So she could have come out of her office?'

'Yes,' he agreed, 'she could. But equally, she could have been one of the Chancellor's staff, and have come out of his room.'

'The Chancellor wasn't there, so that's less likely. Mr Brady, you told me yesterday afternoon that you didn't recognise the woman, but was she completely unfamiliar to you?'

He sighed, frowning. He closed his eyes, imagining. 'I suppose,' he ventured, 'I might have seen her before, but I've seen most people in this place. I've been an MP for twenty-five years.'

'Do you know Ms Repton's PPS?' I asked.

'Doctor woman?' he asked. 'Remind me. What's her name?'

'Michaela Satchell.'

'I know her,' he admitted, 'but she's not someone I see very often in the Commons. Ministers' PPSs are dogsbodies, Mr Skinner, like a senior officer's batman in the forces. They're unpaid, doing the job because it's on the ladder, albeit the lowest rung. They scurry around in the background, but stick to their own side of the House.'

'The woman you saw,' I asked him, bluntly, 'could that have been Dr Satchell?'

Merlin Brady shook his head. 'I know how important this is, Mr Skinner, and I would really like to help you . . . if only to help persuade you to join my team . . . but honestly, I cannot say yes, and I cannot say no. I have no idea who she was.'

I gave up the fight. 'Okay,' I sighed. 'Thanks for trying.' I turned towards the door, then paused. 'I'll get back to you on the other thing.'

He smiled again. 'But don't build my hopes up?'

'Something like that.'

'He knows,' Neil exclaimed as soon as we were outside. 'He knows that this is a murder investigation, doesn't he? Even though we didn't say so.'

'Yes,' I admitted. 'I told him yesterday that she'd been attacked. At the time I didn't see it as a risk, and I've been proved right.'

'Just as bloody well!' he exclaimed. 'He didn't strike me as a Lothario,' he murmured. 'He didn't strike me as anything, truth be told. He's just an ordinary-looking bloke; how he got to lead his party defeats me.'

'It defeats most people.'

'What the hell can a wolf like Siuriña Kramer see in him?'

'Loneliness,' I replied. 'It emanates from him; inside he's a shy man who just wants to be liked. My suspicion is that she realised it from the start, and latched on to him. Even though he was a backbencher when it began, he'd been around for a long time. And even though he wasn't seen as a leader then, he had influence.'

'Poor sod,' Neil murmured. 'Now that she's the Prime Minister's wife, she won't need him any longer.'

'My thoughts exactly.'

'It's a pity he couldn't help us identify the woman in the corridor.'

'He didn't say yes, but he didn't say no. Let's busk it and confront Satchell; see how she reacts.'

'How do we find her?'

I'd been wondering that. Satchell's world had been turned upside down in the previous few hours. Her personal power base had gone; there was no point in trying Downing Street, or even Norman Hamblin. She was just another . . .

'We page her,' I exclaimed, remembering something I'd seen happen while I was waiting for Aileen. 'Simple as that.'

We walked back to the Central Lobby and straight up to the reception point. I could see the corridor that leads into the Commons chamber; the doors were open and there was someone in the Speaker's chair, but with very few people to keep in order, as far as I could see.

There were two men on duty, bright eyed and eager to please. 'Yes, gentlemen,' one of them said as we approached. 'How can I help you?'

'Will you call Dr Michaela Satchell MP, please?' Neil replied.

'Certainly, sir. And you are?'

'Constituents,' I shot back. 'She's expecting us.'

'But she isn't,' Neil murmured as we stepped away from the counter.

'Trust me,' I said. 'Her brain will be so scrambled she'll assume she's forgotten.'

It didn't take long to prove me right. 'Gentlemen, Dr Satchell is in Portcullis House,' the helpful receptionist called out. 'She apologises and asks if you could meet her there, in the courtyard.

You'll have to go back outside, and cross the road, I'm afraid. Members of the public can't access it directly from here.'

McIlhenney stepped back towards him and spoke quietly to him. I saw a warrant card being flashed, and the usual change of expression.

Portcullis House connects to the Commons by the same colonnade that we had used earlier. We found our way back quite easily; we stepped off an escalator into the vast central atrium of the newest building in the parliamentary complex, just in time to see Mickey Satchell trotting down the stairway that faced us.

She turned towards the street level entrance, expecting her visitors to arrive from that direction.

I tried not to startle her but she jumped nonetheless as we walked up to her and I called out, 'Good afternoon, Dr Satchell.'

She spun round to face us. Stylistically, she had known better days. Her hair wasn't quite dishevelled but it looked as if it had been patted back in place, and all the eye make-up in the bag she carried couldn't disguise their puffiness.

'Mr Skinner,' she murmured, frowning, as if she was trying to work something out. 'I'm sorry,' she continued, 'I can't stop; there are people coming to see me, constituents . . . today of all days. I'd forgotten all about them.'

'No you hadn't,' I told her. 'I'm sorry about the deception, but we need to speak to you again and I couldn't allow you the option of avoiding us.'

I'd expected a protest, but there was none; not the faintest sign of annoyance, only confusion. 'This is about Emily?' she replied. 'But surely, now that she really is dead, this is a matter for the police.'

'I am the police,' Neil pointed out.

'As for me,' I added, 'I'm still wearing my Security Service hat, even if it doesn't fit me too well. Yes, this has become a murder investigation, but it's still a very discreet one and it's still in our hands.'

'You surprise me,' she admitted. 'I thought that our new Prime Minister . . .'

I smiled. 'Would have got me out of here sharpish?' I suggested. 'Left to his own devices he probably would have, but the Commissioner of the Metropolitan Police saw it differently. Where can we talk?'

'Do you want to come up to my office?'

I looked around; the space seemed to have been designed for casual meetings, with coffee tables gathered around a cafeteria at the far end. Very few of them were occupied. 'Nah,' I murmured. 'Let's go along there, Dr Satchell. As far as the world knows, we really are constituents.'

She nodded agreement and led the way, bustling through the courtyard with an air of ownership. She chose a table that was as far removed as possible from any other in use. 'Would you like coffee, gentlemen?' she offered, in a voice loud enough to carry to the closest groups, acting out the part of a welcoming MP.

I glanced at Neil; he shook his head. 'No, we're fine, thanks,' I said, then waited until she was seated before taking one myself; Skinner, always the gentleman.

'How can I help you?' she began, the volume much lower, leaning forward, almost hunched over the table. 'I don't know what more I can tell you. I found Emily, I made a tragically wrong diagnosis, and I yelled for help. Roland Kramer took over from there, he called in the Security Service and you got involved.'

'For my past sins,' I agreed. 'Okay, Dr Satchell, you've told us that you saw Ms Repton in her office yesterday morning at around ten o'clock and never thereafter, until you found her, not dead as you thought, but dying as we know now.'

'That's right.'

'You are absolutely certain of that?' I asked.

'One hundred per cent,' she insisted.

'How are you physically, doctor?'

'What do you mean?'

'Are you in good health?'

'Yes. Why shouldn't I be?'

I frowned. 'I've been told that you have a history of problems related to drug abuse.'

Her face twisted into a look of fury. 'And who the fuck told you that?' she hissed.

'You know I'm not going to say. But you're not going to deny it, are you? You can't imagine that you'd get to be the Prime Minister's PPS without being rigorously vetted.'

'No, I'm not going to deny it; it happened, but I was young and, like many junior doctors, under tremendous workload pressure.'

'It was severe, though,' I continued. 'You were hospitalised?'

'Hospitalised, treated and discharged. Like I said, it's ancient history, and if one word of it gets into the public domain, I will sue your arse off.'

'It won't get there through me,' I assured her, 'but if it did through any other source, suing would be pretty pointless, because it's true. Anyway, I ask you again, did it leave any residual problems? Memory loss, for example.'

Satchell shook her head, vigorously. 'Absolutely not. Why do you ask?'

'Because I have a witness who saw someone remarkably like you coming out of the Prime Minister's room at ten fifty-ish yesterday morning.'

As the last vestige of anger left her face and as it paled, I knew the gamble had paid off. I waited patiently, watching her trying to frame her reply, looking for a way to extricate herself from the fairly deep metaphorical shit in which she stood.

It took an age, but I gave her all the leeway she needed. 'I didn't go in,' she murmured when she was ready. 'I took someone there, but I didn't go in. It might have looked like I was coming out of there but I didn't go in.'

McIlhenney threw her his most sceptical glance, and he's an international-class sceptic. 'You're going to have to talk us through that one,' he drawled.

'I know it sounds odd,' she conceded, obviously agitated, 'but it's true. Emily called me, and said that a man would ask for me by name, in the Central Lobby. I was to meet him there and take him to her room.'

'A man? Help us here; what was his name?'

'She didn't tell me,' she insisted. 'All she said was that a man would ask for me by name at the desk.'

Neil's look was full of scorn. 'Tall man? Short man? Black man? White man? Thin man? Fat man?'

'None of that. All she said was that a man would ask for me.'

'And we can confirm this by going back to see the people at the reception point in the lobby?'

'Well, no,' she admitted. 'As it happened he didn't ask for me. I went straight there; being Monday morning the lobby area was quiet. I was the only person there, and he came straight up to me.'

'This is all so implausible, Dr Satchell,' I murmured, 'that it's probably true. How did Ms Repton call you?'

'On the internal line.'

'Which of course is untraceable. You'd never seen him before, is that what you're telling us?'

'That's right.'

'Then describe him please,' I said, my sarcasm level rising to match McIlhenney's.

She looked me in the eye, as if she was trying to summon up some defiance. 'You know Chewbacca in *Star Wars*? The Wookie?'

'Yes.'

'Well, he looked fuck all like him,' she retorted, drawing an involuntary smile from McIlhenney that vanished as quickly as it appeared. 'He was nondescript; a couple of inches shorter than you, Mr Skinner, but much less shop worn and twenty years younger; early thirties, maybe a little older, dark hair, clean shaven, clear eyed. The type I never saw at all when I was in medical practice because he was exuding good health. Do you want me to do an Identikit picture for you?'

'No thanks,' I replied. 'I'll just dig out my passport photo from the nineties. You've just described me.'

I wasn't kidding; I was sure that's what she had done, but she didn't bite, holding her ground instead. 'Well, that's the best I can do,' she snapped.

'Then let's move on. You led this man whom you'd never met, whose name you didn't know, into a private part of this building, right up to the PM's door . . . but you didn't go in?'

'No, I just knocked on the door, then opened it. He stepped inside and I closed it behind him.'

'How did you even know that the Prime Minister was in there?' I challenged her.

'As I opened it, I heard the sound of the toilet flushing. The plumbing in here is still Victorian; it isn't discreet.'

'Did Ms Repton ever leave the seat up?' Neil asked casually.

She looked at him, down the full length of her nose. 'What woman does?' she murmured.

Twenty-Eight

Whether Mickey Satchell had been in the Prime Minister's office didn't concern me. Not that I believed it; I couldn't see any conscientious PPS just opening the door and shoving a person she didn't know inside without checking that her boss was still okay with it. I reckoned she'd been caught in a lie, denying that she'd seen Emily after ten o'clock, and that her account was the only way she could see to wriggle out of it.

Truth or not it was academic; whether she'd been in there or not, Brady had spotted her at ten fifty; if he had got the time right, her boss's phone records indicated that she had been active after that.

What was relevant was that there had been no sign of her, or the mystery visitor, on the CCTV footage that we'd been given to review.

Once Satchell had left us and headed back to her office, Neil suggested that we go to his to consider our next step. But I already knew what it would be. We stayed at our table and I called Amanda Dennis's private number.

'You know we're still on the case?' I asked, as she picked up the call.

'Yes, Feargal told me; in fact he asked my permission.'

'That was damn proper of him,' I grunted. 'You never asked mine.'

'I know you too well,' she laughed. 'Short of your wife going into labour, nothing would drag you away from this now. And even then . . .' she pondered.

'My wife isn't going into labour,' I retorted. 'In fact she's getting on a train in a short time from now and heading down here. Feargal's agreed that she should do the post-mortem.'

'Is she indeed?' Amanda murmured. 'Now that I didn't know. People won't be happy about that.'

'I don't imagine they will be,' I agreed, 'but it's the right thing to do. Those people are interested parties at the very least; the alternative would have given them ministerial oversight of the process, and that is certainly not appropriate.'

'Agreed. They won't be happy, as I said, but they can't doubt your wife's suitability for the task. Will she be assisted?'

'This is England,' I pointed out, unnecessarily. 'There's no legal need for a second pathologist to be present. But if Sarah wants one, I'm sure she'll be able to call on one of her academic colleagues . . . as long as he isn't on the Home Office panel.' I paused. 'But that's tomorrow's business. I have other pressing matters. The CCTV you sent me; where did it come from? Who oversees the coverage?'

'The man I mentioned earlier, Rudy Muttiah, the Parliamentary Security Director; I believe the cameras are operated by contractors, but he'll be able to tell you.'

'Did you see that footage?'

'I still haven't seen it; I had it sent straight to you. Why?'

'Maybe nothing; most likely a technical hitch, or,' I added, as the possibility struck me, 'carelessness on our part. I'll need to look at it again. Where do I find the Muttiah man?'

'His office is in Portcullis House,' she volunteered.

'Happy coincidence: that's where we are now.'

She gave me a direct dial number; I called it straightaway.

'PSD's office,' a male voice announced. If treacle had a sound, that's what it would have been.

'Hello,' I said. 'I'd like to speak with Mr Muttiah, the Parliamentary Security Director. My name is Skinner; I believe that Sir Feargal Aherne may have mentioned me to him.'

'Yeah, he did,' molasses man replied. 'This is Rudy; I have a small team and today it's off sick, hence I'm answering my own phone. What can I do for you, Mr Skinner?'

'Commander McIlhenney and I need to ask you about the CCTV footage we reviewed yesterday, but not over the phone.'

'Where are you?'

'In the same building as you, or so I'm told. In the courtyard.'

'Come up to the second floor; I'll meet you at the lifts.'

We had to look around to spot the elevators, which were tucked away in the opposite corner of the atrium area, then had to wait for one to arrive. I am not the most patient man in the world, as everyone but my younger daughter Seonaid will admit . . . Seonaid being the apple of my eye, and the only person in the world who can make me do exactly as she wants when she wants . . . and so I was fidgeting impatiently when it did open its doors, even more so when it went down instead of up.

When finally we reached the second floor and stepped out, Rudy Muttiah's smile raised my irritability level by a couple of notches. *Why are you fucking smiling, mate?* I thought. *The Prime Minister got killed on your watch.*

He defused me pretty quickly, though. 'Am I glad to see you guys,' the grey-suited man said, and he meant it.

Undistorted by the digital machinations of a mobile phone, the richness of his voice possessed a soothing quality.

And something else; the sigh that it carried made me realise that while Neil and I had been hung out to dry, potentially, by being handed an assignment that, if it wasn't unprecedented in its sensitivity and importance, was at least in the same ballpark as JFK and his brother, we were not alone. Rudy Muttiah might not have been an investigator, but his arse was on the line as well.

He was a big guy, an inch or so taller than me, and I'm no midget. His skin was a deep bronze hue that was a perfect match for his voice. His thick black hair showed not a trace of grey, and yet the lines around his eyes suggested that he was in his forties. I tried to guess his racial make-up but his Yorkshire accent kept getting in the way.

He read my mind. 'Dad Sri Lankan,' he volunteered, 'Mum from Sheffield. Come on, my office is just along here.'

We followed him, turning left, then going halfway down a passage that was open on one side, overlooking the courtyard, and with opaque glass walls on the other. He stopped at a door with no adornment other than a number, two hundred and twenty-two.

'This is me,' he said, as he led us into a wide open area, with two desks, neither occupied, and a meeting table. The wall beyond had two doors. They weren't glass; they might have been real rosewood. The parsimony of my Scottish soul made me hope that they were a cheaper alternative, but the opulence of the rest of the Westminster complex made me doubt that.

'Your absent team?' I asked, nodding at the vacant desks.

He nodded. 'Bloody flu,' he growled. 'Come on through.'

He opened the door on the right and showed us into his private office. His desk was set at right angles to the door, allowing him a view of the House of Commons . . . that is to say the parts that weren't covered in scaffolding. I glanced around. There was a framed photo on the desk, a woman and two young children, and on the walls two framed artworks that I realised were old vinyl album covers, *London Calling* by The Clash and *Too Much Too Young* by The Specials. I know a bit about music; it didn't take me long to make the connection.

He saw me looking. 'You know The Clash song "Rudie Can't Fail"? It's been lodged in my head for the last twenty-four hours: this Rudy has failed and he's been shut out. That's what I'm feeling. Whatever happened over there, if it's down to a failure in security, then I should be dealing with it.'

'How much have you been told?' Neil asked him.

'The Home Secretary called me yesterday morning; he told me there had been an incident in the Prime Minister's Commons office, but that it was being contained. The detail I got later, from the news, after she'd been taken to hospital. Then I had a call from the head of MI5, asking me for security footage of the area in the House that leads to the senior ministers' office corridor.'

'Do you control the cameras over there?'

'Control? On a day-to-day basis, no. Am I responsible for them? Yes. The CCTV monitoring service is contracted out to a private firm but they report to me. When Mrs Dennis called me . . . she called me herself, how bloody usual is that? . . . she asked me to supply her with the footage within a specific time-frame. I called the service manager and had it set up; told him to copy personally that period of the recording and make it accessible through a link. I assume that all happened because I've heard nothing since.'

'It happened,' I confirmed. 'We've seen it. Now we'd like to speak to the person who put the clip together.'

'Do you have a problem with it?'

'I don't know,' I admitted. 'Let's call it a potential anomaly for now. Is there any way someone could have been in that area of the House without being picked up by the camera?'

'None,' the Security Director replied, firmly. 'Are you suggesting that happened?'

'That's how it looks,' I told him.

'Come see this,' he said. There was a second doorway, between the two framed album covers. He opened it and led us into a room that was slightly bigger than his own. The wall that faced us was covered completely by monitor screens.

'That gives a complete picture of the House of Commons. Each one of those screens has a feed from a different camera; they're interlinked and they have night-vision capability. Trust me, suppose a mouse came out during the night looking for cheese in the cafeteria, we'd catch it in the act. There's only one corridor that isn't covered: the one where the senior ministers' offices are located.'

'Does that include the stairway that leads down to the private entrance, or does that have a camera?'

'No. It used to, that and the corridor, but around fifteen years ago, at the time of the Iraq war, the prime minister of the day got a bit sensitive and had the coverage removed. He also put his own protection people on the private entrance. These days it's staffed by parliamentary police officers, but nobody's ever got round to putting the cameras back.'

'I see. How do we get to talk to your manager? Are you okay with that?'

'I will be,' he replied, with a smile, 'when you tell me what exactly you guys are doing.'

'We're investigating the murder of Emily Repton.'

His eyes widened, the creases around them deepened. 'Fuck!' he murmured. 'I'll get him across here.' He returned to his office; I watched from the doorway as he picked up one of the three phones on his desk and punched in a number. 'Joe,' I heard him say, 'spare me a few minutes, please. Yes, I know it's going to be hell on earth this afternoon, but I need to see you. Now, please.'

He hung up. 'Not happy, but he'll be here.'

I nodded. A few minutes to kill, so I decided to catch up with something else that was on my mind. I called Norman Hamblin from my mobile; Cerberus put me through at once.

'How goes?' I asked.

'Speedily,' he said. 'The new PM is reshaping his Cabinet already. As expected, Ellis is the Deputy PM, staying as Chancellor. Michael Darkley, one of his cronies, is the new Foreign Secretary, called in from the back benches. Radley has resigned, to the surprise of many people. I don't know who the new Home Secretary is yet.'

'What about the Defence Secretary, Wheeler?' I asked.

'The former Defence Secretary,' Hamblin countered. 'He's being replaced by Bernice Crichton, another Kramer acolyte; the problem is that I can't find him to break the news.'

'He's still missing?'

'I don't know if he's ever been officially missing, Mr Skinner, but if you're suggesting that his absence is disturbing, I agree with you.'

Twenty-Nine

*T*he man who burst into Rudy Muttiah's office was his polar opposite. He was short, fat and whey faced; where the Security Director's suit was Savile Row, his looked as if it might have come off a rack at the 'final reductions' sale at the very last BHS store to close its doors.

As for his voice, it was an impatient south London whine. 'I hope this is urgent, Mr Muttiah,' he began. 'Of all days,' he moaned. 'We're expecting a new Cabinet any minute and the place will just light up.'

'Live with it,' big Rudy replied, curtly. 'These gentlemen need to speak with you.' He glanced at Bob. 'This is Joe Coffrey, CCTV manager. Use this office for your chat, guys,' he added. 'I need to step downstairs anyway.'

It occurred to me that he didn't want to be within earshot of our interview with the TV man, even through a thick wooden door.

'Thanks,' Bob said. Then he smiled. 'We won't make a mess, I promise.'

'What is this?' Coffrey exclaimed as he looked up at us. His eyes sought mine, as if he felt in need of a friend and hoped I might be one. I looked down at him, with the same stony expression that big McGuire and I used to sow the first seeds of fear in the so-called *hard men* we encountered on the streets of Edinburgh twenty-odd years ago. It was probably unnecessary, but I didn't like the guy.

He gave up on me as a bad job and turned back to Bob, to find that his smile had vanished too.

'What is it?' the wee man repeated, then finally asked a very obvious question. 'And who are you?'

The twitch of my friend's eyebrow was almost imperceptible but I saw it and understood that he wanted me to take the lead. 'I'm Commander McIlhenney, Metropolitan Police.' I showed him my warrant card, holding it up and making sure that he read it. 'My colleague is attached to the Security Service. We're the people for whom you copied a section of CCTV footage yesterday.'

He gulped.

'Before we begin,' I paused, giving him time to think 'Begin what?' 'is there anything you'd like to say to us, anything you'd like to volunteer?'

'Such as?'

'Such as, might you have made a mistake with the timeframe of the section you supplied?'

'But he couldn't have,' Bob interrupted. 'We checked the time on screen at the beginning and the end, remember.'

I nodded. 'Right enough, so we did. That makes it all the more difficult to explain.'

'Explain what?' Coffrey squeaked. Rudy Muttiah liked his office cool, but he was sweating.

'I think you should sit down,' Bob said to him. 'In fact, I insist on it.' He pulled up the only guest chair in the room and put a hand on his shoulder, pressing him down.

'We have a problem with your tape extract,' I continued. 'We know that two other people walked along that corridor yesterday, *en route to the Prime Minister . . . sorry, the late Prime Minister's office, but there isn't a sign of them on your footage. So explain to us, Mr Coffrey, how that could have happened. Before you say anything,' I added, 'you need to realise that this is a very serious matter, the most serious that either of us have ever encountered in our long careers.'*

'He means tell us the fucking truth,' Bob murmured. 'We know the tape was doctored, and neither of us believes for a minute that you just did it off your own bat. Who told you to do it?'

Something happened then that wasn't an edifying sight, or sound, or any other sort of sensory experience. It had never happened to me with a witness before, and when I asked him afterwards, Bob admitted that it was a new one for him too.

Joe Coffrey pissed his pants.

'He told me I had to do it,' he wailed. 'He'll come for me now you know, and he'll find my family. He'll never believe I didn't tell you.'

'In which case,' Bob said, gently, 'you've nothing to lose by telling us now. You have a lot to gain, in fact,' he added. 'Once you've shared it with us we'll be on your side. Take a look at us. Do you think we can't take care of the guy who scared you?'

The sad wee fat man looked up at him; his eyes were as moist as his trousers, but I could see relief in them as he shook his head, slowly.

'Come on then,' Bob continued. 'What happened?'

'He came into my office about half past twelve,' Coffrey began. 'He didn't tell me his name, just showed me a badge. He said very soon I was going to be asked for footage of a section of corridor in the Commons building covering an hour or so that morning. He said that there were a couple of people on it who his boss didn't want to be seen, and so he wanted me to erase them; he wanted me

to tamper with the recording.' His voice rose, as if the notion was outrageous. 'I told him I couldn't do that. I said I had a duty to my employer and to Mr Muttiah to keep the record intact. I asked him who his boss was and why he thought he could give me such orders.'

He shuddered. 'He said I didn't need to know that. Then he said that my first duty was to myself and to my family. I have a picture of my kids on my desk; he took out a gun and he tapped it against the glass. "If you don't do as I say," he told me, "first it'll be them, and then it'll be you." And he meant it, he meant it!'

He looked up at me, searching for sympathy; I let him see a little.

'No,' Bob replied, 'he made you believe that he meant it, and that was all he needed to do. The badge he showed you: could you read a name on it?'

'There wasn't time. I saw it for less than a second.'

My friend took out his Security Service warrant and showed it to Coffrey. 'Did it have that crest on it? Can you remember that much?'

He nodded. 'Yes it did, I remember that much.'

'Can you describe the man?'

'Not really; he was leaning really close to me and his eyes were all I could see. He had a dark suit on, but so do most men in that place.'

'How about his accent?'

'Not London; West Country possibly. I'm rubbish with regional accents.'

'Could it have been Welsh?'

'It could have been anything but Scottish or Scouse; them I do know.'

I could tell from Bob's frown that he had someone in mind.

'When you doctored the record,' I said, moving on, 'did you do it on the copy or on the original tape?'

'On the original,' Coffrey replied. 'He made me do that; he was watching me all the time.'

'With a gun to your head?'

'No, he'd put it away by then, but I'd got the message.'

'So the original is gone for good.'

'I'm afraid so.'

'We know one of the people on that section; we believe the other was a man.'

'That's right. But I'd never seen him before. He was a stranger in the palace; I can tell you that categorically. If he'd been here before, I'd have seen him and I'd have remembered.'

Bob held up a hand. 'Do you have him on any other cameras?'

'Sorry, no. We did but the man made me delete them all, even the one that looks at St Stephen's Entrance.'

'Bugger,' Bob grunted. 'So we have no visual. Can you describe him?'

'Oh yes. He was wearing a light-coloured suit, beautifully tailored, with a Nehru collar rather than lapels; it was a sheer material, so light it shone like silver. He was with Dr Satchell, so a height comparison lets me estimate that he was around six feet tall.' He glanced at me. 'About the same height as you, Commander, and a bit shorter than you, sir. What else? Black patent shoes, hand-made for sure.'

'He was wearing a suit,' I said, 'but no overcoat? It was a bit parky yesterday morning.'

'He did have a scarf on,' Coffrey volunteered. 'I forgot to mention that. A big thick woollen one, predominantly black, with red and cream ribbons and a crest. I couldn't see the detail, but *there was blue in it. It belongs to one of the Oxford colleges, but I can't recall which one.'*

'I can.' I looked at Bob, whose face was wreathed in a smile that was positively beatific. 'I played on a private golf course once, a while ago now. The guy who owned it had that crest in every one of the flags. The blue you describe is on the left-hand side and it's background to a silver lion rampant. I know the college you can't recall. It's Balliol.'

Thirty

'A few years ago,' I told Neil, after the unfortunate Mr Coffrey had limped damply back to his office, 'around the time I had that bit of bother with someone trying to set me up on a corruption charge, the thing that you and McGuire helped me out with, Andy Martin and I had to sort out something, a child kidnap case. It took us to a Highland estate belonging to Everard Balliol, John Balliol's father; in fact, he helped us out with the conclusion. The detail of that never made the papers.'

My friend had the sense not to press me to share it with him. 'Everard was a Texan, an industrialist who started in oil, then just proliferated, into everything that was upcoming and sexy. He was a genuine billionaire, not just a millionaire with bullshit and a PR machine. He claimed descent from the King of Scotland whose name he bore, and he backed that up by buying as much of the damn country as he could. He was also as crazy as the proverbial bedbug. When I saw the first *Men in Black* movie, where the guy turns into a giant cockroach at the end, it made me think of him.'

'What happened to him?' Neil asked.

'He was murdered for a few dollars and a pile of jewellery by one of the Korean bodyguards he kept around him. I read about it at the time, then I thought no more about it. I didn't realise he had a son . . . for he was as gay as he was crazy. I'm sure the Koreans did more than guard his body . . . but I Googled him in my hotel last night before I met Amanda and sure enough, he married a country singer in his mid-thirties, had a kid with her, then sent her back to Nashville and, presumably, the boy to boarding school.'

'And it's him who brought the Spitfire propulsion system to our government, the son?'

'In exchange for another billion or so and a passport, that's right.'

'Which left him happy as Larry, presumably.'

'That's right,' I continued, 'and the announcement was good to go. So why did Emily Repton call him in to see her a few hours before she was due to stand up and make it? But did she?' I pondered aloud. 'Or was he wished upon her? If so, by whom?'

'Reasonable questions all,' McIlhenney commented. 'Do you have any answers?'

'To the last one, yes, that's fucking obvious: by the person who wanted the tape erased. And the way I see it, that can only be one man: Roland Kramer. The guy who leaned on poor wee Joe Coffrey: Security Service badge, dark suit, armed in the House of Commons, and likes to wave his weapon about; that can only be one of two men, the pair who were on guard yester-day morning, and I'd put your last penny on it being Kramer's minder, the fella he called Daffyd.'

'Wouldn't Coffrey have known him?'

'Why should he?' I countered. 'He's never under CCTV surveillance, only in the corridor.'

'And we're going to prove all that exactly how?'

'I'll get it out of him,' I promised, 'don't you worry about that.

Coffrey will identify him, with Amanda and me in the room to shore up his courage. But before we go there, I want to nail down the sequence of events that led to Balliol being in her room.'

Neil stared at me. 'What have we got here?'

'You know as well as I do. We have the Prime Minister being fatally wounded in her room by the billionaire who is about to hand our nation the world's deadliest nuclear strike force. And we have the Home Secretary, her inevitable successor, sending an armed man to cover it up by threatening the family of the only man who could prove that Balliol was there.'

He whistled. 'As big McGuire would say: fuck me!'

'I wish he was here. I could use another pair of heavy hands. Yes,' I added, 'I know we can call in Met officers if we need them, but we don't have time to bring them up to speed. We've got to do this on our own. Pretty soon, mate, we've got to split up, but before then, I have a couple of calls to make, as soon as we're back in your office.'

The first of those was to Amanda Dennis, to update her on what we had discovered. I thought about calling Feargal Aherne too, but decided that he was better off not knowing of my suspicions until I was able to prove them.

'I want your man Daffyd,' I told her, once I had finished. 'I plan to reintroduce him to the man Coffrey.'

'I want Mr Daffyd Evans too,' she said. 'The stunt with the gun in Kramer's Commons room was not acceptable from a Security Service employee. However, there are two problems with that. One is that I can't find him; he isn't picking up calls to his mobile, or answering the home number that we have on file for him. The other, even more frustrating, is that when my assistant called Kramer's private office to ask for their help in locating him, she was told that he doesn't work for me any more.'

'How can that be?' I asked.

'He's been transferred to the Downing Street staff, effective immediately, reporting directly to the new Prime Minister. If Mr Coffrey's story is true . . . as I'm sure it is . . . the means of proving it is out of our reach. The tracks have been covered.'

'What if I intercept him somewhere, in a public place, with Coffrey?'

'I wouldn't do that. You'd be putting the man at risk . . . and yourself too, possibly.'

Frustrating, but she had a point. Kramer had reached the top of the pyramid of power. If I was correct, and he was complicit in the attack on Emily Repton, he would go to extremes to protect himself.

'Okay,' I said, 'forget Daffyd Evans for now. We don't need him anyway; we have another route to the truth. Where can I find John Balliol?'

'You'll need to be careful with him too,' she warned.

'I plan to be,' I promised. 'I'll take him when the time is right, and that will be when your forensic team can give me evidence that puts him definitely in that room. Until I have that I want to put eyes on him, that's all.'

'I hope I can help you with both of those. The physical evidence is less certain without a comparator but I can probably locate him for you. Balliol's essential to the national security; that puts him under the protection of my, of our, service, and by implication our surveillance. He owns considerable property, but since the Spitfire project began he's spent most of his time in the Aldermaston complex.'

'If he's living within it that'll be a problem.'

'Then let's hope he isn't,' Amanda murmured. 'I'll get back to you. Anything else?'

'Lots,' I retorted. 'First there's Nicholas Wheeler, the soon-to-be former Defence Secretary, if he isn't already. I need to speak to him, but nobody can find him, not even Hamblin.'

'When was he seen last?'

'Sunday, as far as I know.'

'The obvious place to start is with his protection officers; they're not under my control, but I can arrange for one of them to call you. Next?'

'The incoming call on Emily's mobile that you told me about yesterday, the one from the pay-as-you-go card bought in Clapham. Has the originating phone been used since?'

'No, nor will it be. We've made every effort to trace the buyer, but it's not going to happen. Why? What's your thinking, Bob?'

'My thinking is that Kramer's involved; a pound to a pinch of pigshit that if you did find the buyer of those SIM cards in Clapham, he'd look a hell of a lot like Daffyd Evans. But why? Why did Balliol suddenly turn up in the Commons, and in her office? And why has Wheeler gone missing? I need to find him, Amanda, I really do . . . that's assuming he's still alive.'

'If he isn't, that would be rather extreme.'

'Yes,' I concurred, 'but if he turns up suffocated in a suitcase that he might or might not have locked himself into, you heard it here first.

'The Balliol information, please,' I continued, 'and Wheeler's protection people, soon as you can . . . Director General.'

I sensed her smile at my use of her formal title. 'You're getting a buzz from this, aren't you?' she said. 'You like this life.'

'I am too Goddamn old for this life,' I insisted, 'and I want to get back to my real one.'

'You and your wife? Feargal's probably still chortling over her doing the autopsy.'

'He better not laugh too loud. If this all goes tits up and Kramer settles into the big chair, nobody will be out of his reach.'

'I know,' she said, grimly. 'And I'll be first in line for the axe.'

'I don't think so,' I countered. 'Second maybe, but I know who'll be first.'

Thirty-One

It didn't take long for the first part of my prophecy to be proved correct.

'Cabinet Secretary,' I began, as my call to Hamblin was connected.

'That won't be me by this time next week,' he responded, solemnly. 'The head of the Civil Service has been instructed by the newly appointed Cabinet Office Minister to provide her with a list of suitable replacements.'

'Her?'

'The newly ennobled Lady Kramer; she'll be introduced to the House of Lords tomorrow.'

Is he crazy? I thought. *What will the media do to her if it comes out that she's been fucking the Leader of the Opposition? Unless . . . Kramer really doesn't know about them.*

For a moment I thought about sharing my knowledge with Hamblin, but decided very quickly against it. I'd made a promise to Merlin, but apart from that . . . he was too honourable ever to use it, but if Siuriña Kramer ever suspected that he knew about her, he might be at risk of a sudden unpredictable misfortune.

'That's too bad,' I said, instead. 'I'm sorry to hear that.'

'Don't be,' he replied. 'I'll be bought off with the customary peerage which I will use to secure some non-political director-ships. They'll be lucrative and they'll have the added benefit of keeping me out of my sister's clutches for as long as possible.'

'But for now, you're still in post?'

'Yes. Between you and me, my colleague said he would take as long as I wished to compile his list, but I asked him not to delay: I want to be out of here. Until then, though, I am still in charge. Do you need my help?'

'If you're able. I have a picture of the last hour and a quarter of Emily Repton's life leading up to her sustaining her fatal injury. It's not complete but I'm getting there. Now I'd like to be able to look back a little further. Is it possible for you to access the phone records of Number Ten, and to check whether she made any calls from there before she left for the House in the morning, and in the twenty-four hours before that?'

'I can do that,' he said, 'but on whose authority is the request being made? For the record, you understand.'

'Would it cover you if Sir Feargal Aherne called you himself to ask for your cooperation?'

'Let's assume that he just did,' he said, decisively. 'Miss Fortescue can be trusted.'

'Miss Fortescue?'

'The guardian of my outer office; most people lack the courage to ask for her name.'

'Me among them,' I chuckled. 'She is pretty formidable.'

'She'll be leaving with me. Her pension is maximised, and she doesn't like the make-up of the new Cabinet. I did point out that as a civil servant that has nothing to do with her, given our political neutrality. Her reply was that her dislike isn't political, it's personal.'

I had barely hung up the phone I'd been using when my

mobile sounded. I checked the screen; it showed 'Number withheld', but in my world many are.

'Mr Skinner?' a male voice asked.

'That's me.'

'My name is Sergeant David Donaldson,' he continued. 'I'm one of the Defence Secretary's protection team. I've been told that I should speak to you, but I wasn't told why.'

'Then let me explain, Sergeant. I need to speak to Mr Wheeler, but I'm having trouble finding him.'

'Are you aware that Mr Wheeler has been replaced as Defence Secretary, sir? My colleagues and I are attached to the job, not the individual, so he isn't my responsibility any longer.'

'I know that, but he was in post the last time anyone clapped eyes on him. I've been trying to find him for the last twenty-four hours and I'm drawing a blank. When was the last time you saw him?'

'When he stood us down, the night before last. He has a flat in Smith Square; our squad maintain . . . maintained, I should say now . . . a constant presence while he's there, two officers, one resting, one on watch. Unless he tells, told us, to go away.'

'Did he do that very often?' I asked.

'Latterly it was quite a common occurrence,' Donaldson replied. 'He has a new lady friend, and she's very . . .'

'Shy?' I suggested.

'You could say that. Discreet might be a better word. I've never seen her,' he admitted. 'I know who she is because I read the bloody gossip columns, but we were always gone by the time she arrived.'

'How did you feel about that, professionally?'

'Truth be told, uneasy. But Mr Wheeler is a very persuasive

guy, and when persuasion didn't work, he was the boss. He told us to go, we went.'

'And that's what happened the night before last?'

'Yes,' the sergeant said.

'What time?' I asked.

'Just after twelve thirty. There was a phone call, on the half hour. He took it and then he came out and stood us down.'

'When do . . . did you usually pick him up after you'd been sent away?'

'That would depend on him. Yesterday he told us that he wasn't going into the House until a couple of hours before the PM's defence statement. We were supposed to pick him up at one, but . . .' he paused. 'That got cancelled. My colleague, Sarfraz, had a text from him mid-morning; it said that he was going away for a couple of days of what he called "private reflection", and that he'd call us when he needed us.'

As he spoke, Sergeant Donaldson sounded more and more hesitant and less and less confident.

'Yes, okay, we were worried,' he admitted, anticipating my question, 'but it's happened before. Nick never believed he was a target for anyone; constant security was tedious for him. He's been known to do that sort of thing before, to bugger off for two or three days at a time when there's a sniff of the other, so when he sent that text to Sarfraz it didn't ring any alarm bells. Now, of course, our boss is Mrs Crichton and he's history.'

'Let's hope not,' I said.

'Are you saying we should have taken it seriously?' the protection officer asked, anxiously.

'I'm making no judgement,' I replied, 'but others might. You and your mate might want to do what you can to check the origin of Sarfraz's message just to make sure it came from Mr Wheeler's phone.'

'We will, sir. Thanks for the warning. I hope he is all right, but knowing him, I'm pretty sure he's under a duvet somewhere with Her Royal what's-it.'

It would have been nice to think so, but I didn't, not for a moment. That possibility had been explored and discounted. Nick Wheeler had disappeared, and who had benefited from his absence? Roland Kramer had, in that he'd been given a free run to the leadership, but that alone didn't answer the big question. Why?

I was still thinking about that when Amanda called me back. 'My people think they've found Balliol's base,' she told me cheerfully. 'He owns a cottage on the edge of a village called Silchester, not far from the Aldermaston establishment. His name is on all the utility bills including the telephone. We checked activity on the line yesterday morning. Calls were on divert to his mobile; there was one, at nine fifty-five from a mobile number. It was another one-off, a pay-as-you-go, but one of the batch from the Clapham purchase. Are you pleased with that, Bob?'

'More than. Thanks. We'll take it from here.'

I sat silent for a while, as Neil caught up with his day job, reading reports from a couple of his undercover officers. As he did that I was thinking about the game that had begun the day before, only to reach a tragic and momentous conclusion that afternoon. I thought about all the moves and all the players and most of all about the man who had emerged on top of the pile.

In the end, according to Hamblin's source, Leslie Ellis, the Chancellor, had backed off from challenging Kramer. Had he seen that the numbers were stacked against him or had he been bought off? With what? A title? The Chancellor of the Exchequer is effectively the Deputy Prime Minister; whatever Emily Repton had called Kramer, while she was alive Ellis had been her de facto number two, in terms of the power that was vested in his office. Kramer might have hung the ribbon round his neck, but it had changed nothing.

And Wheeler's disappearance? What the hell was that about? There's a danger in my job of becoming too conspiratorial, of letting your imagination run riot, chasing after it, and losing yourself. Forcing myself back to the path of realism, I decided that Sergeant Donaldson was right, and that in the words of the song that's the embarrassing ringtone to my phone, the one I really will change soon, there's always a woman to blame.

I turned to Neil, as he put the last of the reports away in a box file. 'Fancy a drive to the country, Commander?' I asked him.

Before he could answer, my attention was captured by the television mounted on his wall. The BBC News channel was switched on, but the sound was muted as Roland Kramer came into shot, at the podium from which we had seen Grover Bryant make his exit a few hours before, above the caption 'New Prime Minister'.

I grabbed the remote and hit the mute button to restore the sound that we had silenced earlier.

'. . . not a moment for which I ever wished, but it falls upon me to take up the burden left by my late and lamented predecessor. Consequently, I have to tell you now that my first act in the House of Commons as Prime Minister will be to make the announcement which she was scheduled to make yesterday before the chain of events that ended her life, events for which no satisfactory explanation may ever be found. I will not anticipate what I will say tomorrow, other than to forecast that it will take the United Kingdom and indeed the world into a great new era. Thank you.'

He turned and walked away, and as he did, the seed, of a glimmer, of a whisper, of the faintest notion, began to form itself in my mind.

'I wonder,' I whispered.

Thirty-Two

When I'd finished briefing Neil on John Balliol's likely location, and he had gone to take care of his part of our investigation, a wave of tiredness washed over me. It didn't hang around for long, but there was no denying its presence. You'll be aware that I don't admit to the effects of advancing years, just as McIlhenney ignores the restrictions and implications of his diabetes, but they exist for both of us, no question.

I like to relax with exercise, so I decided that I would walk to the Savoy, it being not far from the Met's new headquarters if you head along the Embankment. On the way I munched on a chocolate bar that I'd bought in the canteen, an old-fashioned lump of Cadbury's that the Americans haven't ruined yet, and I thought about seeing Sarah and about how much I love her. She and I have endured some tough times over the years, but we're still around and from now on, God help anyone who tries to get between us.

I thought also about the surprise I was going to spring on her, and wondered how she'd react. The one thing I knew for sure was that she wouldn't be overwhelmed by the importance of the task. I hadn't asked for her just because she's my wife, but because I really do believe she's the best in the slicing and dicing business.

When I'd booked the hotel the clerk had asked for a contact number. I wasn't about to give them my mobile so I gave her the Security Service public number and said that if necessary I could be reached through the Director General's office. When I registered, the people at the desk made a big fuss of me so I guessed that they'd checked me out. I didn't mind that at all; it was my way of warning Amanda that the bill was coming her way!

I hadn't asked for anything fancy, but they gave me a suite, with a view of the river, a big step up from my serviceable but small room in the hotel above a pub. The place was so swish that I felt shabby, and as for my travel-weary clothes, I took care of the latter by using the butler service to have my suit pressed and almost everything else I had worn laundered, and having them procure me a new white shirt from their favoured shop in Jermyn Street, immediate delivery.

As for myself, I soaked in the jacuzzi-style bath for twenty minutes, and took a restorative half-hour catnap. I even had a brief dream; it featured Emily Repton, alive and nasty, as she had been on our first encounter, Roland Kramer, trapped fearfully in a corner by something unseen, Nicholas Wheeler, a face I know only from the media, and bizarrely, Everard Balliol, leering at me as I missed a putt on the golf course on his Highland estate.

He was the one who disturbed me most of all. I awoke with a question in my mind that had nothing to do with the Repton investigation. I'd read of his murder and been unmoved. Everard had been a bully and a tyrant, a man I'd judged to be capable of anything; in short, a dangerous geezer. In my experience people like that are also very careful.

Would Everard really have allowed himself to fall victim to

an opportunistic attack by a member of his own staff? The guy I'd met would not, I judged. So what had really happened to him?

But that was for another day. I rose, shaved, dressed in my new shirt, a blue silk tie, my valeted suit and my shiny, polished shoes and went off to King's Cross Station in an Addison Lee car, to meet my wife.

Happily the train was on time, and the night wasn't too cold. I swept her into the taxi, but didn't tell her our destination. She didn't twig to it until the driver turned off the Strand. She stared at me as he pulled up at the hotel entrance.

'Here?' she exclaimed. 'You bring me here and you didn't warn me? I'd have . . . my hair's a mess, look at how I'm dressed.' Then she smiled. 'But what the hell? I only have three outfits I can get into anyway, and I can do something with my hair.'

'You don't need to do any of that stuff,' I assured her. 'In fact you can dine stark naked if you want. We're eating in our suite; you'll like the view. Come on.'

Her case was small and had four wheels, but a porter commandeered it as soon as we stepped into the foyer. It was unnecessary, but what the hell, it was just another fiver, small beer in that place, I guess.

'This is lovely,' she declared, as she stepped into our accommodation. The lights were low, the curtains were undrawn and the Thames flowed before us, beyond the trees.

'This is the Winston Churchill Suite,' I told her. 'Before you ask, there isn't even a hint of cigar smoke.'

She looked around. 'They could fit his whole family in here,' she murmured. 'Bob, you are a darling man, but are you ever going to tell me what this is about?'

'Let's eat first. Get naked if you want, but you might prefer to wait until the waiters have left.'

She compromised by wrapping herself in one of the hotel's soft white bathrobes. I wonder how many of those hang in wardrobes around the world.

I had ordered a light supper, given the hour, with sparkling water. Obviously Sarah wasn't drinking wine so far into her pregnancy . . . in fact she stopped on the day she did the test . . . and I show solidarity with her, in her presence. It was even less of a hardship than usual; I wanted to keep a clear head.

Finally when we were done, and had seen enough of the passing marine traffic, it was time to come clean.

'So,' she asked, 'what is this all about? Are you preparing me for news I don't want to hear that you're going to accept this job offer of Aileen's?'

'It isn't her offer,' I pointed out. 'It comes from Merlin Brady, the leader of her party.'

'The left-winger everybody says isn't electable?'

'He probably isn't,' I admitted, 'but I've met him and I like him. He's a sincere guy; hopelessly naive, but sincere. His isn't the only offer, as it happens; I discovered yesterday that our cunning First Minister's been plotting to get me in there as a cross-bencher, in the hope that I'll back his objectives.'

'You are in demand,' she murmured, tugging the robe closer around her. 'Come on, man, out with it, which one are you going to take?'

I smiled into her eyes. 'I'm not going to take anything that you don't want me to; you know that.'

'That isn't an answer,' she pointed out. 'You're tempted, aren't you?'

I nodded. 'I'm flattered; that much I will admit. Not by Clive

Graham's machinations, I'd never go for that, since it would be fundamentally dishonest, but as I said, I do like Brady, and I can see that he has a job that needs doing. His leader in the Lords is very able and very useless at one and the same time. I'm not a member of his party and I've never voted for it, but if the objective was to remove the son of a bitch who's just slithered into power, that's something I would love to do.'

I winked at her and grinned again. 'But I might be able to do that,' I told her, 'without joining Merlin's team. A lot has happened in the last thirty-six hours, and I'm wrapped up in it.'

I took my temporary MI5 badge of office from my pocket and laid it on the table. Sarah picked it up and studied it, a frown forming then deepening as she read it, and absorbed its meaning.

'She's pulled you in!' she exclaimed, indignantly. 'The Dennis woman has been trying to recruit you since you left the police, but I didn't think you were interested. In fact,' she said, and there was a challenge in her voice, 'you promised me that you weren't.'

'I haven't broken that promise,' I assured her, 'but this was something I couldn't refuse. Since midday yesterday, Neil McIlhenney and I have been investigating what has turned out to be the killing of Emily Repton.'

'I think you'd better . . .'

I nodded as her whisper faltered, then I took her through the whole story, step by step, move by move. When I'd finished she was silent for a while, then said, 'You think this man Balliol killed her? Is that what you're saying?'

'That's what the evidence suggests, and more than that, there's further clear evidence of a conspiracy to cover it up. Neil's on Balliol now; I'm not going to move yet, but when we're ready we'll take him. I need to get somebody else out of the game before then.'

'Is this dangerous?' she asked.

'If I thought it was,' I replied, 'you wouldn't have set one tiny toe outside of Gullane.'

'Then why am I here?'

'Why do you think?' I grinned. 'I want you to do what you do best . . . well,' I added, after a moment's reflection, 'second best. A prime minister deserves the top people, even after she's dead.'

Thirty-Three

*L*ou called me at five minutes to midnight; by then I'd been watching John Balliol's so-called cottage for four and a half hours. That might have been what Bob had called it, and the sign at the end of the drive might have read 'Greystone Cottage', but in reality it was a substantial country house, set in a few acres of land.

There was a rough track along what I took to be a boundary, from the satellite image that I'd printed out. After I'd sussed the place out, as carefully as I could in the darkness, I'd found a spot where I could park up out of anyone's sight, and from which I had a clear view of anyone arriving or leaving the house.

I'd come prepared for a siege; sandwiches, fruit, diet Red Bull and other sugar-free drinks, biscuits, and also a supply of plastic bottles to piss in, as necessary. In truth I was excited. I hadn't been on a proper stake-out in years. I'd gone along on a couple of occasions when the time had come for my undercover officers to take their targets down, but then I'd been more or less an observer. Being involved, keeping concealed watch on a suspect was different, something I'd enjoyed in the junior ranks, and which I thought had been gone for good.

Mind you, while I was up for the task, I wasn't quite sure why

I was doing it. Given what we knew about Balliol, my view had been, 'Get him, sweat him, close the case,' but Bob hadn't wanted to do that.

'Too many imponderables,' he had said. 'We have no physical record of Balliol being in Repton's room, only the word of Mickey Satchell and the intimidation of Joe Coffrey. They're both flakes, the sort of witness you dread exposing to an aggressive defence counsel. Coffrey's terrified, and Mickey will probably say anything she thought would benefit her career. I want the whole package, and most of all I want the whole story.

'Look, Neil,' he had argued, 'we have a certain advantage here. Nobody knows what we're doing, other than Hamblin. I don't want to blow that, and that's what we'd do by hauling in Balliol for questioning at this stage. For that's all it would be; he would hide behind the most expensive lawyers he could find and would be back on the street in half an hour. For now, let's just watch him, see where he goes, what he does, whom he visits, who visits him.'

I could have stuck to my guns, and overridden him; I was a serving police officer, he was a civilian with an uncertain legal status. But I didn't. If I took my case to Sir Feargal, I wasn't sure he would back me, and anyway, Bob was probably right; he usually was.

So there I was, munching a banana by moonlight at damn near midnight when my phone flashed in its dashboard socket; 'Louise', the screen proclaimed.

'I just found your note,' she said, when I answered her summons. 'Underneath the half-bottle of Lanson, which is currently chilling. You're involved in an operation and don't know when you'll be back? How many CID wives are spun that story, I wonder, with or without the champagne persuader? It's lucky for you I know that

Bob Skinner's involved. With him, anything's possible. That man will never change.'

Although my wife and Bob go back more than thirty years, to university when he was a final-year student and she was a fresher, straight from school, I've never asked either of them about the extent of their relationship, because it's ancient history, and frankly because I don't want to know, but it's pretty clear from what she's told me that they had the hots for each other.

It didn't last because Bob had another girlfriend, Myra, who became Alex's mother, a girl he'd known from his school days who was a student teacher through in Edinburgh, sowing plenty of her own wild oats, or so I've heard. When they parted it was amicable; Lou's acting ambitions were very strong by that time, and Bob's heart was set on a police career. His loss, eventually my gain.

'Is he with you?' she asked.

'No, this is a solo mission.'

'So he's tucked up in bed somewhere,' she laughed, 'while you're freezing your nuts off watching some low-life scum.'

'Not low life; far from it, in fact. And as for big Bob's surroundings, not any old surroundings; the Savoy, no less.'

'Bloody hell, we can't afford that, and we're not skint.'

'There's a reason for that,' I assured her. 'Sarah's with him. And we can afford it,' I added. 'I promise you a night there, soon.'

'You will be held to that, McIlhenney. Where are you anyway? Or is that hush-hush too?'

'I'm somewhere south of Watford,' I replied. 'At least I think it is. You know my geography; it's shite.'

'Why did you take my car, and not your own?'

'It's compact, it's unobtrusive and finally I've found a use for its four-by-four capability.'

'Don't bend it.'

'I'll try not to; if I do, the Met'll fix it. Enjoy the champagne.'

'I may keep it for your return. One glass won't hurt you. Take care. Night, love you.'

'You too.'

My job satisfaction dimmed more than somewhat as I ended the call, wishing I was back home . . . even though one glass would probably hurt me, my diabetes being just a wee bit more problematic than I let on.

Greystone Cottage seemed to have settled down for the night, after a pretty unremarkable evening. The only three arrivals had been a van, delivering sushi, according to its side panels, a motorcyclist, dropping off a pizza order, and finally a sleek dark BMW saloon. A dark-haired woman in a tight-fitting black dress had emerged from the back seat, door opened for her by the peak-capped driver, and gone inside, her only luggage being a small vanity case. I fired off several frames with my Nikon, hoping that its night setting would steal enough light from the open door of Greystone Cottage to yield an identifiable image.

I took an educated guess at her function, and her profession, reminding myself of the fundamental truth that while money can't buy love, it can rent some pretty spectacular alternatives.

Through an upper window, I had caught a glimpse of a man I took to be Balliol, from his age and general description. He'd been pacing up and down, a phone pressed to his ear; the call lasted for over ten minutes, and he wasn't smiling when it was over.

The food orders had been accepted by a black-clad oriental . . . or possibly by two for I couldn't be sure that it had been the same man on each occasion. Bob had told me that John Balliol's father Everard had maintained a cadre of Korean bodyguards. It seemed that his heir was keeping up the family tradition, a remarkably generous act, given that one of them had gone rogue and killed his employer before vanishing without a subsequent trace.

Twelve thirty came and went, then 1 a.m., with one light showing through a carelessly drawn curtain. Finally, at one ten, that went out also.

Greystone Cottage had settled down for the night; I took a piss in one of my bottles, set my alarm to wake me at five thirty, and then followed suit.

Thirty-Four

I felt guilty about arguing Neil out of hauling John Balliol in for questioning, and even more so about asking him to camp outside the guy's house, but I had convinced myself that if we were ever going to get to the truth of Emily Repton's death, it would be through him.

That said, I didn't feel so guilty that it got in the way of my enjoying my night in the opulence of the Savoy with my lovely wife. Sarah loved it too, once she had come to terms with the job she was being asked to do the next day.

The river was still flowing slowly towards the sea when we woke next morning. I had just ordered breakfast when Neil called my mobile. If you can sound stiff in a phone call, he did, and tired too.

'There's nothing doing,' he reported. 'The curtains are all open now, the ones I can see, and I have a good view into the house. Balliol doesn't appear to have any staff other than the three Koreans I've counted so far, unless you count the woman who left ten minutes ago in the same Beamer that dropped her off last night.'

'Koreans?' I said.

'Family loyalty, I guess.'

'Will you be able to ID the woman?' I asked.

He recited the registration plate of the vehicle that had picked her up. I noted it, to be passed to Amanda for tracing.

'I have a couple of images too,' he added. 'I have a usable one from this morning.'

'Send it to me, if you can; I'm sure you're right. She's not his chiropractor. But she has been inside the house; that could be useful. Anything else?'

'Just one observation,' he replied. 'So far, I've got five people inside the house, including the lady, who did not just come for dinner, I imagine. Given that, they had a hell of a lot of sushi and pizza delivered last night, more than enough for that number of people.'

'Maybe he's throwing a party for the Aldermaston Spitfire team after the announcement this afternoon,' I suggested.

'Trust you to curb my enthusiasm,' he grunted, 'but you could be right.'

But maybe I wasn't, I thought, after I'd signed off, promising Neil I'd get down there as soon as I could to relieve him. I suspected that I'd slipped down Lou's Christmas card list by several notches, and she's not someone I'd ever want to upset, not again.

I passed on the registration number to Amanda; yes, she was up and about that early, or at least her mobile was. I forwarded Neil's photograph too. It may have been we were miscalling the woman by labelling her as an escort, but anyone who leaves a billionaire's pad in a hundred-grand auto wearing a five-grand designer dress in perfect make-up and with not a hair out of place at 7.45 a.m. is unlikely to be an amateur, whatever her game.

'Who's that?' Sarah's question took me by surprise, I hadn't heard her leave the bedroom, but she had and was looking over my shoulder at my phone.

'It's not Mother Teresa.'

'Dunno,' my wife murmured, 'she looks as if she could perform miracles.'

I let that one pass. While she went off to shower and get ready for her day, I called someone else I hoped would be an early riser. And he was; Sir Feargal Aherne had been in his office since seven, he told me, perusing the morning's media.

'Have you seen the coverage?' he asked.

'No, but I can guess how it looks. I had a call from my managing editor on the *Saltire* yesterday afternoon. It went to voicemail, and I chose not to return it.'

'Probably wise,' the Commissioner observed. 'It's as if everything happened so fast yesterday, the PM's death followed almost immediately by the coronation of Kramer, that it took the news desks by surprise. But now they've caught up and the questions are coming thick and fast, demanding to know what happened to Emily.

'I've agreed with Kramer and the Mayor that everything will be channelled through my press office for the moment. I've instructed that we hold to the line that there will be no detailed statement until the cause of Ms Repton's death is established by post-mortem examination.'

An alarm bell rang in my head. 'Hold on, Feargal,' I said. 'I don't want Sarah besieged by a howling mob of journos.'

'She won't be,' he assured me. 'The media will expect the autopsy to be performed at the Westminster Mortuary, which is state of the art. It won't be. I had the body transferred during the night to the facility in Papworth Hospital near Cambridge; that's where it will be done.'

'You'll need a police witness at the autopsy,' I pointed out, 'but Neil McIlhenney's keeping an eye on John Balliol and I plan to go down there to relieve him.'

'I know,' he said. 'This is a prime minister we're dealing with. I propose to observe myself; I think that's appropriate. I will collect Professor Grace from the Savoy at nine thirty, if that's okay with you.'

'It's fine; it leaves both of us free to concentrate on the jobs in hand.'

'Is there anything else you need from me?'

'In an ideal world, I'd like you to detain Mickey Satchell. She's the only witness to Balliol entering Repton's room, given the destruction of the CCTV evidence, but I suspect she's going to decline to identify him. We caught her off guard yesterday, but she's had a chance to regroup.'

'Why would she refuse?'

'As soon as she does, she incriminates herself as part of a conspiracy.'

'That's what you think this was?' Sir Feargal exclaimed. 'A conspiracy to murder?'

'That's the way it looks.'

'Are there witnesses against her?' he asked.

'There is one, who may be able to put her outside Repton's room, when the man we think was Balliol entered. He only saw her, not him.'

'Is this witness reliable?'

If we'd been on Skype, he'd have seen me wince. 'I think so, but that's when it gets really hairy. At this stage, Feargal, you don't want to know any more than I've told you so far. I don't want to involve my man unless it's unavoidable; if I can find physical evidence that puts Balliol in the room, where he's supposed never to have been, that'll be enough for us to detain him meaningfully, without involving anyone else.'

'Then let's hope for the best.'

'Yeah,' I sighed. 'Let's hope. In the meantime, there's someone else I want to confront, or at least meet: Nicholas Wheeler. He's been missing from his apartment for forty-eight hours, his car's gone too, and I'm having trouble buying his protection team's assumption that he's holed up with a woman, licking his wounds. His career as a minister may have hit the buffers, but he's still an MP. As such he has an agent in his constituency; I checked with her last night and she told me she didn't know where he is either.'

'Could she have been told not to say?'

'It's possible, if she's a very skilled liar, but there was anxiety in her voice and I don't think she was faking it.'

'You see him as part of this conspiracy?' the Commissioner asked.

'He could be. He's one of a very small circle of knowledge on Spitfire.'

'So was Emily Repton; she was about to announce the new weapon system in parliament, and the man Balliol was its parent, so to speak. Why conspire against her?'

'That I don't know,' I admitted. 'It's the missing piece. Kramer will deny all knowledge; now he's in the big seat we probably won't even get to put the question. His bodyguard Daffyd Evans, the man we suspect of forcing Coffrey to take Balliol's visit off CCTV, he's not contactable. I've spoken to the Chancellor, who more or less shrugged his shoulders, fed me a line about challenging Kramer for the leadership and then did nothing when it came to the crunch. If I'm going to get inside this thing I need to speak to Wheeler. He may know nothing that'll solve the mystery, but I need to ask.'

'There's one way, you know,' Sir Feargal murmured, 'that might help you find him.'

'Go on,' I said.

'Where's his car, Wheeler's car, do you know?'

'I've never asked the question. What's the relevance? Do we even know he has one in London?'

'He has; it's an original Mark Ten Jaguar, bloody big beast, and it's housed in a secure garage below his apartment block. I know this, because it became a matter of concern to the protection group.

'The Defence Secretary is always viewed as a high-risk target, always has been for as long as the post has existed, first for the generally disaffected and in the modern era for global terrorism. His protection officers don't like him driving alone, but Wheeler has always insisted on going off piste on the road, as he does with his love life.

'The strongest representations were made to me about it. I tried to persuade him, but he insisted on a degree of freedom and personal privacy. He laughed, and said that even if he did have a detective with him in the car, he'd still be at risk because of the way he drives.

'He's a pleasant young man, but he wouldn't be persuaded. I went over his head; I went to the Prime Minister's office, but Ms Repton refused to intervene.'

'So?' I asked. 'How did you get around it? For it's clear that you did.'

'I did what I did when a similar situation arose during my time as head of the Police Service of Northern Ireland. A particularly recalcitrant minister of state in the Northern Ireland Office took exactly the same line as Mr Wheeler. The reckless bugger had a mistress and thought we didn't know about her,' he explained.

'Even in the modern era in Ireland, with a much lower threat level than at the height of what they still call the Troubles, the man's behaviour was suicidal. So I told my security people to put a tracker in his car, without him ever being aware. And I did the same with Wheeler. I had to be a little discreet, since technically it involved breaking and entering; his protection officers don't even know it's there.'

'You put a bug in a Cabinet minister's car?' I laughed.

'Yes,' he declared, with something like pride in his voice. 'I won't have anything happen to these people on my watch, not if I can prevent it. Most modern vehicles have trackers fitted anyway; his, being a vintage model, didn't.'

'How effective is it?

'If it's tucked away under six storeys of housing, there might be a loss of signal. But if it isn't, we should be able to find it. I'll put people on it as soon as they come in, and get back to you as soon as I can. I agree with your summary; finding Wheeler has become imperative.'

I left him to keep this promise and went to tell Sarah of the arrangements he had made for the autopsy. Then I did the obvious; I called all of the personal numbers I had been given for Nicholas Wheeler, his flat, his home in his Gloucestershire constituency, and his mobile, to check whether he'd surfaced overnight. The home numbers went to voicemail, and the mobile was switched off.

I rang his agent too, on the mobile number she'd given me, but all I got out of that was an earful from an irritable husband, a crusty sod who snapped that his wife was in the lavatory, and that she hadn't heard from her boss since the last time she and I had spoken. He added that as far as he was concerned, Mr Wheeler could stay absent without leave for as long as he liked, as his business took up far too much of his wife's off-duty hours. I had some sympathy with that view; during my marriage to Aileen, she had seemed to spend half her life on phone calls with her agent. At least that's what she told me; maybe it had been Joey Morocco.

Breakfast arrived just as Sarah emerged from the bathroom. We took time to do it justice, and I studied her carefully as we ate. I had begun to worry that I was asking too much of her. She was excited by the job in hand. Was she too excited? That was my worry.

As often she does, she read my mind. 'Relax,' she said. 'I'm fine. I'm a doctor, remember; I know how to monitor myself and I do, on a daily basis. My blood pressure is on the low side of normal, and I had a kidney function test last week which was clear on all counts.'

Reassured, I took some time to glance at the newspapers that had arrived with the breakfast trolley. Sir Feargal hadn't exaggerated. 'PM Death Mystery' in the *Daily Telegraph* was the most restrained headline I saw. Even the *Financial Times* was excited. 'Repton Passing and Kramer Accession Rock Markets', it declared.

Most of the stories quoted Grover Bryant's Downing Street announcement and no more, but *The Times* may have been his favourite, for its political editor carried additional lines in his piece. They didn't say much, but made it ominously clear that Bryant would not be content until the full circumstances of his half-sister's death had been established.

Nevertheless, the tropical illness story seemed to be holding, just. 'Inexplicable', the *Sun* described it, breaking its usual syllable limit.

In a few hours' time that would all change, once Sarah had done her work. How would it be announced, I wondered, and by whom? My guess was that Kramer would insist on taking the lead, setting the agenda rather than reacting to it.

Events were finely balanced for our new Prime Minister; his rush to make the Spitfire announcement interested me. I've learned a bit about news management since I joined InterMedia and one principle that I understand is that if there's a big story that you have an interest in burying, the best way to do that is by finding another one.

The truth about Emily's death would have to come out in some form, but as long as Balliol couldn't be linked to it, and as long as no motive emerged, Kramer's version would be accepted.

He was the man perched at the top of the pyramid, as I had observed. It was built of pebbles, but as long as they all stayed in place, he would be fine.

The first one shifted when my mobile rang, and I saw that the caller was Hamblin.

'I have some interesting news for you,' he began. He was a man so not given to excitement that when he did show some, it had a hint of hysteria. 'The Number Ten phone records; I have gone through them and one call stands out, made by the Prime Minister on her private line, at twenty-five past midnight, to Nicholas Wheeler, at his flat.'

'Oh yes,' I exclaimed, his excitement infecting me, 'and as soon as it was over, Wheeler kicked out his protection officers. What about hers?'

'I have no idea,' Hamblin replied, 'but I did summon the night duty police officers as soon as their shift ended this morning. Miss Fortescue sent for them, privately. Under, shall we say, forceful questioning, one of them admitted that he let

Ms Repton out of Downing Street, by a back entrance that goes into Horseguards, at twelve thirty-five. This has happened on other occasions, he confessed.'

'Oh you fucking beauty,' I laughed. 'Are there any politicians in Westminster who aren't sleeping with other politicians?'

'I believe you Scots have a saying,' he murmured, 'of which the punchline is, "Damn few and they're all dead." Am I right?'

'Close enough for the cigar, Cabinet Secretary. We know that her protection team dropped her at the Commons at a quarter to ten. Did they pick her up from Wheeler's?'

'No, she seems to have walked back. She re-entered the building by the front door at ten to eight, carrying a Costa coffee beaker and a bag that the night duty officer thought contained croissants. She'd have been unobserved by the media at that time.'

'I hope she enjoyed them,' I told him. 'They could well have been her last meal.'

'Does that take you forward, Bob?' he asked. We had attained solid first-name terms, a major advance on our first encounter.

'Oh yes, it does. Think about it. Emily spent the night with Nick Wheeler; twelve hours later she was dying and he was missing. I don't do coincidences, Norman. It leaves me hoping that another pebble will be dislodged. When it is, the whole damn lot might come tumbling down.'

Thirty-Five

I was more than a wee bit grumpy when Bob called me just before eight; my enthusiasm of the night before had vanished, as gradually I had been reminded of the realities of being in the field (almost literally in this case) with only a watching brief. The big man's calmness didn't help. His equanimity had been restored, but a night in the Savoy will do that for you every time.

Mine had gone to hell in a handcart. It rolled even further down the pathway when I broached the theory that there might have been more people in the house than we knew about, based on the amount of food that had been delivered. His instant response, that the team from nearby Aldermaston would have something to celebrate in the afternoon when Kramer took the wraps off Spitfire, was one that would have occurred to me had my brain been working even at seventy-five per cent efficiency.

Still, I was chuffed with what I had achieved, particularly the clear, identifiable shot of the lady who had visited Greystone Cottage overnight. Even in early breaking daylight she was a looker. Balliol's accountant? They usually carry briefcases, not make-up bags. His companion? Probably. A performance bonus for one of the Koreans? Unlikely.

She may have no part to play in the story, I thought, woozily, but if Bob's friend Amanda, or my boss Sir Feargal, could trace her, she might be able to tell us how much of that sushi had gone in the fridge.

Yes, I really was feeling woozy for an hour or so after Bob ended our update with a promise to come down to relieve me as soon as he could. I'd miscalculated the amount of food I'd need, given that I'd managed a bit less than two hours' sleep through the night, and my blood sugar levels were in danger of joining my equanimity on that handcart to hell.

I do have tablets for the condition, a drug called chlorpropamide that's supposed to help my pancreas produce more insulin, but it's an aid not a cure, and if my sugar levels were getting low, what I really needed was a bag of boiled sweets, something I did not have.

Or maybe I was just having a panic attack, for the sound of wheels crunching along the drive snapped me back into wakefulness and made me put my problems on hold.

I trained my binoculars on the turning circle in front of the house, just as a small white hatchback came into view, then drew to a halt. As a man climbed out of the driver's seat I grabbed my camera, focused quickly through its long lens and was able to fire off several shots as he straightened up, then walked towards the stone steps that rose up to the portico. The door opened as he approached and he stepped inside; not a casual caller then, someone who was expected.

And someone who was familiar to me; I'd seen him before, I knew it. A young man, early thirties, with fair hair. I studied the images I had captured on my Nikon's small screen, and chose the one that gave the best view of the caller's face. It wasn't as well defined as my shot of the woman, but I zoomed it in and peered at it. Yes, familiar, but what was the context?

And then I remembered. When I'd recruited Shafat Iqbal, my

undercover currency trader, he'd been positively vetted. That means we hadn't simply looked at his financial affairs, we'd looked at him too, without his knowledge, followed him during his off-duty time, to ensure that he really was who he claimed to be.

I'd seen all the photographs, including several of his fiancé; a couple of those had included a white car, a BMW hatchback. I couldn't remember the registration plate, but I could remember its owner, and I was looking at him in those images; James Ellis, the son of the Chancellor of the Exchequer.

But what the hell was he doing there?

My first instinct was to call Bob, but I thought better of it almost at once. Instead I set out to answer the questions that I knew he'd be bound to ask, and one in particular.

I took my phone from its holder in the dashboard and flashed through my contacts, stopping at one who was listed only as 'SI', then hitting the call button.

'Sergeant Iqbal,' I began as he answered, 'it's Commander McIlhenney. Can you speak?'

There was traffic noise in the background, but his voice was clear. 'Yes, boss,' he replied: I don't like being called 'guv', or 'guv'nor' and all my people know it. 'I'm cycling to work, but my helmet's Bluetooth. What's up? You're not going to pull me in, are you? I'm nearly there, boss, honest.'

'It's okay,' I assured him. 'This is something else; I'm going to ask you a couple of questions. They cannot be discussed with anyone else, repeat anyone. Understood?'

'Got that, sir.' His breathing was heavier as if he was pedalling up an incline.

'In your household, yours and James's, has there ever been any discussion of something called Spitfire? That's discussion to which you'd been a party, or discussion that you may have overheard?'

'Hold on,' he gasped. 'Big hill; I'm going to pull over.' I waited until he was ready, letting him gather his breath.

'Not directly,' he replied, his voice almost back to normal, 'but there was one time, I walked into the kitchen on Saturday morning. James and his dad were there, and I heard Les use that word. James started to reply, then stopped again. He just said, "Nah, nothing," or something like that. I thought no more of it.'

'Okay. Second question. Has a man named John Balliol ever been mentioned there?'

'John Balliol?' he repeated. 'An American? Sharp-dressed fellow?'

'That fits his description; thirties, intense look about him.'

'Yes, he has. Not only mentioned,' Iqbal added, 'he's been there, let me think, three weekends ago. He arrived mid-afternoon on the Sunday; Les took him into his study and James joined them there. I wasn't invited.'

'Was there anyone else at that meeting?'

'Was there ever. The Home Secretary turned up, complete with a minder; that's the man who became Prime Minister yesterday. Not just him, either; Radley, the Foreign Secretary, he was there too.'

'Anybody else? Any other Cabinet ministers?'

'There was another guy; he was last to arrive. He turned up in a bloody big classic Jaguar. Lovely car; light blue. I don't know what he was, for we weren't introduced, but when James met him at the door he said, "Hello, Nick." Then he took him into the meeting.'

'How long did James stay in there?'

'All the way through; afterwards I asked him what it was about. All he said was that it was government business, and that his father wanted a note kept of the meeting.'

'Isn't that what the Civil Service is for?' I pondered.

'I had the same thought,' Iqbal said. 'Commander,' he paused as a heavy vehicle passed by, waiting for its noise to fade into the distance, 'what's this about, and why is our unit interested in it?'

'We're not,' I told him, abruptly. 'I am. Do you know where James is now?'

'I don't. All I do know is that he left earlier than usual this morning. I asked him what was up. He glowered and said, "Crisis bloody management." Then he was gone. Is he in trouble, boss?'

'I don't know. Don't ask him either, ever. This conversation never happened, Shafat. I am very serious about that.'

'Understood, boss.'

'On your assignment,' I asked, to get him off the subject, as much as for any pressing need to know, 'you said you're nearly there. Can you put that in a timeframe?'

'There's a meeting next Wednesday. Once I find out who's going to be there, I'll know better. If we get all the right people in the room, that could be the moment to close them down.'

'OK, report back as soon as you do know.'

I ended the call and looked back at Greystone Cottage. The white Beamer was still there, but one of the Koreans was standing in the portico. On guard? That's how it looked.

I went back to my phone and called Bob. 'I think you should get down here,' I said, 'soon as you can. James Ellis is paying a surprise visit to his friend Balliol. When you come, bring me some sandwiches, bananas and boiled sweets. I'm staying for the duration.'

Thirty-Six

Amanda Dennis is a hard person to surprise, in my experience, but when I called her just after Sarah had been collected by Sir Feargal, I pulled it off twice; first when I told her about Emily Repton's early hours' walkabout habit, and again when I revealed her destination.

'She was eleven years older than him,' she exclaimed, more than a little naively, I thought.

'Did you really say that?' I laughed. 'A woman who had a relationship with her son's pal?'

'I suppose,' she conceded. 'But . . . my God, I hope the new administration takes a more responsible approach to personal security than hers did.'

'Give her a break; Wheeler too,' I argued. 'Single people in the public eye must have a hell of a job sustaining a private life, politicians more than any other. If they want to get laid they can hardly do what Balliol did.'

'Oh no?' she chuckled. 'You should see some of the stuff we have on file.'

'Have you traced that woman, by the way?' I asked. 'The one Neil photographed?'

'Her and the car. You were right, it was private hire and so was she. Her name is Amelie Tinker, she's Spanish and she's pretty exclusive. She lives in Madrid, and uses an agent, who provides her services to men with net worth of no less than twenty million sterling. Five grand a night plus a business-class air fare might be a lot to ordinary mortals, but it's pocket change to the likes of Balliol. By the time we traced her car, it was on its way back to its base from Gatwick and she was in flight.'

'If we need her can we reach her?'

'I'm sure we can,' she said. 'One call to her agent should be enough; he won't want to get on the wrong side of the likes of us. If it isn't, I can call my opposite number in the Spanish Interior Ministry; but the agent will know that, so he'll cooperate.'

'Keep that on hold for now,' I replied. 'I've just had Neil on the line; there's something else we need to find out if we can. Why did James Ellis turn up at Greystone Cottage half an hour after Señorita Tinker left?'

'The Chancellor's son?' she exclaimed. 'What the hell's he doing there?'

'A bit of crisis management was what he told his boyfriend. I'm now wondering whether it relates in any way to a gathering held three Sundays ago in the Chancellor's house in Wimbledon. There were five participants: Ellis, Kramer, Radley, Wheeler and Balliol. They met in the Chancellor's study and the minute was taken by Ellis Junior.'

'They met without Emily Repton?'

'Yes, and I can only assume that they did it away from Westminster so that she wouldn't find out about it, and maybe also to keep Norman Hamblin in the dark.'

'A secret within a secret?'

'Yes. I really do need to gather these people in now; Balliol at the very least.'

'Then I have some good news for you,' Amanda exclaimed. 'We have grounds. The CSI team has put him in the room. They found a right palm print on the back of the toilet seat; the right index finger matches the print that Balliol uses to access the development lab at Aldermaston.'

If she hadn't been on the end of a mobile phone connection, I'd have hugged her. 'Lovely,' I whispered. 'How did you get hold of that?'

'I have a colleague in the Ministry of Defence. Sometimes interdepartmental cooperation works, Bob. Now tell me, how do you want to go about this?'

'As quietly as we can,' I replied. 'Ideally Neil and I would go in there, arrest Balliol, and take him somewhere, probably back to Westminster since that's where the crime took place, for questioning.'

'What stops it from being ideal?' she asked.

'Those Koreans,' I replied. I smiled. 'Okay, there are only three of them as far as Neil can tell. He and I aren't so old that we can't handle them, but a uniformed presence might deter any . . . unpleasantness.'

'That would raise the visibility of the operation,' Amanda pointed out.

'I think we're past the point of discretion,' I countered. 'We have grounds to arrest Balliol on suspicion of murder, without the need for a warrant. I'll ask Neil to get some officers from the local force to attend, complete with lights and sirens.'

'Leave that to me,' she said. 'What will you do about James Ellis?'

'If he's still there when we go in? Nothing, unless he gets in the way. We've got no grounds to detain him.'

'How will you get Balliol back to London?'

'In the car you're going to send for me. You can do that, can't you?'

'No problem.'

As she spoke, my phone buzzed, telling me that another caller was trying to reach me. I asked her to wait while I checked the screen. It was the Commissioner, calling, I supposed, from his car en route to Cambridge with Sarah.

I put Amanda on hold, and took his call. 'Bob,' he began. His voice was a little raised; he sounded excited. 'My people have located Wheeler's car. It's stationary, in the grounds of Greystone Cottage.'

'Jesus,' I exclaimed. 'Wait a second, Feargal; I have Amanda Dennis on hold, and I'm going to try to make this a three-way call.'

I fiddled with my mobile, and managed to pull it off. When we could all hear each other, I asked the Commissioner to repeat his message.

'Nicholas Wheeler's with Balliol?' Amanda murmured. 'Let me line this up in my head. Emily spent the night with him. She left before eight to walk back to Downing Street and he went AWOL. Three hours later, Balliol was shown into her office and tried to kill her. Now we discover that Wheeler went to his place.'

'Yes,' I said. 'That call she had from the untraceable mobile: we thought it had to be from Kramer, but could it have been Wheeler who made it?'

'In these new circumstances, that might be a reasonable assumption,' Sir Feargal observed. 'What are the consequences?'

'Amanda and I are agreed that it's time to arrest Balliol; that's what we were discussing. I'd say that if we find Wheeler there we take him too.'

'Do you have grounds?'

'Has that always worried you in the past?' I challenged him. 'I've arrested people in my time just because they were out of place.'

'Touché,' he conceded. 'Bob, given your shady authority in this matter, I think you can pretty much do what you like. You should call in any support you feel you need, either from the local force or from the Met; this is no time to be getting prissy about territorial boundaries. But do it fast; as soon as the professor has completed her examination and established the cause of death, I will have no alternative but to go public with it.'

'Understood. Sarah,' I asked, 'can you hear this?'

'Yes,' she called out.

'Then do us a favour, honey. I know you're always meticulous during an autopsy, but double-check everything this time.'

'You mean go as slow as I can get away with?'

'You said it, not me.'

I disconnected the Commissioner from the conference call and went back to Amanda. 'How soon can you send your car?' I asked. 'I need to get down there now.'

'If you're ready, I'll give the order now. Do you want the driver to be armed? I'm thinking about the unpredictability of Balliol's Korean entourage.'

'Not unless I am too. I always feel safer when I'm the one holding the firearm.'

'That will be arranged,' she said. 'Twenty minutes at the outside. It'll be a black Range Rover. Big enough for you, McIlhenney and two detainees.'

'Good enough. I'll call Neil now while you make arrangements for the uniforms. I heard what Feargal said about using the Met, but it'll be quicker if we rely on the locals for the show of force.'

I let her go to do her thing and called Neil. I updated him on the Wheeler development, and promised that I'd be with him as soon as possible . . . with his sandwiches and boiled sweets straight from the Savoy. I was about to tell him about the uniformed presence when he cut in.

'Hold on, Bob,' he murmured, quietly, 'there's action here: someone else arriving. I've got eyes on him now. Bloody hell!' I heard him whisper. 'Is that who . . .'

'Who?' I hissed, impatiently.

'I've only seen the man once,' he replied, 'on Monday morning in the House of Commons, but I'm pretty sure it's Kramer's bloke, Daffyd Evans.'

'What's he . . .' I began, then stopped, for I knew I wasn't going to come up with an innocent explanation. If it was Evans, and Neil wouldn't have made the identification without being more than 'pretty sure', it added a darker shade to the situation.

'Wait for me,' I ordered. 'Do nothing else until I get there, but leave your phone on and make sure it's charged. I may use it to pinpoint you when we arrive.'

I called Amanda back at once and told her of the new arrival. 'That changes things,' she declared, instantly. 'It'll be two cars, for I'm coming myself, with support. Daffyd will definitely be armed; therefore we will be too. He may have Downing Street protection, but in these circumstances I'm going to regard him as one of mine who's gone rogue.'

Thirty-Seven

She called off the blues and twos. The arrival of Evans was a direct link to the new Prime Minister, and made discretion mandatory. Amanda insisted on it. Not only would the arrival of a noisy contingent of the local Mr Plod have spooked everyone in the house, she declared, it would have introduced unscreened witnesses to a situation that of necessity had to be contained.

As a former police officer I might have taken issue with her, but I didn't. The vast majority of the women and men I'd known, worked with, and commanded were honourable people who would keep their mouths shut when required, without question, but if there was ever someone I wasn't sure of I never took a risk. If we'd called in uniforms from that location, I wouldn't have known any of them.

Two cars, black Range Rovers with a menacing look about them, arrived at the hotel; the back door of the first opened and I slid in alongside Amanda, seated directly behind her driver. The rear car, I'd noted, also had two occupants.

'Everybody armed?' I asked as we moved off.

She nodded, and opened a box-like compartment on the floor of the vehicle; it contained three identical handguns and three magazines. I took one out and studied it; a Browning Hi

331

Power, tried and trusted. I knew the weapon, having fired it on the range more often than I care to remember, and in action that I'll never forget.

'If Evans tries to leave before we get there,' she said, 'I'd like McIlhenney to intercept him at the gateway.'

'Not going to happen,' I replied, firmly. 'Neil's unarmed, he's had little or no sleep, and he's not in the best of shape. I'm not putting him at risk. If Evans leaves, we let him go. I'll find him myself, later, if necessary. But if he doesn't leave,' I added, 'how do we handle him?'

'That will depend on how he handles us. If he behaves himself, we'll take him back to Thames House for interview.'

'And Balliol, Wheeler if he's there, James Ellis?'

She bounced it back at me. 'What do you think?'

'We should separate Balliol from the others; he has to be cautioned formally at the scene by Neil, then he should go to a police office . . . the Met HQ or Westminster Police Station, whichever Feargal says . . . for interview and charge. Wheeler and Ellis go to Thames House with Evans.'

She nodded. 'I'll go with that. This situation is not the norm for me; it makes me all the more pleased that you agreed to come in on it.'

'I'm not sure I was given a choice,' I reminded her.

'Come on,' she chided me, 'you could have walked away at any time; you didn't want to, that's the truth of it.'

She took a tablet from her bag, one of those big Apple Pro jobs that don't make sense to me when for the same money you can buy a proper laptop. 'Take a look at these images,' she said. 'You haven't met any of these people, so you should have sight of them before we get there.'

She fired up the device and opened a folder containing three images; each was of a man, all in the same age bracket.

'James Ellis,' she began. Having met the father recently, I looked for signs of him in his son. They were there, but only around the eyes and ears. He had a more prominent nose and while his fair hair was starting to recede, he had a long way to go before he caught up with the Chancellor. Also he looked to be much taller. Les was a smaller bloke, about Sarah's height without her heels.

'What does he do, exactly?' I asked. 'PR you said, but what does that mean?'

'He's the founder and sole director of a public and media relations company. At least that's what it calls itself on its corporate literature; it also has a lobbying division that it doesn't advertise overtly, and that's where James is most active.'

'Who are his clients?'

'Multinationals, but none in the financial sector; that would have the potential to compromise his father.'

I looked at the second face, one I'd seen before on news bulletins and once in a vacuous celebrity magazine that I'd picked up in the hairdresser's, in the absence of anything more sensible, for example a golf magazine, or a brochure for a yoga retreat in Wales, or a flyer for a cruise to the Antarctic, or even the *Daily Star*.

Nick Wheeler was an exceptionally good-looking guy, no question about that. Aged thirty-four and yet he didn't have anything like a wrinkle on him, not even laugh lines around his eyes.

'Does he have a grotesquely ugly portrait in his attic?' I asked. 'Like Wilde's Dorian Gray?'

'No,' Amanda assured me. 'He is as he looks; a charismatic young man, and brilliant with it. He chaired his family catering firm, briefly, after his grandfather died, but sold it when he was elected to parliament. There has never been a breath of scandal about him, never.'

'There will be, if his relationship with Emily gets out. His grandfather,' I repeated. 'What about his parents?'

'They died when Nick was eight, in what appeared to be a suicide pact. The autopsy revealed that his father had inoperable metastasised lung cancer and that his mother was in the early stages of motor neurone disease. They'd have been in a race to the grave, but decided to cut it short. Nick was raised by his grandfather, also named Nicholas. They were very close.'

'How did they do it? Mum and dad?'

'With a heavy dose of sedatives and carbon monoxide; they locked themselves in the garage while Nick was with his grandparents and turned on the Jaguar's engine. It didn't take long.'

'Jaguar you said?'

'Yup, a Mark Ten. The very same car that the tracker placed at Greystone Cottage.'

'Bloody hell,' I exclaimed. 'If I'd been Grandad Wheeler I'd have tipped it into a crusher, there and then.'

'He didn't, though. He kept it as a weird kind of memorial to them and left it to young Nicholas.'

'That reminds me of Dali, the artist. When Gala, his wife, died he put her body in his Cadillac and drove it to her mansion. Her tomb's in the cellar and the Caddy's still there, or was the last time I visited, in the garage as part of the exhibition for the tourists.'

'Nick takes it a stage further.'

I whistled. 'Driving around in your parents' coffin: I can't get my head round that.'

I turned to the third image. John Balliol was the antithesis of

Wheeler, dark haired, pale skinned, pinched features; he was smiling but it was narrow, suspicious, as if he was searching the camera lens and the person behind it for ulterior motives. No, I'd never met him before nor heard of him before the previous Monday, and yet I did feel that I knew him.

His father, the billionaire Everard, and I had crossed paths a couple of times, and his memory lingered with me. He was a far different character from the image offered by his son in that photograph, big, outgoing, ebullient, challenging, aggressive, dominating, egomaniacal, the sort of guy you hope will never run for prime minister, or president, or any office to which a beguiled, hypnotised populace might be reckless enough to elect him. I am no psychiatrist but I have met some crazy people in my time; I had always reckoned that Everard was borderline at best, well over the border at worst.

Peering into his son's eyes on that tablet screen, I thought I saw something I recognised.

When we were out of London and halfway to Silchester, I called Neil. I was concerned when he picked up the call. He sounded dog tired, and that is unusual. In fact, it was a first.

'How are you doing, mate?' I asked.

'Okay,' he replied, 'but the sooner you get me a sugar hit, the better.'

'It won't be long,' I promised. 'Has anything happened since we spoke last?'

'No, it's as it was; no new arrivals, no departures.'

'Good. If Evans leaves I need you to photograph his departure. Video it if your camera will do that, but make sure he's clearly identifiable. Whatever happens, in half an hour I want you to leave your position and meet us at the entrance to the grounds. We join up there.'

'And do what?'

'Lift everybody inside.'

'Including James Ellis?'

'Absolutely; we can't get round that one, Neil. I don't see it compromising your man, though.'

'Let's hope not. I value him as an officer and I like him as a bloke.'

Amanda and I didn't speak much for the rest of the journey. The Security Service will never admit to having an armoury, so I wasn't prepared to take those fictional weapons on trust. I checked all three of them carefully, but they seemed to have been well looked after and properly oiled. I inserted the magazines and put them back in their container.

The Range Rover's satnav found Greystone Cottage easily. McIlhenney was waiting for us at the gate as we drew up. I opened the door of our vehicle and he slid in beside us. He didn't look too bad; a shade pale, made more noticeable by his black polo neck and jacket, but he'd managed to shave, spruce himself up, with facial wipes, I guessed, and squirt on some deodorant.

I gave him the bag of food that I'd brought. He went straight for the boiled sweets. 'Soor Plooms,' he exclaimed when he saw the packet. 'Where the hell did you find these?'

He ripped it open, took out two of the green boilings and jammed them into his mouth, sucking as hard as he could, trying to draw sugar into his system.

As I was helping restore Neil's levels, Amanda had summoned the two men from the second car. 'Quiet but firm,' she instructed. 'No weapons displayed, but keep them handy. I think you all know Daffyd Evans, our former colleague. He may have gone over to the other team, and he's the reason we're here in support rather than the police.' She paused.

'That said, I want to play it by the book as far as we can. We're here primarily to arrest John Balliol, the owner of this place, on suspicion of murder. Commander McIlhenney should have the lead in that; we'll just round up the dross, including Mr Evans. Understood?'

The three men nodded; so did Neil, who was still working on the sweets.

We re-formed our small convoy and headed up the driveway that led to the so-called cottage. James Ellis's BMW and Evans's car were blocking half of the turning circle, but that didn't bother our drivers. They drew the Range Rovers up side by side at the end of the approach road so that nothing could leave.

As they did so I took the pistols from their box and gave one to Amanda. She put hers in her bag; I chose a clip-on holster from the box and put it behind my back, as I always did on armed duty. My reasoning is that if the weapon goes off by accident it's better to shoot yourself in the arse than the other option.

The driver armed himself too, and we stepped out, walking three abreast towards the small mansion, with Neil and me in front, flanking Amanda.

We hadn't reached the third of the steps up to the portico before the front door opened and three black-clad orientals stepped out. They weren't wearing badges saying 'Korean' but I knew that's what they were.

Everard liked to play games with his when he had an uninvited caller. He'd tried it on me once, a mistake on his part. I eyed the three of them. The oldest of the trio looked familiar from times past and I wondered if he was thinking the same about me.

As we reached the top step, the youngest of the trio moved

half a pace forward, blocking our way. Neil moved across to confront him.

'I'm Commander McIlhenney, Metropolitan Police,' he announced. 'We're here to detain Mr John Balliol in connection with the murder of Ms Emily Repton in the Palace of Westminster, two days ago. Please step aside, for we will enter.'

The man stood his ground. 'Warrant!' he shouted.

I saw a vein stand out in my friend's neck. He didn't reply, not immediately; instead he seized the Korean by his tunic, raised him up and head-butted him, right between the eyes.

'That's my warrant,' he said. Then he dropped him like an eighty-kilo sack of spuds.

They call it the Glasgow Kiss, but trust me, we're pretty good at it in Edinburgh.

'Fuck me, Bob,' Neil murmured, 'I don't think the glucose balance is quite right yet. I'll need another couple of those sweets.'

Our three companions moved round behind us, sweeping Balliol's other attendants aside.

'Paul, you stay here,' Amanda ordered. 'Secure this door. Mark, Ian, find the back entrance and make sure nobody leaves that way. Gentlemen, let us apprehend Mr Balliol.'

She led the way into the house, and into an entrance hallway. There was a double doorway on our right; one half was open, framing a figure that I recognised as James Ellis.

'What is this?' he protested.

'I'm a police officer and this is an arrest, sir,' Neil replied. 'We're not here for you, but get in my way and we will be. Mr Balliol; where is he?'

For a moment, Ellis stood his ground, until I caught his eye and shook my head. Reluctantly, he stepped aside. I went first, my hand behind my back, gripping the butt of the holstered Browning, just in case Evans was waiting with ideas of stopping us.

He wasn't; Balliol was alone, standing by a tall marble fireplace but eyeing the bay window as if it was a means of escape. Neil stepped past me and repeated his announcement, told him that we were there to arrest him in connection with the murder of Emily Repton and then cautioned him formally.

'You do not have to say anything but it may harm your defence if you do not mention, when questioned, something which you later rely on in court. Anything you do say may be given in evidence.'

The man was being taken into Neil's custody but throughout the process he ignored him and stared at me with eyes that seemed all-too familiar. 'Are you Skinner?' he whispered, with a hint of incredulity in his tone.

'That's impressive,' I acknowledged. 'How come you know me?'

'My father spoke of you, a lot. He had a file on you, on his computer; he showed it to me. I was never sure whether he admired you, hated you, or was afraid of you. Maybe he was all three, but he wasn't afraid of much. All he ever said was that he was a better golfer than you, but you were a better putter.'

'He was only half right there. Yes, I met your dad,' I admitted, 'mainly on the golf course. The only thing I'll say about him was that he played to his handicap and he didn't cheat.'

'That was his handicap. He was a very moral man with old-fashioned ideas. When I was a kid, on one of the rare occasions I was home from school, a guy, one of the local pushers, sold me some pills, Quaaludes. My father found them, and got the truth from me; the guy was never seen again.'

'Old-fashioned ideas didn't keep him alive, though,' I countered. 'But he's not why we're here,' I added. 'You know why; you've been told.'

'I'm saying nothing until . . .'

'I know, I know, until you have a lawyer. But you haven't arrived at a police station, sunshine, so technically you don't have a right to one. Even then, Commander McIlhenney can keep you waiting for thirty-six hours for a brief, since killing the Prime Minister is by any definition a serious offence.'

'I didn't kill Ms Repton,' he murmured.

'You say, but the thing is, we have a whole long list of people we know didn't do it; yours is the only name that isn't on that list and you'll have a hell of a job persuading us to put it there. But that isn't for now, John, that can wait. Our immediate priority is rounding up your other house guests, without any unpleasantness.'

He shrugged. 'Carry on.'

'Help would be appreciated.'

'Mr Skinner, in a few hours I'm going to be the most famous man in this country and free and clear of any charges. So why the hell should I help you in any way?'

'Possibly to stop me from going Old Testament on you.'

His eyes narrowed. 'You might at that: my old man reckoned you would. Ah, what the hell. Upstairs, bedroom facing you; you'll find Wheeler there, and probably the other man.'

'Daffyd Evans?' Amanda asked.

'If you say so. I don't know his name. He's Wheeler's nurse, that's all I know.'

I didn't like the sound of that; in fact I disliked it so much that I took the stairs two at a time till I reached the top, then threw the door that faced me wide open.

Wheeler was lying supine on a king-size bed; his arms were

spread out, and his wrists and ankles were secured to its four corner posts by plastic restraints. His golden skin was dulled and his eyes were no more than slits.

As I burst into the room Daffyd Evans was hovering over him, with his back to me. As he straightened up, startled by the noise, and turned to face me, I saw that he had a large syringe in his right hand, and that a pistol hung beneath his left armpit in a shoulder holster.

'Drop it,' I snapped, drawing my Browning as I spoke.

He smiled at me. 'Well, well, well. It's the awkward copper. I'll be happy to accommodate you, Mr Skinner, however you'd like it, just as soon as I've given our friend here his medication.'

As he was speaking he had moved round to the other side of the bed, putting it between us.

'Drop the syringe,' I repeated, slowly.

'I don't think so,' he replied. 'You're a policeman, Mr Skinner, a retired chief constable, a desk jockey. You've got a policeman's mentality. All I'm doing is administering a sedative; there's no threat to life, so we both know you're not actually going to shoot me.'

He leant towards the semi-conscious Nicholas Wheeler, grasping his left forearm, his thumb on the plunger of the syringe, and directing its needle towards a bulging blue vein.

'You got that one wrong, mate,' I said, and then I blew his right kneecap off.

Thirty-Eight

I *heard the shot just as I reached the top of the stair; then I heard the screaming. I suspect they heard that in Aldermaston.*

The door was open. I saw at once that Bob was all right and that Nick Wheeler had been restrained and incapacitated in some way. That left only Evans unaccounted for, but it wasn't until I reached my old boss that I could see over the bed, and realised what he had done.

Roland Kramer's minder was thrashing on the floor clutching his shattered right knee, still screaming as he banged his head backwards against the heavy curtains as if he thought that generating a second pain source would offset the first.

'You took your time,' Bob said as he cut the first of Wheeler's restraints with a tiny pair of scissors he'd produced from somewhere.

'Those Soor Plooms you brought me,' I complained. 'Did you not read the packet? They were sugar free. So I'm still not exactly stable.'

'Take it out on Evans,' he grunted as he cut another of the plastic bracelets.

I moved round and crouched beside him, feeling my knee settle into something wet. I glanced down, saw that it was blood, and gave myself a pat on the back for having the foresight to put on an old pair of chinos for the stake-out.

'Shut the fuck up,' I told him, a little brusquely perhaps, but his yelling was getting on my nerves. He was bleeding like something hanging upside down in a halal butchers, so I stripped his belt from its loops and used it as a tourniquet, forcing him to straighten the wounded leg in the process.

The knee really was a hell of a mess; Bob's a crack shot, as he's had to demonstrate a couple of times during his career, with unfortunate outcomes for the shootees.

I could see bone, and splinters of something that was once patella; the bullet might have penetrated the joint or ricocheted off and buried itself in the carpet, but I couldn't be sure of either. I did look around for it, though, and that's when I saw the syringe lying on the floor.

'What's in it?' I asked.

'Thiopental,' he gasped, though clenched teeth. 'Anaesthetic.'

'I know what thiopental is. Do you want it?'

He nodded, his eyes pleading with me. 'But not the whole lot.'

I could see why. There were thirty millilitres of solution in the syringe; I've done a field first aid course and know that given a five per cent mix, that was a potentially lethal dose. I injected one-third of it into Evans' veins and he was unconscious in seconds.

'They weren't messing about,' I told Bob, as he freed Wheeler. 'The guy would never have come round if he'd had all of that.'

I stood up slowly, my balance felt a little uncertain. 'I need to find the kitchen,' I told him. 'There must be sugar somewhere.'

There was, in brown cube form. I laid a couple on my tongue and let them dissolve. As they did, I sneaked a quick look into the fridge; some of that sushi delivery was there, so I helped myself.

As I walked past the drawing room where we'd found Balliol I saw that he'd been joined there by Ellis and the three Koreans, under the guard of Paul, Mark and Ian. The guy I'd banjoed glowered at me; if the handkerchief he had pressed against his nose had once been white, it wasn't any more.

Amanda Dennis had joined Bob upstairs. 'Daffyd's going to need medical attention soon,' I warned them. 'That anaesthetic won't keep him under for ever.'

'I've made arrangements,' she said. 'A private ambulance is on the way already; there's a Ministry of Defence hospital unit at Frimley Park in Surrey; it'll take him there and he'll be operated on by an army surgeon. Then he'll be held incommunicado under ministry police guard. Suppose Kramer goes looking for him, he'll have trouble finding him.'

'What about him?' I asked. Wheeler was showing signs of being more responsive than when we'd found him.

'Take him home,' Bob said. 'Have a doctor look him over, then have one of our trio downstairs babysit him until we're ready to talk to him, or vice versa, depending on how long that stuff takes to wear off.'

'What about Balliol?' I asked.

He looked me in the eye. 'He's in your custody, Commander,' I knew there was a 'but' coming, 'but we don't have time to play by the rules. I don't believe we have time to take him to Westminster Police Station or anywhere else; we need to interview him right now. You can charge him when you're good and ready; that doesn't matter.

'Kramer is covering his arse here; everything will be deniable as far as he's concerned, unless Balliol and Ellis incriminate him. It all goes back to him, and I will nail him, but I need to do it before he stands up to make the Spitfire announcement in four hours' time. After that he really will be untouchable.'

Thirty-Nine

Balliol's self-confidence was impressive; in that respect he reminded me even more of his father. He sat in a small room off the entrance hall, dressed in a white silk shirt and pale blue tailored trousers that had probably cost twice as much as my suit. I had decided to interview him there, rather than in his main lair, the opulently furnished drawing room. He gazed at Neil and me, as if he was daring us to begin.

Through the window I could see a private ambulance as it drove away, with a still-sedated Daffyd Evans inside. Wheeler, who was rapidly regaining his senses, had left a few minutes before in another, bound for his Smith Square flat in the care of Ian, the Security Service operative.

Balliol's assurance cracked just a little when I said, deadpan, 'It's best that you leave us alone now, Commander,' and Neil did just that, equally grim faced and without a word.

I hoped it would look menacing to our interviewee, but the truth was that his departure wasn't a tactic. I had persuaded him, not without difficulty, that he should go home for a while to freshen up. The sugar cubes had put him back in balance . . . although I knew I was going to be reminded of those sugar-free Soor Plooms for years to come . . . but he'd had

345

a tiring night and needed some down time.

'So how the hell,' I asked, as the door closed on my valiant friend, 'does Nick Wheeler MP come to be upstairs tied to a bed, drugged up to his eyeballs?'

My prisoner looked back at me. I wasn't sure how it would go. He wasn't going to incriminate himself, I was sure of that, but if he judged that a show of cooperation might look good later on . . .

That was the choice he made.

'His nurse brought him here,' he replied, 'the day before yesterday. He told me that he'd been at a party, that he'd seriously overdosed and it needed to be hushed up. I agreed that he could look after him here . . . although at this stage of the game, it was a complication I didn't need.'

'The Spitfire game?'

'I'm sorry,' Balliol drawled, 'but that's a state secret, for a few hours yet. I've told you about Wheeler, but I'm not going to talk about that, or anything else.'

'That's what you believe,' I retorted, 'but you've just made your first mistake.'

'What was that?' he asked.

'You opened your fucking mouth,' I chuckled, 'even if it was to say you were saying nothing. That's a sign. People who really are in silent vigil, they keep it zipped.' I drew a finger across my lips. 'On the telly they say "no comment", but in real police situations they don't speak at all. You have to draw it out of them with pliers . . . not that I go in for that stuff, mind you.

'There are damn few of those in my experience, strong silent types. Most subjects want to talk to me; they want to show off, they want to tell me how clever they've been, or how ruthless, or how violent. It's a game of course. They want me to work for it; yell at them, threaten them, bang the table.'

I smiled. 'I don't play, though, not any more; at least I didn't when I was a serving cop in an active role. My technique was to wait my subjects out, to frustrate them by saying nothing at all.'

I locked my eyes into his. 'It also scared the shit out of many of them,' I added. 'They wound up telling me things I'd never even imagined them knowing.

'One bloke actually told me about a murder nobody knew had been committed; a very wealthy man hired him to kill his mother-in-law and get rid of her body. He was very efficient; we'd never have found her if he hadn't drawn me a wee map.'

I laughed. I'd made the story up but Balliol seemed to have bought it. 'The wealthy, John, they think they can get away with anything. You should know that; you did.'

He stared back at me, his mouth tight. He seemed to have taken my advice. I decided to open it by massaging his ego; that can work just as well as squeezing a man's scrotum . . . a practice I never tolerated, by the way.

'How much are you worth now?' I asked. 'I know the media reported that you inherited six and a half billion dollars from old Everard, but how much are you worth today? Have you grown your inheritance or eroded it?'

'The media got it wrong, as usual,' he replied, indignantly. 'I inherited closer to ten billion, net, from my father. When you have that much wealth it's hard to measure it,' he smirked, 'or to count it on a given day, but I reckon I'm worth fourteen billion as I sit here, patiently indulging your bullshit.'

'So you're a better man than your father ever was?'

'I didn't say that,' he countered. 'I have clearer vision than my father. I don't allow myself to be distracted by a pointless obsession with family history, or by a mad dream to regenerate

Scotland by buying as much of the place as possible then building new townships to lure emigrants back to the country, and factories to give them employment.'

'As far as I recall,' I said, 'he started to fulfil his mad dream by building a golf course on a piece of land that could only be reached by air.'

'He did, but golf was another of his obsessions. He thought the world was ready for another Bobby Jones. He hoped it might be me for a while; he dragged me on to the course every day I was home, but I never broke eighty in my life and the lowest handicap that even he could manufacture for me was thirteen, at a course he owned in South Carolina, where the worst golfer in the world wouldn't have played off any more than twenty.

'Eventually he gave up on making me a top golfer and he more or less gave up on me. He never brought me into any of his businesses, or gave me any preparation for the future.'

'He thought he was immortal,' I ventured. 'And he was, as you say, more than a little obsessional, in the way that Genghis Khan was a little obsessional, or Napoleon, or Henry the Eighth. He never introduced you to any of his enterprises?'

'I knew what they were: petrochemicals, software development, armaments, aviation, publishing, but not much more than I'd have picked up by reading the *Financial Times* or *Forbes* magazine. The one thing he did tell me about was laser propulsion.'

I raised an eyebrow: not for effect, it was spontaneous. Were we starting to get somewhere? 'I thought that was your project?'

'Latterly, yes, but it was brought to Dad by a man called Sigmund Podolski. He had a proposal that needed funding for the creation of a new engine system. His vision was that it would power spacecraft and would advance man's exploration of the solar system by decades, by slashing the time needed to reach planets. "Mars in a month," he told my father, and gave him a video presentation that showed exactly how it would work.

'Dad was very impressed; he asked me what I thought, first time ever. I told him that before we go to other worlds we need to master our own.'

I nodded. 'You saw the military capability right away, didn't you?'

'Of course. I didn't spell it out for my father, because I didn't think I needed to. Wrong, John. A day or so later he told me that he was going to fund Podolski's project, but that it would be vested in a trust that would be administered by an international commission for the benefit of all mankind. Not for the Balliol family and certainly not for the USA, oh no. In fact, he told me that he intended to structure all his wealth.

'My future role would be as its manager if, he told me, I was up to it; if I wasn't, he was going to leave me nine million dollars, one tenth of one per cent of his fortune, and his South Carolina golf course in the hope that one day I'd get down to single figures.'

'Is that when you decided to kill him?' I asked casually.

He stared at me, then laughed. 'You don't expect me to admit to that, do you?'

'No,' I said, 'and frankly I don't give a fuck one way or another; but you did, I know it, you know it. You paid one of his bodyguards to fake a robbery and kill him . . . maybe paid him around nine million dollars and a golf course, or the equivalent? There would be a degree of irony in that . . . before he could complete your disinheritance. Did the Korean live to enjoy his pay-off? Somehow I doubt that.'

'Speculation, all of it,' Balliol scoffed.

'I told you,' I repeated, 'I don't care. How about the man Podolski? Is he still alive?'

'No, he died four months ago. There was an accident in Aldermaston; nothing made the press.'

'Here's some more speculation: by then his death didn't matter. You had built your team in Brazil, and adapted Podolski's engine for other purposes.'

'Something like that,' he admitted. 'We hadn't got all the way there. We needed more than was available in Brazil, and doing a deal with its government was out of the question.'

'Why Britain? Why not simply take it to the Pentagon?'

'God forbid. That really would have been besmirching my father's memory. There's one thing you may not know about him, because it was excised from all his official biographies.

'He fought in Vietnam, in the early days of the war. No, "fought" is the wrong word. He was part of a three-man CIA assassination team sent into Cambodia in nineteen sixty-seven to assassinate Prince Sihanouk, because he was perceived to be pro-Chinese.

'They failed; the other two guys were killed and Dad was captured. He was tortured, but he had very little to tell them, so they tried to use him for propaganda purposes. At first the US government denied his existence; then they said that he was a deserter from an infantry unit who had gone over to the other side, and they made no attempt to extract him. He was a prisoner for three years, until Sihanouk fell.

'He was succeeded by a general called Lon Nol; he was pro-American, and sent Dad back to Saigon, quietly, without any fuss. Of course, he was an even bigger embarrassment then. The CIA continued to deny his existence; he was sent back to the States with a quarter of a million dollars in hush money, which he used to build his fortune . . . after he'd changed his name.'

'He wasn't always Balliol?' John had been right; there had never been a whisper of this in anything I'd ever read about Everard, and some of that was classified.

'No, he was born Everard Morrison. He took Balliol from one of my great-grandmothers, on his mother's side. So you understand now why he was pathologically anti-American, and more than a little crazy, as you inferred. I didn't like the son of a bitch, but it wasn't his fault, not all of it.

'Because of him I could never have taken what I had to a government as untrustworthy as the US. I did think about Russia, but not for long. Instead I approached the United Kingdom. They were only too pleased to see me, even though it was very hush-hush. I named my own price, which all in all I thought was pretty reasonable.'

'What was that?' I asked.

'Didn't they tell you?' He looked surprised.

I smiled. 'Yes, they did,' I admitted. 'A billion and a passport.'

'That was the headline figure, but there was something else. Ten per cent of all defence expenditure on Spitfire and all future orders for limited versions for export sales to friendly governments . . . including the US . . . will come to me.'

That was news, but I wasn't letting him see it. 'You must have caught the Prime Minister on a good day,' I said.

'I didn't deal with Locheil,' he replied. 'I did my business with a cabinet subcommittee of three people: Kramer, who was Chancellor then, Monty Radley, Foreign Office, and Les Ellis, who was Defence Secretary.'

In my head, more pieces began to move; the picture was almost complete. As I'd told him, he'd wanted to talk to me all along. He'd wanted to boast. He'd been easy, really.

Up to that point.

'So why in God's name, when the whole project was about to be complete, did you go and kill Emily Repton?'

'I didn't,' he insisted.

'Come on, John,' I exclaimed, 'you stuck a blade in her head.'

'Then prove it; you can't even prove I was there.'

'You took a piss in her toilet, or was it a whizz? Did stabbing her scare the shit out of you, literally?'

The slightly crazy eyes blazed, his mouth closed tight, and he settled into his chair. The interview was over.

Or so he thought: I wasn't quite ready to give up. 'We can put you in the room, John,' I insisted. 'We have a fingerprint in the toilet.'

'Maybe you do; but that won't be enough. It doesn't have a date stamp on it, does it?'

'Then there's the CCTV.'

He laughed. 'Oh yes?' he challenged. His confidence had returned and that worried me.

I nodded. 'I know you've been told that's been wiped, and it has, but we have the man who was coerced into wiping it.'

'Yeah,' he retorted, 'and what if he went home last night to his sad little divorced man bedsit to find a bag of cash, an air ticket to paradise, and a link to half a million dollars in a bank account that you will never trace? If that happened. whatever he told you yesterday he won't be saying today, or ever again.'

Fuck, I thought. *We should have locked Coffrey up*, for the mockery on his face told me he wasn't lying.

I tried to let nothing show on mine. 'Also we have Mickey Satchell,' I continued, 'the MP who took you to the Prime Minister's room.'

'And you're as sure about that,' he said, 'as you were about

352

having the man you allege fixed a tape that I was never on?'

'Are you boasting to me that something has happened to Dr Satchell?' I leaned towards him. All of a sudden squeezing his baw-bag until those damned smug eyes popped right out of his head seemed like an attractive proposition.

'I'm telling you nothing at all, Mr Skinner. Not one fucking thing . . . apart from this. You're not going to believe it, and why should you because nobody else does. I . . . did . . . not . . . kill . . . Emily . . . Repton!'

Forty

I stomped out of the little room, leaving Paul to guard our smug prisoner and went back to the drawing room, where Amanda was waiting with James Ellis. My phone was in my hand, calling Neil. I heard a hiss of tyre noise as he took my call.

'Mickey Satchell,' I told him urgently. 'You need to find her; have people check the Commons but I doubt she'll be there. If she isn't, send officers to her home; tell them to kick the door in if they have to. I have grounds to fear for her safety. Use your own people if you can; if not, well . . . use your own judgement.'

'Understood,' he replied. 'Did you get this from Balliol?'

'Let's just say that a suggestion was made. Check Joe Coffrey's workplace and home as well, but I doubt that you'll find him. There's every chance he's in warmer climes by now . . . unless he's dead in a ditch on his way to Heathrow or Gatwick.'

'They're not kidding, are they?' Neil grumbled.

'No, they're not, but I'm about to have a serious chat with the weak link. Let's see what develops from that.'

I was looking at James Ellis as I spoke and as I put away my phone. 'Crisis management, you said; you were bloody right there, mate, but this one is out of your control.'

'Crisis management,' he repeated. 'Oh dear: Shafat.'

I hoped he didn't notice the tightening around my eyes. I had intended not to expose Neil's man, although it would be difficult not to, but I might have given him away with one careless remark. 'Who?' I asked, doing my best to look puzzled 'That's one of the things your consultancy does, isn't it? Crisis management?'

'Yes,' he murmured.

'Then surely that's why you're here. We have a dead Prime Minister, a live prime suspect and you're in his house, along with a semi-comatose man who was a member of the government twenty-four hours ago. If that's not a crisis, Mr Ellis, I don't know what is. So what is your function here?'

'I was sent to advise Mr Balliol.'

'About what?'

'His reaction to the Spitfire announcement when it's made.'

I'd dropped a small clanger earlier; his was a beauty.

'You know about Spitfire?' I asked him, slowly.

He gulped, as he realised the extent of his mistake, and nodded.

'Who told you?'

'Dad. My father. The Chancellor.'

'You make him sound like the Holy Trinity. Did he send you down here?'

'Yes.'

'What orders did he give you?'

'He said that whatever happened I was to keep Balliol stable, and away from the media.'

'Stable? He had doubts about his stability?'

'The man killed the Prime Minister!' Ellis shouted. 'Does that sound normal to you?'

The door was open. I reckoned that Balliol must have heard him but there was no sound from the other room.

'He says he didn't,' I told him.

'She was alive when he went in, she was dying when he left. That's what Dad said.'

'I see,' I murmured. 'The Chancellor believed that and he ordered you down here to look after him? My colleague and I interviewed Mr Ellis yesterday morning but he didn't say a word about it to us. It looks as if we need to speak to him again, under caution this time.' I paused. 'Before we get there, though, were you aware of Nicholas Wheeler's presence in this house?'

'Only after I got here.'

'Too bad you weren't here earlier,' I grunted. 'You just missed Balliol's call girl; seems she was quite a sight.'

I'd thrown that one in, with all the subtlety of the old fisherman in *Jaws* chucking lumps of bait off the back of his boat. Ellis sank his teeth into it.

'She wasn't Balliol's woman. He hired her, sure, but she was for Wheeler.'

'Wheeler? He was out of his skull.'

'I don't imagine that'll be clear in the photos the Korean took; he'll look like any other bloke being fucked senseless by an expert.'

Thank you, James, I thought, reading the same words in Amanda's smile.

'Who told you this?' she asked.

'John Balliol. He laughed about it.'

'Which Korean took the photos?'

'Three. They're all called Kim,' he explained. 'Balliol calls them One, Two and Three, in order of seniority.' He glanced at me. 'Kim Three's the chap your colleague damaged.'

'I might damage him some more when I'm through with you,' I murmured.

Amanda stood. 'I'll take care of that,' she said, briskly, 'with Mark's help. Those pictures will be secured. Then I might reach out to Señorita Tinker's agent,' she added, for Ellis's benefit. 'I suspect she'll be happy to cooperate with us, to save her career.'

'The man who came here this morning,' I continued as she left, 'the guy who has a sore leg now. Think about this, Mr Ellis, but do not think, for one second, about lying to me. Have you ever seen him before?'

He nodded.

'Where and when?'

'He came to our house once, Dad's house in Wimbledon, about three weeks ago. He was a protection officer, for Roland Kramer.'

'Why was Kramer there?'

'To meet with Dad.'

'Anyone else?' I ventured, trying to avoid Ellis guessing that I knew the story.

'Yes. Monty Radley, Nick Wheeler and John Balliol; they gathered to discuss Spitfire, to agree its deployment and to confirm the financial deal with Balliol.'

'You know that much? Were you in the room?'

'I took the minutes, typed them up when the meeting was over and gave everyone present a copy. All five people signed all five copies.'

'What about the Prime Minister? Was she there?'

'No, she didn't want her hands on it, she had said. Nick Wheeler did volunteer that he was honour bound to report back to her. Kramer didn't like that; there was an argument between them, in fact. It got heated, and that's unusual for Nick.'

'Did you keep a copy of the minute?'

He shot me the look of a hunted man. 'God, no. Dad even

insisted that I destroy the notes I'd taken and the document I'd created on the computer, and watched me do it.'

'What about the agenda?'

'There was a technical report by Balliol, and a series of videos of Spitfire in action, including a simulated mission to Ascension Island filmed by an on-board camera: that's around seven thousand miles and it took fifty minutes, including a period of deceleration for simulated payload delivery. It was breathtaking, unimaginable. When it was over, nobody could speak for a while.

'When they could,' he continued, 'the final detail of the financial arrangement with Balliol was settled and included in the document and the name of the project was confirmed. Balliol wanted to call it "Ozymandias", but everyone else agreed that was a terrible idea. Radley suggested "Thatcher" but he'd had a couple of drinks by them so nobody took any notice.'

'Is there any way you could recover the document you typed?' I asked.

Ellis shrugged. 'I don't think so,' he replied. 'They say these things never vanish completely, but Dad had me trash it, then empty the trash can, and delete the entire history of the day's activity. Maybe an expert could recover something even after all that, but the first problem he'd have to solve would be how to get hold of Dad's laptop, for that's what I used.'

'That might be possible,' I said, but with no optimism. 'Is that it?' I asked. 'Are we done or is there any other information you're holding back?'

'That's all I know; I promise.' He looked up at me. 'Can I go now?'

I laughed, a touch scornfully. 'What do you think?'

Forty-One

When Amanda returned, she was holding an SD memory card, and wearing a satisfied smile. 'Our young friend with the sore nose didn't take much persuading,' she said. 'He has no employment rights in the UK, and the prospect of deportation and repatriation didn't appeal to him, possibly because he has a North Korean passport and defected from an international gymnastics event in Brazil two years ago.'

'Did he say who ordered him to take the photos? Did he actually say it was Balliol?'

'That he didn't do; he said that the instructions came from Daffyd Evans, before he left here yesterday and before Señorita Tinker arrived.'

'Translate that and he's saying they came from Kramer. If I'd known that at the time I might not have let Neil give him that anaesthetic, not until I'd made him admit it. How secure is the guard on him?'

'It's secure until the Prime Minister or the Defence Secretary order it to stand down, or until the new Home Secretary removes me from office and cancels your commission.'

'Any one of those things could happen,' I said, 'when word of what happened here gets back to Number Ten. So it had better not. Is there somewhere we can lock the Koreans, also Balliol, and our boy here?' I added, jerking a thumb in the general direction of James Ellis. 'I'm sure that Paul and Mark can handle themselves, but we're looking at five against two when we go.'

'Where are we going?'

'Wheeler's place; there's a document that I need to get my hands on. Balliol has a copy, but he's not going to tell us where it is, not at the very earliest until Kramer stands up in the Commons and makes Spitfire official.'

She pocketed the SD card and grabbed her bag. 'Let's go,' she declared. 'I'll brief the boys.' She hauled Ellis, who looked scared and bemused, to his feet. 'You with me. I'll drive,' she added over her shoulder as she frog-marched him from the room, to hand him over to his guards.

When she returned I made a show of protesting that I'm a terrible passenger, but she didn't buy it. It was her car and she was the boss, so I was consigned to the front passenger seat.

She was running on adrenaline and confidence as we set off, but it didn't take long for me to realise that she was scared too.

'What are we into here, Bob?' she asked. 'What has happened? Boil it down for me.'

'We're looking at the murder of the Prime Minister, by John Balliol, and an orchestrated campaign to cover it up, led by her successor and the Chancellor, involving the kidnap and potential blackmail of Nicholas Wheeler, a Cabinet Minister. Explain it any other way if you can.'

'I can't,' she admitted.

'Was Evans actually going to kill Wheeler?'

'Neil knows more about that anaesthetic than me, but he reckons that if he'd given him all the contents of the syringe, he'd have gone to sleep for ever.'

'You've got us that far,' Amanda said, 'now tell me: why? Why did Balliol kill her?'

'I don't know. Maybe it wasn't meant to happen, but with the Balliols, father and son, nothing can be dismissed as impossible. Jesus, Joseph and Mary, the man's developed a weapon system that's going to change the entire world order, so what's a wee bit of murder to him?'

'But you say he denies it,' she pointed out, cautiously.

'So did Peter Manuel.'

'Who's he?'

'A mass murderer from close by my home town, before my time. He showed the police where he'd buried a poor girl victim, but he still denied doing it.'

'Is he still in prison?' she asked.

'Oh yes. He was buried there, after they hanged him.'

My phone sounded in my pocket. It hadn't locked on to the car's Bluetooth. I took the call, putting it on speaker. It was Neil, still on the road.

'Mickey Satchell,' he sighed, with a tone of inevitability in his voice that told me what was coming, until he proved me entirely wrong. I'd been expecting her to have been found dead in her bath with an armful of morphine, a bellyful of whisky, and a suicide note left on her computer confessing to killing Emily during some trivial argument. But no.

'I tried calling her in her office in Portcullis House,' Neil said, 'but got no reply. The Commons switchboard couldn't find her either. I was on the point of sending those guys to kick in her door, but something made me call Hamblin before I ordered that.

'He knew where she was all right; I've never heard a man sound so cynical. She's the new Home Secretary. It'll be announced in an hour or so, before the Commons sits this afternoon.'

'Bought off,' I exclaimed. 'She's such a weak character, that possibility never occurred to me.'

'There's more to come,' Neil retorted. 'John Balliol's being given a peerage and a seat in the Cabinet. They're going to call him Secretary of State for Innovation; that'll be held back until after the Spitfire announcement.'

I looked sideways at Amanda; her knuckles were white on the wheel, a worrying sight, since we were doing ninety. 'They really have locked it up,' I growled, 'haven't they?'

Forty-Two

The extent of the cover-up made us worry even more about Wheeler's physical safety. To be sure, Amanda called Thames House from the road, and ordered that two more operatives be sent the very short distance to the former Defence Secretary's flat to treble the guard on him. Then she drove even faster.

Happily all was quiet in Smith Square when, to my relief, we arrived. With Daffyd Evans in hospital, incommunicado, and Balliol and Ellis locked up in Greystone Cottage, there was no way that news of our intervention could have made it to Downing Street. The minder's absence would be noticed sooner rather than later, but I hoped that Kramer would be too busy preparing for the big announcement in the Commons, less than two hours away, for it to become an issue.

When Ian let us into the penthouse flat, we found Nicholas Wheeler looking a hell of a lot better than when last we'd seen him. A Security Service-approved doctor was with him, packing her kit away in a bag as we came into the room.

'He's fine,' she told Amanda. 'I've given him a shot to help his recovery from the drug. He might be a little nauseous for a while, but that'll pass.'

As she left, Wheeler pushed himself out of his soft cream

chair and extended a hand in my direction. 'Thank you,' he said. 'It's been made pretty clear to me that you saved my life.'

To my surprise, I felt a little embarrassed. 'Forget it,' I mumbled. 'It's what we do.'

'That man was there to finish me off, wasn't he?' he continued.

I nodded. 'He knew how much was in the syringe. Proving it, though, that'll be a different matter. I can tell you now that his story, if he says anything, will be that you're a junkie and that he was trying to wean you off your addiction to thiopental.'

'Who is he?' he asked.

'I'm not going to tell you,' I replied. 'It's possible that you might be required to pick him out in an ID parade. The last thing I want is to prejudice any prosecution.'

'You can identify him, can't you? Even if I can't.'

'Yes, but only as the man who was about to inject you. I can only place him in that room, not here, and not as your abductor.'

'I'll be struggling to do that myself,' Wheeler confessed, as he dropped back into his chair. 'I never saw him properly.'

'Not even when he attacked you?' Amanda exclaimed.

'No. He came out of the lift wearing a balaclava; he hit me and I remember nothing in any detail, just haziness and dreams, until I started to come round in that place this morning. I'd let him come up because he said he was from Number Ten and had a document from Emily.

'I was here on my own, you see. The night before I'd sent my protection officers, Dave and Sarfraz, away, so I could have some privacy. They were due to collect me later to take me to the Commons for Emily's statement.' He paused, peering at us as if we were slightly out of focus. 'What happened about that? Did she . . .'

'Ms Repton is dead, Mr Wheeler,' I told him, speaking softly, hoping that I sounded sympathetic. 'She was found in her Commons office, unconscious, with a blade embedded in her skull. She never came round and passed away yesterday morning. It's our belief that what happened to you was part of a cover-up.'

I stopped, letting silence fill the room, watching Wheeler as the shock hit him. 'She's . . .' he murmured after a while.

'I'm afraid so,' I said. 'We know why you sent your protection people away. It was Ms Repton's privacy you were really protecting, not your own. We realise that.'

'And the statement?' he whispered.

'Spitfire hasn't been announced yet,' Amanda told him. 'You've missed a lot. Roland Kramer is now the Prime Minister, and you are no longer Defence Secretary. The statement that was to be made on Monday will happen this afternoon.'

'Ahh.' He gave a great gasp and sagged into his chair, his head falling backwards against its cushion. For a moment I thought he'd passed out again, until he continued. 'Oh no it won't. Not the one that was supposed to be made.'

'Yes,' I whispered, as my lurking, unspoken, theory of everything came to proof.

'Emily came here early on Monday morning,' Wheeler said, his voice strengthening. 'She and I, we were close; not in love, or anything as dramatic as that, but we were close colleagues and we were confidants.'

'The royal-ish girlfriend that the tabloids are all over,' I said, 'she's just a smokescreen, I take it?'

'Yes; a friend, a partner at public events, but no more than that. Emily and I were in a loose relationship, outside our offices; I could never go to her place, obviously, but occasionally she'd escape from Number Ten and come here. That's what happened on Monday morning.' He stopped and looked at us, more sharply than before. 'How much do you know about Spitfire, Mrs Dennis, Mr Skinner?'

'All of it,' Amanda replied. 'Up to and including the meeting in the Chancellor's house where the final decision was taken and the deal done with Balliol. You were at that meeting; you signed the minute.'

'Yes, I was and I did,' he confirmed. 'But I was there as . . .'

My phone rang. I checked caller ID and saw 'Sarah'.

'Sorry, I have to take this,' I murmured. 'Honey,' I said as I picked it up, 'what's up? Are you finished?'

'Yes,' she said, 'but there's something I need to know. Were any crime scene photos taken?'

'Of course, but by me, not a CSI photographer.'

'I'd like to see them, not necessarily all of them, just the ones that show the body . . . the victim,' she corrected herself, 'in situ at her desk. Can you mail them to me? To my phone?'

'Sure,' I replied. 'Hang up and I'll do just that.'

I walked over to the room's big picture window, ignoring its panoramic view of Westminster Abbey and the Houses of Parliament as I selected the images Sarah wanted from their folder and fired them off, one by one, to her email address. I didn't have time to wonder why she wanted them.

When I was finished, I turned back to Wheeler and Amanda. 'Apologies, but that was necessary. Please continue. You were at Ellis's meeting . . .'

'Yes,' he said, 'with Les, Roland, the foul Radley and John Balliol. Les's son was there too, and Kramer's creepy minder, although he stayed in the hall.' That told me there was no chance of him picking Daffyd out of a line-up. They'd met before; defence counsel would walk through it.

'What the rest didn't know,' he went on, 'was that I was there with two hats, mine and Emily's. She inherited the Balliol project from her predecessor, George Locheil.

'He had agreed to the deal and to the cost but he wasn't involved in any of the discussion with Balliol. George is a cautious guy; he wanted to leave himself wiggle room. He wanted to be sure that if anything went badly wrong, like blowing up bloody Aldermaston by accident, the blame would fall on Kramer, Radley and Ellis, not on him.

'Emily took the same line, but for a different reason. She was always ambivalent about Spitfire at best. Its potential frightened her; it brought with it power that she wasn't sure one person should have. In that, she was out of step with Kramer and Ellis, and Radley too. They were zealots, all of them.'

He paused. 'Sorry, can I get myself some water. My throat, it's very dry.'

'Where's the kitchen?' Amanda asked. 'I'll fetch a glass.'

'Mr Skinner,' Wheeler whispered, as she left. For the first time I appreciated how young he was. 'You are real, aren't you? This isn't part of my nightmare, is it? Emily really is dead?'

I reached out and squeezed his hand. 'I'm afraid so, lad. She is, and you're not. But I've got the fucker that killed her, and now I'm going to get the people who sent him.'

'Here.' Amanda returned and handed him a glass of water. 'Sip it,' she warned. 'Remember what the doctor said about nausea.'

'I will. I don't feel anything at the moment.' He took a sip. 'Back to the meeting,' he said, revived. 'Emily wasn't invited, but Roland did tell her about it. She asked me to attend and to report back to her, but not to rock the boat. So I did, I agreed the deal and signed the minute. But I told Roland I'd convey the terms of the agreement to Emily, and I added that the final decision had to be hers alone, as she was the Prime Minister and she held the nuclear codes.'

He sipped some more water, rinsing it around his mouth before swallowing. 'Roland didn't like that. He insisted that the decision we'd just reached could not be overturned. I begged to differ and we had a bit of a shouting match. It was loud enough for his minder to come in to find out what was going on, but Les shooed him away.'

'That matches what James Ellis told me this morning,' I said.

'You've seen James?'

'He was in the house where you were held,' Amanda volunteered. 'Do you have your copy of that document?'

He nodded. 'It's in my safe, set in the floor under the rug beside my desk. Emily asked me to keep it here.'

'What happened on Monday?' I asked, moving him on before he tired.

'Emily came here; she walked, as always, and I let her in. When she called, she'd said she couldn't sleep on her own and wanted company, but I could see it was more than that. She had barely taken her coat off when she said, "Nick, I can't let our country do this. I'm going to override the Spitfire agreement, whatever the unholy trio may say. Are you with me?" As if I wouldn't . . .'

His voice broke, and so did his composure for a second or two. 'I just hugged her and said, "Thank you for doing the right thing." Then I asked how she was going to go about it.

'She had thought that through,' he continued. 'We sat down with my laptop and drafted the statement that she'd have made, if she'd been allowed to do it. By three a.m., we were finished. She printed out two copies, and then we grabbed as many hours' sleep as were left to us. She left at seven thirty to walk back to Downing Street.'

'What did she do with the copies?' I asked.

'She took them with her.'

'You don't have one?'

'Not printed, but it'll still be on my computer. Give me a moment.' He rose, none too steadily, and went through a door at the far end of the living room, returning a few seconds later, clutching a slim laptop in a hard blue case. He fired it up, found what he was looking for and handed it to me.

Amanda joined me on the sofa; I angled the screen so that we could both see without distortion. There was a file on the desktop, named 'Spitfire'. I clicked on it, and it opened. We read it, in solemn silence.

Mr Speaker, I wish to make a statement of vital importance to the nation and to the world.

Just over two years ago, in the administration of my predecessor, senior ministers, specifically the Foreign Secretary, the Defence Secretary of the day, and the Chancellor of the Exchequer, were approached by an entrepreneur, Mr John Balliol.

Mr Balliol, a man of great wealth, had been funding private research, in Brazil, on a new type of laser propulsion. Initially it was seen as having value in space exploration, but as Mr Balliol's team progressed their work, it became clear that the system's potential was far greater.

PAUSE

Projectiles using the laser propulsion drive could operate within the atmosphere and beyond, at speeds far greater than anything previously contemplated. Unmanned, and operated remotely, they could deliver, undetected, a payload to any target in the world in well under two hours, and return to base.

PAUSE

I have to advise the House that a research and development programme, which was carried out in total secrecy at the Aldermaston Weapons Establishment, is now complete. This country has in its possession a craft of immense power that makes all other weapon delivery systems virtually obsolete. It is ready for deployment carrying a full range of weaponry, both conventional and nuclear.

PAUSE

'It has been given the name Spitfire, for sentimental and historic reasons. I have to say that I find that inappropriate since the original Spitfire was built purely for defensive purposes; today's is the opposite. It is an offensive weapon of terrifying capability.

Mr Speaker, honourable members, we now find ourselves in possession of what is the ultimate deterrent.

PAUSE

However,

PAUSE AGAIN, BRIEFLY

I do not believe that we, or any other nation, is sufficiently responsible to be the custodian of such a system.

PAUSE

Consequently, I intend to place the Spitfire system in the hands of the United Nations, and to seek the adoption of an international treaty, under which all nations would pledge never to develop a similar system for military purposes.

PAUSE

I will ask the Foreign Secretary to convene an immediate meeting of the Security Council to discuss my proposal. I have already spoken with the Presidents of the United States, Russia and China. All three declared their support for my proposal and undertook that they would be co-sponsors and signatories of the United Nations treaty.

PAUSE

Technology can never be uninvented, but it is my belief that if Spitfire is maintained under international control, for use purely as a deterrent to the ambitions of rogue states, we will enter an era when all other nuclear arsenals in the world can be dismantled.

I commend this statement, etc.

There have been a few occasions in life when I have been rendered speechless, but I can't recall another when I found my hands shaking at the same time, and a cold fist gripping my stomach.

'No other copies?' I whispered, when I could, looking at Wheeler.

'None. She might have photocopied it in Downing Street, but I can't imagine her doing that.'

'Then why did she make two?' I wondered. Seeking an answer to my question, I called Neil McIlhenney, and asked him to do something for me.

When that was done, I made another very simple request of Amanda. I didn't need to explain its purpose; she'd guessed. Her mind really is disturbingly similar to mine. If we ever did work together full-time we'd be seriously dangerous.

Forty-Three

I was emerging from the shower when Louise handed me the phone. 'It's you know who,' she announced, more than a little tetchily.

When I'd arrived home she'd been less than impressed by my appearance, and by what I'd told her was mud on my trousers. She'd been about to put them in the washing machine when I snatched them from her grasp.

'They're for the bin,' I told her. 'They were past their best anyway; that's why I wore them.' The truth was that I didn't want her to see the colour that would have come out of them, even diluted by water and detergent.

'So are you,' she complained. 'You're too senior an officer for all-night gallivanting; and you're too old for it too.'

'That's not what you said when we were in that club in Barbados last winter.'

'Hmph,' she snorted, managing to grin simultaneously at the reminder. 'I want you fit to go back there. By the way, is that a lump on your forehead?'

I took the phone from her without comment, having pushed my luck enough for one day.

'Things are moving on,' Bob told me. 'There's something I'd like you to do.'

'What makes you think I'll be let out to play?'

He told me what needed doing.

'No problem with that. I can handle that from home.'

As soon as I was dried, shaved, suited and shod, I shut myself in the room that Lou and I use as an office and went to work. I had to make a couple of phone calls to source the information and numbers I was after, but after pulling a bit of rank I got them.

Emily Repton's chief protection officer was a man named Rob Hull. He'd been a uniformed inspector before being approved for protection duty, but rank counts for less in that division than in the rest of the Met.

He was guarded when he answered my call to his service mobile; not many people have the number. 'Rob here. Who's calling?'

'Commander McIlhenney. You know who I am?'

'Yes, sir; who and what. How can I help you?'

'What you don't know,' I told him, 'is that I've been seconded to investigate the death of the former Prime Minister.'

'Oh yes?' Suddenly his level of interest sounded higher than a payday loan. 'It needs investigation, does it? At commander level.'

'Subject to autopsy findings, it's being classed as suspicious.'

'Good,' he retorted. 'I liked the boss and I didn't swallow that virus story for a second. What can I tell you, sir?'

'Let's go back to Monday morning. You and your colleague went with Ms Repton from Downing Street to the Commons, yes?'

'We did. The car dropped us at the side entrance; Barry and I walked her upstairs and into her office.'

'Did you encounter anyone else?'

'Yes, we did,' he replied at once. 'Ratty and his guy were leaving for an engagement locally just as we arrived.'

'Ratty?' I repeated.

'Sorry, sir. Mr Kramer, the Home Secretary; Prime Minister now. First name Roland, so the guys in the group call him Roland Rat. He was a character on breakfast telly, way back,' Hull explained.

'Yes, I knew that. The only rat who ever joined a sinking ship, they said at the time. Did they stop and talk?'

'They stopped,' he replied, 'and they talked. Ratty said, "Good morning, Prime Minister," with a bit more enthusiasm than he usually shows. Emily looked up at him, then she said something in reply. I couldn't quite hear all of it, but I did hear Nick Wheeler's name mentioned. He was her bit on the side,' he added. 'I can tell you that now she's gone. She thought we didn't know, but we did. When she was done, she tapped Ratty's chest with a big envelope she was carrying, handed it to him and carried on up the stairs.'

'Then you saw her into her office and left?'

'Yeah,' Hull sighed, sadly. 'And we never saw her again; bloody shame. Yeah, the boss was all right. We'll miss her, Barry and me.'

'Where are you now?'

'In limbo, sir, we're being replaced. The new man doesn't want any of her old staff. He has his own bloke, and he'll pick the team.'

I thanked him and let him go, then went through to the kitchen to tell the headmistress, as I like to call her, that I was going back to team up with Bob, wherever he was.

She smiled. 'Go on then,' she said. 'Whatever this is, it has you so pumped up that you'd never forgive me if I gave you detention.'

Forty-Four

Neil joined us at Wheeler's flat. The news he brought was what I'd expected; finally, I reckoned, I'd got something right.

'Emily gave Kramer a copy of her statement as he left for his Prison Governors engagement,' I said. 'He read it on the way there and I imagine he hit the roof. He told Les Ellis and they made a plan.'

'Radley too?' Neil asked.

'You met him,' I replied. 'He couldn't plan his way out of a phone box. Nor is he a man for a crisis. No, I think they kept him out of it. My guess is that after speaking to the Chancellor, Kramer called Emily on his private mobile, and asked her to meet with Balliol, either to brief him in advance or to give him a chance to talk her round.'

'Do you think they sent him in there to kill her?'

'I wouldn't put it past them; they were ready to eliminate Nick here. But on balance I don't think they did; my assumption is that Balliol lost it when she told him he was missing out on his share of a few billion pounds' worth of arms sales and went over the top. I believe that, because things happened very fast when it was discovered. Amanda was called in, rather than the police, with a view to containing the situation, until they could come

375

up with an alternative account of what they thought was the Prime Minister's death.'

'True,' she agreed. 'Containment was the first word Kramer used.'

'He thought you would follow orders, to the letter,' I continued. 'He didn't anticipate you bringing me in, but it would have been dangerous to forbid it. It would have looked suspicious. So I was given forty-eight hours to sort it out, something they were sure I'd never do. Even before I'd begun they were fixing the evidence. Evans was sent to intimidate Coffrey into doctoring the tape, then he came here, and took Mr Wheeler out. Your car was in the garage, yes?' I asked.

The young MP nodded. 'My lift is private and goes down to the garage; all the protection people knew that.'

'That's how he got you out of here,' I declared, 'and down to Greystone Cottage. They kept you under there, until they figured out what to do with you.'

'What about the three phone calls Ms Repton made to his mobile?' Amanda asked.

'It was on charge,' Wheeler volunteered. 'Switched off.'

'And the woman?' Neil murmured.

'She was either to set him up for blackmail,' I replied, 'or to discredit his reputation after they'd killed him. The latter probably, given the amount of juice in that syringe. Drug-fuelled orgies? The tabloids love them. Chances are he'd have been found dead in another location, and the photos would either have been there or would have been leaked afterwards.'

Wheeler stared at me; he was astonished. 'What photos? What woman?'

Amanda took the SD card from her pocket and handed it to

him. 'You may examine these later, or you may choose not to. Either way, you must destroy them.'

'You've seen them?' he asked.

'I had to,' she said. 'I'm sorry. The woman is not identifiable, but you are: all of you,' she added. 'They'd have killed you, because they had to, and then, with these images, they'd have buried you.' Amanda turned. 'What do we do with all this, Bob?'

'We wait for your man to get here, then you all leave the room while he and I have a word. After that, we go and face the . . .'

Mobile phones: they are a blessing and a curse but usually the latter. I gave a shout of exasperation as mine demanded my attention, but cooled it when I saw that once again it was Sarah who was calling me.

'Hi,' she said, quietly. 'Are you alone? Because you might want to be when I tell you what I have to. You can be pretty spectacular when you explode.'

'Hey,' I exclaimed, 'you're not . . .'

'Hell no! My waters are a way off breaking. But I have finished the autopsy on the late Emily Repton.'

I walked through to the kitchen, without a word to the other three. As I left them I heard the door buzzer sound: the man from MI5, I hoped.

'Right,' I murmured. 'I'm alone. What have you got for me?'

I didn't explode when she told me. I couldn't; I was altogether too fucking tired. Instead, I told her what I wanted her to do.

And then I went for a very private chat with the man from Thames House. I was smiling when it was over, and as we left Smith Square.

Forty-Five

Norman Hamblin met Amanda, Neil and me at the entrance to the Cabinet Office, then led us directly through the building, into 10 Downing Street, and onwards, upwards, to the Prime Minister's private quarters.

Roland Kramer was waiting for us, alone, in his sitting room: a clock on the mantelpiece showed two fifty-five. 'I can give you fifteen minutes,' he said, brusquely, brimming with confidence. 'I'm making the Spitfire statement at three thirty. Mrs Dennis, you say you are in a position to report on Ms Repton's death. I'm pleased to hear that; it needs to be cleared up.'

'I agree, Prime Minister,' she conceded, 'but that may not be so easy.'

She was carrying a document case, from which she produced a tablet. 'The post-mortem examination of Ms Repton's body is complete. The pathologist, Professor Sarah Grace, has submitted a written report but she has also delivered a summary by video, from the mortuary where it was carried out. The simplest way to proceed is for me to play it to you.'

She switched it on, placed it on a coffee table so that we could all see it, and pressed a button.

Sarah's face appeared on screen, still at first, but when

Amanda hit the 'Play' arrow, in full video mode.

'*Good afternoon,*' she began. '*I am Professor Sarah Grace, head of Edinburgh University Forensic Pathology Unit. I was instructed by the Commissioner of the Metropolitan Police Service to perform a forensic examination of the remains of the late Prime Minister Emily Repton. This is now complete. I have submitted my full report to the Commissioner; this is a summary of its principal conclusions.*'

I sneaked a quick glance at Kramer; there was tension about his eyes, as he stared at the screen, no question about it.

'*Ms Repton died from the effects of a profound injury to the brain caused by the penetration to a depth of four point two inches of a narrow blade, following a violent blow. There were no other injuries, and none of the defence wounds often found in victims of a knife attack. This was a single, fatal, penetrative impact.*

'*I have autopsied more stabbing victims than I care to recall, and in every one resembling this I have been able to declare uncontrovertibly that death was the result of a homicidal act.*'

She paused; for effect. '*In this case I am unable to do so.*'

I'd seen the video earlier; I'd known what she was about to say. As she dropped her bombshell I kept on looking at Kramer, and saw a tremor run through him that could only have been one of relief. His mouth twitched at the corners, as he suppressed a smile.

'*Ms Repton was in excellent physical condition,*' Sarah continued. '*All of her major organs were perfect . . . with one exception. When I removed the brain and was able to examine it closely, I found something that had not been visible on the scans made at the Royal Free Hospital because of bleeding.*

'*There was a large tumour attached to the primary motor cortex in the frontal lobe of the brain, the area that controls motor skills. This had been neither detected nor treated, but it was so advanced that its effects could have been catastrophic at any time.*

'For example, at times of stress, it could have induced seizures that might have been taken for violent epileptic fits, in the grip of which the sufferer would be liable to lose all control of her movement and would thrash around, violently, in all directions.

'While I cannot state definitively that this happened, I believe there is a probability, rather than a possibility, that Ms Repton plunged that blade into her own head.' I looked at Kramer for a third time. The smile had forced its way on to his face.

'In support of this,' Sarah continued, *'I would point to three factors. I am advised that only Ms Repton's fingerprints and DNA were found on the letter-opener that killed her, and that those prints were clear and unsmudged.*

'Also I have examined photographs taken of the scene, with the victim still in situ at her desk. Her Red Box is there, and in front of her there is a pile of envelopes. On close examination, and enlargement of the images, it can be seen that these have been slit, but that their contents have not been removed. This indicates that Ms Repton sustained her fatal injury while opening mail.

'Finally, the position of the wound indicates that if it was inflicted in that way, the victim would have been holding the blade in her left hand. It is a matter of record that Emily Repton was left handed.'

She paused again, this time to gather herself. *'I repeat that I can't say, beyond a doubt, this is what happened. It is possible that she was stabbed by someone else. However, all the circum-stances I have described indicate otherwise. That is what Sir*

Feargal Aherne will say when he announces my findings later this afternoon.'

The recording ended, Sarah's face was frozen once more on the tablet until Amanda picked it up.

'So, Mr Skinner,' Kramer boomed, 'the crime wasn't a crime after all.'

'Not that one,' I agreed, 'but the cover-up, that was. Terrifying wee Joe Coffrey into editing the CCTV to take John Balliol and Dr Satchell off the version that was given to us. Removing from Emily's office the printed copy of the statement she would have made that afternoon, the only copy other than the one she'd given you earlier. The abduction, drugging, forcible detention at John Balliol's house, and attempted murder, of Nicholas Wheeler, who knew what the Prime Minister had intended to do that afternoon. All of those things are crimes.'

'Which you will never prove!' Kramer barked. 'Or ever allege again.'

'You know it's all true, and Les Ellis knows it, because you two ordered it, all of it. You did that because you thought that Balliol had indeed killed her. You sent him in there to persuade her to change her mind, and the next thing you knew, she had a blade in her head. That's why you went to such lengths to conceal his presence there.'

'If so, it isn't relevant; there was no crime,' he protested. 'Balliol denied it from the start, did he not? You must have interviewed him; you know that.'

'Yes, but the point is, until a few moments ago, the evidence said he did, and you believed it. Balliol told me as much himself. And you were glad, because it took Emily out of the way and left you with your hands on the world-changing weapon she was going to give away.'

'It wouldn't have come to that,' he said. 'Les and I would have confronted her before she made the statement and forced her to amend it or resign.'

'Forced her? At knifepoint? And what would you have done about Nick Wheeler?' I glared at him. 'Maybe Daffyd Evans can tell us.'

The Prime Minister's eyes gleamed; his narrow smile was deeply unpleasant. 'I doubt that he will,' he murmured. 'He's been taken from the hospital where you sent him, on my orders. You'll have difficulty calling him as a witness, although I promise, you would be wasting your time! It's over, Mr Skinner,' he said, quietly. 'Face it, it's over.

'Mrs Dennis, you can keep your job; in fact I'd be obliged if you would remain as Director General. Mr Skinner, you may keep your temporary commission . . . or you're free to accept Labour's offer of a peerage, which I know about, and to waste your time crusading from the Opposition benches.'

He glanced at the clock. 'And now you must go, for I have to get across to the Commons and complete the job of saving Spitfire for the nation. Come and watch me. There's a spectators' bench on the floor of the chamber. I'll arrange for you to be seated there.'

'You know,' I said, grimly, 'I think we will. I warned you, Kramer; you're my next project.'

The people downstairs wanted us to leave by the way we had arrived, but Hamblin, who was clearly demob happy, counter-manded them, and we made our exit through the iconic front door, under the gaze of the media mob gathered to record the comings and goings as Kramer completed his ministerial team.

'Let them make what they will,' the Cabinet Secretary said

happily, 'of the head of MI5 and the rest of us coming out of here together.'

He fell into step with Amanda, Neil and me as we walked through the gates and on towards the Palace of Westminster. Once we were out in Whitehall I dropped a pace or two behind, and made yet another phone call on the move to the man from Thames House who'd arrived at Wheeler's flat, and one more, a last one, after that.

As Merlin Brady answered I decided that yes, on balance, I do come down on the 'blessing' side of the argument.

Forty-Six

There really is a spectators' bench that's as close to being on the floor of the House of Commons as makes no difference. Sitting there is like being an MP without having to bray cheers and abuse and wave an order paper.

Amanda and Neil had decided to pass on witnessing Kramer's triumph and go back instead to their respective offices, but Norman Hamblin talked us through the officials and into the chamber.

We arrived at three twenty-five. At that time half of the green benches were unoccupied but they began to fill with remarkable speed, like an extraordinary stream of scurrying early-morning commuters that I witnessed once in a railway station in Surrey, when I was down there for a police conference. In the blink of an eye it was standing room only in the Commons.

Our vantage point looked down the length of the House and slightly across to the government front bench. There was a solemn murmuring, a deep-throated hum, from that side, as Kramer entered, squeezing past his Cabinet colleagues to his position at the Dispatch Box. From the Opposition benches there was silence.

Finally, Mr Speaker stood. I expected him to yell, 'Order!

Order!' but he didn't. Instead he intoned, 'Personal statement, Mr Merlin Brady.'

Kramer had been half out of his seat. He looked bewildered as he stared up at the Speaker's chair, but sank back down, as the leader of the Opposition rose to his feet.

'Mr Speaker,' he began, 'I thank you for this opportunity to bring to this House matters which I believe deserve its attention.'

The hum that had seemed to hang over the chamber like a swarm of very small bees fell silent instantly, as members on both sides tried to figure out what the hell was about to happen.

'I must begin with a confession,' Brady said. 'For some time, I have been in a personal relationship with a lady; an improper relationship. However, I do not believe that it is one that requires my resignation.'

'Then sit down!' a deep voice yelled, from the benches opposite. That did draw a cry of 'Order!' from the chair.

'Not yet,' the Labour leader riposted, mildly. 'Over the last few months that relationship has brought me information that I might not otherwise have had, but I have rarely used it, for fear of compromising the other person. This afternoon, however, I received something from her email address, which I am assured is genuine.

'The fact that I have been sent it can only mean that she wishes it to be brought into the public domain without further delay, and in particular before the Right Honourable Gentleman, the Prime Minister, makes his much-vaunted announcement.

'What I have here, and I say again there is no doubt as to its authenticity, as I believe another Right Honourable Member of this House can confirm, is the text of the statement that the late Prime Minister, his much-lamented predecessor, would have made if she had not been struck down,' he paused, a crucial telling pause, 'by fate.'

'I have no doubt that our former Right Honourable Friend would wish me to share her thoughts with you, even after her death.'

Kramer jumped to his feet. 'Mr Speaker, I must protest! This cannot be allowed!'

'Ah, but it can, Prime Minister,' the wee guy in the black robe barked back at him, 'and it will. Be seated and let the Right Honourable Gentleman continue.'

He stood his ground. 'I will not!' he shouted.

'I warn the Right Honourable Gentleman,' the Speaker said, quietly. 'Be seated.'

'This is good,' Hamblin whispered, alongside me. 'He's not kidding.'

The Prime Minister's face was puce, veins stood out on his neck. He had lost it; he had fallen totally, absolutely out of touch with the plot. 'I will not!' he repeated.

'Then you leave me no choice. I name Mr Roland Kramer! Serjeant-at-Arms!'

'What does that mean?' I asked Hamblin, as the House erupted in tumult.

'It means he's kicked him out,' he replied as the black-robed official took Kramer's arm and drew him away, his face paling as he realised the enormity of what he had done. 'He's ejected the Prime Minister from the Commons. I never thought I'd live to see the day.'

'The leader of the Opposition may continue,' the Speaker said, calmly. 'Order! Order!' he added, waiting for silence before resuming his seat.

Brady nodded his thanks, drew a breath and began. 'She

would have said,' he boomed, his voice stronger and more forceful than I had ever heard it, 'Mr Speaker, I wish to make a statement of vital importance to the nation and to the world.

'Just over two years ago, in the administration of my predecessor, senior ministers, specifically the then Defence Secretary and Chancellor of the Exchequer, were approached by an entrepreneur, Mr John Balliol . . .'

I doubt that the House of Commons has ever been more silent than it was as Emily Repton's last gift to the nation was read out.

The moment continued as Brady resumed his seat, and as Nicholas Wheeler, who knew where to find me, caught my eye, then that of the Speaker, and rose to his feet.

'Mr Speaker,' he said, 'I can indeed vouch for the authenticity of that declaration, as I helped my late friend and leader draft it.

'To help ensure that her wishes become the agreed policy of this House, I propose to challenge immediately for the leadership of my party, that opportunity having been denied me yesterday by my involuntary absence from parliament, the reasons for which will, I promise this House, become public.'

Forty-Seven

'Are you finally going to tell me?' Sarah asked, sipping mineral water in the dining room of the Savoy. 'How did you do it?'

'Very simply, for those who know how,' I replied. 'One of Amanda's geeks hacked into Siuriña Kramer's email account and used it to send Emily's statement to Brady, with a covering message telling him that it had to be revealed before Kramer stood up in the House.'

'You used the poor guy?' There was a hint of disapproval in her voice.

'Not at all. The opposite; I made him a fucking hero. I called him and told him how it had got there; I told him the whole story. He'd known for a while that Siuriña was playing him, but he'd gone along with it for the sex, which he said was a lot better than the information she pretended to feed him.

'I called Nick too, and told him what had happened with Kramer. He was primed for action.'

'Will his challenge succeed?'

'Absolutely. Amanda has reached out, shall we say, to the lady in Spain; she will make a voluntary statement in return for not being extradited on conspiracy charges. It'll name James

Ellis as the man who hired her. He's singing like my granny's canary already.

'Nobody died, other than Emily, and that was pure misfortune, so nothing will ever come to court,' I told her. 'That would be far too messy. But Kramer will step down tomorrow morning, as will Ellis and Mickey Satchell.

'I'm not certain what'll happen after that, but the expectation is that Nick will be elected leader and invited to form an administration. Kramer will set a record as the shortest-serving Prime Minister of all time. Not even in Italy can they match someone having only two days in office. Norman Hamblin will carry on, of course; they can't afford to let him retire.'

'And what'll you do?' she asked, reaching across the table to take my hand, before it could wrap itself around the flute of champagne that she'd insisted I have. 'Will you stay here or will we go home?'

'I called Merlin an hour ago, and told him "no thanks"; too much excitement for me.'

'And Amanda?'

I took my plastic card from my pocket and gazed at it. 'Be in no doubt,' I said, 'I know where I belong and that's with you, not her.'

Then I put it back, grinned at her and winked. 'But you never know. It might come in handy in the future.'

Don't miss the latest gripping novel in the Bob Skinner series . . .

A BOB SKINNER MYSTERY

Quintin
Jardine

When a rich man dies by poison, there are many suspects . . .

A BRUSH WITH DEATH

When millionaire Leo Speight is found poisoned at his Ayrshire mansion, Police Scotland has a tough case on its hands. Speight was a champion boxer with national hero status. A long list of lovers and friends stand to benefit from his estate. Did one of them decide to speed things up? Or was jealousy or rivalry the motive?

The Security Service wants to stay close to the investigation and they have just the man to send in: ex-Chief Constable Bob Skinner. Combining forces with DI Lottie Mann and DS Dan Provan of Serious Crimes, Skinner's determined to see Speight's murderer put away for a long time. But there's a twist even Bob Skinner couldn't see coming . . .

Available now to buy and download in eBook.